Seven Years of Famine

A Novel

Shady Grove Press, LLC

Seven Years of Famine

Issued in print and electronic formats.

Library of Congress Control Number - 2018902824

Fiction – General

Shady Grove Press
Deerfield Beach, FL

Shadygrovepress.com
Shadygrovepress@gmail.com

Gregory Thomas Jeffers is a philosopher, historian, farmer, and former Wall Street financier.

He is the author of:

"*Prosperous Homesteading*" - ClubOrlov Press

"*Duress and Desire*" - Shady Grove Press, LLC

"*Stones in the Garden*" - Shady Grove Press, LLC

The Best Books… are those that tell you
what you already know.
—George Orwell

Great is truth, but still greater, from a practical
point of view, is silence about truth. By simply not
mentioning certain subjects… totalitarian
propagandists have influenced opinion much more
effectively than they could have by the most
eloquent denunciations.
—Aldous Huxley

Force and mind are opposites;
Morality ends where a gun begins.
—Ayn Rand

I offer my heartfelt thanks to Michael Redmond, Robert Kissel, and Ethan Freeman for many years of the fearless co-examination of everything, and to Jim McCreary, editor extraordinaire, for his generous assistance.

Chapter 1

Steel grey clouds crowned the Manhattan skyscrapers, but there was no rain. *That sky looks grim*, Hank thought to himself, as he peered out of his bedroom-suite window. *Incredibly beautiful, but grim.* The luxurious 5th Avenue penthouse apartment he and his beautiful third wife called home looked out over New York's Central Park with a spectacular view of the Great Lawn and beyond. The light of the rising sun poking through the clouds in spots and reflecting off the buildings along Central Park West exaggerated the effect, and while it might dazzle the tourists, Hank paid it no mind. It was all old hat after all these years, but the clouds and the doings of nature were another story. While the neighborhood where he lived now was a long way from his boyhood days in the Flatbush section of Brooklyn, Hank had always dreamed of living in the mountains of the American West. It was an odd dream for a man who had become a Wall Street "Master of the Universe," but he was a rather bizarre and quirky man.

His father was a *garmento*, one of the thousands of first- and second-generation American Jews who made their living in the clothing, or *schmatta,* business in Manhattan's garment district. His mother was a seamstress who worked from home and kept the family together, always pushing and prodding her three children to out-work, out-study, out-hustle, and out-play anyone or anything that came their way. Aaron "Hank" Katz had worked his way through City College, and after graduation, went to work for Woolf Abrams & Company, which at that time was a small stock brokerage company in lower Manhattan. Over the next 50 years—*has it really been 50 years?*—the Firm prospered and grew as Hank worked his way up through the ranks, and finally to Chairman & CEO. He was a multi-millionaire many, many times over, a titan of the financial world, CEO of one Wall Street's most prestigious investment banks, and a generous philanthropist.

Although 72 years of age, he was fit and active, and with his third wife—who was 26 years his junior—Hank cut an imposing figure in New York Society. He was only 5'8", plain-featured and had a shiny pate from over 40 years with male pattern baldness, but the force of his personality left people with the impression after they had met him that he was tall, dark, and handsome.

Hank had two small dogs that he showered with attention and training. They were not show dogs, just a couple of dogs he got from one of New York City's animal shelters, and he walked and curbed the dogs himself. Hank enjoyed his image as a "man of the people" and made a point of letting others know that he was as humble as the day he left Brooklyn. For instance, Hank liked to walk to work when the weather permitted but would gladly ride the subway down Lexington Avenue to Grand Central Terminal and walk underground to his office when the weather was less cooperative. This had the effect not only of reinforcing his down-to-earth image with the people of New York, but also served notice to the executives of Woolf Abrams that if the Chairman doesn't take a car service to and from work, neither do you. Hank was known for running a tight ship, and that meant turning off the lights, reusing paper clips, and flying coach.

Although the day was chilly and gray for this time of year, no rain was called for in the weather report, so Hank decided to walk to work. It was 7:00 am as he left his building—in his nondescript trench coat and wool ascot hat he could have passed for a cab driver—carrying a briefcase and his morning paper. The morning research call at Woolf Abrams started at 7:45 am, and Hank liked to set the example for the firm's 5,000 employees by always being there to hear it. He walked south on 5ᵗʰ Ave., then east on 57ᵗʰ Street until he got to the east side of Park Ave., after that he headed south once more toward his office eight blocks away.

The curb in front of Woolf Abrams's office building was crowded with taxis and Lincoln Town Cars dropping off and picking up commuters, clients, and customers of the firm. The building was open 24 hours a day, 365 days per year. There was always a market open somewhere, and someone on Woolf Abrams' trading floor would be trading those securities when those markets were open.

Hank was crossing Park Avenue when two men climbed from the back of one of the taxis waiting in front of Woolf Abrams' offices. They remained on the sidewalk as Hank walked south on the east side of Park, and as Hank approached them, the man closest to Hank walked away from the street and toward the buildings along Park, while his companion remained at the curb, next to the open door of the cab. Most witnesses would later recall nothing of how the two men got there, only that they fled in the back of a taxi, with a gun pointed at the head of the driver.

Why would these buttoned-down professionals, the "suits," members of the corporate establishment, notice two "little brown men," as they were later described, who dressed like—and appeared to be—street vendors? These little brown men were invisible to the suits. The invisible little brown man closest to the office building was the first to open fire on Hank Katz. He strode smoothly and briskly to intercept Hank. His right hand came up holding a 9mm automatic pistol and in one quick motion—Pop! Pop! Pop!—he shot Katz three times in the chest. Katz staggered backward but did not immediately fall to the ground. He just stood there with a blank expression on his face as the man who fired the shots calmly walked back to the cab, and the other invisible "brown man" stepped forward and opened fire.

Boom! The report of a .357 magnum's muzzle blast is very different from the report of a 9mm automatic pistol. The shot struck Katz in the belly, causing his body to double over and fall forward to the ground, head first. Katz may or may not have been dead at this point; in either case, witnesses said that he did not put his hands out to catch his body and protect his head as he fell. His head plowed into the sidewalk with a sickening thud, though none of the witnesses would remember hearing it. They did *see* it, however, and no one there on that New York City sidewalk would ever forget the way the second shooter, the other "little brown man," walked next to Katz's lifeless, blood-spattered form and emptied his revolver into Katz's head, pulverizing it. The ricochets of the bullets zipped off in all directions after they passed through his flesh and hit the reinforced cement of the sidewalk. The killer then flashed a second weapon—witnesses described it as a semi-automatic handgun—pointing it at the many innocent bystanders gawking in shock and horror. People ducked, dove, and fell to get out of his line of fire, but with his work finished, the killer fired no more shots. The assassination was a success, and little brown man number 2 climbed into the back of the taxi where little brown man number 1 was waiting, holding a gun to the driver's head. The cab joined traffic and drove north on Park Avenue as if it had just picked up a fare headed toward the airport. The crowd around Katz waited several seconds before getting up, and it took another 15 seconds before the first of 715 calls to NYPD emergency 911 service came in.

Chapter 2

NYPD Detective James "Jimmy" Bannon was just
finishing up a session with his doctor when the call came that
a homicide had just been committed in broad daylight in
front of dozens of witnesses on Park Avenue in mid-town
Manhattan. Bannon's first thought was that an angry
socialite had just whacked her cheating husband. In that
neighborhood, that would be the equivalent of giving out
speeding tickets on the Autobahn. This was the east side of
Manhattan; there just wasn't that much violent crime going
on here. But Bannon had always liked that Mafia term—
"whacked"—it just had a nicer ring to it than "kill" or
"murder" or "slay." It was a real New York expression, one
that all of the detectives in homicide enjoyed saying out loud,
especially when the "whackee" was some piece-of-shit mob
guy who had it coming. It didn't matter that the perpetrator
might also be a piece of shit mob guy—with any luck he'd
get his sometime soon. Of course, the Mafia has not been
active since the ubiquity of security and cell phone cameras,
not to mention the FBI's organized crime task force—all
very bad for the Mob's business.

Bannon didn't want any of the guys to know that he saw a
shrink. They would think he had gone soft, that his job was
getting to him—that the blood, the guts, and the gore of
working in homicide had taken its toll. But that was not the
reason he was seeing the therapist. Bannon's father had died
six months earlier, and the younger Bannon never got to say
some of the things he would have liked to say to his father
before the old man passed—like what a miserable drunken
failure of a father the man had been to Bannon and his
brothers and sisters. Bannon's mother took the easy way
out—she died in self-defense when he was in high school.

His phone rang again.

"Bannon here."

"Jimmy?" A voice on the phone said. "You better look sharp when you get here! The media is here big time. And I'm not fucking kidding ('um not fugin' kidin')! We got some uniforms holding them back with some (crime scene) barriers but the victim was some kind of big shot, and all hell is breaking loose down here!"

"I heard… you're at the corner of 48th & Park, right?"

"Yeah, we won't be hard to find."

They weren't.

Bannon approached the crowd with his shield dangling on a small chain around his neck. Once he got the attention of the "uniforms," he was ushered past the barriers and inside the perimeter of the crime scene. Jimmy approached the victim from behind, at the victim's feet. From that angle, he could see blood on the ground around the body, but he had seen worse. His first thought was that the victim had been shot in the heart; when someone gets shot in the heart the heart stops beating, and the blood does not get pumped out of the body, it has to leak out via gravity. He didn't get a better look before he was interrupted.

"Jimmy! Wow, that was quick. Victim's name was Aaron Katz, aka 'Hank,' least that's what his ID says. It's not a driver's license, it's some kind of corporate ID. Here, it's got his picture on it, not that you're gonna recognize him. He took some in the head when he was down."

Bannon approached the body. He saw the briefcase that Katz had dropped when he was hit in the chest. It was close enough to Katz's hand to make one think he had held it until he died—as if he had something important in it. Bannon got a good look at Katz's head, or rather what was left of it. The coroner's report would later state that Katz had been hit in the head with at least four rounds delivered at close range from a high-powered handgun, but that he had been dead already. One of the shots that struck his chest had pierced his heart.

"Anything up with the briefcase?" Bannon said.

"Nope, we looked inside, just a newspaper and a bagel. Witnesses said the shooters never touched him, didn't take anything, just BAM! BAM! BAM! And then they drove away in a cab, although not before scaring the shit out of some of the people first. One of the perps pointed his gun at some of the people on the sidewalk. I think he just wanted them to stay the fuck out of the way and mind their own business. Either way, they got the message, and he didn't shoot any of them. Several of them are going to require first aid for some nasty bumps and bruises they got when they dove into the cement."

Bannon did not recognize the voice immediately. He looked up and saw it was coming from the new detective, Steve Solano. Solano was well spoken for a New York City detective. His diction and pronunciation sounded more like an investment banker's than a cop's, but he was learning to curse.

With enough time, we will ruin him as a human being, too, thought Bannon.

"Aaron Katz, aka Hank Katz, 72 years old, CEO of Woolf Abrams. That's their office building there," he pointed to the marble lobby with the drop-dead gorgeous receptionist trio staring out the window in shock. They looked like something out of one of the old Robert Palmer music videos he watched when he was in 6th grade.

They still looked damn good, Bannon thought.

"He's a big shot, megabucks, society player. Everybody knows him. Everybody loves him," Solano continued. There was a brief pause during which Solano and Bannon looked down at the body of Hank Katz and then back to each other. Solano shrugged and added, "Almost everybody."

"What a fucking job they did on him," Bannon said to no one in particular. "Well, someone wanted him dead, and the perps weren't taking any chances. Multiple entry wounds. They really whacked him."

He stopped and looked up into the air as if struck by something. They did "whack" him, didn't they? Very publicly, just like the way the old-time gangsters carried out their murders—to gain the most effect when making an example out of someone.

Bannon looked over at the body. The guys from NYPD's crime lab were on the scene now. They would collect video evidence from the security cameras, photograph the body from every conceivable direction, and collect and collate all of the pertinent physical evidence and data to help the homicide detectives put together the puzzle that was every murder. Although it appeared that each bullet had passed completely through Katz, they might get lucky and find a fragment, or even a complete bullet lodged in his body, clothes, or briefcase.

Now came the detective work. It was like the play, "Six Degrees of Separation," by Sam Shepard. Somebody who Katz knew, or somebody who knew somebody who knew Katz, or somebody who knew somebody who knew somebody who knew Katz, etc., had killed Katz.

Bannon's team had interviewed over 50 witnesses in the Katz murder, ranging from the street vendor who sold Katz his bagel, to the beggar he gave the change to, to the woman who was just about to greet Katz on the street, Stacy Mendelsohn. She was an Assistant District Attorney with over 30 years under her belt, prosecuting sex crimes and murders for the city. This ADA had seen some of the most brutal cases of rape, murder, and mayhem imaginable—but she had seen them in the form of police files, not from within speaking distance of a victim while the crime was being committed. The victims in her cases told her their terrible stories—or if they were dead, the evidence told their stories—in the safety and comfort of her mid-town office. Nothing she had ever experienced prepared her for the sound of gunfire only feet away, and the sight of blood and human brain tissue spattered across the sidewalk and on the clothes of the unfortunate onlookers. The result of the crime, the mutilated body of Hank Katz, had indeed made a life-changing impression on this formerly ambitious career girl/social climber.

Bannon knew Stacy Mendelsohn, or knew of her, in any case. Mendelsohn was from a prominent New York family and on her way up in the DA's office, perhaps one day on her way to the Mayor's Mansion, but there had been a hiccup along the way. She had been the lead prosecutor in a famous serial rape case back in the late 1980s, a crime spree that had terrorized New Yorkers for two years during her early career with the District Attorney's office.

Although the rapes had ceased in 1988, an arrest was made in a 1990 sexual assault case in which the accuser claimed that the married man she had been having an affair with had groped her. The accuser had conveniently forgotten to mention that she and the accused had been having a sexual relationship for over two years. The investigators never bothered to investigate the accuser's background, which included arrests for stalking, in-patient psychiatric care, treatment for Borderline Personality Disorder and depression, and accusations of sexual assault against no less than five former lovers. The accused was promptly arrested, and because of his good looks and Wall Street position, he made it onto the cover of one of New York's infamous tabloids. One of the victims of the serial rapist came forward and identified him from his picture in the paper as the man who had attacked her.

The man, Roger Barrack, would soon be charged with that crime as well. His attorneys were successful in bringing to the court's attention the history of the initial accuser, and, after she was confronted with this evidence, she withdrew her accusation, and stated under oath that her motive for reporting Barrack to the police initially was that she was angry that he would not leave his wife. For perjury and filing a false police report, she received a six-month suspended sentence, and was ordered to undergo psychiatric evaluation and care.

The prosecution continued in the other case, and after two mistrials due to hung juries, Barrack was convicted of rape, solely on the eyewitness testimony of the victim. He received the maximum sentence—25 years to life in a maximum-security prison. The ordeal had bankrupted Barrack. His wife divorced him. His children's lives were devastated. During his first month in custody, the man had been gang-raped in the prison laundry.

While recovering from his injuries in the prison hospital, he was approached by an attorney from the **Innocence Project,** whom he had contacted during his third trial, about appealing his conviction by using a then-new scientific technology called Forensic DNA, which could prove his guilt or innocence irrefutably.

The evidence was collected, and an appeal was filed to have Barrack's DNA compared with the DNA found on the victims. Over the next two years, Assistant DA Mendelsohn and her team vehemently fought this appeal, and the new technology, in the courts, noting that the victim had "positively" identified her attacker, and that a jury of his "peers" had found him guilty beyond a reasonable doubt. But finally, on the eve of a historic court decision, Mendelsohn relented, allowing the DNA findings into evidence. It had become impossible to impugn the new technology when other District and State Attorneys throughout the country had begun to use the technology to make convictions, just as Mendelsohn's team soon would.

There was only one problem: Barrack had committed suicide several days earlier, in a successful effort to provide the proceeds of a life insurance policy to his destitute family. He had jumped off a 5th-floor cell block walkway, landing head first on the cement. Because the policy had been in effect for nearly ten years, there were no grounds for the insurance company to withhold payment. His ex-wife and children received the proceeds from the $2.5 million policy.

The defense and prosecution were each provided with the results of the DNA comparison. Mendelsohn's staff nervously assembled in her office. This was indeed a make-or-break "Moment of Truth." Either they had served the interests of justice by prosecuting and convicting a sadistic and inhuman madman, or they had caused the torture and death of an innocent man and destroyed the lives of an innocent man's wife and children. After all, the DA's office had brought three trials, with all of the force, power, and weight that only the government can, thus breaking Barrack financially, and leaving him less capable in each succeeding trial of defending himself. As Mendelsohn read the report, she felt as if she had been punched in the stomach. She couldn't breathe, her bowels became watery, and her head pounded as she read the one paragraph statement that concluded that Roger Barrack could not have committed the rapes.

She felt little regard for Barrack or his family, or the victim, or for the fact that a serial rapist had been on the loose with no one looking for him (the rapist had moved on to Florida and had raped and killed a ten-year-old-girl several years after Barrack's conviction) while Mendelsohn and her team defended their "victory" at trial. Mendelsohn knew her political career was in trouble. That was her overriding concern.

Her staff knew at once the contents of the report. Before a word could be offered to console each other, a loud voice said:

"Are you Stacy Mendelsohn?"

"Huh?" was all that would come from her at the moment.

"Stacy Mendelsohn, you have been served, and are compelled to answer the complaint and civil action enclosed within," the man with the loud and authoritative voice said as he handed her a summons to appear in civil court.

Mendelsohn looked around at her staff as they wandered off to begin to come to terms with their role in the wrong that had been done to Roger Barrack, his family, and the people of New York. But lawyers being lawyers, most were able to get over it quickly.

Besides, this was Mendelsohn's problem.

Mendelsohn looked down at the affidavit and complaint. It was a lawsuit brought against Mendelsohn, the DA's office, the police department, and the City of New York by Roger Barrack's widow. The District Attorney's office and its deputies and assistants were statutorily immune from personal liability, provided there was no malice. What a laugh! Malice is the very base of the criminal code. In any event, the prosecutors could be called to testify in the case against the city. And while Mendelsohn herself was personally shielded from civil liability—under the law in every state of the union prosecutors have little risk, even in cases with incredible wrongdoing—the City of New York was not. Her career never recovered. She went on to prosecute homicides after the litigation was settled, but after some very unflattering press, her shot at the political brass ring had been shut down. Now pushing 60 years of age, she went on with her work with the DA's office but was never again given a high-profile case. To assuage her bruised ego, she spent her free time volunteering for "Friends of Israel."

Although he was a career police officer, Bannon didn't particularly like law enforcement personnel, and he hated lawyers outright, particularly prosecutors. He felt they were a step or two lower than child molesters.

Didn't anybody notice that on Monday, these guys were working for the DA, willing to burn someone alive for jay-walking, and on Tuesday, they were high paid defense lawyers, willing to defend child murderers and mob hit men,

18

as long as the price was right? At least cops didn't pull that shit. At least cops stayed on this side of the line. Not these fucking low life prosecutors. This was all just training for the time when the big payday came.

Once indicted, you either took a plea or you went to trial—and trials cost money. There was a sign hanging from the wall in Bannon's office that said: "A jury is a group of twelve people brought together in a court of law for the purpose of determining which side has the better lawyer." Everyone in this business knows that money does wonders for a defendant's chances. The prosecution has unlimited money to spend when it wants a case badly enough. That is not usually true for the defense.

In Bannon's opinion, most people had a false sense of confidence that the justice system was there to protect the innocent and punish the guilty. The justice system was there to win, and neither side gave a good fart about guilt or innocence. Considering how fallible human beings were, it didn't take a genius to figure out that, often enough, innocent people would wind up convicted and punished, and guilty people would be acquitted and freed. Once you figured this out, it was hard to like lawyers.

Chapter 3

Walt and Jenny Thomas sat on the comfortable couch in their TV room watching the news. The lead story, of course, was the Hank Katz murder. Walt and Jenny sat unblinking in rapt attention as the news story ran. When the news anchor moved on to a political story Walt got his cell phone out and texted his brother Jason, "important, call me."

Jason had retired with his second wife to a farm in Kentucky and had made some adjustments and changes in his life, including fathering three more children. He had one son from a previous marriage. Jason and family did not have commercial TV, and rarely followed the news, and had only a single pre-paid cell phone for the entire family. Walt often teased his brother that he was positively primitive. But Jason did have Internet service at the farmhouse, and the only way to get in touch with him was via VOIP or voice-over-internet-protocol. The service Jason used also had the ability to receive and send the ubiquitous cell phone SMS texts. Since Jason almost never answered a phone call directly, Walt had gotten into the habit of texting Jason and waiting for a callback. To Walt's surprise, Jason was calling him now.

Walt answered the call, "Hey, brother."

"Hey, what's going on?" Jason was in a jovial mood. He was always in a jovial mood. But so too was Walt. It seemed the brothers were genetically cheery, though Walt's spirit had been darkened by loss a few years back, and clouds would often gather over his mood.

"I thought you should know. Your former boss was murdered today, right outside your old office building."

This caught Jason off guard. He answered reflexively.

"Which one?"

"Hank Katz."

"You're kidding me!" Jason was stunned. "What happened?"

"Two guys walked up to him on the street in broad daylight, in front of like 50 witnesses, and shot him to death."

"What the hell?" Jason had been floored by the news and was just now catching up. "Did they catch them?"

"No," replied Walt. "They got in a taxi and drove away. They had a gun on the cabbie and got out after a few blocks. The cabbie called the police. I am sure they will get them. There has to be DNA and lots of other physical evidence in the back of that cab, not to mention all of the cameras in Manhattan. I mean, come on."

"Holy shit."

"I thought you would want to know."

"Yes, thank you for telling me. I just… can't believe it."

"Are you going to come up for the funeral?" asked Walt.

"Well, it is not like we were particularly close personally, even when I worked there. So, no, I don't think I will be coming up for another funeral."

Walt understood. Jason and a dozen of his childhood friends had had a very close call with the 9/11 terrorist attacks. They had flown back to New York to attend the funeral of the father of one of their friends. The man had had an outsized impact on their young lives, as their Little League coach. The funeral was on the morning of September 10, 2001. Some of the friends flew out that evening, some first thing in the morning. Jason was on a flight that took off from LaGuardia Airport a little after 1 am on September 11, 2001. While all of the childhood friends landed unharmed or were left stranded in New York after the nation's air travel was shut down, it was still a life-changing experience. Jason had been staying in Manhattan, and after the funeral had taken a train to Grand Central and headed downtown to see an old friend and colleague who worked in 7 World Trade Center, the "other tower" that was not hit by an airplane, but which collapsed anyway. After leaving there, Jason had run into several friends and acquaintances on the street, many of whom worked in the doomed Towers, and perished the following day.

After that experience, Jason had lost interest in flying to New York.

Chapter 4

It had been three days since the Katz murder, and Stacy Mendelsohn was waiting in her conference room at the DA's office to be interviewed by Bannon and his team. When he entered the room, she found herself impressed by this homicide detective. He was well dressed, a first, really, and had shaved that morning, another first for a detective, in her experience. After the introductions, the questions:

- Did she walk that way to work every morning?
- Yes.
- Did she recognize Hank Katz?
- Of course.
- What do you mean, "of course"?
- It is a small community. My father and Hank Katz were involved in the same charities.
- What community? Which charities?
- The New York Jewish Community. They raised money for various Jewish causes and were very active in the community here in New York, and also were involved with issues regarding Israel.
- Did you see the gunmen?
- No, I was looking up at Hank and about to say hello when he was shot. It was so loud, and happened so fast, that I could not comprehend what had just occurred. I came out of it when the gunman started waving a gun at everyone.
- What else can you tell us?
- Not much. At that point, I fell to the ground to avoid being shot myself.
- How long before…

Bannon's phone rang.

"This is Bannon." He spoke into the phone, then listening to the caller for about 30 seconds, his face impassive.

"We are on the way," said Bannon, as he clicked off his cell. He just stood there long enough to gather his thoughts and scramble the thoughts of everyone else in the room.

"What's up?" asked Solano after an unbearable period of silence.

Bannon made to speak, then paused again, and then realized that Mendelsohn worked for the DA's office.

"Three guys using automatic rifles just got out of a taxi over at the Waldorf and killed Alan Levin, several members of his entourage, and two uniformed cops," Bannon said, and paused as he looked back and forth to Mendelsohn and Solano. The three were stunned. "I don't know, we'll see. Anyway, we gotta go."

"Alan Levin?' Mendelsohn shrieked. *"The* Alan Levin?!! What the…"

Mendelsohn never got to finish her sentence. At that moment there was an earthshaking explosion so powerful that it rattled the windows and shook the building. The three law-enforcement professionals knew that the terrorist attack that they all had been waiting for, any day and every day since the 9/11 attacks, was underway.

Chapter 5

Alan Levin was one the most powerful men in Hollywood. Now in his early 70's, he still exuded the boyish charm he had when his first blockbuster made him a household name over 40 years ago. He was funny, easygoing, and extremely polite. Not the brooding genius, nor the spoiled Hollywood mogul. He was just a regular guy—with a billion-dollar net worth and a knack for making great movies.

He had come to New York on a spur-of-the-moment thing. When you're Alan Levin, spur of the moment is not a problem. He flew his private jet into New York's LaGuardia Airport, where several limousines waited to take him and "his people" to the Waldorf. Although he had a beautiful apartment in Manhattan, the media reported that he only planned to be in the city one night and was going to 'rough it' at the Waldorf with his staff. He loved New York, especially in the fall, though it wasn't quite autumn yet, and after checking in and signing autographs and having his picture taken with a passerby in the Waldorf lobby, he had planned to take a limousine out to the Bensonhurst neighborhood in Brooklyn for some *real* Italian food. Not that shit they called Italian food out in L.A.

As he passed through the revolving doors, he heard a series of loud bangs—POW! POW! POW!—that sounded like the special-effects gunfire from some of his movies. Actually, it had been the sound of a CAR-15 assault rifle fired gangland style from the window of a taxi that had pulled up alongside two policemen assigned to patrol in front of the Waldorf Astoria's Park Avenue entrance, several blocks north of the place where Hank Katz had been murdered. Both cops went down like scarecrows that fell off their support poles, collapsing in odd contortions on the sidewalk, and the cab continued north on Park Avenue. With everyone looking to the northeast corner of Park Avenue, where the officers' bodies now lay with parts of their heads missing and large pools of blood gathering, no one noticed three small, dark-skinned men—a witness would later describe them as "little brown men with straight black hair, maybe from India or Pakistan or someplace like that"—as they quickly ran up and opened fire on Alan Levin with fully automatic AK-47 assault rifles. Levin's body danced as more than ten rounds hit him in less than a second, and then his body crashed down to the sidewalk in a heap.

Bannon found the "little brown men" description of the witnesses somewhat amusing—sort of like "little green men," only closer to home. But of course, he worked in homicide, and homicide detectives have strange coping mechanisms.

Unlike the Katz murder, the shooters fired several rounds into the crowd, killing three people and wounding seven. Bannon wasn't sure if they were firing into the crowd or if they intended to kill another member of Levin's entourage. In any case, Sammy Stearns, Levin's money man and financial partner in many business deals, died along with Levin in a hail-storm of bullets in front of the lobby of the Waldorf Astoria.

The shooters ran back to the south end of the block and got into a taxi that raced North on Park Avenue. This taxi wasn't as lucky as the Katz get-away car. As they turned east on one of the side streets of Manhattan's east 50s, they ran into a traffic jam caused by an NYPD patrol car blocking their escape at the end of the street. Police were converging on the cab, by foot and patrol car, from every direction.

The men in the cab did not attempt to flee. The responding police officers were taking cover behind parked cars and the cars that were abandoned by their drivers in the middle of the street. All of the officers were pointing their service revolvers and 9mm semi-automatic pistols at the taxi, screaming at the tops of their lungs for the men in the cab to throw out their weapons and come out with their hands in the air. More uniformed officers arrived, forming a ring around the taxi, and with police at either end of the street and the buildings on either side of the cab, there was nowhere for the men in the cab to go, no way to escape. They were surrounded.

One of the officers, newly elevated to sergeant, took charge of the uniformed police ringing the car. He shouted into his collar-radio transceiver for the other officers to hold their fire to avoid shooting each other, or a potential hostage in the form of the cab's driver, and to try to take the men alive. The sergeant could see the men in the cab. They appeared to be laughing amongst themselves, as if this were all very amusing, and the driver seemed to be in on the gag. The sergeant spoke into his radio that he was going to give the men an opportunity to surrender, though all the officers on the scene were aware that just 75 feet away was a car full of cop killers.

The men in the cab stepped out of their vehicle, and the sound of automatic weapons-fire filled the air. All of the men in the taxi, including the driver, were firing westward at the police officers there. Those officers returned fire while the sergeant screamed into his radio for the officers on the east side to take cover to avoid being struck by their fellow officers, but this was in vain. One of the officers to the east of the taxi was struck in the head and died instantly. It didn't much matter. They were all about to become dead men.

The taxi exploded with such force that a water main 12 feet underground was broken and exposed, flooding the area. The multimillion-dollar townhouses for 100 yards in either direction and on both sides of the street had their exteriors and roofs shorn off by the blast. The 55 police officers who were surrounding the taxi were killed instantly in the blast, along with 400 civilians, some living in the demolished townhouses, others felled by their curiosity and their desire to see what the commotion was.

Over the next few days, New Yorkers would be a lot less interested in police activity than they had been before.

Chapter 6

Bannon and his men never got to the blast site. The Manhattan FBI office had cordoned off the area and asserted control over the investigation. Within hours, National Guard troops were patrolling the streets. Bannon was busy enough without having to cover the investigation into the Waldorf Area incident. That was now someone else's problem.

During the three days that followed the blast, and within a week of Hank Katz's murder, five doctors, three lawyers, seven prominent businessmen, and one Broadway producer were killed in much the same manner and style as Katz had been. In each case, two or to three "little brown men" walked brazenly up to the victims in public places and shot them to death in a disturbing display of brutality. Each victim was shot over ten times, receiving multiple body and head wounds. The message was clear—if you were a target, you would not survive the attack. All of the victims were white, male, educated, and wealthy—and they were all Jews.

Bannon hadn't met with the FBI yet, but he knew they were coming. Then "The Tape" arrived.

It was delivered to one of the local TV stations, by one of New York's ubiquitous bicycle couriers, and forwarded to the NYPD, which made several copies, and then forwarded the original to the Feds.

The tape showed a young man speaking into the camera with detailed information about each of the murders— "assassinations," as the tape's narrator called the killings— that would have been unknown to any person except the killers themselves.

So, the tape was authentic.

The young man spoke in unbroken English, with no trace of a foreign accent, unless one considered his New Jersey

(*Noo Joisy*) diction "foreign". He delivered this short explanation for the murders:

"This message is to all who give aid and support to the terrorist state, Israel:
You are considered enemy combatants, and legitimate military targets. You will be killed, you who have caused the deaths of Muslim women and children. We are prepared to strike you in your homes, your businesses, your synagogues, and your schools. Your money has paid for guns, grenades, rockets, and tanks that have killed and maimed our people. This war we wage will not be measured in days but in the blood of those who have raised their hands against us, and who have taken our homes like thieves in the night. We will have our homes again, and you will sleep in your own blood."

The Feds refused to release the tape to law enforcement agencies, confiscated the copy that the TV station that had received the original tape had kept, and warned the TV station managers that all other copies had better be turned over as well. So much for the "Freedom of the Press."

The battleground of the Middle East moved first to North Africa, then to Europe, and had now come to America. Within a week of the blast that killed 55 police officers on Manhattan's upper east side, another 24 police officers were assassinated while on duty. Though this was never reported in the media, rumors swirled. Officer funerals were not permitted to be the spectacle that deaths in the line-of-duty had historically been—that was just too dangerous—but it was hard to sweep the killings and the funerals under the proverbial rug.

Cement traffic barriers surrounded police stations and officers were stationed behind sandbags, or were ensconced in armored personnel carriers, but the assassinations of patrol officers in the New York Metropolitan region continued unabated. 233 NYPD cops quit their jobs or had been fired for absenteeism within a week of the blast, and NYPD job applications dried up. All of the metro area municipal police forces were in similar straits. People seemed far less interested in carrying a gun and a badge when the bad guys started working together in teams and shooting back in deadly earnest. Wearing a police or firefighter uniform was suicide, and the officers still showing up for work refused to wear them. Tourism came to an abrupt halt. Grand Central Terminal was otherworldly, empty even at rush hour, as were the subways. Broadway couldn't give a ticket away and within a week had shut down altogether. Life had changed in New York. A bunker mentality had taken hold of the population. And in addition to the killing of uniformed police officers, every few days another well-to-do Jewish professional in the metro New York area was murdered in cold blood.

Chapter 7

Walt Thomas was sitting in front of his computer surfing the web when reports started to come in that a major "destructive event," perhaps an earthquake, had hit Tehran, Iran. He thought little of it. Earthquakes happen, after all, and thankfully they usually happened to someone else. About 15 minutes after the first reports of Iran's "destructive event," news reports started to come over the web that a major "destructive event" had just been reported in Israel. Within minutes, all news sites were saying that perhaps a nuclear catastrophe had taken place, and then reports started to come in that Pakistan and Saudi Arabia had sustained nuclear blasts as well. Walt reached for his cell phone and called his son.

"All circuits are busy. Please try your call again later."

He waited a minute and redialed his son.

"All circuits are busy…"

Walt got up from his computer, walked to the kitchen and out the back door to his car, and raced down the hill to the local grocery store, less than a mile away. Most of Walt's family lived in Florida, where a hurricane had once left them without power for six weeks. A volunteer fireman and former Boy Scout, Walt understood emergencies—people still needed to eat, drink, wipe their asses, and wash their hands. He ran into the store to buy supplies of every type, only to find that he was not alone. Other quick-thinking people had had the same idea, and were quickly emptying the aisles. Still, Walt had been fast enough. His cart was piled to the limit with non-perishables. When he got to the check-out counter, Walt was impressed to see that they were still accepting credit cards.

The first report of Iran's "event" was 62 minutes old. The first mention of "nuclear" was less than 42 minutes old.

From the grocery store, Walt drove to one of the gas station and convenience stores that he owned on the other side of town. The clerk behind the counter was listening to an Indian pop recording, and seemed to have no idea of the events of the past 90 minutes. Walt pushed him around the store, packing a week's worth of bread, milk, and eggs into a box for him, and told him to get his family together. The clerk had no idea what Walt was talking about, but seemed to get the idea that something was amiss as Walt shooed him out the door and into his car. Walt also insisted that the clerk fill up his gas tank before leaving. Then Walt headed back inside the store to gather what he could. When the clerk came back with a handful of cash to pay for the gasoline, Walt practically shouted at him.

"Go *home*! There is no time! Go home!"

The look on the man's face was an expression that Walt would not soon forget.

I wonder if the electricity in his house will still be on when he gets there. Then he went back to worrying about his own house and family.

The lights were still on at the station, so Walt filled his car with gas, grabbed ten five-gallon gas containers from inside the store, and filled them with diesel fuel. He walked back into the store, locked the front door behind him, and turned off the pump lights and all of the indoor lights except the night-lights that were always on for security purposes.

Walt looked up as headlights came into the pump island area of the station. It was his son Manny and daughter-in-law, Danielle. Manny stopped the car right in front of the door and got out of the car. "Wait here, but get behind the wheel," Manny said to his wife.

Walt strode to the front door and unlocked it, and Manny stepped inside.

"Holy shit!" said Manny

"Holy shit is right," replied Walt. "Go out back and get every box that will hold something and bring it in here. We'll take all the food and all of the drinks up to the house. Fill the rest of the jerry cans that are out in the garage with diesel and put them in the back of your truck. And go tell your wife to top off your tank. *Hurry.*"

Father and son proceeded to load all of the canned goods, candy, packaged food, beef jerky, refrigerated foods, snack bags, donuts, sugar, ice, soaps, batteries, and the other various and sundry products one would expect to find at a gas station's convenience store, into cardboard boxes and large plastic garbage bags. Not a word passed between them. They left the fragile Styrofoam coolers for last, and then packed them separately with ice. After they emptied the store's contents into their vehicles, Walt locked the gas pumps, turned off the switch to the pump, and then flipped all of the breakers in the main electric utility box, thereby killing all power to the building. He hoped that people would look at the empty shelves and the dark building and perimeter and assume there was nothing left to steal. Of course, there were still 20,000 gallons of gasoline and diesel fuel in the tanks in the ground. But without a key for the fill valve, and some specialized pumping equipment, that fuel would not be easy to steal. He located a piece of plywood that had come with some of the wood pallets that the food was delivered on, spray-painted large block letters in bright orange—"SORRY NO GAS"—and placed the makeshift sign in front of the front door. Then he locked up behind him. Manny was still loading boxes into the back of his truck.

"When you're finished, take everything up to the house and bring it into the kitchen. We need to do an inventory. OK?"

"OK. Where are you going?"

"Down to the shop to get every tool that we might need that I can fit in the car, and anything else I can think of. I'll meet you at the house in an hour. Tell your mother to wait there for me and not to leave the house until I get home."

"OK," said Manny.

Chapter 8

The edges of the scenery were a little sketchy. He lay on his back in a field of lush green grass with red and white clover in full flower. Springtime. He didn't remember how he got here. He was just here. He lay back in the grass and took in the puffballs of white clouds in the bright blue sky. He could look up at the clear sky, right into the sun itself, in fact, without needing to blink or even squint. *That's strange.* He took in the movement of the clouds as they weaved in and out of the space above him. Then, overcome with thirst, he rose from the grass and walked diagonally down the hill towards the woods that hid a freshwater brook that over eons had cut the ground into a deep crevice. The stream water splashed over rocks made smooth by the passage of time, sand, pebbles, water and ice, freezing and thawing. Bright green moss grew on the rocks that bordered the stream. He wanted to walk to it to drink but suddenly, he was paralyzed with fear by an explosion. No, not one explosion; one after the other; the sound felt like it was crashing through his head. Instead of wanting to drink from the stream he felt a terrible urge to vomit.

"Roone!"

He heard someone calling his name, and felt the terrible blasts and the urge to vomit again.

"Roone!"

He was going to her. To the person calling his name. He opened his eyes and gagged. Bang! Bang! Bang!

"Roone! Wake up!" the voice shrieked from the other side of the door.

Roone recognized his girlfriend's voice. He swung his feet to the floor, feeling somewhere between still drunk and very hung over.

Pilar was pounding the door so hard that it was rattling in its metal frame. That was impressive, given the heavy-duty doors of the student dorms and her diminutive size. "What the fuck?" Roone muttered to himself. He was too ill, his head in pain, to scream over the sound of the pounding. He wobbled upright and then walked unsteady to the door, his eyes barely open, his hair pressed flat onto the side of his head by the pillow. He felt like hell, but right now he was willing to do whatever it took to end the awful racket.

Roone unlocked the door and turned to head back to his bed, with Pilar hot on his heels. Either he didn't notice that the hallway was dark, and Pilar was holding a flashlight, or he was just too sick to care. Roone kept the hurricane shutters on his window closed, so he was used to darkness in the room.

"Oh, my God!" said Pilar.

She was dumbstruck. The room smelled of the alcohol that Roone had secreted and aspirated from his lungs.

"Have you been sleeping all day?!"

"Ugh..." Was all Roone could muster. All he could think about was getting back to his bed.

"Ugh?!" shrieked Pilar. "Get up! World War III has started! The Middle East just got nuked and there is no electrical power!"

"Wha...?

"You didn't notice it is pitch black and that I am holding a flashlight?"

Roone started to mumble.

Pilar ignored Roone and opened the door to the Jack-and-Jill dormitory bathroom. She headed toward the shower and turned it on and felt the water. Miraculously, it was still warm. Then she turned to the cheap particleboard shelving, retrieved a bottle of ibuprofen, and shook out four capsules.

"Get in here and get showered and sober!" She turned on a dime to retrieve her hung-over boyfriend from his bed, but almost ran into him as he stood in the bathroom doorway.

"Here, take this," she said forcefully, handing him the ibuprofen and turning to fill up a cup with water from the sink in the tiny college bathroom. The light from her flashlight danced around and made Roone even more nauseous, if that were possible. She handed him the water cup, and pushed him towards the shower while holding her flashlight so that he could see. Of course, he could have navigated this bathroom in complete darkness while drunk as a sailor—as he had proved on any number of occasions.

He stood in the shower as the water beat him into wakefulness and said, "Now what the fuck is going on?"

"World War III has started. I was driving back to campus when the radio stations reported that a nuclear war broke out in the Middle East. I was about an hour away from campus. At first, the news said that an earthquake hit Iran, but within 20 minutes or so they corrected that and said a major nuclear event occurred in Iran, Israel, Pakistan, and maybe Saudi Arabia. I came back to my dorm and packed my things. The phone networks are overloaded, so I couldn't call you. Just as I was leaving the electricity went out. The whole campus is locked up with traffic. I walked over here."

Roone stood frozen in place, like a wax statue dripping with water and standing motionless in the resulting puddle beneath his feet. Pilar could tell his brain was still addled from the binge-drinking episode the night before.

"Wait. There was a nuclear war in the Middle East, and the power is out here?"

"Yes. And there is no cell service."

"Pilar… are you sure about this?"

"Roone, there are thousands of kids crying their eyes out right now down in the quadrangle. The traffic lights don't work, and traffic is at a standstill. There is no electric power, no cell phone service. And you slept through it all, drunk as a fucking monkey. Well done."

Roone was impressed. Pilar never used profanity.

Pilar grabbed the only towel that was hanging over the rack. It was moist, maybe even slimy. She wondered when it had been washed last. Despite recent events, Pilar was left to marvel, if only for a moment, at Roone's lack of concern for such details. He was unparticular in a way that she found both revolting and extremely attractive. If Roone ordered his eggs at the local diner sunny side up, and they came back scrambled he never seemed even to notice. If a waitress poured cola into his glass of sweet tea, Roone would drink that as if that is what he wanted. Pilar could change plans at the last minute and Roone followed right along as if nothing had happened. There was only one thing that Roone was consistent about—and that was his attraction to Pilar. He adored her.

Roone was a 6th-year senior. He had taken a year and a half off from school to travel and work. Now, at 24, he was a hard-assed and full-grown man. Mature, self-possessed, and ambitious, Roone did everything to excess. He worked hard, studied hard, drank hard, and what was most important to Pilar, Roone loved hard. He loved everything about Pilar; he loved her voice and her accent, he loved the way she walked, the way she smelled, and the softness and tone of her skin. He kissed her so much he practically drooled on her everywhere they went. They had met a little over a year before, when Pilar came to the summer session as a freshman. She was 17 then and he was 23. They met in Calculus I. Pilar had been born and raised in Buenos Aires, but her family had moved to Ft. Lauderdale when she was 13, and that's where she went to high school, excelling in math and science. Roone had just changed his major to mechanical engineering. He was late to the program and would need to complete a full summer program on either side of this regular school year if he hoped to graduate.

The moment Pilar saw Roone for the first time she broke out in a sweat. He was over a foot taller than she, thin but muscular, and dressed in flip-flops, jeans, and a plain white

T-Shirt. Roone's body was a walking testimony to his athleticism and physicality. He was unlike any of the boys or men she had met in her young life in Buenos Aires or Ft. Lauderdale. But if Pilar was taken with Roone, that attraction was a beach breaking ocean wave compared to the tsunami coming back at her from Roone. He didn't so much pursue her as commandeer her, and Pilar reveled in the light Roone exuded in her presence. She was now just 18 years old, but she felt there would be no other men for her, ever. There could not be others. Roone was a force of nature.

Pilar left him there, retrieved underwear and a t-shirt from his dresser, unceremoniously threw them at him, and headed back to look for a shirt and pants. Before she could find something, he was standing next to her rifling through his dresser. He dressed quickly, though he was still unsteady on his feet. Then he collected a bag from the shelf on the top of his closet, gathered some clothes and gear that were hanging below, and pulled some others from inside his dresser. He put on his work boots and threw his sneakers into the bag, tossed Pilar a jacket that belonged to his roommate, and said, "Let's go."

"Go where?"

"Well, we can't stay here."

"Why not?"

"Didn't you just say that the grid is down and a nuclear WWIII is underway? There are 20,000 students here and another couple million people living in the city. We have to get the hell out of here."

"Roone, five minutes ago you could barely stand. Now you've got an adrenaline rush and you're ready to go commando?"

Roone laughed out loud.

"What the hell is so funny?" Pilar fumed. "What the hell is wrong with you?"

"I am sorry baby… when we say, 'going commando', well, that is an old joke to describe the practice of not wearing any underwear." Roone pulled his boxer waistband up and out of his pants. "See? I've got underwear on. I am pretty sure you meant 'off-grid,' or maybe 'bug-out?'"

For Pilar, English was a second language, and though she spoke it well, her native tongue was Spanish. Colloquialisms and slang were often misunderstood.

"What's the difference? You know what I meant," Pilar asked. "It's all that survivalist stuff from that stupid Sociology course."

The college offered a "lay down" elective called "Survivalist and Prepper 101: How to Survive Societal Breakdown." It was one of the most popular lecture courses on campus. Pilar had no interest in zombie apocalypses, epidemics, or a collapse of the financial system. She much preferred art, fashion, and design. But Roone was taking the course, so she took it just to be near Roone.

"Yeah, well, I think nuclear war qualifies. We can't stay here."

"Where should we go?"

"To my father's place." And with that Roone was already in motion and out the door, with Pilar and her flashlight right behind him. There were several men with flashlights ahead of them, working by the door of the dorm elevator. Roone paused for a moment to see what was going on. A muffled voice came from behind the elevator doors.

"What's going on? Can you help us or not?!"

"We're working on it!" one of the workers screamed to the people trapped on the elevator. "Just hang in there! We will get you out!"

"Holy shit, this is real!" said Roone, as he grabbed Pilar's hand and headed off to the stairwell. "Now you know why I always hated elevators. We gotta get the hell out of here."

It was true. Roone hated elevators and steadfastly refused to use them. Pilar thought it was just another cute idiosyncrasy of Roone's. He seemed to have dozens of them.

The stairwell was 20 yards or so to their right. Roone's dorm room was on the 5th floor. The couple entered the cement structure of the stairwell that was built as a fire exit for a building that couldn't burn.

"What? Roone, campus traffic is at a standstill. Nothing is moving. The traffic lights don't work. We can't drive anywhere."

"We're not driving. We're walking."

But they were not walking; Roone was bounding down the stairs with Pilar trying to keep up. He waited for her under the battery-powered "fire exit" sign and held the door open to let some light in. Pilar joined him at the exit and turned off her flashlight.

As they left the dorm building, they were greeted by a throng of college students in the fading light typical of an early fall or late summer's day in Atlanta, GA. The dorms and other college buildings were dark, and the students must have felt that there was safety in numbers. Roone walked purposefully at the edge of the crowd, avoiding eye contact with those gathered there, with Pilar hot on his heels. As Pilar looked around, she could see that many of their fellow students were in tears, embracing each other in a show of emotion and affection, breaking often to recheck their cell phones in vain, and then coming back for another hug and another outburst of tears.

Roone looked out at the crowd and now felt real fear for the first time, though the expression on his face told of a man who seemed unconcerned with what the students were doing or how they felt. At least his head was feeling better now. Either the ibuprofen was kicking in, or the shower helped, or perhaps the adrenaline rush cleared the fog of his hangover. He paused to pick up a fist-sized stone that was lying in the roadside gutter, loosened from a drainage culvert. He placed the stone in his backpack.

"What's that for?" Pilar said as she struggled to keep up with Roone's long and purposeful strides.

"Research."

"Where are we going?"

"First, to the student union building."

Now she understood why they were walking the direction they were. The student union was a block away, and the campus exit that would take them north was in the opposite direction. They arrived in a few moments. The building was dark, and the glass doors were locked with a chain holding them together.

"It's locked," said Pilar.

"No shit," replied Roone.

He looked around. The crowd of students three blocks back was much bigger than it appeared to be when he had left his dorm. Roone wondered what the hell they were doing. They were gathering in the square that was situated between the four largest dormitories on campus. There must have been several thousand people just wandering around aimlessly.

"Wait for me across the street past the parked cars under those trees. You see 'em?"

"What are you going to do?"

"I gotta go talk to my guidance counselor," Roone said as he rolled his eyes.

Then he pulled her close and kissed her on the lips and then her neck.

"I love you, baby," he whispered into her ear. "Now just go wait over there. I'll just be a minute."

Pillar did as she was told. She could see Roone from where she was standing, and watched as he took his backpack off and walked up and down the sidewalk in front of the building. He returned to the front doors, set his backpack on the ground, and retrieved the rock he had picked up from the road. He took another look around, launched the rock through the glass of the student union doors, and then turned and ran to where Pilar was standing.

"What the hell do you think you are doing?" Pilar hissed.

"Shh," Roone replied and held his finger up to his lips. It was twilight, and since they were standing in the shade of the trees, someone happening on the scene would never see them, but a security guard stationed there would have been able to watch Roone cross the street. After several minutes, Roone was satisfied that no one was coming after him and that there were no flashlights illuminated inside the building.

"Here, take this stuff and jam it in your backpack if you can, and carry the rest," said Roone as he emptied his backpack on the ground in front of Pilar. "Give me your flashlight. You see that bench at the bus stop up there?" Roone pointed two blocks further up the street on which they had been walking. "Wait for me there. I will call you from those trees, OK?"

Pilar started to object, but Roone was already bounding across the street and into the student union. Pilar collected the clothes on the ground and tried to fit them into her backpack, but there wasn't enough room, so she balled them together and jammed them in as best she could, but did not try to close the zipper. Then she walked off to the bus stop. It took her a couple of minutes to get there, and she was seated on the bench for a couple of minutes more when she saw Roone running up the street on the other side. He seemed to be weighted down a little, but he ran like a gazelle and joined her without bothering to run to the trees.

"Come on; we've got a few more stops to make."

Pilar did not stand up. "What the hell do you think you are doing?"

Roone took a look around. No one was following him. This was as good a time as any, so he sat down and took a deep breath and exhaled.

"I don't mind sleeping here if you don't. But I think things are going to get pretty uncomfortable very quickly. What I had in mind was to go out to the strip and visit 'Sonny's' before anyone else gets the same bright idea. They have hiking gear and sleeping bags. We can be at my father's farm in 10 to 15 days."

"Why don't we just stay here?" Pillar asked.

"Where? At the dorm? What are we going to eat tomorrow? Think about it. Thousands of students are going to be looking for breakfast tomorrow morning. The cafeteria won't be open. What will they eat? Now think about the 'boyz in da hood' over there," and with this, Roone nodded his head in the direction of the housing projects south of the university campus. "Do you think the police will be able to handle them after they haven't had anything to eat for a day or two? Shit, the police can't handle them now. There's some stuff we need and that I would like to pick up before everyone else gets there."

Pilar ignored this cryptic last line, focusing on the rest.

"The power might come back on."

"Yeah. And it might not. I am leaving. Right now," Roone said as he stood up. "I want you to come with me, but it is up to you." He was bluffing like a master poker player, and she knew he was bluffing. "I'm leaving. You coming?"

He wouldn't have left her. But he needed to end this negotiation now. He started to walk away, and she got up and ran after him. She grabbed him roughly by the hand and spun him around and then dove into his arms. She was crying.

"You are scaring me," she sobbed.

"Good. 'Cause I am scared shitless right now. We need to move—*now*. And we need to be at my father's farm *before* we get tired, *before* we get hungry, and *before* we get sick or weak. Do you understand that? We can always come back. We won't always be able to go."

"Ok," said Pilar, but she looked like she was close to melting down into little more than a puddle on the ground.

"Can you hold it together for just a little bit? We need to get away from downtown Atlanta. I raided the canteen at the student union. I have enough calories in this backpack to get us to my father's place without starving if that is the way it has to be. But it would help if we had some water and a couple of real hiking backpacks and real sleeping bags and a real portable shelter. I want to go over to 'Sonny's Sporting Goods' before other people get the same idea."

"You mean you are going to rob Sonny's."

"Robbery is when you use force to take something from a person, so no, I am not going to 'rob' Sonny's.' If there are any people there, I am not going anywhere near the place. But if this thing just happened, I might get lucky. Maybe the staff went home early. Maybe Sonny can't make it back to the store 'cause he's stuck in traffic, or maybe a lot of things. If I can, I am going to break into Sonny's and steal some stuff that we are going to need. If not, we are going to have to make other arrangements."

"I think you have lost your mind. What if the power comes back on tonight or tomorrow? You are going to be arrested, and that is only if you are not shot as a looter."

"The power ain't coming back on. And I am not going to loot the place, OK? I am going to 'borrow' a couple of things. Now let's go."

Roone strode off, and Pilar followed. Her gut told her to go to Roone when she heard the news, and her gut was telling her to stick with Roone now. This was *her* man. As she caught up with Roone, she took his hand, and he turned and smiled at her.

"We are going to walk all night, or at least most of it. Are those sneakers comfortable?"

"Yes, very."

"Well, OK then. Let's do this."

Chapter 9

Roone's visit to Sonny's was uneventful and productive. They waited until nightfall, sitting quietly in an alley a block away, behind a large cardboard box, and using some collapsed cardboard to keep their butts off of the dirty ground. Roone left Pilar with instructions to return to campus if he was not back in an hour. But he was back in less than 20 minutes. The staff, in their excitement, had left both the back door and the front door unlocked. Roone bolted through the store by the light of Pilar's flashlight. He grabbed two sleeping bags, two hiking-sized backpacks, and an LED headlight—there was only one—along with some batteries. It was all he could carry. He figured he would bring this stuff to Pilar and then head back for a second visit to collect a few other things. That didn't go as planned. After returning to Pilar, he heard a group of young men traveling up the avenue where Sonny's and the other stores that served the campus were situated. Going by the voices, these were local thugs, not college students. Roone decided they needed to get to the highway, I-75 north out of Atlanta, where there might be safety in numbers. The danger lay between here and there. But it wasn't far, perhaps a half a mile east on 10th Street NW, where they could pick up the ramp that would bypass I-85 and lead them directly to I-75.

The plan was to hitch a ride in exchange for some of the packaged food that Roone had liberated from the student union. That plan went out the window as they approached the highway. It was a parking lot. The cars were not moving an inch, but the good news was that their headlights were still illuminating the roadway. It would have been unnerving to have to walk through the caverns of the highway in the dark. But Roone's real fear was that the local hoodlums would take the opportunity to drop rocks and other projectiles from overpasses and retaining walls onto the masses of office workers fleeing downtown.

This was an exodus. That is the only word that would describe it. Tens of thousands of people, most of them in business attire, were walking out of downtown heading in all directions. It was an impressive sight—a sea of humanity was walking home out of one of America's largest cities in the light of thousands of automobile headlights.

"Why aren't the cars moving at all?" asked Pilar.

"All the cars that were low on fuel before the blackout ran out, and blocked the other cars, and eventually all of them will run out of gas. I am sure intersections are piled up with car wrecks. Drivers abandoned their cars, making the situation worse. Maybe things will clear up outside the city."

"Well, what's your plan?"

"I want to make it to Marietta tonight, but I don't know, and I don't have much of a plan other than to get the heck out of here. Even when we get wherever we are going, we can't both sleep at the same time. One of us has to keep watch. Tonight, we have to walk 20 miles. Tomorrow we need to make 30 miles."

Pilar took a deep breath and exhaled.

"Hey, sweetness," Roone said in a comforting voice as he squeezed her hand. "We are young and in good shape. The record for miles walked in 24 hours was something like 180, so 20 tonight and 30 tomorrow is no big deal. All we need is a good sleep in between. We will be fine."

"Roone, this isn't a game. This isn't a lab for that idiotic course. For all we know, we could be next. And I have no way to reach my parents to tell them that I am OK and to see if they are OK."

Roone kept his head down for a few moments as they walked.

"I know. But right now, it helps to focus on what we are doing. There is nothing we can do about anything else. The most important thing to do is to survive this. This city is going to boil over sometime in the next few days. We can't be here for that."

Roone and Pilar were walking along the western shoulder of the southbound lane of I-75, surrounded by people doing the same thing. Roone wanted to cross the highway to the northbound shoulder, because the glare from headlights was not helping his hangover, though the air and exercise did. Most of the people stuck in traffic had turned off their motors, and some had turned off their headlights. Roone figured in a couple of hours it would be dark, and that these cars would be right where they were now.

"Hey, Roone!" someone shouted from behind them. "Roone!"

Coming up behind them just off the shoulder was Max Pennington, a fraternity brother of Roone's before he left school for his "gap year," which turned into a year and a half. Max was a freshman when Roone was a junior, and now both were seniors, but when Roone returned to school, he did not return to the fraternity. After meeting Pilar, the fraternity just didn't hold that much appeal for him anymore.

"Hey, Max!" Roone called back as he walked backward within the flow of people.

Max was hand in hand with a young Asian woman. The two weaved into the crowd to walk with Roone and Pilar.

"Hey man," said Max, as if they had just bumped into each other at a local bar, though he was a little bit winded from running. "I saw your head sticking up above the crowd, and I hoped it was you. We have been trying to catch up to you for the last five minutes."

"Hey, Max. Where were you? Or where are you coming from?"

"We went down to the zoo just to change things up. All of a sudden, people started heading for the exits. Our cell phones were not working, and we had no idea what the hell was going on. By the time we got back to our car, the traffic was stopped cold. The car radio worked until about 90 minutes ago. When the power in the city went out, the radio went dark too."

"Holy shit."

"Yeah, man. Holy shit."

"Max, this is my girlfriend, Pilar."

"Hi, Pilar. This is my friend, Akiko. She is from Japan. We just started dating."

"Hi," Pilar and Roone said to Akiko together.

"Hello," Akiko replied. Roone wondered whether she spoke English.

"Bro," said Max. "We gotta get across the highway. This side has retaining walls up ahead somewhere, and I don't want to get hit by people throwing rocks. Some of the locals were throwing bricks and rocks down onto the people walking on the highway. We saw one guy get hit in the head right in front of us. He's dead. He has to be. His brains were right there on the ground."

"Shit, I was worried about that. OK. Let's get moving."

The two couples pushed their way off the shoulder and into the five southbound lanes of stalled traffic, and then crossed the median on the inbound shoulder.

"I think we are better off walking here," said Roone. "Fewer people, and it will be harder for someone to reach us if they throw something big."

Roone was helping Pilar over the median guardrail and Max was helping Akiko; when the girls were over Roone set a brisk pace north.

"Where are you going?" asked Roone.

"My parents live in Chattanooga, maybe a little over 100 miles from school. How about you?"

"My father and stepmother live in south-central Kentucky. Probably 300 miles."

"Ugh. That's a hike."

"Yeah," Roone said as he smirked at Max and rolled his eyes. Max got the message. No point in scaring Pilar. "So, you guys didn't even stop back at school?"

"No way," replied Max. "After we saw that guy get killed, we decided to make tracks the hell out of Atlanta, and we won't be coming back until the power is back on."

"Well, you can't make it to Chattanooga tonight. We are trying to get up to the suburbs around Marietta. You are welcome to camp with us. One of us can stand watch while the others sleep, and the girls can share the other sleeping bag."

"Sounds good to me. Do you know how to get to your father's house?"

"I think so. I would know the way cold if I were driving. Walking will be a little more interesting, but I think we will find it. How about you?"

"My parents live off of I-24 outside Chattanooga, on the way to Nashville. No problem."

"From your lips to God's ears," said Roone.

A little after midnight the four college students came upon the I-75 exit for Marietta, GA., north of Atlanta. There were still people walking along the highway, and some of the cars were already empty and abandoned. The highway had been a parking lot since they started.

"I am still a little wound up. I don't know that I could sleep. Does anyone feel like pushing on?" Roone asked.

"I don't think I can sleep," said Pillar.

"Ok with me," said Max as he sought confirmation from Akiko.

Akiko just nodded.

"There is a wildlife preserve ahead right off the highway," said Max. "I don't know exactly how far or if we can even make it, but they might have water."

After a half hour's walk, they pointed Pilar's flashlight at a sign. "Rockridge Forest, 4 miles."

"That's gotta be it."

They walked on in silence. No one mentioned anything about not being able to sleep.

"We will not be able to find any of the facilities in the dark," said Roone. "We might as well walk on until we feel like stopping. I will take first watch."

They walked for another hour, bounding across the landscape of the concrete jungle of northern Georgia despite the hour and the distance. Youth was being served this night. Unceremoniously, Roone picked a place to wander off the highway and into a thicket of southern white pine. They could not see that on the other side of the trees was another construction project or that they were still a couple of miles south of the Rockridge National Forest. Roone asked everyone to be perfectly still and to listen. All understood what was being asked. None of them moved so much as a muscle as they listened intently to be sure they had not stumbled into trouble. There was no sound.

Roone and Pilar unpacked the sleeping bags and laid them right next to each other.

"I'll take first watch. You guys get some sleep. I will wake you up in 2 hours," Roone said this last line to Max.

Pilar opened her sleeping bag and motioned with the flashlight for Akiko to join her. Akiko responded by sitting down on the other sleeping bag and looking up at Max, in silent communication that she would be sleeping next to him tonight. Max understood the unspoken signal perfectly and lay down next to Akiko. She slid in next to him, and he closed the flap over the both of them, and lay on his back as Akiko lay on her side with her head on his chest.

Roone came to Pilar, and she stood up. They embraced, and Roone buried his face in her fragrant neck. After some time, they broke, looked down at Max and Akiko snuggled into one another, and smiled at each other.

"I guess they are taking their friendship to the next level," Roone whispered into Pilar's ear. "I love you, baby. Get some sleep. We've got a long walk ahead of us."

Pilar hugged Roone tightly, and he wrapped her up in his long arms, and then guided her to her sleeping place. She stood up on her tiptoes and kissed him again, and then got into the sleeping bag.

The four college students continued their trek north on I-75 at first light. They changed their minds about looking for the public facilities at Rockridge Park, electing to get farther outside the metropolitan area. They would need water. Roone had taken a quart bottle of bleach from the student union canteen to purify surface water, but they did not have anything to hold water in. There was no shortage of plastic bottles littering the side of the highway, and soon they found eight, 16-ounce bottles complete with tops.

There were lots of people sleeping in the cars that were stranded on the highway. Daylight revealed that more than half of the cars had at least one person in them. Roone noticed that most of the people in the cars were either older or very overweight. He figured that the people who were young and fit enough had taken steps toward self-rescue. Those who could not rescue themselves waited in their cars to be rescued. The line of stranded cars on the highway stretched as far as the eye could see.

"What are all of these people in these cars going to do?" asked Pilar.

"I don't know. Where the hell are the authorities? You'd think they would be working to clear the highway," answered Roone.

"Hey, Max!" Roone said so that Max could hear him. Max and Akiko had fallen back a bit.

"Yo!" said Max and he and Akiko hurried to catch up.

"We need to find some water."

"Yeah, I know. We can't keep this pace without water, and we can't carry enough to keep the pace. We are going to have to find it along the way."

"I was thinking the same thing. Maybe the water is still on at these roadside gas stations. If it is, we can drink deep and carry the water internally and then if we have to, we can collect surface water and purify it."

"Man, last night the road was packed with people on foot," said Max as he stopped and looked back toward Atlanta. "Where'd they all go?"

"I was thinking the same thing. I bet most of them were commuters, and got off the highway and walked towards home, wherever that is, and the others are probably taking it easy and resting before the final leg home. I don't think many of them are walking all the way to Chattanooga."

"Or Kentucky," replied Max.

"Don't fucking remind me."

"You are welcome to come home with me. But it is 20 miles out of your way, which means an extra 40 miles of walking if doubling back is your only option."

"Dude, I am hell-bent on getting to my Dad's. But thanks for the offer."

"Well, we still have at least two days' walk to Chattanooga."

"I would say three or four."

"Yeah. I was just being ambitious and optimistic."

"Young man! Young man! Can you help me?" A woman's voice was coming from up ahead somewhere. "Young man!"

A woman was waving from the passenger window and looking into the side mirror at Roone. Roone and Max approached the car. Pilar and Akiko faded back.

"Yes, ma'am?" said Roone from the edge of the shoulder.

"Young man, does your cell phone work? I need to call my son."

Roone breathed in and out. It was just an older woman sitting alone in a car.

"Uh, no ma'am. Cell phones are not working at the moment. There is no electric power."

"What? No cell service and no electric? What the heck is going on?"

"You haven't heard anything?"

"Heard what? I was driving down the highway going to my son's house in Riverdale. And then the traffic just stopped dead. I must have fallen asleep. I ain't never heard o' no traffic jam taking all night."

"Ma'am, there was a nuclear war in the Middle East last night. Within an hour or two the electric grid went down. I don't know why or how they might be related, but that is what everyone seems to agree happened. The cars on the highway all the way down to Atlanta have not moved an inch since yesterday. I think you are going to have to walk."

The woman looked at him as if he had been catching flies in his mouth and scratching his ear with his feet.

"Walk? I can't walk! I'm fifty years old, and I'm a big woman. I wouldn't make it to the next exit."

Then she opened the door of the car and, with great effort, stood up for emphasis. She was an impressive specimen. She appeared to be a perfect square—five feet, four inches by five feet four inches and about half as thick. Her garments, a mauve top and black pants that stopped just below her knees, were made of a synthetic material that stretched to give her ample bulk room to maneuver. Her feet were shod in a pair of glittery gold flat shoes that had been crushed and distorted by her weight. Her feet, ankles, and knees looked like a massive sleeve of dark hanging deli cheese that was pile-driven into her shoes, with her flesh spilling out and over the confines of her footgear.

"Well, ma'am, then you are going to have to wait until the authorities get here."

"When the hell will that be?" Her bright white teeth and blood-red tongue were a powerful contrast to her dark skin color, and together with the animated way that she spoke Roone was reminded of the mother of a childhood friend. It was an effort not to smile at the memory. His friend's mother was a gentle and kind soul.

"Ma'am, I am sure they will be here soon. If we see them as we walk, I will be sure to tell them to come looking for you. What is your name, please? So I can tell them when I see them?"

"My name is Lorraine Washington."

"OK, Lorraine, I will be sure to send them right here as soon as we find them. OK?"

"OK, thank you, young man. That would be very nice of you."

As they walked away, Max said, "Dude, what the hell are you talking about? Who are we going to tell to help Lorraine Washington?"

"No one. There is no one to tell, and there is nothing we can do for her. Do you think the four of us could carry her? Or would you have preferred that I told Lorraine that she was probably going to die here? Look around you, man! There are thousands of people in these cars. They just happened to be in the wrong place at the wrong time—no one told them WWIII was about to break out, so they didn't pack for the occasion. They have no food, no water, and most don't even have a change of clothes. Worse, many of them are incapable of walking more than a few hundred yards. There is nothing we can do about it."

Max looked dejected and said nothing, and fell back a few steps behind Roone. Akiko took Max's hand, and Pilar caught up with Roone and took his hand, and the four hiked in silence.

Chapter 10

Miriam Weiss ran as fast as her middle-aged body could manage down the hallway to the front door of their apartment, where she stopped and fumbled for her keys. The door opened and Martin, her husband of 12 years, stood before her. Miriam collapsed into his arms. After a moment's embrace—an embrace infused with the emotional component of unimaginable tragedy—she opened her eyes and saw that they were not alone. More than a dozen members of their Schul, or Jewish Temple, were behind Martin. It was standing room only in their New York City apartment.

When Miriam and Martin finally broke their embrace, their twin daughters, aged 11, ran to them, with one daughter seizing Miriam and the other Martin. Miriam looked back into the apartment and the people sitting and standing there and to their anguished faces and their tear-filled eyes. The parents comforted their children individually and then came together in a family group hug. After some time, Martin peeled away. He had only just gotten home himself, perhaps a minute before Miriam, and had found the throng of people that were now in his home waiting for him in the lobby of his apartment building. Similar scenes were playing out all across the New York Metropolitan area that night. He and his friends had ridden up to his floor in two separate elevators, in a state of shock. They walked in silence behind Martin to his apartment, where he paid the children's nanny and sent her home to see to her own family. The nanny sprinted off. She must have been watching the news. Seconds later Miriam was at the door. Miriam and the nanny could have passed each other in separate elevators.

Martin was a highly educated Wall Street professional with advanced degrees in mathematics and business and a Doctorate in economics—but that was only what he did for a living. His passion was his faith, and the history of the Jewish people. Several years earlier he had been ordained as a Rabbi in the Orthodox tradition and had taken an unpaid position as Rabbi for a small Orthodox congregation on the Upper West Side neighborhood of Manhattan.

When meeting Martin, few people guessed at first that he was an observant Jew, much less a Rabbi. Of course, the "kippah" that he wore on his head at all times soon showed his convictions. While soft-spoken and kind of spirit, Martin was a bear of a man. Barrel-chested, and with shoulders that looked like they belonged on a man felling trees rather than leading a Jewish community in prayer and observance, Martin could have passed for a retired Iranian wrestler, or perhaps a Greek arm-wrestling champion. In fact, he did have serious training in several martial arts disciplines. After people got to know Martin, they came to see him as a leader who was filled with goodwill towards his fellow man—Jew and Gentile alike—but the first thing that impressed was always the obvious brute strength of his physique.

Martin wasted no time and addressed those assembled. "I can only say that I have heard the reports. It seems that all of you have heard them as well."

There were a wail and cry from one of the women who was standing in the back of the apartment as she fell to the ground. Several others knelt down beside her.

"Her daughter is in Israel," Miriam whispered into Martin's ear.

Martin closed his eyes and winced.

A knock came at the door, and since the door had not fully closed from Miriam's entrance, the new guests gently pushed the door open. Martin turned to see a young couple in tears standing outside his front door. The woman was in obvious distress. Perhaps it would be better to say that she was in agony. Her husband was holding her around the waist with his left hand and on her upper arm closest to him with his right. Had he not held her tightly his wife would not have remained standing. Martin knew that her parents lived in Israel.

"Please, come in," was all that Martin could think to say at the moment.

He turned to the people who had already arrived and said, "I know that many of you do not know if your family members and loved ones living in Israel are alive or have perished. It may be some time before we know exactly what has happened. It is widely reported from every major news source that Israel, Iran, Saudi Arabia, and Pakistan have all experienced significant nuclear events."

Cries of despair filled the room. Martin continued.

"I know you have come here to be with your people in this time of great tragedy, but this is not the time to comfort each other. This is a time for action. We have no idea who or what has caused these events, and we certainly cannot trust in the veracity or accuracy of future reports. This could be the end of a nuclear war—or just the beginning. New York City could very well be next."

Distraught as the members of this group were, it had not occurred to any of them that more nuclear attacks could take place. It stood to reason that in any nuclear war the northeast coast of the United States would be high on the list of potential targets. Such reasoning forced all of the people in Martin's apartment to concern themselves with the immediate future rather than the immediate past, if only for a short while. Still, no one said anything in response, so Martin continued.

"We, Miriam and the girls and I, are going to leave the city tonight."

Martin's good friend, Jeffrey Levi, spoke up. "Where will you go? It is a madhouse out there! We walked up here from Murray Hill. There must have been a hundred thousand people standing around Grand Central trying to get in! You could never get near the place. I am sure that Penn Station is the same. We are trapped."

"We are going to walk out of the city," responded Martin. "Perhaps we will get lucky and be able to hitch a ride along the way. If not, then not. But we are not staying here."

"Rabbi, with all due respect," said Rachel Rosenthal, a professor of mathematics at City College. "A thermonuclear bomb would immediately kill almost everyone within 5 to 20 miles of the detonation point, and radiation sickness would eventually kill everyone for 50 miles in every direction. If an attack were to occur, there would surely be many bombs deployed."

"Yes, I am sure that is true, and all the more reason for us to put as many miles as possible, as quickly as possible, between the city and us. We are leaving immediately. I am not telling any of you what you should do. This is a decision each family will have to make for themselves, taking into consideration your circumstances. But it is not just a nuclear attack that we must fear. Tomorrow the banks will be closed. The cash and credit cards in your pockets are essentially worthless. The international banking system, the SWIFT payment system for settling international trade, along with domestic shipping and trucking, all of this has already ceased to exist. Everything we know as money is an IOU of an IOU of an IOU going out to infinity. That IOU chain has been broken. There will be no stuffing the shaving cream back in the can. Everything we ever knew no longer exists."

"How can that be!?" shrieked Ruth Solomon, an incredibly wealthy elderly woman whose late husband built his fortune in New York City real estate. "I think you are overreacting, Rabbi."

"Well, I may well be, Mrs. Solomon. And I sincerely hope that I am. In that case, I can always walk back and see all of you for Shabbos. But I doubt I will be coming back. There are 50 million human beings living within a 200-mile radius of here. Perhaps more. There will not be a scrap of food on the shelves anywhere. The region is entirely dependent on food transported in on trains, trucks, and ships. I don't think anyone is going to be willing to travel to New York City anytime soon, with the possible exception of the National Guard. No, we—my family—are leaving right now. Anyone here who wishes to walk with us is welcome to come, but I cannot guarantee that I can be of assistance to you. Anyone who wishes to walk with us must be able to keep up as we will not stop for anything."

Miriam was staring in wide-eyed disbelief at her husband.

"Please," Martin said looking back at her with a pleading expression on his face. "Pack two changes of clothes and as much food as can be effectively carried in our backpacks, along with our sleeping bags and the necessary toiletries. Put on comfortable walking shoes and layers of clothing that can be removed. Please. There is no other way."

Miriam and Martin had been committed hikers for many years, though that had slowed when the girls were very young. For the last two years, they had made overnight trips to Bear Mountain State Park by train. All had backpacks, sleeping bags, and hiking shoes. Still, Miriam hesitated. Miriam herself was an adjunct professor in the Sociology Department at Hunter College, where she taught Women's Studies. Miriam quickly calculated that this was not the time to question Martin's judgment. She and the girls departed for the bedrooms.

"I wish I had more to say to all of you. I wish I could be a comfort to you now in your time of sorrow and anguish. I hope all of you will understand that my first responsibility is to my family—Miriam and the girls. Every single action I take from this moment forward will be taken with their future in mind. If any of you wish to come with us, you will have to leave your life here with what you have on at this moment, and I don't recommend that. I think we have enough food in the pantry to feed all of us for a day, perhaps even two, but you will need coats and hats and comfortable shoes and many other things, and I just don't know when we might find such things. Those of you who are not coming with us are welcome to everything and anything we leave behind in the apartment. May God bless you and keep you."

And with that Martin was no longer their Rabbi. He was a refugee.

The young man who came to the apartment last with his distraught wife spoke up. "Rabbi, my parents live in Riverdale. Which way are you walking?"

"Up the West Side Highway, across the bridge and hopefully on to the Saw Mill River Parkway or the Hudson Line tracks. I hope to make it to Westchester County tonight."

"We will walk with you as far as Riverdale. We live in a small studio apartment. I doubt we have even a day's worth of food at home. We will leave with you when you go."

Martin clapped the man, David Rosen, on the shoulder, and said as he walked away, "We leave in 15 minutes."

Chapter 11

It had been less than three hours since the reports of
nuclear explosions in the Middle East came through. The
Internet was still operating, though many websites were not
responding and those that did took a long time to load. The
phone system was overwhelmed by the surge in traffic, and
calls would not go through. Walt marveled that the Web was
working at all. Still, there was no official word from the U.S.
Government. The reports were coming from the social media
platforms, bloggers, and the international news services. The
trains coming north from Grand Central Terminal were
packed, standing room only. The express to Tarrytown just
disgorged its passengers, many of whom did not live in
Tarrytown, but as no one had any idea who had nuked who
or what and who was going to be next, many people were
afraid that New York City might be the next nuclear attack
target, so they fled to Grand Central Terminal upon hearing
the news, and took the next train headed out of the city,
without concern as to where the train was heading, so long as
it was heading away from Manhattan. Of course, on any
other night every train would make five to eight round trips,
but not tonight. Every departing train was on a one-way trip
out of the city. The railway employees operating those trains
were not about to head back to Grand Central Terminal. Most
of the workers on the Metro-North line lived north of
Manhattan. The crew on this train had gotten on at the
Tarrytown station. They now abandoned the train and headed
off to the cars they drove to work that day, heading for home.
The same was true of all of the Long Island Rail Road and
PATH trains. This had the effect of stranding nearly all of the
two million people who commuted to and from New York
City every weekday.

By the time Walt and Manny had finished emptying the small gas station convenience store, the traffic on Route 9 heading north was at a standstill, bumper to bumper. They needed to get across to the southbound lanes, which were still moving slowly. Since there was no way for the drivers of the cars in the northbound lanes to open a space for Walt to cross to the southbound lanes, he had to improvise.

Jumping out of his car and flashing his Firefighter's badge, he approached the young man in the driver's seat of the car in front of him.

"Hey man, I need your help," Walt shouted to him to get through the closed car window. The man lowered his window. "We need to open a lane here for emergency vehicles. I need you to pull into the southbound lanes until they pass and then back up into your spot after they pass."

Then Walt headed into the middle of the southbound lanes holding up his badge. To his great relief, the woman in the next car stopped. He wondered how much longer a badge would have any effect. Walt pointed to the driver of the car behind the northbound vehicle he needed to move to remain where he was and flashed his badge again. There was a family in that vehicle, and the young man in the driver's seat signaled his understanding. Walt then motioned to the man in the northbound lane, who then started the laborious effort of getting his car out of the bumper-to-bumper traffic and into the southbound lane. It took a few back and forth full rotations of the steering wheel, but he got it done. Manny drove through the space, and Walt sprinted back to his car, got in, and shot across the gap in the traffic. The drivers of the cars he just commandeered looked after him, not sure of what just happened. It didn't matter. Northbound traffic didn't move an inch, and the driver who had made room for Walt performed a parallel parking maneuver back into the space he vacated.

After traveling at a crawl in the southbound lane of Route 9, Walt turned onto Pocantico Street heading toward

Beekman Avenue. Eastbound traffic was at a standstill, so Walt turned right on Beekman and headed toward the Hudson River and River Road. He was the only car headed in this direction and soon arrived at the "H-bridge" that straddled the railroad of the Hudson Line, which ran along the east side of the river all the way to Grand Central Terminal in midtown Manhattan.

As he came to the crest of the northwest portion of the "H," Walt saw hundreds of people milling about the train station platform and the street in front of the station. A northbound train was stopped on the tracks with its doors open, but it did not appear that anyone was on the train. He turned left and left again to come down the northeast ramp, where a police officer was directing traffic. Walt was a pillar of the community and knew everyone. He flashed his lights at the cop, and the cop recognized the car—he had gone to high school with Walt's son Manny—and trotted over.

"Hey, Mr. T. Hi ya doin'?" The police officer, Santiago Perez, had been with the Tarrytown police force for nearly ten years. His manner and voice were as if he were directing traffic out of a church parking lot on a Sunday.

"Hey, Santi. I'm good," Walt called him by his nickname. "What the hell is going on here?"

"The express train arrived a little while ago," the officer said. "It was packed like a sardine can. Like nothing I have ever seen before. We are treating over 50 people who overheated or got crushed. There must have been 5,000 people. Maybe more. On a train with the capacity for less than 1,000? Freaking crazy."

"Holy shit!" Then, after a brief pause as he looked back on the scene, "Is there something wrong with the train?"

"We have no idea," said the officer as he took off his hat and rubbed his crew-cut head. "We can't find any of the people who worked that train."

Walt looked back over his shoulder at the crowd.

"The crew probably got on here this morning," Walt said, speaking to himself as much as to the police officer. "So, their cars were here." He paused. "They're gone."

"Yeah, that's what our sergeant said."

"The train's crew are already in their cars and are trying to get home. That train ain't going anywhere unless your guys know someone who can drive a train and is willing to head into the city."

"We got our own problems," said officer Perez. "What if every train coming out of Manhattan dumps 5,000 people here? Where the hell are we going to put them? We don't need that train coming back here every two hours with another 5,000 people, not to mention all of the other trains."

"What about the commuters trying to get back home to Tarrytown?"

"They are on their own. I can tell you that not many of the people that were on that train there were locals. They were just people trying to get out of the New York City."

"Holy shit…" muttered Walt. Then he picked up his voice and directed it to Santi. "I am going to my shop to pick up a few things. Is it possible to get across Broadway?" Route 9 was called "Broadway" in Tarrytown. "Route 9 is completely stopped over in Sleepy Hollow."

"We cleared the Main Street intersection for emergency vehicles. That includes firemen. I will radio up that you are coming that way."

"Thanks, Santi. Good luck."

"You too, Mr. T."

Walt's mind raced as he processed what he had just seen; if people were fleeing the city like that, they must be afraid that New York would be next. But Tarrytown is only 25 miles north of mid-town Manhattan. If New York City were to be the site of the next nuclear attack, 25 miles was not far enough away.

Walt's house was only a quarter of a mile up the hill, but it was a steep hill. Carrying everything up the hill would take him, his wife, their son, and his wife a dozen trips—and that was if no one else discovered the treasure trove he had in his car. But Walt made it home through the Main Street intersection, his car loaded with goods from his trip to the grocery store, his gas station and convenience store, and from the workshop. In addition to groceries and fuel, he had brought many things that might prove valuable in the future: hand tools, a few more diesel storage cans, paper, pens, and a .357 magnum handgun and two 9mm automatic pistols he kept in a safe at the shop because his wife hated guns and refused to allow them in their home. She did not know about the .223 caliber assault rifle he had purchased over a decade earlier, which was in their clothes closet behind the suits that he never wore. He had only three boxes of ammo for the .357, but he had 750 rounds for the 9mm pistols, and a thousand rounds for the rifle in an ammo can along with three 30-round clips. He wondered how long the ammo kept for, as he had purchased all of it at least five years ago. He had not fired any of the weapons since attending the firearm safety class required for a pistol permit, but he knew his way around firearms.

He pulled into the driveway of the large home and spacious lot, through the stone pillars and back to the car park off the kitchen. A stone wall separated the car park from the circular driveway. Walt wanted all of the privacy he could get. Jenny was outside waiting for him and ran to him as he stepped out of the car.

"Oh, thank God! I can't get through to anyone on the phone!"

Jenny was near hysteria. Walt did not try to comfort her. He was in crisis management mode. He grabbed her upper arms and held Jenny still and waited for her to make eye contact. She finally did.

"Five thousand people crammed onto a train meant for less than a thousand just arrived at the station. Most of them are not locals. You know what that means? It means we are going to be overrun with people coming out of the city."

"What?!"

"The train that brought them here was abandoned by the crew. But there will be other trains, and I bet each one will be packed with thousands of people. They won't all land here in Tarrytown, but I expect more than a few will. Others will land all up and down the Hudson Line." Walt was referring to the small towns along the river in Westchester County, N.Y. There were a half a dozen of them to the south. "And there will be thousands and thousands more making the trek on foot."

"So?" Jenny was starting to calm down.

"So, we don't have the resources to feed and shelter them. This will be the largest refugee crisis in the history of mankind. And it is going to happen right in our front yard."

Chapter 12

Traffic was at a standstill as Martin and his family, accompanied by David and Rachel Rosen, walked west on West 87th Street. They stayed one block north of the major crosstown street where traffic could travel both ways.

"Are your parents at home?" Martin asked David.

"Well, they are not out of town that I know of. I hope they are home. My father sees patients at Albert Einstein medical center, but his surgeries are scheduled early in the morning and he is usually home by 3 pm."

Martin only nodded his head and kept up a brisk pace, a pace so fast that his wife and daughters were forced to break into a short run every few steps just to keep up. Martin did not slow down. This was the pace that must be kept. He expected to cover nearly four miles each hour and to rest for five to ten minutes before continuing on another four-mile stretch.

"Do you really think there will not be any food or supplies being brought into the city?" asked David.

"Well, have you noticed that the cars on the street have not moved an inch since we started walking west? I bet that right now all lanes, northbound and southbound, of the Westside Highway are being used by northbound vehicles, and that none of them are moving, either," responded Martin, his breathing heavy. "We will know in a few minutes. If that is true here, it will likely be true for every other access road in or out of the city. Trucks heading south have been forced to turn around."

Martin and David set the pace up front. The flow of people walking towards the West Side Highway picked up considerably. Miriam and Rachel walked hand-in-hand behind the men, and the twins also walked hand-in-hand behind their mother and Rachel, who cried as she walked. As

87th street came to an end, the Westside Highway came into view, and as Martin predicted, the southbound lanes were filled with cars pointing north—though no vehicles were moving on either side of the highway. Here the group merged in with other people who were walking and turned north on Riverside Drive. Traffic was at a complete standstill, and the number of pedestrians seemed to grow by the minute.

"I don't think we will be hitching a ride anytime soon," Martin said loud enough for the group to hear him. "It does not take many abandoned cars on the highway to make it impossible for anyone to drive out of the city. Or into it.

"Eventually everyone will abandon their cars and walk. It would take a month to clear all of the cars even if they could get every tow truck in the city on it. And they can't. The tow trucks are stranded behind all of the abandoned cars, too. As are all of the tow truck drivers, all of whom have better things to do right now. Like taking care of their own families."

"Holy shit," muttered David. "I didn't think of that."

"There will be nothing coming into the city or Long Island by road. It will have to be by water. I doubt the trains will be running any time soon. I don't think electric service will be on much longer, and everything depends on the duration of that. We need to be in Yonkers before that happens." Yonkers was the first city to the north of the New York City, directly bordering the borough of the Bronx. "From there I think it is less than 15 miles up the Hudson River along the tracks to Tarrytown."

The parade of humanity walking up the West Side Drive seemed to belong to the fit and the young, though Martin noticed that some of the drivers, mostly portly office workers, were abandoning their cars. He assumed they were trying to get to their homes in Westchester and Fairfield Counties. Martin reasoned that most of them would make it home—eventually—and that most of them would die there—eventually. They were not in any physical condition for self-rescue. He brought his concerns back to himself and his wife and children. The people all around him were God's children, not his.

David Rosen walked in silence beside Martin, thinking carefully about Martin's commentary. David was an only child from a good family and had recently completed the master's in business administration program at Columbia University. His father was a general surgeon, and his mother a psychiatrist. They had met in medical school. His parents were not religious Jews, but David became observant after meeting Rachel, and his parents welcomed his new-found convictions. Her family became observant during her parents' lifetime—her grandparents had not been observant—and kept kosher at all times, not just in their home. The Holocaust had had the effect of refocusing many secular Jews back to their Jewish heritage. Rachel's parents had retired to Israel a little over a year earlier, thus fulfilling a lifelong dream. David blanched at the thought and slowed his pace a bit. Martin did not and pulled ahead of David.

"Rabbi," David said as he jogged to catch up and walk abreast with Martin. "Where are you going? You are welcome to stay the night at my parents' house. They have a huge house, and no one lives there but the two of them."

"We are going to make it to Tarrytown tonight," he said between heaving breaths. They were practically jogging and were all carrying loaded backpacks. "A brother of a good friend of mine lives there."

"What if they aren't there?"

"Yes, well, that occurred to me. If they are not there, we will apply to the local Temple for any assistance they might give us. But we will stay just long enough to get a night's sleep and continue north."

Martin's train of thought was more than a little frightening to David, as he had not thought past getting to his parents' house in Riverdale, which was not much more than ten miles north of midtown Manhattan.

"You think New York City could be next?"

Martin took a deep breath.

"David, every second that goes by with us still standing here sharing existence gives me hope that will not be the case. But it does not matter. There *is* no New York City anymore. Come on; you just finished your MBA! You know enough about how the system works. The money that lubricates our economy and maintains law and order is only an infinite series of IOU's. Once a significant link in that chain of IOU's is broken, the whole chain falls apart. Look around you!"

David did so. They were in the middle of a sea of humanity walking on foot out of Manhattan. Martin continued.

"None of these people is ever going to make a mortgage payment, car payment, or credit card payment ever again. This is not 9/11, where 3,000 people were murdered, and several buildings got knocked down, and the stock exchanges were closed for a few days. Millions of innocent people have been murdered in the name of 'national security.' The political and philosophical implications are mind-boggling— this might well be the end of the nation-state as a political entity—but the consequences for the average person living in the industrialized West will be much more tangible and acute in the short term. As of this moment the financial system of banks, cash, paychecks, loans, and credit cards no longer exists. The stock market will never open again. The banks will never open again. Ever. The cash in your pocket is worthless. Everything is surreal now because it has only been a few hours since the news of the bombings, and people are not hungry yet. In a day or two, the crisis will no longer be surreal. It will be very real."

"Come on," David pleaded. "If there are no more bombs, if the U.S., Europe, Japan, and China are not involved, why would things be so dire here?"

"Because North America has 450 *million* people, most of whom think that food comes from a grocery store and water comes from a faucet," Martin replied impatiently. "These are people who think you stay warm in winter by turning a dial. And because there are over 100 nuclear power plants in the United States, and many of them will be at serious risk of catastrophic failure."

Martin caught himself and relented, continuing in a softer tone. "It would be a wonderful thing if the United States and Europe remained free from nuclear attacks. But even if we are very fortunate and none of the nuclear power plants experiences catastrophic failure, that does not mean that oil from the Middle East or bananas and coffee from Central America will be on the menu anytime soon, because they surely will not. But consumer items like bananas and coffee are not the issue. The issue is trade. How will people pay for food, water, and clothing? How will international trade be settled and paid for tomorrow? Are those sellers going to accept 'trust me, I will pay you next Tuesday?' I hardly think so. Are buyers able to pay COD? Not unless they have a hell of a lot of gold on hand and the ability to exchange one for the other. Eventually, international trade will happen again, but not in the volume that we have grown accustomed. And just who will be going to work tomorrow or the next day? How will they be paid? With checks drawn on banks that will never open again? Remember, our currency is loaned into existence, and as I said, not a single person you will meet is going to make another mortgage, car, or credit card payment—and that is the end of the money supply and the monetary system. All of the major currencies that were in use a few hours ago no longer exist. The government will not be able to put it all back together quickly enough to stuff the genie back in the bottle—no matter how many people they kill. Our money is backed by the full faith and credit—that means the taxing muscle, the ability to force people to pay taxes with our currency just to live—of the U.S. government.

Most of that comes from income taxes collected from people within the confines of a monetary and banking system that no longer exists. Millions of people are abandoning the only lives they ever knew, as we speak. In just a few days those who remained behind will be far more interested in staying alive than in earning a paycheck that they cannot cash, drawn on a bank that will never open again, to pay for the very things that the system rests on."

Martin looked at David and awaited his response. There was none.

"And that's just us, at the individual level. What about international trade? The entire world has settled their trade accounts with U.S. dollars paid through the SWIFT payment system. That system required everyone to suspend disbelief, the way you do when you watch a movie, and accept bytes on a screen as payment for something genuine—let's say two million barrels of oil or 40 tons of bananas or coffee. Reality has just set in. Sellers with two million barrels of oil will still want to sell their oil, but they will insist on some other form of payment. Until that gets worked out, and that is if it ever gets worked out in any time frame that is meaningful to us, international trade is kaput, and with it the U.S. dollar. Here, do you have any cash on you? It doesn't matter. Just pretend you have cash because no one is going to be willing to take it as payment anyway. Ask the next ten people you see if they will sell you a bottle of water for $100. Would you sell a can of the soup you have in your backpack for $100?"

David stared ahead and scoffed to himself and then smiled.

"No. I guess I wouldn't."

"Just wait a few days," said Martin. "And see what you will be willing to do for a can of soup."

David turned his head to look at Martin who was looking back with a smirk on his face, his eyes unblinking, his head nodding, and then Martin added, "Humpty Dumpty sat on a wall. Humpty Dumpty had a great fall. All the king's horses and all the king's men couldn't put Humpty together again—especially after one or two nuclear power plants cook off. We have to get to a place of safety."

"Where would that be, Rabbi?"

"There are lots of safe places, but as a practical matter the answer is *not here*."

Chapter 13

Jason was steaming hard-boiled eggs for snacks for the next day. Or at least he was trying to. The pot seemed to stop agitating. He ignored the pot and opened the refrigerator door.

The light in the fridge was out. Jason looked back at the stove. The indicator light that warned of a hot cooking surface was not on.

Wow. Never blew the stove breaker before, Jason thought to himself.

A quick trip to the home's electricity panel box told him it was not a tripped circuit breaker. The electric service was down.

He returned to the kitchen, removed the steaming pot from the electric range, turned the burner dial to the "off" position, and headed out to the summer kitchen. There was an old camp stove standing by out there. He thought for a moment of firing up the wood cook stove that stood in the middle of the kitchen, but the evening was just too warm, and he didn't want to build a fire big enough to bring the wood stove up to cooking temperature. He decided against that. The stainless-steel outdoor wood-fired cooking station was standing at attention just outside the back door, but Jason just didn't feel like splitting kindling and lighting a fire. Finally, he brought in a 20-pound tank of propane from just outside the kitchen door to fuel the camp stove, twisted the regulator to attach the propane tank, turned the stove dial to start the flow of gas, and lit one of the burners with a long lighter designed for the purpose.

His wife and infant daughter were out for the afternoon and evening visiting at the home of some friends, and Jason was home with their 10-year-old boy and 8-year-old girl. His older son from a previous marriage, now 24 years old, was away at college. It was late October, and the sun would be going down soon. Illumination was not a problem—Jason had many hobbies, and one of those was collecting kerosene lamps and lanterns. He had enough lamps, wicks, and kerosene to keep them in light until hell froze over. But lamplight would not keep the chest freezer cold. The freezer held the meat from a large hog and a good-sized beef calf, and that meat was at risk. It would stay frozen for a day or two, but not beyond that.

The family lived on a 160-acre farm out in the country. The nearest small town with any commerce was nearly 20 miles away. He had only just recently finished porting his cell phone over to a free VOIP, (Voice-Over-Internet-Protocol) account. The only problem with that was that, with the power down, the internet router in the pantry was also without power, and since his only option for making phone calls was VOIP, he was not only in the dark, but also was unable to make phone calls. He had a pre-paid cell phone for use in an emergency, like calling AAA if his truck broke down, but the farm was so remote that there was no cell signal there, so that pre-paid phone was of no use. Not only was he in the dark, but he was also incommunicado with the outside world.

It was early evening. It would be dark in an hour or so, and his wife was not due home until after 9 pm. He figured it was probably just an accident or a downed transmission line and hoped the lights would be back on by dark.

The kids were a little rambunctious, without their TV, pads, and computers, so he ushered them out of the house and told them to play on the swings. That lasted 12 minutes. They had come back in the house, torturing him about the electricity, and darkness was fast approaching.

"Well, we can go to bed and hope the power comes back on sometime tonight, or we can get in the truck and drive to the WigWam," he said to the kids. The WigWam was a local gas station and convenience store.

"Can we get ice cream?" asked his 10-year-old son.

"Why not?" he replied. "Get your shoes on and let's go."

The gravel drive that led to the country road where their mailbox stood was almost a third of a mile long. Streetlights are not a regular feature out in the country, but Jason could see that the other farmhouses along the two-lane highway were also dark. The occupants of these homes sat outside and waved as he drove past. It was 8 miles to the WigWam and while driving along the two-lane country road he passed some people sitting outside their darkened homes. No one was talking on or looking at cell phones. The cell towers must have lost power, too.

Jason pulled his pickup truck up to the fueling islands at the gas station. The WigWam store was dark. The front door had a sign that said, "Closed." Not "Sorry—We're Closed." Just, "Closed." Well, it had been over two hours since the lights went out. He guessed they had just given up on waiting for power and had shut down early. He turned around for the 8-mile drive back to his farmhouse. On the way home, he passed several families sitting outside the fronts of their homes. They waved as he passed. Not one of them was using a cell phone. Something didn't seem right. People in the country will always wave and smile to a neighbor driving by. Well, they did wave, but they didn't smile. He didn't stop to talk, chalked up the somber expressions to the inconvenience of the blackout, and hoped that by the time, he returned home that the power would have come back on. He arrived home to find that it had not, so without further discussion Jason and the kids turned in for the night.

When his wife Ellen and their baby daughter returned home, the house was quiet. Jason was asleep and breathing heavily, lying naked on the bed without even a sheet to cover him. The farmhouse was not equipped with a central heating and cooling system, so sleeping naked was Jason's response to warm and humid evenings. Ellen typically wore one of

Jason's t-shirts. She put the baby down in the crib next to their bed, slid in next to Jason, and turned in for the night too.

Chapter 14

Walt was sitting at his computer desk trying to connect to the various news sites on the Internet, but none of them would load onto his screen. He tried his cell phone again, and now he got nothing—not even the "all circuits are busy" message he had gotten earlier. He went back to the spaghetti and meatballs that his wife placed before him. Walt took his fork and stabbed it down into the slippery mass of cooked pasta noodles and began to twirl the fork expertly in his hand to take a bite of his supper. As he brought his fork to his mouth the electric power went off, and even though he had thought it probable that they would lose power, it still came as somewhat of a surprise. Still, he was ready. He had a small LED flashlight in his pocket. He put his fork back down in the bowl, reached his hand into his pocket, took the flashlight out, and flicked it on. Then he stood up and headed out to the kitchen, bringing his bowl of pasta with him. He could see the light from Jenny's flashlight as she was coming down the stairs. Manny was standing outside the kitchen in the car park, enjoying the night air with his wife. The flashlight that Walt had given him was in his pocket, but he didn't bother to take it out. He could see his father's flashlight through the screen door to the kitchen, as well as the light from his mother's flashlight through a window as she came down the staircase. They met in the kitchen.

"Well, that's that," said Walt.

"Whaddaya mean?" asked Manny.

"I thought we would lose power," said Walt. He then turned to his wife and said, "Hey, Jen. Kill your flashlight. We only need one at a time."

Jenny turned off her flashlight.

Walt and Manny sat on the stools of the breakfast bar in the kitchen. Walt turned his flashlight off. The darkness was more comforting than the harsh light of the LED bulb. For a few minutes, no one said anything. The air was soft and still, and at first, the atmosphere brought back a childhood memory to Walt of waiting in the dark with his parents for the fireworks displays over the Hudson River on the Fourth of July, but after a while, it was just dark. Manny spoke first.

"Now what do we do?"

"Well, first off. We can't stay here."

"Where is there to go?" Manny asked, and then pointed out, "We don't even know what the hell is going on."

"We know that something big, perhaps nuclear war, happened in the Middle East. We know that there are thousands of people down by the train station with nowhere to go. We know that a train came out of the city filled with people trying to get as far away as possible. That train is still down at the train station and did not return to Grand Central because the crew abandoned it. We know the power is off. We know we live in the largest metropolitan area in the United States."

Manny sat back against the backrest of his stool, tried to get comfortable but couldn't help fidgeting and finally leaned over the table-sized breakfast bar with both of his elbows resting on it. Walt continued to lean back in his seat and seemed to take comfort in looking at the tops of his engineer's boots. Manny waited for his father to finish his train of thought, but it seemed Walt had finished.

"What are you trying to say?" asked Manny

Walt looked up at his son, and the two shared a short laugh. This last line was an attempt at a little gallows humor from an old inside joke.

"I wish I were trying to say something else. Eight million people are living in New York City, with another three or four million living on Long Island. What if the power is still out in 24 hours? How about 48 hours? 72 hours? If the power remains out, millions of desperate people are going to be walking up and out of New York City and Long Island. What do you think that is going to look like?"

Manny breathed in and held his breath for a few seconds, pursed his lips and tickled his nose with his mustache, and breathed out.

"We got a problem," said Manny. "We got a big problem."

"Yeah. We do. Geographically speaking, Westchester County is an 11-mile wide funnel with the Hudson River on one side and the Long Island Sound on the other. Millions upon millions of people are going to come walking through here. Are they bringing port-a-potties with them? Or are they going to shit wherever they can? What are they going to eat? Where are they going to sleep?"

Manny moved as if to speak, but Walt held his hand up and continued.

"I will tell you where they are going to sleep, eat, and shit—in the houses and commercial and apartment buildings here in Westchester and over in Fairfield County. Some will move on. Some will squat right here. Many of them will have guns. They will only pretend to ask if they can sleep somewhere or have something to eat. If someone says no, they will burn the house down, and the next door they knock on will be more receptive."

"We will defend ourselves," replied Manny.

"How?" ask Walt

"We have guns."

"Oh, great. So, we're gonna shoot the first ten people and leave their bodies out there on the front lawn as a warning? I guess we could always eat them. If we leave them to rot, we will all die of disease. If you don't plan on eating them, you must be planning on organizing a burial detail. I hope you have a backhoe with a full tank. We will be the first in the neighborhood to have our very own mass grave in the backyard."

"Alright, wise ass. What do you think we should do?"

"We have to leave. We can't stay here. And before we leave there is something I have to do."

Chapter 15

The morning light broke the darkness in Jason's bedroom and stirred him from the night's sleep. He looked over to the nightstand on his side of the bed. The LED lights from the computer charger were still dark.

Oh, shit. We are going to have to deal with the meat in the freezers. Farm life tends to focus the mind thus, but instead of getting up and after the day's tasks, he settled back into his pillow. He heard what appeared to be a knock at the front door, but convinced himself that he was still sleeping, and that he had dreamed that. Another series of raps brought him to wakefulness, wondering who could be knocking at his front door at dawn. He got out of bed, grabbed the pair of jeans he had worn the night before and a t-shirt, rubbed his eyes, and walked out of the bedroom as he pulled his arms through the shirt's sleeves and headed down the short hallway to the front door. There was an Amish man—Jason could tell by the hat—standing at the front of the porch with his back turned toward the front door. His Amish neighbors were diligent about respecting the privacy of others. Even from behind, Jason recognized the neighbor's oldest son, Noah, waiting there on his porch. Jason opened the door.

"Good morning, Noah! Come on in. I was not expecting you for another hour. I was just about to make coffee."

Noah turned around when he heard the door opening and nodded when he made eye contact with Jason then raised his right hand in a quick wave but said nothing. He took the screen door in his hand as Jason let it go, and followed Jason in.

Noah often helped Jason around the farm. And today they would be working hay—cutting, raking, and baling. It seemed there was always a field ready for one stage or another in the process from late spring to mid-autumn.

"My father sent me over early to see what you thought about what happened yesterday," Noah said to Jason's back.

This was a first. They had lived here for three years and Abraham, Noah's father, never had sought Jason's opinion about events before. Jason stopped, and with a quizzical look on his face turned to Noah and asked, "What happened yesterday?"

"You haven't heard?" Noah said as his hands came up just a bit from his sides with his palms facing Jason. "My father says World War III started last night—a nuclear war. Everybody in our church is talking about it. But we don't know what to make of it, and my father sent me over here to see what you might have to say."

The words coming out of Noah's mouth, said in the gentle manner typical of Jason's Plain People neighbors, pierced Jason's heart and mind and scattered his thoughts. It took him several more seconds to process what he just heard.

"Where did you hear this?" Jason asked, still having difficulty and not fully able to wrap his mind around what he was hearing.

"Everybody seems to know it," replied Noah, looking down at his boots. Noah always took his boots off before coming in their house. In his excitement and fear, he had forgotten this time to take them off. "All of the English are sitting outside their houses talking about it, and it seems as if all of our church members have gathered in my father's shop. I am surprised you didn't know."

"I have not heard a thing. The power went out last night, and we went to bed early."

"Hi, Noah," said Ellen in a quiet, I-am-not-quite-awake kind of voice, as she shuffled into the kitchen from the hallway behind the men. "What's going on?"

Noah just stood there and said nothing, but his eyes traveled back and forth from Jason and Ellen.

"Noah came here to tell us that World War III broke out last night," said Jason.

"Hold, on. What?" Ellen asked in a raised voice.

Jason and Ellen looked wide-eyed at each other, and then at Noah, and said nothing more. Noah collected himself and said, "My father asked me to come over here and ask you what you thought about the nuclear bombings."

Ellen was wide-awake now.

"*What* nuclear bombings?" She was on the verge of screaming.

"Easy honey," Jason said to her, and then turned to Noah.

"Noah, I have no idea what is going on in the world. Ellen was out at a music jam session last night with the baby, and I was home with the kids. We don't have TV, and I was not surfing the Web, so I have not heard or seen any of the news reports. The lights went out yesterday, and our phone works over the Internet, and that requires electric power—so no one could call us. This is the first we've heard about it. So please. Tell us what you know."

"Well, I don't know very much," Noah said, exasperated. "That's why my father sent me here. It seems there was a nuclear war in the Middle East last night."

Jason retired to his bedroom to get dressed for a visit with his Amish and Mennonite neighbors, while Noah stepped out on the porch to wait. Ellen waited in the kitchen for Jason to come out of the bedroom. The kids and the baby were—miraculously—still asleep. Jason appeared in the kitchen in clean blue jeans and a dull grey shirt that buttoned up the front. An outsider might have mistaken him for an Amishman or a Mennonite, but thanks to his full beard and mustache and belt instead of suspenders, none of the local Anabaptists would make that mistake. Jason attended a Quaker Meeting, and though he had no belief in the deity described in either the Old or New Testaments he had quietly taken on a manner of wearing plain clothing with solid grey shirts. Though it was not the garb worn by members of the local Amish church group, it was close enough to confuse outsiders.

Quakers referred themselves as "Friends", and to their loosely affiliated organizations as the "Religious Society of Friends." They had fled persecution in England and Holland, and had organized the colony of Pennsylvania as a safe place for Quakers and other persecuted Christian denominations. At the time of the American Revolution, one out of every three Americans identified as Quaker. By the early 21st century, only 1 in 300 Americans identified so. The Anabaptists, on the other hand, were thriving. Early in the 20th century, the American Anabaptist population was estimated to be about 5,000. By the early 21st century their ranks had swelled to 500,000.

In the 18th century, the Pennsylvania Quakers took in Anabaptist communities from the Continent—the Amish, Mennonites, Dunkards, and Hutterites—among many other denominations that were fleeing religious persecution in Europe. So, Jason felt he could relate to them. Step by step, he had fled industrial society's economic and social oppression. And although he did not convert and join an Amish or Mennonite church, the people here had accepted him and his family as friends and neighbors—although in the early days after their arrival, the Anabaptists' welcome to Jason and his family had been more reserved than the welcome which the Quakers had given the Anabaptists back in colonial Pennsylvania. Still, Jason and Ellen had felt welcome among them. But Jason was not too sure he would be welcomed today.

Noah was on the front porch waiting as Jason stepped out of the house. It was cool, so Jason wore his black felt hat. In his dark and plain clothes and black hat, Jason looked as if he might be attending a funeral—and the thought saddened him as it crossed his mind. It was likely that thousands, and perhaps millions of people, had died in the bombings.

"Noah, if you don't mind, I'd like to ride with you. I will walk back if you can't take me. I think it best that I conserve whatever fuel we have."

"Don't worry, I already figured on that," Noah replied. "I will run you back home."

Jason got in on the left side of the buggy, because the driver sat on the right over the buggy's brake pedals, such as they were. Noah's wasn't a true "buggy." A buggy has a framed black tarp covering it, and a glass windshield to keep the driver and passengers warm and dry. The vehicle Noah and Jason were sitting in was open to the elements and was more often called a "spring wagon." It was comfortable enough—as long as it was not raining, and the occupants had a heavy wool blanket to cover their legs if the weather was cold. Whether it got its name as a wagon appropriate for fine spring weather or because it was a just a wagon box that rested on axle springs, Jason didn't know. He just knew that he loved to ride in them, and so he had one of his own, that he used around the farm. He rode now with Noah because it would take more time to catch his buggy horse and harness and hitch him to the wagon than it would for Noah to bring him back home. As they drove down the long gravel driveway and through their woodlot to the paved two-lane highway a third of a mile from the house, it occurred to Jason that he was being summoned.

Abraham's farm was perhaps three or four miles away using the paved roads, though it was only a little over a mile away "as the crow flies," or if you had a horse to carry you through the woods and farmland that lay between. Noah typically rode his horse—a young quarter horse gelding that was coming along nicely as a cattle horse—over to Jason's house, but today he had arrived in the spring wagon pulled by "Trigger," the family's Standardbred gelding.

Jason was unquestionably being summoned.

The Standardbred breed of horse was the fastest gaited pacing horse in the world—some had been clocked at over thirty miles per hour at a trot and, in horse racing, these horses were known as "trotters." Trigger himself had been born and bred for the track, but had failed to make the grade, and had been sold at auction, and then sold again by the auction buyer to Abraham. Still, Trigger had a brisk and beautiful gate, and Noah and Jason arrived at the Yoder family farm in less than fifteen exhilarating minutes of fresh air and beautiful scenery. After he had gotten used to buggies and wagons, Jason always felt that cars moved too fast. They got you where you were going a whole lot faster, but you missed most of the details of the scenery that surrounds your life. In a car, when you finally saw something worth looking at, you were already past it. As the buggy turned onto Abraham's driveway, the sound of the wagon's steel rims changed from rickety clanking on blacktop to crunching on gravel, bringing Jason's thoughts back to the matter at hand. Thirty somber men who were congregating around the workshop looked to the spring wagon as it crunched down the gravel drive toward the house and outbuildings. Noah pulled up to the hitching post that was set in cement outside and to the left of the workshop, and he and Jason hopped out. Noah tied Trigger to the post as Jason walked toward the workshop. Nothing in the countenance of the men there gave any indication that something was amiss in the world.

"Hallo," some of the men said in their low-German accented dialect. They always drew out the "o" at the end of it. Jason greeted the men he knew by name and nodded to those he did not but did not offer to shake their hands. Handshaking is not a common custom of greeting amongst the Plain People. If offered, most of them would do so—but with absolutely no enthusiasm. Jason continued into the shop to where Abraham was standing. Abraham was speaking to several men, in the language they used in their homes, as the men gathered around a hay square baler that was in for repairs. Abraham heard the small commotion of Jason's arrival and switched seamlessly over to English.

"Hello there, Jason," Abraham said in his gentle way. Jason noticed he used the English "Hello" rather than the "Hallo" of his German dialect.

"Good morning," Jason replied, speaking to all gathered.

The other men smiled shyly and offered a quiet greeting but demurred to Abraham.

"Well, now. It looks like we've got big doings in the world," said Abraham, looking down and pulling and stroking his long grey beard with his right hand several times before finally just holding onto it, perhaps in an effort to stop from continuing a nervous habit.

Jason never hurried the Plain People—the Amish and the Old Order Mennonites often referred to themselves that way—in conversation or anything else. They would get where they were going in due time. He remained still and waited for Abraham to continue. The workshop became very quiet.

"Anyway, we don't know anything about nuclear bombs and such, and we are wondering what it is that has happened over there. We thought you might know a thing or two about this."

The men in attendance formed a circle around Jason and Abraham. Noah, who spent a great deal of time with Jason and was usually very outgoing, faded back into the crowd. It occurred to Jason that it was very likely that none of these men had seen photos of Hiroshima and Nagasaki, or of the nuclear tests in the New Mexico desert and on the Bikini Atoll. They understood that something horrific had occurred, but they were not able to grasp the scale of a thermonuclear weapon. Worse, their faith contains an "End Times" scenario. Jason was sure that this weighed heavily on their minds.

Jason took a deep breath and mirrored the gentle and unassuming manner of speaking that Abraham used and said, "Well, I don't know what happened. I can tell you a thing or two about thermonuclear bombs if that helps, but I went to bed early last night because the power went out in my house. I don't have a TV. And I have not been able to get onto the Internet. So, I hadn't heard a thing until Noah showed up at my house this morning. Perhaps you can tell me what you have heard."

"The truck driver that delivers logs to my brother's sawmill said that Iran and Israel got into a nuclear war and that both countries have been destroyed. And that Saudi Arabia and Pakistan were also involved and perhaps India."

"So, all we know is what you heard from a truck driver?" asked Jason.

"Well, my brother and his sons heard it too. The trucker was sitting in his cab while delivering logs to the sawmill when the news broke about what happened. He called them to the truck, and they all listened in. I don't think the radio would fool around about something like that."

Jason had to suppress a smile at the mention of "the radio."

"No, I suppose they wouldn't," he said without the slightest trace of sarcasm or patronizing.

"Several of our English neighbors saw it on TV, too, and they told our people about it."

"My sense is that the county people, you know, the sheriff and the fire department and maybe the state authorities, will probably have the most accurate sense for what is going on," Jason said.

"Well, we have not seen hide nor hair of any of those people," Abraham said more excitedly than Jason had ever heard him. "You'd think they would send word."

Jason considered that and said, "Yeah. You'd think they would."

"What do you think all this means for us?" Now Abraham was getting down to it.

"The good news is that you and I are still here talking to each other," replied Jason. "So, no one has dropped a bomb on us. But with the electricity down we have no means of communicating with the outside world. We don't *know* what happened."

"Every news channel on the TV was sayin' that Iran and Israel and a few other countries done nuked each other," said a voice with a heavy Appalachian twang.

Everyone recognized the voice. McCoy O'Neil, son of the largest landowner in the county, had seen the dozens of buggies parked at Abraham's, and decided to invite himself to the gathering. He sat astride his massive spotted draft cross just outside the double door of the workshop. "And it seems there were a lot of excited city folk around our country 'fraid they was gonna be next," O'Neil continued. He seemed to be enjoying himself. "The news said they was runnin' for the hills! And then, just when things was startin' to get good, the power went out."

He seemed more disappointed that he didn't get to watch the exodus of refugees pouring out of American and European cities than about the murder of millions of people.

The circle of Amish men around Jason and Abraham parted so that none of them stood between O'Neil and Jason. The Amish were content to listen and to let the outsiders speak. Jason took a deep breath. This was the last thing he wanted to do, and O'Neil was the last person he wanted to see, but at least here was a first-hand source of the news reports. Neither he nor any of the Amish, aside from the few that listened in on the radio in the trucker's cab, had anything else to go on.

"Hello McCoy," said Jason. "Anything you can tell us of the news reports would be greatly appreciated. I am afraid that none of us had access to a TV yesterday. Did you watch the news personally?"

"You bet I did!" O'Neil seemed to be genuinely enthusiastic about the bombings. "I was sitting there watching FOX News. First, they said it was an earthquake in Iran. Then they said that the Russian military said that Iran and Israel got into a nuclear war. They said Iran and Israel are both gone! Can you believe that? Just plain gone! Pakistan got involved, and they got bombs too! And Saudi Arabia, which don't make no kinda sense cause the Russians said they ain't even got a nuclear bomb, but they said they got bombed anyway!"

"Did the U.S. government say anything?" asked Jason. "Did the president hold a press conference?"

"Nope. The people on the TV said that the president was prolly on his way to Air Force One or already up in the air."

Jason rolled his eyes. Not at O'Neil, but at the events O'Neil was describing.

"Yes," said Jason. "That makes sense. The federal government's plan to survive a nuclear war is to get the president, his cabinet, and the joint-chiefs-of-staff airborne in Air Force One." Then Jason turned to let the Amish men there know he was directing his comments to them and said, "Air Force One is the president's personal air plane. It is a huge jet that can carry enough people to keep the federal government's executive branch—that's the president and his administration—operating."

"I don't know who the president and his people are going to be talking with so's they can operate anything with all the electric out!" said O'Neil. There was no doubt about it. He was thoroughly enjoying himself, but his horse wasn't, and it spun around once and then backed up a few steps. All there caught sight of the handgun strapped to O'Neil's hip as the horse turned.

"Well, I doubt the power is down everywhere in the country," said Jason. "And certainly, the power is not down everywhere in the world. The president will need to speak to the military commanders stationed all over the world."

"Yeah! Maybe the U.S. will get a chance to nuke somebody! Maybe we can get into a pissing match with the Russians or the Chinese." It was no secret that O'Neil hated the federal government with a passion. Sometimes, his commentary didn't make any sense. Other times, it was like a brittle hammer hitting a broad nail directly on its head. Jason always felt that O'Neil was a crazy person, but a very bright crazy person. Intelligence and insanity seemed to go together often enough in history. When Jason first met O'Neil, he was put off by his diction and vocabulary, but quickly concluded that this was cultural, and that O'Neil was extremely well read—but also unstable and potentially violent. Jason avoided him whenever possible and was powerfully relieved when O'Neil came up short in the election for sheriff.

"Anyway, the folks up yonder in New York City sure seemed to be worried. Last thing I saw on the news before the power went out was them piling out of there, 'fraid they was gonna be next. You got kin up there, ain't ya?"

"What time did your power go out last night?" Jason asked, ignoring that last question from O'Neil.

"I don't know exactly. I should have looked on my cell phone because all the appliances with a clock in 'em went out with the power, but I didn't. I am going to guess sometime between 5 and 6 pm."

O'Neil was a showman. In high school, his senior year classmates had voted him "class clown" and "teacher's torment" but also "friendliest." He also had run, and lost, a race for public office as sheriff of the county—but he had just barely lost. And he had served in the U.S Army. He knew how and when to make an exit.

"Well, I got a notion to git in motion," he said with a big smile and a tip of his hat, ever the showman. "I just stopped by to let you know that we got feed corn out in the field. Any y'all need corn can come work for us gettin' it in on shares. Just come by and see me."

And with that, McCoy O'Neil reined his horse around and trotted back out the way he came in. The circle of Amish men closed once again around Jason.

"Well, there you have it," said Jason. "I don't have anything more to add to that."

"Can you tell us anything about these nuclear bombs?" asked Abraham.

"I can tell you that each bomb is certainly cable of destroying a large city and killing millions of people. I can also say with some certainty that a single thermonuclear bomb of the likely yield for bombs used by these nations would not destroy an entire nation the size of Iran, but I don't know how many bombs were used. Israel is a much smaller nation. Between the energy from the blast and the radioactive fallout from a thermonuclear bomb, a small nation like Israel might depopulate within a matter of weeks."

"'Depopulate?'" asked Abraham. "You mean they would all die."

"I mean that to survive the explosion and fallout within a particular radius people would have to be very lucky and then have the wherewithal to flee hundreds of miles away on a moment's notice, into hostile nations who might not accept them. Israel is about the size of the state of New Jersey, one of our smaller states. By way of comparison, Iran is over twice the size of Texas, the largest state in the lower 48."

Jason wasn't sure if any of the men present knew the relative sizes of New Jersey or Texas, but it was all he could think of at the moment.

"Whew…" was all that Abraham could say. A murmur traveled through those assembled.

"But we don't know anything," Jason added quickly. "We don't know how many bombs were deployed, what cities were hit, or how many people were killed."

"So why would the electric power be out here?" asked Abraham.

"That's a good question. I have no idea. There are lots of possibilities. A foreign government might have deployed a software attack on the computers that run the electric grid. Maybe they detonated a high altitude EMP device. Or maybe the physical infrastructure here in North America was attacked." Jason paused and waited to give others an opportunity to speak up. When it appeared no one would, Jason filled the void. "Or maybe it is just a coincidence, and the power will be back on soon. There is no way for us to know. We will have to wait for reports to come in from the outside world."

The circle of men dissipated somewhat with smaller groups peeling off to speak among themselves. Noah stepped forward from the crowd and nodded to Jason to look behind him. When Jason turned, he found Abraham signaling Jason to follow him. The three men stopped to talk after just a few steps, just enough for some privacy.

"I want to thank you for coming this morning, Jason. My people are very concerned. I think you helped them a great deal."

"Well, thanks, but I didn't really have much to say."

"You said enough. More than that, you don't appear to be frightened out of your mind that the world is coming to an end. My people needed to see that."

Jason paused for a moment and gathered his thoughts. "Abraham," said Jason, and here he paused again. "I am very concerned with the challenges I think are ahead of us, but I don't think the world is coming to an end, and I don't think we will be the target of a nuclear bomb here in this part of the country."

Jason paused and considered how to say what he wanted to say next but for a moment said nothing. Abraham peeled off after waiting a few seconds. He could see that Jason had something to add, but whatever it was it could wait. He needed to attend to his people. He then called out to the men to gather around.

"Thank you for coming this morning. I think we all needed to see and comfort each other. I think it is obvious that we are confronted by a great challenge, and I think the next thing to do is to see to our own. This is a time to take stock of everything in our lives. That means we must know exactly where we stand. If nothing comes of this, and

America is spared, and we all go back to work, it won't harm us to have taken these steps.

"I want each of you to go home and take inventory of your livestock, your hay and feed, your stores of food and firewood, clothing, and tools, implements, and hardware—right down to the last nut and bolt, screw and nail. For those of you who work off-farm at day-jobs, and that's most of us, please leave a note with my wife. She has pencils and paper on the front porch for you. Families engaged in farming will need help, and those not engaged in farming will need work, and we will try to match everybody with the type of work needed. We must husband our resources. Thank you for coming."

Sometimes Abraham struck Jason with awe—and this was one of those times. He had aired out everyone's concerns through the mouths of outsiders. All heard the same of what was said and known. The outsiders had given comfort to the Amish men in attendance that the "End Times" was not upon them—and that gave Abraham the moral authority to call his people to action. He was circling the wagons. It was brilliant.

Abraham gently elbowed his way to Jason and took him by the arm and walked to the house. They stopped before they got to the porch.

"Abraham, I think that was a wonderful and smart thing to say at the moment."

Jason was smiling as if he had just heard a political candidate at a campaign speech.

"Well Jason," said Abraham. "Don't be too impressed. I have long feared that we have become far too complacent and needful. I don't fear the End Times. Even if it were upon us, we have lived righteously. What should we have to fear from the Lord's judgment? No, that is not what concerns me now."

Jason waited for Abraham to say what was on his mind, but Abraham just stood there, looking off into the fields beyond his house and stroking his beard. Jason gave him some time to collect his thoughts, but after a bit, Jason felt the need to prod Abraham.

"Well, what is it that concerns you, Abraham?"

"'Concerns' me?" Abraham asked. "No, I am not 'concerned. I am afraid, God forgive me.'"

"Afraid of what exactly?" asked Jason.

Abraham paused, took off his hat and wiped his brow and put his hat back on. Then he looked directly and unblinking into Jason's eyes.

"'Seven Years of Famine,'" replied Abraham, and then he walked off towards his house, leaving Jason and Noah alone.

Chapter 16

Jason rode back home with Noah, pondering the circumstances. Perhaps the electric power would be back on by the time Jason got home, and the news anchors would be apologizing for scaring everyone, and it was all just theatre. Orson Welles would have been proud. But as they climbed the gravel driveway up to their house on the top of the hill behind the woodlot, Jason could see Ellen and the baby on the porch, and the kids playing on the swings. Ellen wasn't staring at her smartphone, and the kids weren't staring at their tablet computers. The house behind them was dark. Even in the daytime, Ellen preferred to have every light bulb in the house burning bright. Jason hated electric lights and preferred kerosene lamps. It would appear that on this score Jason was going to have his way for a while. Jason stepped down from the spring wagon and patted Trigger in silent thanks for taking him home in such a pleasant manner.

Jason walked up to the front porch to talk with Ellen and fill her in, though he knew nothing more than what Noah had told them this morning. For his part, Noah headed off to the barn to harness the horses. Ellen was sitting with the baby on the porch swing when Jason walked up the steps.

Jason got right to the point. "It seems that all the big news services reported that several Middle East countries were involved in a nuclear exchange yesterday."

"Oh, my God," Ellen moaned. "So, it's true."

"Well," said Jason, leaning on the porch railing and lowering his head until his chin touched his chest. "We don't know what's true. Or at least, that was what I tried to remind everyone at Abraham's. But the fact is that reports of nuclear war are everywhere. And now the power is off, and we have no way of contacting anyone to find out what the hell happened."

"Why would the power be off here in the U.S. if the nuclear bombs went off over there?"

"Honey, I don't know," Jason answered. "It is impossible to know anything. The U.S. could be experiencing a coordinated attack on the software that runs the electric grid. Or it could have been an EMP weapon, though I doubt that.

"What do you mean?" asked Ellen.

"Well, human beings cannot feel an electromagnetic pulse," answered Jason. "But some of us should be able to *hear* one powerful enough to knock out large portions of the electric grid. Individually we might not know what the sound was, but if everyone acknowledged that they heard *something,* that would be a clue. No one mentioned it. There would be other clues: Electrical transformers would have burned, and lots of electronic gadgetry would not work. So, we will have to listen to what other people have heard and seen. The thing is, we don't know how broad the grid failure is. It could be just local, though I doubt it."

"Why?" asked Ellen.

"People living in areas with power would still have access to gasoline and diesel. Some of those people would be randomly driving through here. I didn't see or hear a soul on my way over to Abraham's farm. And McCoy O'Neil arrived there on horseback and didn't mention seeing anyone on the road, and there is a 10-mile stretch of a busy state road between Abraham's farm and the O'Neil spread. O'Neil came here looking for harvest laborers to pick field corn on shares. That tells me that perhaps some of their cars and equipment are not working, which would suggest an EMP. Or O'Neil is just being smart and conserving the fuel that is in his farm tanks for more important work. Either way, the O'Neil's don't think they will have access to fuel to run the harvesters and combines. It also tells me that the O'Neil's don't think anyone will be interested in working for cash—so they offered the Amish a share of the harvest. And it's been what? Less than 24 hours! And already the O'Neil's are looking to swap grain for labor? In the case of the McCoy O'Neil, it may be just a case of wishful thinking. He's been hoping for the world to come to an end. He seemed to be enjoying everyone's distress."

"Yeah, well, he certainly is a case." McCoy O'Neil had always given Ellen a case of the heebie-jeebies.

"But there was something Abraham said."

"What does Abraham have to do with this?"

Officially, the Bishop had the final say, but the Bishop had gotten old and feeble. Abraham was only a Deacon, but he was obviously the unofficial leader of the Amish church-group surrounding Jason's and Ellen's farm.

"Nothing, it's just that what he said over there just now made a lot of sense."

Ellen waited, in vain, for Jason to tell her what was said, while Jason examined his boots, his hat, and the feel his beard. Now completely out of patience, Ellen asked, "OK. So, what did Abraham say?"

"Well, he said that all of us have to take stock of everything in our lives. That we must organize so that we waste nothing, and everything that is useful is known and deployed to its best use, and that we must not let an egg break on the ground or let a piece of fruit go bad on the vine or leave a single piece of hay in the field. Or at least that's I what took away from him. He used the biblical line, 'The Seven Years of Famine.'"

"Why would the Amish care if the electric power is out? All of them are off-grid. They won't even notice it."

"Well, they might wall themselves off from the rest of society, but they still depend on the industrial economy. Most of the members of this particular church group living around us work as carpenters and construction laborers. Yeah, they have wood stoves for cooking, heating, and hot water. And they have expansive gardens, pantries filled with food, milk cows, and horses for transportation—and barns filled with hay to feed them. But they need money to buy parts for their equipment and buggies, lubricants and fuel for chainsaws, kerosene for lamps, and tools, not to mention construction materials. They get all of that stuff from outside their community. Even the Old Order Mennonites down in Shady Grove are not immune, even though they won't so much as use a chainsaw or pump motor, and very few of them work off-farm. I am pretty impressed with Abraham. He seems to see the situation for what it is."

"And what is the situation exactly?"

"Unless the electric power comes on soon, and by soon, I mean no more than a few weeks and maybe as little as a week, the financial system as we know it will not be retrievable. That is, if the power remains down, at some point in the very near future it will be impossible to get hundreds of millions of people back to working at their jobs and paying their mortgages, car loans, and credit card bills—even if we can get the system back up again. There is a point of no return. Once people are freed from the idea of being in debt, the very idea of loans and collateral will be impossible to reintroduce, and enforcing collection by seizing collateral on prior debts just won't be possible. The level of force that would be required would destroy society. The only way out of this mess is to get the power on before it is too late."

Ellen and Jason were quiet for a few minutes as they pondered their circumstances.

Jason spoke first. "We have enough firewood for the next two or three years, but I think we should do everything we can to cut firewood consumption. Lord knows where or even if we can get enough gasoline to run a chainsaw," Jason said. "And honey, that hot water kettle was the buy of the century."

Ellen looked up and smiled coyly. It was her idea, and over Jason's objections, to buy the 55-gallon stainless steel wood fired water kettle last year. At the time it seemed like an expensive novelty, but they had soon put it to good use— and with the power out, that kettle just became invaluable.

The family would have an endless supply of hot water for bathing, laundry, and water bath canning, plus safe drinking water, in exchange for the labor of putting up firewood. And since the kettle was stainless steel, it would last indefinitely. In addition to a large firebox wood stove for heat, they had bought and installed a wood cook stove that produced a fair amount of hot water, but not quite enough for a family's needs. So, last year Ellen insisted on buying the kettle, over Jason's objections. This year she doubled down and insisted on an outdoor stainless-steel wood-fired oven, grill, and cooking station. Their farmhouse did not have heating or air-conditioning, and without AC, cooking inside made the house unbearably hot in warm weather. The new cooking station solved that issue, and now they cooked outside from May until October.

"When do you think we will know something more?" asked Ellen.

"I don't know when anything will happen anymore," He said, scraping the clay mud soil from his rubber boots on the edge of the porch. This always annoyed Ellen, but right now she didn't seem to care. "It just seems reasonable to husband our resources as much as possible.

"Then I won't waste any propane canning the meat in the freezer. I will fire up the cook stove."

"Ugh," Jason grunted and breathed out forcefully. "I forgot about that. I have to get the hay in, so I won't be around to help."

"That's OK, I'll manage," Ellen said.

"Good," Jason responded, but his mind went to his older son, who was away at college more than a half a day's drive away. He wondered how long it would take him to walk home. "If we all sleep downstairs near the stove, and we block off the rest of the house, then I bet a small overnight fire will be enough to keep the room comfortable on even the coldest days. Our blankets and bed clothes should be enough, and when they aren't, we will break out the sleeping bags."

"I've been thinking about winter all morning," said Ellen, staring ahead.

"Me, too. But I am more concerned about next spring," Jason said, still looking at his dirty boots. "We have everything we need to get through this winter, I think. Next winter is another story."

"Come on. The power will be back on by then. This isn't the end of the world."

"Maybe not, but it might be the beginning of 'Seven Years of Famine.'"

Chapter 17

Martin and Miriam and their twin daughters trudged on. They parted company with David and Rachel Rosen, in a tearful farewell, in the Riverdale section of the Bronx, one of the five boroughs of New York City.

"Before", Martin had been one of the thousands of well-paid foot soldiers who ground out the work for the "Masters of the Universe". He had recently finished his Talmudic studies, and had been ordained a Rabbi in Israel. Now his schul, or temple, was gone, his friends were gone, and his country was gone.

No, I am an American. I am a Jew, but I am an American.

They walked out of New York City, north along the west side of Manhattan, onto the Henry Hudson Bridge, across the Spuyten Duyvil Creek which separates the Bronx from Manhattan, and then northward along the Hudson Line train tracks on the east side of the Hudson River.

Martin thought that his girls, not yet twelve years old, might make 15 miles if pushed hard. He underestimated them. They made it to the village of Hastings that night, seven hours and 19 miles after leaving their apartment. Mercifully, it was not raining, or the trek might not have been possible. But they were exhausted. Miriam tugged on Martin's hand.

"We have to find a place to sleep for the night," Miriam said.

"Yes, you're right," replied Martin. "See that pedestrian bridge up ahead? That should be the Hastings train station. With any luck, we will be able to shelter there."

As soon as he finished speaking all of the lights on the east side of the Hudson River went dark. A few seconds later, the lights on the other side of the river went out too. To the north stood the massive Tappan Zee Bridge, or at least that's what Martin and Miriam called it, its lights blazing in the darkness. The bridge had a new name, but neither could think of it at the moment.

"Uh-oh," said Martin as he looked around. "This isn't good."

"Well, the electricity is still on up there," Miriam said, nodding to the bridge.

Martin turned to look north, and the bridge disappeared from view, making the darkness absolute.

"Uh-oh," echoed Miriam.

That night they slept in the Hastings train station with several dozen other hikers and were pleasantly surprised to find that the bathrooms still had running water. They slept well enough and woke at the first sign of dawn. After a breakfast of peanut butter and jelly sandwiches, they continued on their way north, up the railroad tracks from Hastings, past the villages of Dobbs Ferry, Ardsley, and Irvington, and by mid-morning had come to the village of Tarrytown, where Martin hoped to seek assistance from a friend's brother.

Jason Thomas and Martin had known each other for over 20 years and had worked together at several Wall Street firms. Both men had keen interests in mathematics and science, and their bond grew as they realized the interests they had in common. Neither missed a science or math lecture, and they often would attend these together, since the opportunities to indulge these passions were plentiful in New York City. Though they came from completely different worlds and social circumstances, and did not socialize outside their spheres of interest, they had become close friends.

Jason had retired to raise horses—or was it cattle?— on a farm down south, and so the math and science "bromance" of these Wall Street co-workers came to an end. Still, they had kept in touch through the years, mostly to discuss their interests, or to share an article or paper, so Martin felt that he could reach out to Jason's brother Walt for assistance. Martin wasn't looking for much. He had planned to stay the night at Walt's house yesterday but had made it only as far as Hastings. Now Martin hoped that Walt might be able to help Martin's family with some food and blankets, after which they would be on their way.

Martin had a general idea of where Walt Thomas lived. With Miriam and the girls in tow, he trudged up from the Tarrytown train tracks to Main Street. The buildings appeared dark on either side of him, and many people were milling around. From Main Street, Martin and his family walked up Neperhan Avenue on the beautiful fall day after the bombings, looking for Walt's house on Maple Lane. Martin recognized the fieldstone wall gate at the head of the driveway, and led his family up the drive, to find Walt standing outside with his son, looking down at a disassembled motorcycle gearbox.

The first thing Martin saw was the revolver holstered on Walt's hip. He stopped, noticing the unmistakable family resemblance to Jason, and spoke up.

"I'm Martin Weiss, a friend of your brother Jason."

"Hello, Martin, a friend of my brother's," Walt replied. "I'm Walt Thomas. I believe we have met before. Call me Walt. Do you know anything about motorcycle gearboxes?" The expression of intense focus had melted into a friendly smile.

"Not a thing," Martin replied, returning the smile.

"Well, then I guess you'd best tell me what's on your mind."

"We've just walked up from Manhattan, and I could use any help you might be willing to give us. I have young children."

Walt looked at Miriam and the girls and smiled. He had never met Miriam before, but he did remember meeting Martin briefly once before. "Please, come with me."

Martin followed Walt into the kitchen entrance of the large house. Walt's wife, Jenny, and son, Manny, were in the kitchen. After introductions, and in the spirit of female camaraderie, Jenny took Miriam and the girls to a guest bedroom on the 2nd floor of their three-story home and showed them the bathroom. Fortunately, Tarrytown was serviced by a reservoir and tank system that was uphill from Walt's house, so the water was still flowing. Walt felt that the water's days were numbered, not that it mattered. It was running at the moment, allowing them to fill all of their containers, as well as their bathtubs.

As Jenny and Miriam departed with the girls, Walt signaled Martin, who followed Walt out to the slate patio off the other side of the kitchen in the backyard.

Martin spoke first. "You don't seem to be suffering here."

"We're not getting on too badly. At least for now," said Walt and paused, spit on the ground and then looked directly into Martin's eyes, and asked, "Where are you headed?"

"I don't know, exactly. North, for now, no other choice really," said Martin.

"Why no other choice?" asked Walt.

"Well, we can't go south back to the city, and we can only go 15 miles east before we run into Long Island Sound, and we can't go more than a half mile west before we will be sitting in the Hudson River. That leaves north."

"Well, I can spare you some food, and there's no shortage of water or containers to carry it in. You are welcome to stay here. We are leaving this evening and don't plan on coming back anytime soon," said Walt.

"Where do you plan to go?"

"South."

"South? To New York City?"

"No. South, down to Jason's farm."

Martin was incredulous. "Do you know how far that is?"

"Pretty damn far," replied Walt. "About 800 miles. Do you know how far winter is?"

"I take your point. But 800 miles is a hell of a long walk."

"Well, I thought about hiking it from here, but gave up on that idea. We need to put some distance between the Northeast and us as quick as possible, and I don't relish the idea of walking with hundreds of thousands of starving refugees."

"Surely you don't think you can just hop in a car and drive?"

"Nope. We're going by water. It's the only way. And we will still have to walk 400 miles or so, but at least we will be away from the largest population center in the U.S., and in a much warmer climate."

There was a period of silence lasting over a minute as each man considered the coming winter.

"So, you have a boat."

"We have a sailboat in the marina at the bottom of the hill," Walt said as he nodded in the direction of the Hudson River.

"Can you make room for us?" asked Martin.

"Do know anything about astronomy or navigation?"

"Not a thing."

"Do you have any experience with sailing?" Walt asked in return.

"No."

"Do you have any deep-sea fishing experience?" Walt pressed.

"None."

"Have you ever even been on a sailboat on the ocean?"

"I took the Circle Line Cruise around Manhattan the day before I got married to my first wife at City Hall."

"That was what, 25 years ago?"

"Coming up on 32."

"Well, that figures all right. We leave tonight. I could use a couple of extra hands. Can you at least handle a gun?"

"A gun?" Martin said as if he had been punched in the stomach. "What would I need a gun for?"

"Never mind. I don't need you shooting one of us by accident."

Walt turned to walk back to the house and then stopped and turned back, almost running into Martin, who was following him.

"Millions of humans beings have been slaughtered by crazy people who thought nuclear bombs were a good idea," Walt said to Martin. "We have had assassinations, one after the other, police killings, and the northeastern United States is probably less than a week away from having some people wind up being slowly roasted over a burn-barrel for dinner. And you don't understand what you might need a gun for?"

Walt was looking at Martin as if Martin had been licking a fire hydrant.

"I am sorry," said Martin. "That was a stupid thing to say. Culturally, guns are anathema to us."

"Oh yeah?" Walt retorted and scoffed loudly. "Well, your 'culture' just nuked at least one country. Maybe two. Someone might take offense to that and want to cut your head off with a kitchen knife. If I were you, I would learn how to use a firearm, and I would make sure my wife and daughters knew their way around firearms, too. Either that or lose the beanie and shave the beard."

Walt walked briskly away from Martin. Martin watched him leave, somewhat stunned by that exchange, and then hurried to catch up to Walt.

"Walt, please. My world has changed a great deal since yesterday. I…"

Walt cut him off by holding his hand up and looking toward the kitchen door. His son Manny was walking toward them.

Walt put his hand on Martin's shoulder and steadied him. It was an expression of solidarity.

"Manny, let's finish packing," Walt said to his son. "And never mind the motorcycle. Let's take the bicycle. After that I want you to give Martin here a quick lesson on firearms while I get everything I will need together." He paused, and then added cryptically, "I want to get the boat packed this afternoon, and I want to be underway before dark. I got something I gotta do."

*****

"What??!!" Miriam shrieked at Martin. "You want to get on a sailboat with a bunch of fucking strange goyim and sail away to go see that geek friend of yours, what's-his-name? Are you crazy? I went along with this little hike with you, but I am not getting on a sailboat to anywhere."

The family was gathered in a guest room at Walt Thomas's house, and while the door was closed, Martin was sure that everyone in the house had heard Miriam.

"Miriam, we need to get away from New York City as quickly as possible. We are less than 25 miles from midtown Manhattan here."

"So?! We can hike up to Bear Mountain. We can stay there until the power comes back on and this whole thing blows over."

Martin had been waiting for this. Until now, Miriam had been unusually calm and cooperative, and Martin felt fortunate that he was able to get his daughters this far from Manhattan before Miriam lapsed into her typical displays of histrionics and resistance to change. Miriam hated change. She was a creature of habit. For Miriam, Bear Mountain was the outer limits of familiar, so that was as far as she was willing to go.

"Stay where at Bear Mountain?" Martin was incredulous. The twins held onto each other for comfort. They were quite used to their mother's emotional outbursts, but they were most definitely not used to hearing their father fighting back. Martin continued.

"Are we going to knock on someone's door and ask them to take us in? They will be strangers and gentiles, too. Or are you planning for us to sleep in tents? We have enough food for another day or two. Then what? These people have the inventory of an entire convenience store at their disposal, and they have been kind enough to offer us passage with them to warmer climes. Do you realize how soon winter will be upon us? Can you imagine what will happen here with no electricity to run the heating and air conditioning and refrigeration systems? With no electricity to pump the fuel that trucks need to make deliveries? People will freeze and starve by the millions. I am not going to risk that for our children."

"How do you know what is going to happen?! What, are you a fortuneteller now?" Miriam was on the verge of hysteria and had reverted to her standard program of passive-aggressive behavior.

"Miriam... you are a professor in the humanities," Martin said as he tried to stroke her ego. Miriam and the women she worked with were very sensitive to condescension from people with STEM—Science, Technology, Engineering, and Math—training and practical skills. "You know how society works. Mankind has always been three meals away from revolution. Well, it is lunchtime. That is, it has been three meal-times now with no power. Things have not fallen apart—*yet*. But by tomorrow morning... We are simply better off on a boat loaded with food and away from people."

"You are not listening to me! I am not getting on any fucking boat, *and that is that*!"

Martin turned to his daughters and said, "Girls. Would you please go downstairs and ask the lady if there is anything you can do to help?"

The girls didn't need to be asked twice and darted from the room.

"Miriam. I am not asking you again. And I am not telling you what to do. You may do as you see fit. My daughters and I will be on that boat. If the power comes back on and it is all a big mistake, we will get off wherever we can, and then come back home. But if the power remains out and this turns out to be a cataclysmic event, which I think is not just possible but probable, I will not be able to protect our daughters or you in this environment. Do you understand what it is that I am saying?"

Martin was always stark, raving calm in the face of Miriam's rage—and it usually only caused Miriam to become more and more unreasonable. For some reason, Miriam held her tongue.

"I want to know if you understand what I am saying. I want to know that I did my best to reach you, to reason with you, but I am not going to fight with you. And I am never going to tolerate any disrespect from you, ever again. You are going to behave reasonably, or I am going to disassociate myself from you—permanently. You have absolutely no leverage whatsoever anymore. There are no 911 emergency services, divorce lawyers or courts, alimony or child support, or emotional support from all those evil and vile women you work with in your 'women's studies' program. You are going to have to learn to be kind and giving, and to be a contributing member of this family. The only person in this world who you can count on for anything at this moment is *me—your husband*. And the only women who will even have a 'husband' from this moment forward are the women who treat their husbands with the respect they deserve. You will learn to treat me with great respect, especially in front of our daughters, or I will leave you on the side of the road. Please let me know that you understood these things that I have said."

Miriam merely looked at Martin with a horrified look of comprehension. Martin maintained firm eye contact and nodded his head once.

"I will take that as a response in the affirmative. Please stay here until you have collected your emotions and can conduct yourself with dignity in the presence of our kind hosts. Or leave. I have said all that I intend to say on the subject."

And with that, Martin stepped out of the guest bedroom, feeling about as good as he had at any time since his daughters were born.

Chapter 18

The Endeavor 37 sailboat was under way via the power of its diesel engine, not the wind. Built in the late 1970's in Tampa, Florida, and the boat had been designed for longevity and endurance rather than speed. Its smooth, shiny gel-coat paint looked impressive, and its fiberglass and white oak frame made it exceptionally strong for a recreational sailboat.

With the small engine running not much above idle, an eerie hush enveloped them as they passed under the new Tappan Zee Bridge, focusing their minds as they listened intently to the near-silence, and wondered whether they would ever see the bridge again.

Ketch rigged, which meant it had two masts, rather than the sloop rigged single mast more often found on this size boat, the Endeavor 37 handled well enough in the Hudson River. Walt had never sailed her on the open ocean. A powerboat owner and enthusiast for most of his adult life, Walt had only acquired the sailboat two years earlier, when he took the boat in trade for a commercial debt and hoped to recoup his losses by selling it. He had had no takers, so he had taken the boat out for day trips, all within 20 miles of his rented slip at the Washington Irving Boat Club, in the shadow of the Tappan Zee Bridge. As he steered the boat through the channel between the bridge's pilings, Walt thought that this unwanted sailboat might well prove to be his most auspicious purchase ever. Looking out over the wheel of the cockpit, he could see a motorboat to his left (or to port, as he reminded himself to use the nautical term), northbound a little over a mile away, with several other boats behind it, also northbound. For now, Walt's was the only vessel heading south.

"Wow," said Martin, looking back at the massive but silent and empty Tappan Zee Bridge. "That was disconcerting."

Walt breathed heavily out of his nose and nodded, making eye contact with Martin. The two men took deep breaths, held them, and then let them out simultaneously. The events of the past 24 hours had been humbling, but the harried pace of events had kept them from thinking about their situation very deeply before now. Some strange primordial emotion seemed to have been triggered in the few moments of echoed silence under the bridge.

Martin had had a full night's sleep, but Walt was operating on just a little over four hours. Even so, Martin looked exhausted, and Walt looked like he had just returned from a weekend at the shore. Still, Walt knew he would need to rest. He signaled Manny over to him.

"You know where to drop anchor?" Walt asked.

"Yeah, I think so. After we leave the channel, when we get to 12 feet of water."

"Perfect. I am going to get a little rest." And with that, Walt headed below to the front V-berth to sleep until Manny woke him.

It was dark in the V-berth when Walt awoke. He looked back and out of the hatch to the cockpit. It was dark there too. He could hear the sound of voices. Walt had woken naturally and felt rested and fully awake. He swung his feet to the deck and fished the flashlight out of his pocket, then headed into the galley, opened a cabinet door, and retrieved a backpack that he had set there when they had loaded the boat. Reaching up and over the electronics, he retrieved a black canvas bag with something heavy in it. He slung both bags over his shoulders and then headed up on deck.

Manny was sitting there in the cockpit with Martin. The women and girls were sitting on the foredeck talking.

116

As soon as Manny saw Walt emerge from the darkness below decks, he stood up and grabbed the dinghy line and used it to pull the dinghy forward to the stern of the sailboat.

"That dark shape is St. John's Hospital," Manny said to Walt as he pointed. Walt looked and squinted his eyes just a little. "We arrived before darkness set in, so I am sure. The shore is less than 200 yards. You will find that strip of sand and trees we were talking about, roughly in that direction." Manny pointed off the stern.

With that, Manny and his father embraced for a long time. When they parted, there were tears in the eyes of both men.

Walt clambered down the transom and gently laid his backpack and black canvas bag down in the boat. Then he climbed into the dinghy in front of the bicycle that Manny and Walt had placed there when they were packing the boat.

"Where are you going?" asked Martin with no small amount of concern.

Walt ignored him and spoke to Manny. "You will hear it, I think. If I am not back within an hour from the start, I guess I won't be coming back."

Martin was not sure what the hell he was hearing or seeing, but whatever it was, he didn't like it. Manny untied the dinghy and cast the line into the dinghy. Walt settled into the middle seat, picked up the oars, put the blades in the water, and set off. The darkness swallowed him within a few strokes.

"What the hell is going on?" Martin asked between clenched teeth as Manny stepped back into the cockpit.

"Look. Take it easy. My father has to take care of something. He will be back soon. And then we'll leave."

Martin, exasperated, wanted to say something, but the way Manny spoke and looked made him think he should keep quiet. He turned to sit back down and saw that Jenny was looking back to the place where Walt had disappeared into the darkness. He couldn't see what she was looking at, but the air was tense, and he heard, or perhaps he sensed,

Jenny, sobbing quietly. Then Manny killed the soft light tubes that illuminated the deck.

Martin sat down worried sick, wondering what he had gotten himself into. Perhaps Miriam was right. Maybe they should have kept on walking.

Manny sat down next to him and put his hand on his shoulder. "Take it easy," Manny said to Martin. "And be quiet. We need to stay dark and quiet until I hear my father calling for us. My father will be back soon."

"What the hell is going on?" Martin did not want Miriam to hear any of this.

"Think about it. You know."

"Is this about your brother?"

Manny scoffed. "Of course, this is about my brother."

Chapter 19

Before Walt could leave, there was some unfinished business he had to settle. There was a man he had to kill.

Five years earlier, his oldest son, Will, then 20, had been shot to death by a police officer. Will was in college and playing football. After a game, he and some friends had driven to the local bar strip and, since they were underage, had sent a friend who was old enough to buy alcohol into a liquor store, leaving Will at the wheel and several others in the back seat. The local police had been called to deal with a bar fight that had spilled out onto the street. One of the officers had motioned to Will to move his car. Another officer, Officer Robert Spinelli, believing that Will was somehow part of the melee and that Will was using his car as a weapon, had fired ten shots at the windshield in front of the driver's seat. Will had died a short time later, bleeding to death in handcuffs while the police ransacked his car. They had found a marijuana cigarette. Later, the media had reported the affair as a "drug-related police shooting."

The loss of a child is the most devastating event that can happen to a human being, and the loss of a child to violence is the worst of the worst. There is no time to prepare, to say "goodbye," or to resolve conflicts. There is only loss, pain, and rage directed at the killer. Walt's rage had churned inside him for the past five years. Every "police-involved shooting" or other perceived government injustice reported in the media sent him into the depths of depression, followed by a sulking rage, and ending in a 24-hour migraine headache, during which Walt could tolerate neither light nor sound. For years he could not walk past the family photos that hung on the wall, inside the kitchen cabinet, on the fridge, or his wife's dresser without breaking down. Slowly his grief turned to anger, and the anger turned into a rage that would not cool.

That man Spinelli had killed Walt's child—and the authorities had done almost nothing. The officer had claimed the standard, "I feared for my life and the lives of my fellow officers." Will had done nothing wrong—he had been following the instructions of another police officer when that "trigger happy Spinelli" overreacted and shot Will to death. Rather than render assistance and try to save Will, the police at the scene had handcuffed him and searched his car. Walt could not get over the vision of Will being left to bleed to death, lying face down on the sidewalk with his hands handcuffed behind his back.

After the shooting, Walt had pressed the issue with the local District Attorney and the State Attorney General, to no avail. The other police officers at the scene had closed ranks around Spinelli, as did the District Attorney's office, providing false and misleading testimony to investigators. Later, as if to add insult to injury, the police officer who had fired the killing shots had received an award for bravery-in-the-line-of-duty from the local Police Benevolent Association. Meanwhile, Walt had dreamed of tying Spinelli to his bed, pinning that award to his chest, and then setting the bed on fire and burning his house down.

Things were different now. Walt's younger son was now a young man. Walt had no children depending on him anymore—he might not get this chance again. Walt decided to settle the score tonight and told Manny that he could not leave with Spinelli alive. Manny agreed. The world was preoccupied. It was now or never. Walt would avenge his son or die trying.

The backpack Walt carried contained six 16-ounce soft-drink bottles filled with gasoline, plus cloth rags he had torn from a bath towel, his loaded Ruger .357 Magnum revolver in a hip holster, three speed-loaders loaded with ammunition, and some matches and a lighter for redundancy—Walt had been a Boy Scout and had learned to "be prepared". Walt also carried a buck-skinning knife on his left hip, along with two sets of handcuffs. In the black canvas bag was a stainless-steel Ruger Mini-14 .223 caliber semi-automatic rifle with three fully loaded 30-round clips. Three clips was half a combat load, but Walt thought that it should be enough, since he was planning an ambush, not a firefight.

Walt set out for shore, to meet his destiny, or to deliver destiny to Officer Spinelli. A lifetime of diaper changes, running alongside bicycles, kindergarten graduation, camping, violin lessons, Little League, and family vacations at the Jersey shore had been destroyed by that "sick fucking cop," as Walt referred to Spinelli, and Walt intended to settle that piece of family business once and for all.

He had thought about using a diesel/fertilizer bomb like the one used in the bombing of the Federal Building in Oklahoma City. He had the diesel and the ammonium nitrate and the knowledge, but he wanted to kill Spinelli personally. He wanted Spinelli to see it coming, to know why he was being killed, and by whom. He wanted Spinelli to bleed to death after being shot. And he wanted Spinelli to bleed to death while in handcuffs, while someone stood by and did nothing to save him. He wanted to kill every member of Spinelli's family, right in front of him. Walt wanted to wipe Spinelli's existence, and that of all his descendants, clean from the Earth.

With just enough moonlight, Walt rowed quietly along near the rocky Hudson shoreline, heading north until he saw the dark shape of the trees between the tracks and sandbar. Walt had been a "river rat" all his life and knew all the Hudson shoreline features near Tarrytown. He felt that at night he could leave his dinghy here in the trees undetected. He could row back to the boat, or even swim in the cold water if necessary, as long as Manny could hear him and give him a flashlight to aim for. But swimming would mean leaving the guns behind, and Walt didn't want to have to do that.

He did worry about getting a flat tire on the way, and had prepared for that, but his tires held up. If he survived, and got a flat on the way back, he could easily walk the return trip, carrying his guns.

It took him 10 minutes to make the sandbar, and another 30 minutes to bike to Spinelli's house. He arrived at about 1 a.m. No one interrupted his trip or sought to stop him.

Walt stared at the house as he walked around the sidewalk adjacent to the property. The house was on a corner. There was no "back yard," but there was a side yard with a children's play set, a patio with a BBQ grill, a table and chairs, an old sandbox, and a pink bicycle with long flowing pink plastic sparklers hanging from the handlebars. His plan was simple—he was going to burn them out. He took one of his gasoline bottles and poured its contents on the window frames along the bottom floor of the house, and across the side porch door leading to the patio area. He ran around the house, setting fire to the window frames, each of which ignited with a loud "whoosh". Then he stood back, lit the rag fuse on another of his bottles, and threw it through the back-door window, spreading flames inside the door. He retrieved two more bottles, lit their fuses, and threw them, spreading flames against the side of the house and inside the dining room. Then Walt stepped back across the sidewalk and into the street, resting his rifle across the roof of a parked car less than 30 feet from the Spinelli's' front door. He didn't have to wait long.

The three Spinelli children spilled from the house, backlit by the fire from the dining room, with their mother and father right behind them. As they came down the short walkway toward the street and the parked car that Walt was using as a rifle rest, Walt aimed and shot the eldest Spinelli child, a girl of 16, in the chest. It was a fatal wound, a heart shot. The noise partly deafened both Walt and the surviving Spinelli's. Officer Spinelli turned in the direction of the rifle shot, trying to collect his wits, and not yet realizing that his daughter lay dying on their tiny front lawn, gasping and bleeding in much the same way that Walt's son had after Spinelli had shot him. Spinelli's eyes widened with terror when he met the Walt Thomas's cold gaze. Walt let a moment pass to make sure that Spinelli recognized him and realized what was happening. Then Walt shot the youngest Spinelli, a girl of 6, right between the eyes. The child went down like a wet ragdoll thrown from a dog's mouth. Walt then shot Spinelli's wife and 12-year-old son in their lower legs. They flopped down in a heap, screaming in agony.

Now Walt came out from behind the car, walking toward a paralyzed-with-confusion-and-terror Officer Spinelli. The light from the house fire made Walt's face easy to see, though Spinelli had to strain to look past the rifle Walt was aiming directly at him.

"You!!" screamed Spinelli.

"Crack!!" answered the Ruger Mini-14. Walt shot Spinelli through the top of his left foot, and Spinelli went down next to his writhing-in-agony wife and son.

"You killed my son!!" Walt shrieked at the downed Spinelli. "Now I am here to kill *your* son! *Your* daughters! *Your* wife! I want you to see it and feel it! I want you to know what you did to me! And then I am going to kill you!!" Walt fired another round into the leg of Spinelli's 12-year-old boy.

"Your daughters are already dead, you fucking piece of shit!" Walt fired several shots into the head of the prone body of the older Spinelli girl, shattering her skull. Then he paced over to the younger daughter's body and fired two shots into her torso. "Ha-ha! How's that fucking feel, motherfucker? Huh?! They're *dead*! How do you like that? Ha ha!! See? I shot them because I feared for my life and the life of my fellow officers!" Walt said, mocking Spinelli. "Hey, why don't you call for backup?"

Mrs. Spinelli began to low crawl toward her younger daughter's body, but Walt interrupted her efforts by firing a round into the back of her knee, the round exiting through the front of her knee joint and splintering the kneecap. Walt then turned, aimed, and fired at Officer Spinelli, striking him in the right kneecap. Spinelli's leg exploded in blood. This seemed to stop Spinelli's backward scoot efforts to evade Walt. Walt turned and fired again at Mrs. Spinelli, striking her in her elbow. He kicked her in the face, took a pair of handcuffs from his belt, laid his rifle on the ground, turned her over, and handcuffed her. He then roughly turned her over again, withdrew his .357 revolver from its holster at his hip, and fired a round into Mrs. Spinelli's shoulder joint. She was now bleeding from wounds in her lower leg, kneecap, elbow, and shoulder. Then Walt picked up his rifle from the ground and holstered his handgun.

"Don't worry, you fucking bitch," Walt shrieked with bloodlust. "You won't die for a while. You will have plenty of time to think about my son. He bled to death, lying on the ground in handcuffs. This piece of shit you call a husband murdered my son."

And with that, Walt spat on her, "Ptuh!"

Walt was crying now.

"He killed my son," Walt sobbed to no one in particular, motioning to Officer Spinelli. He looked up to find the Spinelli boy leaning against the smoldering house. "And now I am here to even the score." Walt emptied the remaining rounds from the 30-round magazine into the body of Officer Spinelli's only son. Then Walt laid down the rifle and reached to his belt for another set of handcuffs. With the cuffs in his left hand and the handgun in his right, Walt approached Officer Spinelli and opened fire, striking Spinelli in the elbow, shoulder, and ankle. He then clubbed Spinelli with the revolver, turned him over and handcuffed his hands behind his back.

It had been less than 2 minutes since Walt had set fire to Spinelli's house, but now some of the neighbors were looking out their front doors, and some were coming down into the street. Walt went to his bike, removed a 30-round magazine from his bag, and retrieved his rifle. He engaged the ammo clip and racked the slide to chamber a round. He then fired several rounds in different directions, screaming like a wild man. The neighbors quickly disappeared.

Walt now approached Officer and Mrs. Spinelli, who were shrieking in pain and agony. He poured the contents of another gasoline bottle onto the bodies of the Spinelli children and set them on fire. He returned to their wild-eyed parents, who were now in shock.

"You think I am going to burn you, too? Fuck you. I hope you survive your wounds and live in agony, though I doubt you will make it through the night. Me? I am going to sit here and tell you what you did to my life."

Walt began to draw breath to speak again when a vision of his son lying in his casket flashed in his mind. His rage boiled over, and he opened the buck-skinning knife he wore on his hip. He tore away Officer Spinelli's boxer shorts, seized his testicles and penis in his left hand, and cut them away from Spinelli's body. As Spinelli shrieked in agony, hands cuffed behind his back, Walt stood back and admired his handiwork.

"Let me know when you are done screaming there, scumbag!" Walt said laughing and holding Spinelli's bloody genitals in his hand. "I want you to die with your balls and your dick in your mouth."

Spinelli's screams began to subside as the blood poured from the wound in his groin. Walt kicked Spinelli viciously in the head until his mouth fell open, and then carefully stuffed Spinelli's genitals into his mouth. After retrieving the last two gasoline bottles from his bike, Walt walked over to a still-very-much-alive Mrs. Spinelli, poured the gas from one bottle over her, and then poured the last bottle's contents over her husband. Walt then stood up straight, looked her right in the eyes, and said, "I changed my mind. Fuck you. I want you two to burn here, now, and then I hope you burn in hell."

Walt struck a match and threw it on the gasoline-soaked Officer Spinelli and his wife. Fire engulfed the couple in a loud "whoosh!" but neither of the Spinellis moved. Perhaps they had passed out or were in shock. Walt was disappointed. He wanted to taunt them as they burned. He stayed and watched until he was sure they were dead. Then he hopped on his bike, as carefree as any nine-year-old on the first day of summer vacation and headed west toward the Hudson River.

The following morning the neighbors crowded the scene of the Spinelli family murders, gawking in horror at the gory spectacle. But most of them knew about the famous case in which a young, unarmed college kid had been shot to death by the man whose charred body, along with those of his wife and three children, still gave up occasional puffs of smoke in the small yard in front of the fire-damaged house. The neighbors clearly had received the lesson.

Chapter 20

Walt arrived back at the riverfront at 1:40 am. The dinghy was right where he had left it, though he could hear people walking and talking along the railroad tracks. He listened intently for a few minutes. Whoever was talking had moved on, so Walt slid the dinghy into the water and walked next to it until the water was up to his knees. Only then did he place the black canvas bag and his backpack in the boat. He steadied the dinghy, took a look at the setting moon for direction, and thought he could see the outline of the sailboat. Then he got into the dinghy and rowed in the general direction of the sailboat. He removed the flashlight from his pocket, set it on flash, and aimed it west. In a few seconds, a flashlight blinked on and off. Walt rowed in the direction of the flash. In a few minutes, he rounded the sailboat and came up astern. Manny was waiting for him on the transom. Walt threw him the bowline, and Manny held the dinghy alongside. Without a word, Walt handed the bags to Manny, one at a time, and Manny handed them in turn back to Martin.

Then Walt took Manny's hand, and Manny pulled him aboard as Walt stepped off the dinghy onto the transom. Father and son hugged each other once again but said nothing. Jenny appeared in the cockpit, still in tears.

Walt and Manny ended their embrace, and Manny scrambled forward to pull the bow directly over the anchor, while his father started the engine and then cranked the windlass to raise the anchor. Manny stayed where he was until the anchor was secured, and then headed back to the cockpit.

"Let's go," Manny said to no one in particular. The small diesel engine propelled the sailboat slowly out into the Hudson River. Walt and Manny watched the depth finder. When the depth increased beyond 15 feet, they made sure that they were safely out of the main navigation channel, and then dropped anchor.

"Ok. Let's get some sleep" Walt said, loudly enough for everyone to hear. "I will take the first watch."

Martin took over the watch from Manny a little more than an hour before dawn. Miriam and the girls were in a dog pile on one of the berths in the galley, with Nicole and now Manny in the other berth.

Shortly after dawn, Walt woke up and left the V-berth at the bow. He headed up topside and took a seat opposite Martin in the bow.

"I don't suppose you saw any street or bridge lights last night?" Walt asked sarcastically.

"You would have heard me," replied Martin in a small voice.

"Huuua. Someone's feeling self-righteous. Right now, the right thing to do is get the hell out of here. We both know that."

"As it stands, we do not have a choice," said Martin. "We live in one of the largest metropolitan population centers in the world, and we are completely dependent on the outside world for all of our material needs."

"And materials will not be making their way into the region on any time frame or in any volume that will matter to the people here," Walt added.

"Yes, I am aware. If this is a coordinated attack on the electrical grid, then most of the people here are going to freeze, starve, or die of dysentery long before spring."

"Scores are going to be settled," Walt hissed as he met Martin's eyes.

Martin shivered. "What's the point of that? If they stay here, they will die. You'd have your revenge. We are human beings, not animals."

"Oh, yeah? Tell me. How do you feel about Adolf Hitler and his merry band of sociopaths? If you could go back in time, would you kill him?"

"Hitler killed six million of my people."

"Hitler killed a lot more than six million people."

"I meant the Holocaust."

"I know what you meant. What I don't know is why you marginalized the tens of millions of other people the Nazis murdered. What, they're not important to you?"

"You are going to moralize with me now? Where were you last night?"

Walt just shrugged and said, "But you would be willing to kill Nazis?"

"They murdered six million of my people. That's a silly moral analogy."

"Silly, eh?" Walt scoffed. "The Nazis killed millions upon millions of people, and all of them were strangers to you. For some reason, some of those strangers are important to you, and you think it's worth killing someone to avenge their deaths. But the guy who killed one of your daughters, you'd let him get away with it? Do you really think that you would just forgive and forget?"

That caught Martin up short. For Walt, this wasn't hypothetical. Walt had lost a son to violence.

"I cannot even begin to imagine what you have gone through," Martin said after a long pause.

"No. That's not true. You *can* imagine. In fact, you just did imagine," Walt was speaking through clenched teeth. His vengeance had not settled the rage he carried in his heart. "You would have no problem degrading your humanity to settle the score with Hitler, and he never laid a finger on your children."

"We must not become like animals."

"Well, that is one way to look at it, but you're repeating yourself, you know that? And you're repeating yourself because these are just platitudes. How's this? We must not allow animals in government costumes—concentration camp doctors, Gestapo executioners, or trigger-happy cops—to kill 'your people' *or my children* with impunity. You do what you gotta do, and I will do the same."

Manny stepped out of the galley and into the cockpit.

"Can't sleep?" Walt asked his son.

"I got enough sleep. Whadya think?"

"I think we should idle down the river to Manhattan and get our asses out to sea." And with that Walt fired up the engine. Manny walked forward to tend to the anchor. Soon they were underway.

"Here, Manny, take the wheel. We will be at the George Washington Bridge in two to four hours, depending on the tide. No point in having all of us on duty at the same time. Wake me up if you are not sure where the channel is. Otherwise, let me rest until we get to Manhattan."

"OK," said Manny as he stepped in front of the wheel.

Walt headed below into the small cabin and went straight ahead to the V-berth beds. There was no sound of snoring. Jenny was awake.

"Walt?"

The tone of her voice stopped him dead in his tracks. He turned to face her.

Jenny's eyes did not search his face. She was not teary or emotional. Her face was expressionless, and her eyes stared into his, unblinking. Cold, stone-like, she waited for Walt to respond.

Walt only nodded to her and said nothing. Jenny nodded back and remained expressionless. After a moment of unspoken communication, Jenny turned with a face as hard as granite, got up out of her side of the V-berth and climbed topside. Walt dove into his side of the V-berth and was asleep in minutes.

They cruised the sailboat under engine power at just a little over idle speed to conserve fuel. Unlike motorboats, sailboats do not gain much in fuel efficiency by increasing speed to raise the hull out of the water and thus reduce drag. Sailboats lose fuel efficiency as motoring speed increases. Besides, they were in no hurry. Depending on the tides, they would either anchor in the shallow waters off of Staten Island or head straight out to sea.

They had an old chartbook of the New York waters—the Hudson River, New York Harbor, New York's Upper and Lower Bays, and Long Island Sound as well as a chartbook of the eastern seaboard—that had come with the boat. Walt and Manny hoped they would not need the charts. Instead, they were relying on the electronic Global Positioning System, or GPS, that was mounted to the right, or starboard, of the wheel. The GPS would not work unless the military satellites circling the earth kept on transmitting. Walt and Manny worried that the satellite transmission would be shut down by the American military. The civilian GPS frequency was separate from the military frequency and could be shut down independently, but at the moment the GPS screen was working, and showing their speed over the Hudson River at four knots—a little less than five miles per hour. That meant the tide was coming in against them. Since they had left about an hour ago, and the watermark on the pilings they passed was not far from the top, Manny figured the tide would turn soon. Their speed should start to pick up gradually after that, as the ocean tides slacken at the top and bottom and are fiercest in the middle of their cycle.

Manny took his eyes off the horizon in front of the boat and looked around. Miriam and the two girls were sitting on the foredeck. They could have been anyone out enjoying a pleasure ride on a friend's boat, rather than refugees fleeing New York City in fear of a nuclear attack. Manny rolled his eyes at the thought. Martin and Jenny were seated in the cockpit area fore, or in front of, the wheel, with Martin looking to port at the New York side and Jenny to starboard at the New Jersey side.

Manny looked at the strange man sitting in front of him. The afternoon of the bombings, his father had asked two family friends to join him on the voyage. He had told them that the New York metropolitan region had far too many people and far too few available resources to weather the crisis that was sure to come even in the absence of a nuclear attack, and that the New York metropolitan area was no place to be if hostilities continued. Walt's friends had rejected his exhortations. No one had taken him up on his offer to join forces for a thousand-mile ocean voyage, to be followed by a multi-hundred-mile hike—uphill no less. Manny smiled to himself. His father had always been on the adventurous side, and that was an understatement. Truth be told, his father was an arrogant, swaggering, hard-drinking, hard-working maniac, who had had enough skill and luck to stay alive despite a seemingly never-ending parade of close calls. Manny could almost see the wheels turning in his father's head.

So, there is a nuclear war in the Middle East? Well, we will get on our sailboat and head out to sea to get clear of New York City, just in case it is next, and then head south to Jason's farm! What else would we possibly do?

Manny was his own man, and would have told his father he was crazy, as their friends had done, if he thought that was the case. But he thought his father's strategy made good sense. It would get them far away from New York City and the Northeast, quickly. If they landed in South Carolina to find that the world had solved its issues without drawing the U.S. into a war or nuclear exchange, well, then they could return home the same way they had left. If not, they could try to trade the boat for provisions—or abandon it if necessary—and walk the rest of the way to Jason's farm.

If everything went according to plan, they figured they would land in South Carolina in six to ten days. If they could then walk 20 miles per day, they would arrive at Jason's farm in another 20 days. They added another five days for all of the things that could go wrong, so the whole trek should take about 25 days. Walt and Manny both felt that in ten days things would not have gotten completely out of hand in the less densely populated South Carolina region, so they should have a good chance of being able to do the walk to Jason's. When Martin and his family showed up at their door after walking out of Manhattan the night before, Walt's and Manny's confidence that they could walk across the Carolinas to Jason's place rose considerably. The bottom line was that they had little choice. It wasn't safe to stay put, and they couldn't carry enough food to walk all the way from New York to Jason's place. So, they had to use the boat to cut down the hiking distance, and then they had to hike. With luck, they might hit a dry spell and do the hiking without a lot of rain or snow.

Manny looked down at the GPS. Each time he did so he fully expected to see the message "searching for satellites" on the screen, indicating that the GPS was no longer receiving a signal. So far, though, it continued to work fine. When he looked back up, Martin was standing next to him.

"Anything I can help with?" asked Martin. Manny shook his head.

"Not at the moment. Don't worry; I am sure there will be plenty for you to do."

The George Washington Bridge loomed in the sky ahead. The Palisades on the New Jersey side had given them all a sense of claustrophobia when they looked in that direction too long. Everyone seemed to prefer the New York side of the Hudson River, despite the natural beauty of the Palisades. They could see the highways, all of them packed with cars and as still as a parking lot. Some people were walking between the cars, but they were too far away to see who they were or what they were doing.

Miriam looked back to Martin, and he met her eyes. She nodded to him, acknowledging his good judgment to leave New York City as soon they could pack and go. He gave her a small smile back, and she turned back to ponder the jam-packed highways. Martin wondered what she pieced together from the previous evening's events. The rush hour into the city would still be underway on any other day, but not in the days after a nuclear war in the Middle East.

They passed under the George Washington Bridge in the same silent awe that overcame them when they had passed under the Tappan Zee Bridge back in Tarrytown. Jenny and Miriam both began to weep at the same moment. Miriam's daughters clung to her in support, but Jenny sat there alone in her grief. While Miriam was overcome with emotion as she took in the eastern shore of the Hudson River and the absence of motion, Jenny's emotions were somewhat more complicated. She had lost a son to murder. The cop who killed her son might not have been charged with murder, but he was a murderer nonetheless. Like Walt, Jenny had dreamed of revenge. Even though Walt had not told her what happened last night, she knew with absolute certainty that Spinelli was dead. She was afraid to ask who else had died, and what Walt had done. She knew her husband well. He was a good man, but he was capable of just about anything when it came to his anger and grief over the loss of his son. Just knowing that Spinelli was dead, and that her son's death had been avenged, was all she needed to know, at least for now. Whatever else Walt might have done to assuage his rage was not something she needed to feel responsible for, and she was not sure she would feel bad about what might have taken place in any event. Perhaps she might even have rejoiced in the slaughter of her enemy's family. This was not a place that Jenny could go right now. It was all she could do to hold on to her sanity as it was.

"Hey Mom," Manny called to Jenny. "Please go and wake up Dad. He wanted to get up when we got to Manhattan."

Jenny went below without answering, or even looking at Manny. She walked forward to the V-berth, where two beds were separated at the head and joined at the feet in the shape of a capital "V" in the bow of the boat. Walt lay there sleeping and breathing heavy. Whatever had happened last night was not affecting his sleep.

When you have been through what we have been through, nothing fazes you anymore. Nothing.

She shook his shoulder gently and called his name, "Walt," in a soft voice. Walt hated to be woken suddenly or rudely. In the past, Jenny would often disregard his sensibilities in this matter and would wake him in any way that her mood struck her. But the world had changed, and she unconsciously recognized the meaning of this change as it manifested itself in her relationship with Walt. And even though Martin was as gentle as a lamb, while Walt was capable of who-knows-what, Miriam was now fully informed of the change, too. The universe had shifted. All of them felt it. Jenny needed Walt. Walt did not need Jenny. No man needed an unhelpful aging woman with a bad attitude, and there was no divorce lawyer available as unspoken leverage. Her cell phone no longer worked. There were no 911 emergency responders to call upon. She would have to control her mouth and her moods. To survive, every man, woman, and child would be forced to cooperate in ways they could not have imagined in their lives "Before."

For the first time in as long as she could remember, Jenny felt fear more than she felt rage. She had raged about her son's murder. Now she feared for herself. She had very little power of her own. She could not use the threat of force to impose her will on anyone. From now on, she would have to make herself useful. The feeling from that realization was unlike anything she had ever experienced.

Walt swung his feet over to the deck and took a few breaths as he tried to clear the sleep from his mind. He awoke knowing where he was, what they were doing, and where they were going. They must be near Manhattan, and Manny had sent Jenny down to wake him. A sense of overpowering relief flooded through him. They had not been stopped by any of the dozens of authorities that might have interrupted their journey. He had hoped this would be the case. Walt reasoned that if they left right away that the authorities would be short-handed and overwhelmed. Stopping sailboats from leaving New York Harbor would be low on their to-do list.

"Are you OK?" Jenny asked in a small voice.

"I am hungry." He paused for a moment and sat perfectly still, stared at nothing in the opposite V-berth, and then asked, "Has anybody been seasick?"

"No. Not yet." Jenny thought that was a strange question but did not say anything. Walt's mind worked in unique ways.

"Hmm. Go figure," Walt said as much to himself as to his wife. "Well, let's see where we are." And with that he headed astern, and up onto the deck and into the cockpit.

"You've been asleep for three hours," said Manny, getting right to the point. "The tide has turned. It is going out. I reckon we are about two hours from the Verrazano Narrows. No more than two. The tide is picking up speed now."

The bridge that connected Brooklyn with the smallest New York City borough, Staten Island, was named the Verrazano-Narrows Bridge. Once they passed southward through the Narrows, they would be in the open ocean, though it was called the Lower Bay. Since fuel conservation was vital, and they had to use the motor until they made it to the ocean, the outgoing tide was a very good thing for them. It would carry them out into the Atlantic sooner than they had expected, with much lower fuel consumption.

There was more good news. When Walt looked down at the GPS, it was still working. Manny followed Walt's eyes down to the GPS and then met them with his own. They smiled at each other.

"Thank heaven for small favors," said Walt.

Walt took over the helm, and Manny went down below to get some sleep. Martin stood up and moved over to stand next to Walt.

"How are you making out?" asked Walt.

Martin shrugged. "I don't know about you, but I don't know what to say, or think, or feel."

"Do you feel seasick?"

"Oh," replied Martin blowing out his cheeks. "I thought you meant something else. No, I don't feel seasick. And it does not appear that my wife or the girls are suffering from it, either."

"Martin, I did mean everything. I wanted to know how you are holding up physically and emotionally. Look, we are both mature men. We have seen a great many things in our lives. But we ain't seen nothin' like this," Walt said in a voice that could be described as amused, or perhaps astonished, or somewhere between the two. "We *need* you to be OK."

Martin did not respond to that. He wanted to ask if Walt had any more stops to make or scores to settle, but he kept his mouth shut. The days of seeking the moral high ground in a debate were over.

"It looks to me like the electricity is out here, too," said Martin. "I don't see a light anywhere, on either side. Even in this bright daylight, we should be able to see something. I don't see anything. You have to wonder what happened. Why is the power out?"

"No, I don't see any signs of electric power, either," responded Walt, as he scanned the buildings to the east in Manhattan. "But we lost power up in Westchester within hours of the news reports. I imagine the city lost power at the same time. And to answer your question, I have no idea *why* the power would be out."

"Well, there are only a few possible reasons. None of them good." Martin was becoming breathless.

"Please. Calm yourself. We are here, and we are safe, at least for the time being. The fact of the matter is that we have no idea what happened in the world the day before yesterday. Yes, we all heard some news reports about a nuclear war in the Middle East, but neither of us talked with anybody who had any first-hand knowledge about that. For all we know it started last week. Perhaps they are still at it. Or maybe it never even happened. Who knows? Maybe an Electro-Magnetic-Pulse bomb hit the U.S. Of course, if that were true, the electronics on the boat shouldn't be working. Maybe the U.S. electrical grid has been hit with some kind of cyber-attack. The perpetrators of that could be foreign *or* domestic if you follow me. Maybe *we* initiated the nuclear war and planted those stories in the media. You know, 'fake news?' The fact is, we have no idea what happened, or what is going on now."

Martin, impressed by Walt's calm demeanor and reasoned explanation, began to speak, "Yes, that's true, and there are other possibilities…" but cut himself off when something strange entered his field of vision as he looked out towards the New Jersey shore. His mind had difficulty processing what he was sure he was seeing. A small, open motorboat that appeared to be crammed with people was speeding towards the Manhattan side, and would cross in front of them at less than 200 yards. As they came closer, the men in the boat came into focus. Perhaps 20 young men, all with jet-black hair and swarthy complexions, were packed, standing-room–only, in the boat. They appeared to be holding rifles, pointed up towards the sky. They looked exactly like the photos the news services published, of fighters standing in the back of trucks as they were being transported in and around places like Syria, Afghanistan, and Iraq.

"Shit!" Walt said out loud. He had seen them, too. "Let's hope they have someplace else to be."

Martin did not respond right away. He kept his eyes on the boat.

"Where are your guns?"

Walt scoffed. "Yeah, now you want a gun? A lot of good they will do us. If those guys want to kill us—they will. They have way more firepower than we do. The worst thing we can do is to appear to be a threat. Then they would have to engage. Let's not give them a reason to stop here. I don't think it's us they are looking for."

The motorboat maintained its speed and course. The men on the motorboat looked at the sailboat for a moment, and then appeared to turn their heads back towards Manhattan as they passed in front of Walt and Martin. As the motorboat approached the Manhattan side of the Hudson River, it turned north.

"What the fuck was that?" Walt said, with heartfelt emphasis on the word "that."

"Holy smokes, holy smokes, holy smokes," Martin repeated with a wild-eyed look on his face.

"Well, that answers that. We don't stop. We are going out into the Atlantic, and we are going to put as many miles between us and here as possible today."

"They can go out in the ocean, too. Can't they?" Martin was nearly hyperventilating.

"Not really. Not in that kind of boat. They could easily capsize, even in here on the river, loaded down like that. Out there they would certainly capsize, or get swamped by a wave, and my bet is the Coast Guard won't be picking up the phone if they call. Whatever they are up to, they will need to conserve fuel. Manhattan is a target-rich environment. The Atlantic is a desert as far as they are concerned."

As Walt was speaking, Martin watched his wife as she kept her eyes glued to the boat with the men holding guns, now off in the distance. Her mouth was wide open, her eyes unblinking. Finally, she looked back and made eye contact with Martin. She said nothing, but the blank look on her face said everything. Martin signaled for her to come back to the cockpit. She and the girls complied. When they got there, they settled on the bench on the starboard side and huddled together.

Walt tapped Martin on the elbow to get his attention.

"You were wondering why the power is out? Well, we just saw a group of armed men that looked suspiciously like what we have come to think of as 'terrorists', on a speedboat racing into Manhattan. You have to assume there are other such groups. The only question is: 'how many?' If there is a coordinated attack going on, and it sure looks that way, perhaps they have seized or destroyed electric generation plants or other grid infrastructure. Maybe they used technology for sabotage, but they might have done frontal assaults on generation facilities as well. Or maybe a full-scale religious war is breaking out. Those guys didn't strike me as do-gooder volunteers out to help bring meals to the elderly in Manhattan. It might be politically incorrect to say, but I wouldn't want that boat and those men responding to a distress call if we were in trouble."

"And there is no way we can know what the hell is going on," replied Martin.

"Exactly," said Walt. "We are on our own."

The tidal current was moving south through the channel at four knots. At 1,200 RPM's, a little over idle, the engine added another four knots of speed. So, the sailboat was moving over the bottom at a little over nine miles per hour. Walt could see that they were somewhere around midtown. He kept a sharp eye out for commercial vessels. He had not seen one operating, though he expected that to change when they got down to the Upper Bay, below Manhattan and above the Narrows.

The sound of gunfire erupted, coming from Manhattan. It didn't sound like a pitched firefight; occasional rifle shots sounded as if someone were taking target practice—or perhaps a sniper was shooting people from safe positions and then displacing to avoid counter-fire. The shooting stopped. Several minutes went by with no more shots fired. Then came a barrage of rifle reports, far too many to count. Sound travels well over water, and all on the sailboat could hear shouts in between the explosive outbursts of the firefight. At times there would be silence, and then more shooting.

The sailboat was moving fast enough that the shooting sounds faded a bit but were still plenty loud coming over the water. At least no one seemed to be shooting at them. Walt did not hear the sounds of rounds passing near them, and there were no splashes in the water around them.

Manny appeared from below and stood in the cockpit with his father and Martin. The three men stared in the direction of the firefight, with only Walt breaking away to check the boat's progress in the channel.

"Holy shit," said Manny.

"Yep," said Walt. "The battleground has come to America—guerrilla warfare in Manhattan. Can you fucking even imagine this?"

"No," said Martin in a dispirited voice. "I can't."

Miriam stood up and led the girls down below. Jenny and Danielle followed them.

Martin called out to Jenny. "Hey, they are going to get seasick down there."

When Jenny turned around, the men could see she had tears in her eyes. Danielle and Miriam also stopped and turned around. They were all crying.

Martin shrugged and went back to looking over the wheel toward the bow.

"I don't think they care about being seasick at the moment," said Manny. "Just sayin'."

"I am sure that's true. I am also sure that when they start to get sick, they won't care about anything else except tossing their lunches."

They were now off lower Manhattan, Walt guessed somewhere north of 14th Street, when they heard gunfire again. This time it must have been near the river. The blasts were much louder and far more terrifying. Given that, Walt thought that they might be taking fire, but again there were no bullets whizzing by and no splashes near the boat. Given the number of rifle blasts, they would have known pretty quickly if they were the intended targets.

"Lord, if you are listening, get us the fuck out of here!" said Walt as he increased fuel to the engine and the boat picked up speed. This was no time to worry about fuel conservation. It was time to survive. In ten minutes, the Battery was on their left. Walt noticed was that all the boat slips were empty, and there were no sailboats at the moorings, or motorboats at the docks. Every boat here had already headed out to sea and away from Manhattan. There were several sailboats ahead and astern of them, so they were not the only sailors on the river. Walt imagined that things had been pretty hectic in the harbor last night after the news hit.

They were now out in the Upper Bay. Several other sailboats were merging in from the starboard and Walt wondered where they came from, as he had not seen them in the Hudson. They must have been moored along the Jersey or Staten Island shallows. There was an armada of sailboats behind them, stretching back toward Tarrytown. There was another armada of sailboats five miles ahead of them. They were merely the lead sailboat in one random pack.

It was mid-afternoon. The Verrazano Narrows Bridge was in sight and on the other side of the Narrows were the Lower Bay and the open ocean.

"I guess we are going for it?" Manny said more than asked.

"Of course, we are 'going for it.' We don't have a choice. The tide is going out, and whatever is happening here, we don't want any part of it."

"Have you ever sailed a boat in the ocean at night?" asked Martin. He didn't wish to sound ungrateful, but the idea of spending the night on a sailboat on the ocean had only been an abstract thought to him before this moment. It was now concrete.

"No, never, now that you mention it," said Walt. "Worse, both of us are going to be asleep when it is your turn at the helm." Walt gave Martin a playful poke to the ribs, and when Martin looked at Walt, Walt winked back at Martin. "What did you think we invited you for?"

Walt and Manny were smiling, first at Martin and then at each other and then to themselves.

"Very funny," said Martin.

Walt and Manny sobered up and looked at Martin with straight faces.

"Are you serious?" asked Martin.

"As a heart attack," replied Walt.

Manny had seen this act from his father many times before. He kept his head down and his smile to himself.

"You would trust me to drive a boat while you slept? Are you crazy? I have never driven a boat before!"

"First off, we don't say 'drive.' 'Steer' or 'take the helm' makes you sound like you know what you are talking about," said Walt, thoroughly enjoying the angst he was generating within Martin. "Besides, this boat is equipped with an auto-pilot. You don't have to do anything except keep a sharp eye out for other boats—and more importantly ships. If you see anything, all you have to do is scream. I will be up here in a flash."

"Ships? Oy!"

"You better believe 'Oy'! A container ship would break us into pieces no bigger than a baseball bat. And we don't want that."

The Narrows were dead ahead.

"Hey, Manny. We are going to put up sail as soon as we clear the Narrows. Tell the women I don't want anyone on the upper deck. We only have two harnesses. I don't want anyone getting swept overboard. We would never be able to get them back aboard."

Jenny and Miriam were just emerging from below deck with sandwiches on paper plates. Danielle was below and was handing soda and bottled water up. Martin was incredulous. Miriam had made sandwiches, or at least had participated in making sandwiches, with no drama involved.

"Good. I am starved," said Walt. "Let's wolf this down before we get to the Narrows. We don't need any distractions in there."

Chapter 21

The workhorses stamped their feet and swatted their tails at the flies and other biting insects that were their constant companions during the warm weather months. The chains and other metal parts of their harness clanked together in a sort of harmony with the creak and strain of the leather bindings holding it all together. The two horses, a soft reddish Belgian mare and a dappled white Percheron mare, had been working together for the past seven years. Both stood over 16 hands and weighed over 1600 pounds. They were working this fine September morning to pull a circa 1920s McCormick No. 9 cycle mower, for the hay season's "fourth" cutting. The first cutting in this region typically was done in late May and early June, and repeated every 32 to 35 days after that, depending on the year's rainfall. If the weather cooperated, five cuttings might be possible, continuing into early November. If the weather did not cooperate, the horses and cows could be turned out on this field for several hours per day to graze off the excess, conserving the hay in the barn, which would be needed to get the livestock through the winter months.

Winter here was short when compared with winters Up North. Pasture grass continued to grow in this region until just before Thanksgiving and began to grow again in March.

The sickle mower clacked and clanged in an unsteady rhythm that sped up or slowed down with the pace of the team which was pulling it. The old Percheron mare, the team's lead horse, set the pace, and was always hitched on the left. Her pace, in turn, was influenced by the horseflies, the heft of the grass, by her never-ending head-butting battle with the Belgian mare to her right, and to a lesser extent by Jason's exhortations.

A sickle mower makes its cut several inches above the ground. The grass is left to lie in the sun to dry into hay which, once cured, can be stored in haystacks in the field, or under cover in a hay barn. These mowers are "ground driven," and work very much like a bicycle, but in reverse. The horses pull the mower forward, forcing the wheels to turn. The wheels turn the "pedals"—in this case, a set of gears and a flywheel— rather than the other way around, and the flywheel pushes and pulls a pitman rod, which moves a mowing bar back and forth to cut the grass. The flywheel and pitman look very much like the rods that turned the wheels on the old-time steam engine locomotives. All horse-drawn equipment collects the energy of the horses' movement in this manner. The only petroleum required to run the equipment is lubricating oil. The power comes from the horses, and ultimately from the grass and grain that the horses eat.

It took the team and their teamster, Jason, about two hours to cut three acres of hayfield. A tractor with mowing implements can cut at 5 times that rate, but Jason enjoyed working with horses, and this was how he worked his farm. Ever cautious not to hurt or overwork the mares, Jason rested the team for two minutes in every ten-minute period while cutting. After they finished cutting in one field, Jason gave the horses a rest for water and grain, hitched them up to a circa-1930s side delivery hay rake, and then headed off to another field that had been cut several days before, where they would rake the hay into long straight mounds of sun-dried grass called windrows. In each field, the tall grass had to be cut, allowed to dry or 'cure' for several days, then raked into windrows, picked up by a hay loader, deposited onto a hay wagon, and transported to a barn for storage. This process required at least three passes over the ground by the horses and the ground driven equipment—four if a hay tedder had to be used to fluff up the cut grass for better drying—before the hay was on the wagon. And that hay still had to be unloaded into the barn for storage. Haying was very hard work, but today Jason did not notice his labors. Today life held new urgency. His mind swirled with the endless possibilities, ramifications, implications, and consequences that the war, or whatever it had been and maybe still was, would have on his family, their community, and on the wider world.

Jason headed back to the barn to drop off the hay rake and attach the hay wagon to the forecart he was driving. The hay loader would then be attached to the rear of the hay wagon. The forecart, wagon, and loader, coupled together in much the same way as train cars are coupled together, would need the power of two teams of horses. Jason went about the task of changing out the double tree that was on the forecart for a "four-horse evener" that would accommodate both two-horse teams on the forecart. Noah was waiting at the barn with a second team of horses. He unhitched the team Jason had been working and led them to a tie on one of the barn posts. When Jason finished attaching the large evener to the forecart, Noah brought his team over and began hitching them to the forecart, while Jason retrieved his team and hitched them as well. They now had four horses hitched abreast. Two horses could pull the combined rig of hay wagon and loader for a load or two, or even three, but there were many loads waiting for them in the field. Four horses could handle the job with relative ease, where two horses were at risk of being overworked. Workhorses had been valuable yesterday, and now, after the bombing, Jason felt that the horses had become invaluable. It seemed to him that everything would be measured from now on in terms of "Before" and "After."

Noah and Jason had been working silently, but now Noah spoke up.

"Many people in our church think that the 'End Times' is upon us."

Jason was still tightening the through-bolt on the forecart's tongue, the long piece of wood that the horses were yoked to by their collars. Noah's voice brought him back to it. This was real. He didn't have an intelligent response. So, he punted.

"Your father doesn't seem to think so. Neither do I. What do you think, Noah?"

"Me?" Noah paused, put his hands on his hips, and looked down at the ground, as if the answer to this question might be written there. When that turned out not to be the case, Noah picked up his head and looked all around him. Noah liked to think before speaking. Early in their working relationship, Jason had been uncomfortable with the pace of his conversations with this 17-year-old man. After some time, both Jason and Ellen had concluded that Noah was not only the most mature teenager they had ever encountered, but also that he seemed to possess the wisdom of an elderly sage. Jason couldn't help but smile as he watched the looks on Noah's face change as his mind worked. Noah's nutrient-dense responses usually packed a lot of meaning into a few words. Jason could tell that the computer running in Noah's head was close to a final calculation of some sort.

"I am not sure what to think just yet," replied Noah. "I may never know. I don't know for sure *what* happened over there. The only thing I know is what I have heard from people who watched TV or read about it on the Internet. But no matter who did what, I don't think the good Lord needs to use man's nuclear bombs as the instrument of his justice. So, I don't think this is the 'End Times.'"

There it was, as always. Noah's short, unassuming preamble, and then—Pow!—his concise, modest, and philosophical conclusion.

For a brief moment, Jason forgot about the world's troubles and marveled at this strange yet insightful young man, who had never flown in an airplane, driven a car, or ordered a book online. Noah always seemed to cut through layers of confusion and obfuscation, arriving at the critical detail, as effortlessly as purple martins cut through the air all around them to catch the insects that flew from the grass as they worked the hayfields.

"Well," said Jason motioning for Noah to jump up on the hay wagon, "now that you put it like that, nor do I."

Jason climbed into the seat of the forecart, settled in, grabbed the reins, and made a kissing sound with his pursed lips to signal the horses to move forward.

The sound of the lunch bell made a welcome intrusion to their labors. Even before Jason and Ellen had ditched their cell phones, the weak cell signal around their farm had made this low-tech communication device necessary. Some of the plain folk had erected bell towers, equipped with a three-gallon sized bell, outside their houses. These bells were smaller than the typical church bell, but big enough to alert the men at work around the farm that it was mealtime. Jason had acquired such a bell at an auction. He then found an old ham radio tower, fabricated a bracket to hold the bell on a hinge, attached a pull rope to the bell, and installed the whole works far enough from his front porch so that the bell didn't blast the people in the house. That bell was calling them now. They left the horses tied to a hitching post and headed off to lunch.

As they approached the house, Jason could see the kids playing outside, and Ellen standing on the porch. Ellen had set the table on the porch for their meal and set a bucket of water out for them to use for washing up. Jason looked at the bucket, and his shoulders slumped.

"Don't tell me the water is off, too."

"No," replied Ellen. "The water is still flowing. But the house is unbearably hot with the wood cook stove fired up. I will be canning all day today and probably tomorrow. I think we will be sleeping under the stars tonight. It's like an oven in there."

Jason could feel the heat pouring out of the house through the front door. They had two wood cooking stoves, one in the "barn apartment" that had been framed out in an old workshop by the previous owners and used as a guesthouse, and another in the kitchen of the main house. Both stoves were fired up to accommodate three large canners, two cast-iron frying pans where ground meat was "browned," and two 5-gallon stock pots where bones and whole poultry were being cooked down to stock and soups before being packed into jars. One of the canners held 19 quart jars, but the other two canners only held seven quart jars. It took 90 minutes at pressure to safely process food that contained meat, and another hour to let the canners cool before opening them. Ellen figured this project would require between 200 and 300 jars—perhaps two full days of cooking and canning from dawn till dusk.

"Well, you are doing a wonderful job, honey," Jason said to encourage his wife. "We are going to need that meat." He regretted this last line. Ellen was prone to anxiety and needed no incentive to worry. Worrying came naturally to her. But Jason noticed that it did not seem to affect her negatively. She was bustling about and in good spirits.

Jason looked out from the porch to take in the position of the sun and guessed it to be about 1 pm—19 hours since the power went down. No one had come bustling up the driveway with news. They were sitting down to a lunch of leftovers from the fridge. Supper would no doubt be the same, but by tomorrow evening what had not been consumed from the fridge would have to be discarded—unless the electric power came on. 19 hours without power will not cause irreparable damage to the system. Jason was just doing the math. He figured three days—72 hours. If the authorities could get the power back on within three days, the system would go on as it had before. After 72 hours, the probability of getting the system back to what it had been, without severe disruption, would decline precipitously with each and every hour. After 10 to 14 days it would take a small miracle, but the system could conceivably be retrieved. But after that…

"Don't look so serious!" Ellen interrupted Jason's thought process. "Let's enjoy some lunch."

Ellen motioned for Noah and Jason to take their seats. Jason sat and looked at the table. In front of him were some lemon slices to flavor the water.

"I was just thinking we won't be getting citrus," Jason said as he reached for a lemon slice and squeezed it into his water. He held up his sandwich and examined it from the side. "Or tomatoes. At least until next year's garden harvest."

"We have 120 quart-size jars of tomatoes in the pantry. You won't have to do without tomatoes. Besides, it hasn't even been a full day. The power could come back on at any time."

The irony of Ellen's role reversal as comforter to Jason's angst was not lost on him. He felt this was as good a time as any to say what was on his mind.

"Yeah, it could. But I doubt it."

Neither Ellen nor Noah spoke. All three chewed on their sandwiches. After a bit, Jason continued.

"I don't think that a nuclear event in the world and the electrical grid being down is a coincidence. In fact, I think that all of North America is without power, and maybe the electrical grid in every industrialized country. The electrical grid was always a soft spot and easy to disrupt. I don't doubt that we have attacked grids around the world in much the way we have been attacked. I don't know the mechanism, or their strategy or agenda—not least because I don't know who did it. A foreign government is most likely behind this, but it could have been done by one or more factions within the U.S.—The CIA, the Pentagon, the Office of Naval Intelligence, the NSA or a small group inside any one of these. Of course, I could be wrong, and the problem is that the entire west or east coast is a pile of smoldering ruins, but I just don't think so. I think this is an attack on the financial and economic system that underpins our military. They, whoever 'they' are, cannot defeat the American military in an all-out war—but they don't need to. They just need to cut off funding to our far-flung military empire. This does that."

"Okay," said Ellen, looking first to Noah and then back to Jason. "But we can fix it, right?"

"Emerson said, 'When you strike at a king, you must kill him.' Whoever did this understand that, and they must feel that they can kill the king, or they would not have done it. Or perhaps they just thought they needed to slow down our military response to whatever happened over in the Middle East. The problem, as I see it, is that we are in a catch-22 with a drop-dead date. We are as busy jamming their grid and system as they are jamming ours. We have nuclear weapons, but they are not much of an advantage at the moment. Unfortunately, our system cannot survive if the current stalemate lasts more than a week or two. We have two ways to lose this conflict: we lose if we engage in a nuclear exchange, and we lose if we cannot restore electrical power. Both sides need to mobilize thousands of engineers and localized electrical power system operators to figure out what the hell the enemy did to bring the grid down. I guess the government can communicate by satellite from various military and government installations that have their own power generation capacity, but to what purpose? All of the software and hardware is distributed all over the place, and most of it has no access to power. Ergo, we need to collect all of our engineers, bring them to a powered government or military installation, retrieve all of their computers and equipment, network it all together, communicate by satellite link because the Web is down, figure out what the hell the enemy did, and then fix it—but rounding up all of the non-military engineers that will be needed to accomplish anything is logistically impossible, though I suspect that all of that is technically feasible. Can we do all of that before the system becomes irretrievable? I don't think so. And even if they were able to get the grid up, there is still the pesky detail of a nuclear war in the Middle East. And there is no guarantee that whoever is responsible won't be able to take the grid down again. Bond payments and oil deliveries, in fact, all international trade, won't be happening anytime soon, so winter is going to starve or freeze millions upon millions of Americans. The economic contraction is going to be biblical. The U.S. will no longer be able to fund its far-flung military empire. The enemy can achieve all of its objectives without firing a shot.

"Think about it: How long will it take the average family to eat all of the perishables in their fridge, and canned foods in their pantry? That is about how long we will have any sense of order. Perishable food will go bad, and the food in transit has already disappeared. The meat and dairy inventories are being consumed as fast as possible in the absence of refrigeration, and there are no replacements. Yes, there is a mountain of grain in storage somewhere in rural America. How is that going to get to the cities? Or to the feedlots, poultry houses, and dairy barns? Many people don't even cook anymore. Without electricity, how are they going to prepare even the simplest meals? They don't have any of the necessary equipment or utensils. People are going to be on the move and exposed to the elements. This isn't a 'humanitarian' crisis. This is a 'humanity' crisis. And frankly, I don't know what to do."

This last line was like a slap in Ellen's face. Jason had always known what to do and always did the right thing, even though she often had fought him over it.

"What do you mean, you 'don't know what to do?'" Ellen was as calm as a Buddhist monk. She reached her hand across the table and placed it on his hand. "You have always known what to do." She smiled at Jason.

Jason wasn't sure if Ellen hadn't taken something, some drug or medication, as she was not typically given to calm and rational conduct when under stress. But there were no such medications in the house. He was sure of that. Perhaps all of the previous drama and histrionics Jason had witnessed with Ellen were reserved for a mock crisis. He did not respond.

Noah looked back and forth at this strange "English" couple. They had moved from somewhere 'out there'—as his people called society—into his community as seamlessly as if Jason and Ellen had been "plain folk" themselves. He wasn't sure if he understood half of what Jason was talking about, but he understood that Jason believed that something terrible was unfolding, and that it might result in the deaths of "billions of people." Noah had never seen a large city and could not comprehend the idea of such vast numbers, but he had a great deal of respect for this Englishman and his wife. They were so unlike the locals that comprised most of Noah's experience with outsiders, or the 'English,' as the Amish called them.

Working side-by-side with Jason out in the fields in blistering heat and bitter cold in the typical tasks of farming—hay work, fencing, gardening, breaking and working horses, barn repair, and construction—had led Noah to know and admire Jason. The fact that Jason farmed with workhorses was a shock in itself. Farming like this is hard work. Most of the local English were immensely obese. The Amish just chalked this up to their habits of watching TV and driving tractors and trucks rather than working with their bodies. The Amish are loath to criticize others openly, but the appalling physical condition of the people living around them was hard to dismiss. Many of the locals waddled from their cars in the parking lots, and had difficulty stepping up on the curb in front of the local hardware store. Noah could not imagine life under the oppressive body weight that his neighbors carried—though it seemed to be OK with them. But Jason and Ellen put up firewood and hay, cooked and heated their home with wood, milked a cow, and worked their farm every day. It took Noah a while to figure out what it was that made these two appear so very different from the other English. Of course, they were fit and trim from manual labor, and this was the first thing Noah noticed. But after getting to know them, Noah concluded that it was not their physical fitness that made them so different, it was their countenances—the looks on their faces as they went about their daily lives. They just seemed well and seemed to feel that all was right with the world. In Noah's experience, this wasn't just unusual for the English. It was unheard of. Sitting here, listening, and watching Jason and Ellen interact, left Noah in the grip of intense sadness for both his friends and his fellow man.

"Well," Noah said, clearing his throat. "I don't know much about what you just said, but I understand that you are very upset. In times like these, we must keep busy, to keep our minds off our troubles, and to keep future troubles off our minds. 'The evil of the day is sufficient unto itself.'"

Jason and Ellen came out of their self-pitying trance and looked up at Noah as if they had just been released from a spell. They looked at each other and smiled, and then turned their eyes back to Noah, shaking their heads slightly in unison at the strange wisdom of this seventeen-year-old man. Noah shifted uncomfortably in his seat, and his face reddened as Jason and Ellen continued with their amused examination of him.

Jason laughed out loud, clapped his hands together once, and then stood up. Noah and Ellen also rose from their chairs. The countenance that Noah had come to recognize in these people was back.

"Well said, Noah!" Jason responded. The weight of the world was suddenly gone from his shoulders—at least for the moment. "Let's all get back to work."

For the rest of the day Jason and Noah worked hay while Ellen emptied the freezer of meats and poultry, cooking and canning it all at a feverish pace. When Ellen rang the bell for supper at 5:45pm, it occurred to her that the batteries in the wall clock would not last forever. She put the thought from her mind. After all, she did have a solution for that.

The ringing bell put the men on notice that they had 15 or 20 minutes to get back to the barn, put up whatever equipment they were using, walk up to the house, and wash up. As Jason and Noah walked towards the house, Jason could see that the house was still dark. It had now been 24 hours or so since they lost power. He put the thought from his mind, by remembering Noah's brilliant exhortation.

Supper consisted of a little bit of everything that was in the fridge: lunchmeats, cheese, left over fried chicken, a crockpot of pork ribs from a few days ago, pasta and sausage in tomato sauce, and a large cabbage slaw with Asian dressing. As Jason perused the options now on the table, his mind wandered to what supper would look like next week. He forced that thought from his mind as well. His children bounced in their seats with the energy that happy children have, even though they spent the day playing outside and helping Ellen as best they could, rather than glued to their tablets.

Ellen placed the spread on the picnic table on the front porch, since the woodstove's heat had made the house, and it was unusually warm for the first day of November. Winter often started fitfully in the American South. She filled the hot water kettle with enough water for their evening showers—a five-gallon bucket of water each—and made sure that a small fire still burned in the firebox beneath it. Jason could see the kettle from the porch and was beyond thrilled with the good fortune of having that piece of equipment. Hot water was one of the mainstays of civilization. Without it, the personal hygiene we take for granted doesn't exist, and the pests and infections that hygiene had vanquished can return, quickly.

With supper concluded, Ellen and the kids cleared the table, and set off to wash the dishes with the luxurious hot water from the kettle. It occurred to Jason that many of his

English neighbors would go unwashed tonight, and perhaps would continue to go unwashed until they could reconcile themselves to bathing with cold water.

"Noah," said Jason. "I know I typically pay you in cash at the end of the day. I don't think cash has any value now. We are going to have to come to a new arrangement. Otherwise, you are going to lose interest in working here."

"I guess we will work something out. There will be plenty of work that will need to be done at our farm. We will have to help each other. I think you are going to become much more important to your Amish neighbors than you were before, and I hope that is okay with you."

"What do you mean?"

"I am not sure, exactly. But after listening to you and thinking it over, something tells me that will be the case. Right now, we have to get your hay into the barn as soon as possible. I am glad this is the last hay cut of the year. The cold weather will be here any time now. If what you say is happening, then we are not going to know what the weather has in store for us anymore. We will have no idea when it is going to rain and ruin all of the hay in the field. I have to go home now and do my chores, but I will be back the first thing in the morning, and I will bring my brothers. We will get you squared away, and then you can bring your teams over to our place and help us with our hay. We only have two teams. With four teams we can get our hay up in a day or two."

"That sounds like a plan," Jason replied with some enthusiasm. He needed the help and would be happy to help in return.

And with that Noah set off to hitch Trigger to his buggy, and head for home.

Chapter 22

Bannon took a deep breath and blew warm air onto his cold hands. He hated this duty with a passion, and couldn't wait to get back to the station, with its electric power generators that were supplying power to the building and its HVAC system. The rest of Manhattan was cold and starving, but critical structures had power, although keeping the generators in fuel had proved problematic. The roads were utterly clogged with abandoned vehicles. Tow trucks worked night and day but moving thousands upon thousands of cars out of the way was a much more significant task than anyone at the Federal Emergency Management Agency, or anyone else for that matter, ever had considered.

It wasn't as simple as having every tow truck in the country descend on New York to clear the highways. The rest of the country had the same problem. Cars, buses, trains, planes, and the people who had been traveling with them, were stranded all over the country. Drivers abandoned vehicles wherever they ran out of fuel. FEMA and the military had an impressive number of tow trucks—for localized natural disasters. But the immensity of the problem in New York just boggled the mind. And of course, Philadelphia, Washington, Boston, Chicago, et al. had similar problems. With the current resources, it would take years to clear the roads.

To Bannon—and to every other municipal employee in emergency services who had been assigned to help untangle this Gordian knot—it was more than surreal. They were trapped in the city unless they walked home. This was true for every civilian commuter as well.

Manhattan doubles in population during a normal workday. Two million people commute into "the city"—which is what everyone, even the residents of the other four New York City boroughs, calls Manhattan—and after the bombings, many of those two million people had been unable to get out of the city. They had had two options: walk home, or sleep in their workplaces and scrounge for food. While many eventually did make it back home, the city remained overwhelmed by those who were unable or unwilling to trek out of there—the obese, the out-of-shape, the prematurely aged, the women in high heels or other impractical footwear, the people who lived too far away to consider walking, etc. The list went on and on.

On the second day "After", the "suicide snipers" appeared on the scene. Perhaps the suicide snipers were tied to the death squads that killed Wall Street bigwig Hank Katz, Hollywood impresario Alan Levin, and dozens of other high-profile New Yorkers. Right now, Bannon and his fellow NYPD officers were dealing with a "terrorist fire team" as they were officially known, or suicide snipers, as the NYPD referred to them.

The NYPD had killed dozens of these snipers, but they also had been losing several of their officers for each sniper killed. The snipers were winning this battle of attrition, thanks in part to their seemingly suicidal dedication. For the NYPD officers, it was just a job. Police officers are civilians. With so many officers dying "in the line of duty", fewer and fewer of them were choosing to show up for work.

Another dirty secret was that not a single practicing Muslim officer of the NYPD showed up for work. For Bannon and many other officers, this was an infuriating development. Lord only knew whose side the Muslim officers were on, but it didn't look good. Bannon suspected that some of the snipers actually were NYPD "absentees".

The snipers appeared to be members of some homegrown radical-Islamist group, who operated in groups of four. One of the snipers would place himself where he could move around easily, and then would shoot any person he could line up in his sights. The other three members of the terrorist fire team would situate themselves so that they could fire on responding police officers. The effect was chilling and immediate. Since nobody had cell or landline phone service to report these incidents to the police promptly, the shootings in the first days after the bombings ran up body counts in the thousands. Many died slow and agonizing deaths because help could not reach them while the snipers were operating.

These sniper teams had virtually shut the city down in the days following the bombings. Even without telephones, the bad news traveled very fast. People hunkered down whenever possible. The police set up battery-powered triangulation listening devices to pick up the sound of gunfire so that they could respond accurately. The terrorists adapted by firing into the air, and then moving out. To make things worse, kids had started lighting firecrackers all over the city. The listening devices could not tell the difference between firearms and firecrackers.

Talk about a shit show.

So now the NYPD was responding to the snipers with APCs, armored personnel carriers. But first they had to navigate the APCs through the vehicle-choked streets, and then they still had to get out of the APCs to engage the terrorists, and the terrorists were not wearing uniforms. Bannon was a U.S. Army veteran and served in Iraq. He had extensive experience with guerrilla warfare. He knew that the insurgents don't have to win. All they have to do is not lose. And right now, they were not losing. Even though the NYPD and the National Guard killed a lot of snipers, there had been no detectable let-up in the number and pace of the sniping attacks. They appeared up in Washington Heights, then down in the Bowery, and then over in the west 40s.

Many of the snipers appeared to be excellent marksmen. Even though they did not have optical scopes on their rifles, and were aiming through "iron sights", they had made some incredible shots—head wounds on moving targets at 300 feet, leg wounds on officers with body armor.

Bannon's team had positively identified this particular terrorist fire team, and had identified all of their positions, using technology that the NYPD and National Guard possessed. The snipers were not able to simply throw down their weapons and fade into a crowd unknown. They knew they were going to be killed or caught. Talk about commitment. They prepared accordingly and arranged their suicide snipers to kill as many officers as possible before they were killed themselves.

Bannon's team was engaged in active waiting, not engaging the snipers per se, but pinning them down and keeping them awake. Everybody has to sleep eventually. The responding officers and soldiers worked and slept in shifts, and the snipers couldn't. After 24 hours, the snipers became only marginally effective. After 36 hours, they were not effective at all. So, the authorities had developed this system of pinning them down and waiting them out before engaging. Bannon and his team were doing that now. Waiting. Resting. Making sure the enemy could not sleep. Many in the ranks were gaining confidence, but not Bannon. Iraq had taught him that guerrilla fighters evolve strategies and tactics much more quickly than command and control armies do. He wondered who had trained the men he was fighting now.

The call came to engage one of the terrorists. Bannon, dressed in full body armor, was on the assault team. They cornered the sniper in a refurbished tenement building on West 40th Street. The authorities had infrared vision and biometrics. The officers knew exactly where their target was and could tell that he had fallen asleep. They would assault the terrorist, first with an anti-personnel grenade, and then with direct action, military jargon for an assault team going in for the kill. There were innocents in the building, so more indiscriminate means of assault were not used.

James "Jimmy" Bannon, the 25-year NYPD veteran, homicide detective, father of three, made his way into the building, along with two dozen other NYPD officers. The

NYPD team had confidence in their tactics. They rolled large shielding devices ahead of them, to protect themselves from the snipers' high-powered rifle fire, and from police grenades' shrapnel. Each officer carried a sidearm in a leg holster, and an AR-15 assault rifle, set to fire three rounds with each pull of the trigger. Every officer also wore ear protection, to avoid being deafened by the concussions and noise from the grenade explosions.

Unfortunately, the terror organization had made some adjustments in their tactics as well. They had set a trap for the NYPD assault team. They simply blew up the building as the NYPD assault team entered it. The blast pulverized the building, along with the tenements on both sides and the buildings across the street. James "Jimmy" Bannon, and the entire NYPD team, died instantly. The blast blew the NYPD team's Armored Personnel Carrier more than 100 feet away, tumbling it over and over, killing the driver. Terrorists: 25 NYPD: 1

Chapter 23

Five days "After", the stretch of highway along northern Georgia's I-75 was utterly still. A wet blanket of eerie silence, punctuated by avian calls from the trees, owls at night and crows during the day, lent a funereal quality to the landscape as dawn broke.

Lorraine Washington had stayed with her car for five days. She walked up and down a short distance from her vehicle, speaking with other stranded drivers during that time. She watched as some of the people near her abandoned their cars after the first night. Each morning another set of people seemed to decide that they had had enough of waiting for help to come and walked off to find food and water.

Each day, Lorraine watched hopefully as helicopters flew overhead on their way into and out of Atlanta. Early on, she had been sure that help would be on the way, but with each passing day, her spirits sagged a little more. The torrent of people fleeing Atlanta the first night and the following morning had slowed, but a steady trickle of white folks continued to ramble out from the city and walk past her stranded car. And each day these people looked a little worse off. Now it was her turn. She was finished waiting. Today, Lorraine was going to abandon her car, her pride and joy, to see if she could find some help. She had eaten nothing during the past five days, had had drunk only a single 64-ounce bottle of soda—and she typically drank one or two of those each day.

The people she saw walking were all heading away from the city, but they were all white folks. Lorraine couldn't recall seeing a single black person walking north, even though there must have been plenty of black folks on the highway. Since there was nobody left in any of the cars near her, the other black folks who had been traveling on the highway when the traffic stopped must have headed south.

She figured her best option was to walk toward Atlanta, toward the helicopters.

Lorraine gripped her car's "Oh Jesus!" handle to help her swing her bulk sideways in the car seat and put her feet on the ground. Then she let go, and forcefully curled her body forward against the thickness of her midsection. Getting into and out of her car always made her light-headed—she needed to breathe out to make room within her body to get into position. Lorraine groaned, stood up, took a few breaths to clear her head, and began to walk south on I-75 towards Atlanta. She was on the section of the highway that ran by Marietta, GA. It was cold, unseasonably cold for Atlanta in early November. She walked for 10 minutes and then rested for 10, then walked for another 10 and rested for another 10. That was the best she could do. Her knees and back hurt—but her feet! Lorraine's feet were killing her. Lorraine had gained a lot of weight over the past ten years, and she suffered terribly from the condition *plantar fasciitis*, painful tendonitis of the tendon that runs along the bottom of the foot. As her foot pain increased over the years, Lorraine had walked less, and eaten more. She had always been a stout woman, but now she tipped the scales at over 300 pounds—and at just 5 feet, 4 inches, that was a lot of weight to ask her small feet to carry.

It started to rain.

"Oh, help me, Lord; help me, Lord," Lorraine mumbled to herself. "Sweet Jesus, help me, Lord. I just need to find some help. Sweet Jesus, just get me to them helicopters. Help me, Lord, and everything will be OK."

Lorraine found herself resting against a stranded car, but she couldn't remember how she had gotten there. She loved cars and knew the make and model of almost every car on the road by sight. Her son loved cars, too. Where was her son? Why isn't he here?

"Sweet Jesus, help me find my son."

And with that, Lorraine pushed her bulk up and off the car. She staggered a few steps. The rain was coming down in a steady, hard, driving downpour. She was drenched. Her glasses fogged, and the rain dripped down into her eyes, and she didn't bother to wipe her glasses or to clear her vision. She walked into the rear bumper of a car and hyperextended her knee.

"Ow-eee!" she exclaimed to no one. She had been walking on the inside shoulder because the cement buttress wall gave her comfort. Now her head swam, and she lunged into the highway lanes, seeking the grass on the outside shoulder.

"Sweet Jesus, just let me rest a minute. Just for a minute, Lord. I just need to rest..." and with that, her legs gave out, dropping her to her knees on the grass next to the outside shoulder of the highway. A jarring jolt of pain screamed from her knee. The rain continued to pummel her body. "I am OK... just a little wet is all, and a little cold, too. I just need to rest."

Lorraine rolled over and laid down on the wet grass, on her back. The rain came down on her face and body, dripped down to the cold earth, and disappeared, as more rain followed the same path. "Sweet Jesus, I'm coming home. Sweet Jesus, take me home. Sweet Jesus..."

Lorraine chanted to herself for an hour and then lapsed into unconsciousness. She was nearly 51 years old, and even though she was diabetic and morbidly obese, Lorraine's body clung desperately to life. After lying there on the cold ground, exposed to the elements for 20 hours, Lorraine Washington finally died early in the morning, on the sixth day "After." Her son would join her in the days to come.

Chapter 24

The prevailing westerly winds caused Walt, Martin, and Manny some difficulty in maintaining a southeasterly heading after they emerged from New York's Lower Bay. After some experimentation, the novice sailors developed a system of combining motor and wind when tacking back east, keeping the mainsail on the centerline. They accomplished this by adjusting the halyard, outhaul and boom-vang lines—for landlubbers, these are the lines that guide and hold the position of the mainsail—while using the engine to power southeast and shutting the engine down when tacking southwest. Walt felt that they were carrying too much fuel on the main deck, and the fuel weight was making the vessel top heavy. They decided to try to consume half the fuel stored in the jerry cans on the deck by the halfway point of their trip, which would leave the boat's fuel tank full for their final approach and mooring in Charleston.

The crew kept their small vessel at sea for the first night. After sunset, a grim and foreboding darkness had swallowed up the contours of the land and shore, triggering a primordial fear that none of them had experienced before. After some discussion, they decided that night sailing was an unnecessary risk. For the remainder of the voyage, they would seek to moor for the night in protected waters. But they struggled to find mooring spots that were both sheltered and far enough from shore to feel safe, so they wound up spending the second night on the open ocean, and the third night too.

In the early afternoon of their 4th day at sea, they determined their position to be ten miles due south of Cape Hatteras, N.C. Martin and Walt examined the chartbook below decks in the galley as Manny handled the wheel in the cockpit. The weather appeared to be taking a turn for the worse. The wind picked up, the temperature dropped, and it began to rain.

"I don't know about you, but I think we should head for the Portsmouth cut," said Martin, pointing to the spot in the chartbook. His tone was both suggestive and hopeful.

Walt replied, "I was just thinking the same thing. We have pushed our luck enough. Who knows what the weather will look like tonight?"

The two men went topside to set a new heading and engage the autopilot. Martin left Manny and Walt, heading back below decks to join the women in the galley and berths. For four days and three nights, the eight people onboard had endured the tight quarters and lack of privacy well enough, but they were ready to be on dry land again. Martin went back to the charts and the old road atlas, which dated from Walt's long-ago stint as a truck driver.

"Hey, Walt!" Martin called out from the galley.

"Yeah?"

"Can you come here for a minute?"

Walt removed himself from the cockpit and descended into the galley.

"Why are we heading for Charleston?" Martin asked.

Walt had to think about that for a moment. "Because Charleston is a big harbor, it's easy to find, it's a good cold-weather port, and because it looked to be about as close to Jason's as every other place in the Carolinas or Virginia."

"I hoped you were going to say something like that," Martin said with a smile. "You know about the Appalachian mountain range? Well, the best path through them into Kentucky for people on foot is going to be the Cumberland Pass. Here, look."

Martin pointed on the road atlas to the area at the intersection of Virginia, Tennessee, and Kentucky.

"Okay. And?" Walt asked.

"Well, I think the sailing leg of our journey is over. Look. The bay on the other side of Portsmouth is Pamlico Sound.

Here is the Pamlico River. The chartbook says the minimum depth in the channel at low tide is ten feet. So, we're good. Now, look here." Martin flipped through the road atlas and pointed as he went along. "The Cumberland Pass is the only way through the mountains. Otherwise, we would have to go around them, almost down to Atlanta, and then back up the other side. That kind of defeats the purpose of taking the boat in the first place."

"Easy now," said Walt. "We needed to get away from New York City and the northeast coast. By starting our walk 400 miles further south, we won't freeze to death on the way."

"I didn't mean to criticize your strategy. I thought enough of it to come with you, though I will admit I had some 'buyer's remorse' along the way. But I am over that now. Today is the sixth day since the power went out. Can you imagine what is happening in New York City? I don't know what we would have done if we had not come with you." Here Martin paused for effect. "Thank you."

"I have no idea why I brought you. I didn't really need your help. But when you showed up at my house the day 'After,' I thought it was fate. Anyway, here we are. And you are welcome. But you really shouldn't thank me yet. We still have 400 miles to walk."

"More like 550 miles," said Martin in a near whisper as he removed his glasses and rubbed his eyes.

"Yeah," said Walt, leaning in and speaking in low tones. "I figured it was something more like that. But if I had told my family how far it was, they wouldn't have come."

"I understand," said Martin. "And there is no point in telling anyone, including my wife, now."

"So, what are you suggesting?"

"Well," Martin hesitated and drew a deep breath. "I think we can make it to Portsmouth before 3 pm. That gives us three hours to cross the sound and run up the Pamlico River, to Washington, N.C., before we run out of daylight. I think that is as far as we can navigate with this boat."

"I see what you're saying," said Walt, looking down at the chartbook. "We can motor at eight to ten knots once we get inside. I don't think we need to worry about conserving fuel anymore. But maybe we should look for a place to anchor somewhere around the mouth of the river. I'd like to be able to see what we're getting into upriver."

"I see what you're getting at," said Martin, as he continued to look at the chart book.

"Besides, I hear the fishing is good this time of year."

"Fishing?"

"Oh, yeah," said Walt. "And I hope you like fish, because I think we only have enough food to last us 12 days on the hike. Maybe 14. And we've got 20 days ahead of us. Man, I hope the bass are biting."

"More like 22 to 30 days, and that's if nothing goes wrong."

"Well, look at the bright side."

"Oh, yeah? What's that?"

"We all will have our teenage figures back by the time we get there."

The sailing party spent the night in Pamlico Sound, on the edge of the channel at the mouth of the Pamlico River. In sheltered water, at a safe distance from shore, they enjoyed their best night's sleep since they had left the marina in Tarrytown. Pamlico sound is only five to six feet deep at low tide, and an Endeavor 37 requires 54 inches of draft. Now was no time to run the boat aground. It wasn't swimming weather, and there were many things on board that they would need for the trek. A cold rain greeted them in the morning. Walt had the third watch and had been fishing. When Manny stepped up on deck, a dozen red drum fish lying on the floor of the cockpit confronted him.

"Whoa! Way to go, Dad!"

When Martin came topside, he saw Manny working the propane burner to fry up a pan full of fish filets, with more fish on the deck, ready for frying. Martin was amazed at the practical skills of his hosts.

"I seem to want to ask how you pulled this off."

Walt replied, "I used a can of tuna fish to attract schools of baitfish, and then I threw a casting net over them. Then I tied a wire leader and a hook to the line on this fishing donut," Walt held aloft a round piece of fiberglass that was shaped like a donut but with a concave edge around the outside and wound with fishing line. "And then I set a hook in the baitfish and set them in the water. We are a little late, last month the fishing would have been much better, but I caught all we need for now."

Martin stood mute, with a bewildered look on his face.

"What?" Walt asked. "What kind of Boy Scout doesn't have a fishing donut in his tackle box?"

"Or a casting net," replied Martin.

"Well, on that one we got lucky," Walt chuckled. "I was keeping crab traps at the dock back home, and I got tired of paying for crab bait, so I bought this casting net just a few weeks ago. Until today, I hadn't thrown one in years."

"Are we planning on carrying fish with us to eat?"

"From your lips to God's ears," replied Walt. "Let's hope the fishing is good along the way. But I wouldn't carry raw fish. That would get nasty fast, though we might cook some and have each of us carry a day's rations. No, these are for trading."

The women and girls came topside, led by their noses to the smell of a hot meal. Manny handed out an endless stream of fried fish fillets, after which everyone went down into the galley to get out of the rain.

"It was dark as a tomb last night," said Walt between bites of fish.

"Thank you," Martin said to Manny, as Manny handed him a plate. Then to Walt,

"Yes, it was. I think this is the seventh day of the blackout." Martin sighed. "It's hard to process all of this. When the sun set over the land, and there was not a single light along the coast. It was surreal. And then the stars came out, and the Milky Way was so clear, without all of the east coast light pollution. That was incredible."

Miriam and Jenny looked at each other, and Jenny broke the silence.

"Right now, a little 'light pollution' would be okay with me. Let's get the hell off this boat and start walking."

Chapter 25

New York City had been very fortunate to avoid a nuclear catastrophe. Within minutes of the bombings, the governor had ordered the Indian Point nuclear power plant, located on the east side of the Hudson River 40 miles north of Manhattan, to begin an orderly shutdown process, to avoid the risk of a nuclear meltdown in a region with 50 million residents. This turned out to be fortuitous. The process of shutting down the plant was governed by procedures promulgated with an eye towards preparing for a natural disaster. These procedures required that the backup generators be engaged to provide power to the plant, independently of the grid. Grid power was lost within hours of the bombings, and Indian Point narrowly avoided an unimaginable disaster.

Stacey Mendelsohn had stayed in her "luxury" apartment building, on the corner of 59th Street and 9th Avenue in Manhattan, since the electricity had gone out seven days ago. If she could have, she would have stayed there for years, but she lived on the 48th floor, and water pressure in New York City only reached the 7th floor, so her voluminous store of water in five-gallon plastic bottles finally ran out, as did her raisin bran cereal supply. The stench coming from her toilet increased the incentive to leave, even though she placed a towel on the bottom of the closed bathroom door to keep the offensive odor from escaping into the living area.

Mendelsohn donned a T-shirt, jeans, and comfortable sneakers for the walk down 48 flights of stairs. Her ever-present Star of David medallion swung back and forth with each step as she descended the dark stairwell, flashlight in hand. She had been careful to conserve the batteries in her apartment, knowing that 48 flights in complete darkness would be beyond her mental state if the time came to descend to the world below.

She made it out of the building, turning south to the 58th Street landing. She then turned right toward the west side of 9th Avenue, walking briskly. The city was eerily quiet, but there were a few people walking on the otherwise silent thoroughfare.

Two young men approached her as she trudged south, and, in the New York tradition, she studiously avoided making eye contact. As the men passed, they looked at her chest. She thought she was a little old for them to be checking out her breasts—they long ago had succumbed to gravity—and she was right. It was her medallion that interested them. The shorter man yelled back to her as he passed.

"Hey, Jew!"

Startled as if the man had smacked her, she spun around, ready to lash out in anger and indignation at the anti-Semite. He waited for her to turn, and to see the gun in his hand.

"Allahu Akbar!" he shouted. Then he shot her in the lower chest. The force of the shot doubled her half over, and she sank down on her knees and rear end as her legs collapsed beneath her. Suddenly she was unable to breathe.

"That's for my brothers and sisters in Palestine," he said with a smile, squatting down to lift up her chin so that he could look her in the eye.

"We won. You're done," he said, and spat on her.

The bullet was a .38 "wad-cutter," a target practice round, not a killing round. Although Stacey was mortally wounded, she spent hours in agonizing pain before she finally bled to death. She never once thought about Roger Barrack.

Chapter 26

Two hours after sunup, the Endeavor 37 approached the small dock in front of the shops in Washington, N.C. Manny stood at the bow with a docking pole, out of habit more than anything. It wouldn't matter if they damaged the sailboat's fiberglass on the docks or ran it aground on the bric-a-brac rocks and concrete that lined the river shore. Beyond the shops was a bridge span which was too low for the sailboat, so this was the end of the line. From here on they would have to walk.

An old man in a blue trucker's cap sat on a bench under an awning in front of the docks. He took a keen interest in the new arrivals but did not get up. Walt waved to the man from the cockpit, and the man waved back. The erstwhile sailors had packed and organized during the trip up the river from Pamlico Sound, and were ready to get off the boat and onto solid ground. Walt killed the engine and called out to the old man.

"Hello, there!"

"You just missed fouling the lines to my crab traps," the man replied, pointing to the port or left side of the boat.

"Well, thank goodness we missed them," Walt called back as he looked up and down the waterfront. It appeared the old man was alone.

"You're not from here," the old man declared.

"No, sir. We are not," replied Walt as the rest of the crew unloaded the stuffed backpacks onto the dock. Walt climbed onto the dock and walked over to the old man.

"My name is Walt. We are just passing through. I caught some red drum fish this morning, more than we can eat before they go bad. I would like to trade them for some things we need."

The old man's eyes widened. "What're you lookin' for?"

"I need a couple of lighters, or a box of scratch-anywhere matches, bleach, batteries, a roll of twine, and a few flashlights, or maybe an old-fashioned kerosene lantern, and a big tarp."

"You goin' campin'?"

"Something like that."

"How much fish we talkin' 'bout?"

"Go look in that cooler," said Walt as he nodded to a white cooler standing alone on the dock. "You can have the fish, the cooler, and the ice. They should keep for a few days in that."

The old man walked over to the cooler and looked inside at the six sizeable red drum fish sitting on the last of the ice from Walt's convenience store back in Sleepy Hollow, N.Y.

"I can get everything you asked for except the lantern," said the old man turning to Walt. "I need an hour. Do we have a deal?"

"You come back here with the goods, and the fish are yours," replied Walt.

"What I mean is, I don't want to come back here and find you traded the fish to someone else."

"Oh, I get you now," said Walt. "Here's the deal. I will not trade these fish to anyone else for one hour."

The old man approached Walt and held out his hand in the time-honored tradition of coming to an agreement. "My name is Ned Perot. I will be back within the hour."

"Okay, Ned. Before you go, where is everybody?"

Martin walked over and joined Walt and Ned.

"Everybody's home," said Ned. "The summer season is over. Most people living in Beaufort County are elderly and retired, there aren't many families living here anymore. Well, there ain't many white families. Black folks still have kids. Most folks are just home waiting for the lights to come back on."

"Seven days," Walt said, incredulous. "That's a long time to sit around and wait."

"Don't I know it," Ned chuckled and took his hat and rubbed his shiny head with his right sleeve. "My wife and I are down to eating the last of the canned food in the panty—we ate creamed corn for breakfast—Lord knows how old those cans are, so I put some crab traps out this morning, and I expect to put out some fishhooks."

"So, there is no food in the stores?" asked Martin.

"Not a thing since the lights went out a week ago."

"Is the water still running to your house?"

"Yeah, we still got water. But…"

Martin interrupted him. "What about the people? No trouble with law and order?

"Oh, there was some trouble for the first two nights. The state police shot two black men for looting or resisting arrest or something like that, the night the power went out. But who knows what went on there? The next night two state police cruisers and four state troopers got burned to a crisp up on Highway 264. I don't know what happened exactly, but it's a pretty grisly scene and ain't nobody come to clean it up. I guess both sides got the message. There ain't been no more police shootings and there ain't been no more looting. What good is a TV without electricity? Anyway, things have been quiet since then."

The men stood there for a moment in quiet contemplation.

"We've got some other stuff to trade," said Walt. "We are looking for eight bicycles."

"Well, that would be a tall order here."

"I got two, 20 lbs. tanks of propane and a third tank that is half full. I expect it's worth its weight in gold at the moment."

"I expect you're right. Of course, you can't carry gold where you're goin'. But I will see what I can do," Ned said as he looked straight into Walt's eyes and nodded once. And then he was off.

"Anything else on your mind for trading?" Martin asked.

"Not really. I was hoping to trade the boat, but I don't think these people need another boat." Walt swept his hand to draw Martin's attention to the boats docked along the riverfront. "Not that bikes are going to be that helpful. One flat will put us back on our feet, one crash and it might be the end of the hike."

"Well, let's see what he comes back with," Martin said.

"We can always take the sails down and use them for a tent," Walt said. "I will cut the lines off before we leave. Rope might come in handy."

"Something else he said struck me."

"Yeah? What's that?"

"He said that most of the people living here are elderly, and except for the African American community, there are few families here. Older people live in small towns and the countryside. Young people live in the cities."

Martin looked down at his feet and said nothing more.

"Martin," said Walt, losing patience. "I got things on my mind. What's the problem?"

"We've been on a boat provisioned by an entire convenience store, so we are not feeling the pain yet. But now, seven days in, the cities have no food, and Ned is eating creamed corn for breakfast. My people live in cities. The only people with a shot at surviving the coming winter will be people with access to food. Whoever heard of a Jewish farmer? There won't be a Jew left. Who are my daughters going to marry?"

In exasperation, Walt did a combination scoff and sigh, and made a motion with his hands, as if to say, "I give up."

"Ya know, you are a fucking ray of sunshine this morning, Martin. But isn't that why we are heading to Jason's farm? So that your daughters live long enough to get married?"

"Yes, it is, and thank goodness we have a place to shoot for, and people who might be willing and able to help us, and that we lucked out and showed up at the doorstep of a friend's brother, who just happened to own a fucking convenience store full of food, and a fucking sailboat to carry all of it. That's a lot of shit that had to go right."

Walt was bemused by this and paused for dramatic effect.

"Wow. Rabbi. That's the first time I've heard a man of the cloth say 'fuck' since I was an altar boy. But I think you need to take it easy there, pal. We can't worry about the whole world and the next 20 years at the moment. We don't have enough food, we are facing a 550-mile hike, and winter is right around the corner. We still need a few more things to go right if we are to survive long enough to make it to Jason's."

"And what if we get there and some crisis has befallen Jason? What then?"

"Now you are truly getting on my nerves," said Walt, visibly irritated. "You are welcome to stay on the boat. It's yours if you want it. Maybe you can make a living as a fisherman. But I'm going to my brother's farm, and on the way, I am going to hope for the best. Believe me; I am freaked right out of my fucking skin. I got a mother, two brothers, and a sister in South Florida. I have no idea what their status or condition is. I've got a son, and a daughter-in-law worried sick because, incidentally, she's pregnant. My wife is an emotional train wreck on a good day, and I can't even begin to understand how she's made it this far without coming apart at the seams, but there it is. And you want me to worry about billions of strangers? Some of them will make it. The rest of them will not. What the hell do you want from me? I don't have the fucking bandwidth for this shit right now. Those people are God's children, not mine."

Walt started back for the boat with Martin hot on his heels.

"Hold on, Walt. I am sorry to burden you with my concerns. I was being selfish and not thinking. It won't happen again."

"Look, Martin. You're a good guy. I know you were always tight with my brother, and he thinks very highly of you. But right now, the only 'your people' you've got are us. We're 'your people' now. I am sorry I got a little short with you just now. But can we talk about this on the hike? We are going to have lots of time where it will be nice to focus on other people's problems rather than our own."

"Yes, of course. And congratulations. Mazel Tov! A first grandchild is such a blessing."

Walt, a man capable of murder and mayhem, just stood there, blankly looking at Martin, who was a mountain of a man, who could break Walt in two, but who wouldn't harm a fly. After a few moments, both men began to smile. Then they started to laugh. "Is it me?" Walt asked. "Or was this the weirdest conversation ever?"

Walt put his right arm around Martin's shoulder, and Martin shifted and put his right arm around Walt's shoulder, and the two men embraced.

When they broke their embrace Walt said to Martin, "Our job, our sacred responsibility, is to get our children through this, and to live long enough to see their children come into the world. Life will go on. The only question is: 'Whose life?' I think it should be us. Our lives and our children's."

The two men held each other by the shoulders, looked deep into each other's eyes, and had a meeting of the minds.

Miriam and Jenny, now seated where Ned had been sitting when their boat came to the dock, had been watching their husbands for the last several minutes, and though they couldn't hear the conversation, there appeared to be a good deal of emotion involved, ending with a heartwarming hug. Jenny smiled at the scene. Miriam seethed with resentment.

"Well, I don't see any bikes," said Martin.

"I took a shot, I didn't expect an old man to miraculously turn up eight bicycles. Let's see what they've got."

Ned came back with another older man, who he introduced as his brother-in-law, Elvin. Ned possessed everything that Walt wanted for the fish, and while he was unable to procure bicycles, Elvin wheeled a shopping cart filled with items they hoped to trade for the propane tanks: a first aid kit, socks, coats, down vests, gloves, baby wipes, other cold weather clothing items, and two two-person tents that were light enough for hiking.

"They must have knocked over a store," Walt whispered to Martin.

Walt already had a first aid kit, but he took everything that Ned and Elvin brought, and directed them to the propane tanks. Elvin wheeled the shopping cart over, picked up the tanks, and shuffled off.

"Where are you making for?" asked Ned.

Walt showed him on his old road atlas.

"That's quite a walk," said Ned. "Walk four blocks north up that street, away from the river. Pick up highway 264, and follow signs for Greenville, Raleigh, Durham, and then finally Greensboro. Your map will have to take you from there."

Walt and Martin bid Ned goodbye, and walked back to where their crew had gathered. Walt felt the need to give the group a little pep talk.

"Well, we've made it this far, and we've got quite a journey ahead of us. As you can see, the grid is still down. We have to accept the fact that this is a self-rescue mission. There is no one to call for help. So, think before you do anything that might cause an injury. We may see desperate people on the way, but if we are to survive and make it to my brother's farm, we must harden our hearts and push on without stopping to get involved with strangers and their problems. We have our own problems. We need to cover about 25 miles per day if we are to make it to Jason's farm before winter. Let's go."

Miriam couldn't take it anymore. She exploded on Walt.

"Who are you to tell me who I can and cannot help? Who the hell do you think you are? You can't tell me what to do! I will do what my conscience tells me to do!"

Then Miriam turned to Martin and said, "This is just too much! I am a strong and independent woman. I am not going to be treated like a child!"

Martin's emotional state was unsteady enough this morning without any help from Miriam, and he was simply unable to respond. Walt gave Martin a moment to speak to his wife, but he remained silent. Walt did not.

"You are absolutely right, Miriam. But I am not talking to you, and I am not telling you what to do. I am speaking, as the head of my family, to my wife, my son, and my daughter-in-law. We are leaving now, and we are not stopping and getting involved in the lives of strangers. I wouldn't dream of interfering with your conscience or the way you wish to live your life."

And with that Walt walked in the direction that Ned said would lead them to the highway they needed to follow, and Jenny, Manny, and Danielle cast their eyes down and followed Walt, leaving Miriam, Martin, and the girls standing on the waterfront. Miriam looked at Martin, her expression not so much pleading as demanding. Martin refused to acknowledge Miriam's presence.

"Girls," he said to get the twins' attention. When they looked up, he smiled at them and said, "Let's go. We have a long walk ahead of us."

Martin put out his hand, and Aviva took it. Hanna walked around Martin to take his other hand, and Martin and the girls started walking after Walt and his family. Miriam stood dumbfounded for a few moments, and then donned her backpack and hustled to follow the group before she lost sight of them.

Within a few blocks, they arrived at the scene of the burned-out police cruisers. Several human remains, charred beyond recognition, were piled on top of each other, their bodies positioned in alternative directions, on the sidewalk. Walt and Manny approached the bodies. Martin stood back from Walt and Manny, and the women and girls walked on.

"Their duty belts are gone, but that looks like a badge, or what's left of one," Manny said, pointing to a piece of mangled and melted metal. He picked it up. "Yeah, it's a badge. I guess these are the troopers."

Walt looked around at the sickening scene, and then at the dreadful expressions of the charred corpses, lying face up and stacked together on the sidewalk in front of a large pane glass store window. On that window was a bright red spray-painted message that Walt understood perfectly. It read,

An eye for an eye
Mother Fucker

Walt turned back and walked toward Martin, who stood there motionless and expressionless, lost to the world. As Walt passed Martin, he added, "and a tooth for a tooth."

This seemed to wake Martin from his trance, and without missing a beat, he replied to Walt without turning,

"'Put your sword back in its place, for all who draw the sword will die by the sword.'"

Walt stopped and called back to Martin, "Yeah, but between now and then maybe I just wanna gloat about it. And what the hell is a Rabbi doing quoting Jesus of Nazareth?"

Martin turned around and caught up with Walt. He shrugged his massive shoulders and said, "That's a good question. It was the first thing that popped into my head. Go figure. How about this: 'Thou shalt not kill.' Moses."

And then Martin hurried off to catch up with his daughters.

"Oh, yeah? 'Fuck you.' Hillary Clinton." But Martin was out of earshot.

And then Walt had a thought.
Moses? I thought that was God? Ah, never mind.

Chapter 27

He was accustomed to being poor; he knew nothing else. But poor is a relative thing—he always had enough food to eat and a clean and warm place to sleep. Billions of others in this world could not claim as much. Coming of age in early 21st century America, he had enjoyed few of the advantages his childhood friends had had in his small, New England hometown. He, his father, his father's father, and his father before him had been born into uneducated, working-class families—wage slaves in the industrial factories and construction crews of modernity. During the good times "Before," such families had followed the advertising, and spent more of their limited resources on things like beer and cigarettes than on their children's education, their homes, investments, and retirement savings. So, his lineage had not improved its lot very much during the 20th century. They had occupied the lowest rung of "White" America's economic ladder. No, they were not as disadvantaged as some of his fatherless black childhood classmates had been, but they were still poor. Though their family had been in America for over two centuries, none of his ancestors had ever owned a home, or a share of stock.

As a child, he often had wondered why other children got dropped off at school in shiny new cars, had fashionable clothes and branded sneakers, and went on ski vacations, while he and his sister had none of these things. Christmas was especially difficult; he and his sister spent the two-week school vacation socializing with friends, but when the other kids gushed about their new skis, and how they handled on the slopes, and how much fun they had on vacation at mountain retreats that seemed like fairytales to him, all he could do was smile and say, "cool." Christmas never was like that for his sister and him. The gifts they received were necessities like shoes, jeans, underwear, socks, and perhaps a coat. Neither his dim-witted father nor his complaining, chain-smoking mother could provide more than the meager basics. He often thought: *We look the same as they do, we go to the same school, play the same sports, why do they have so much, and we have so little?* But he did not dwell on this—it did not harm his spirit nor crush his joy in living—and he accepted his position without resentment. These formative experiences turned out to be excellent training for enduring privation. Enduring privation appeared to be his chief purpose in life. This was too bad, because right now he wished he had gotten more training in practical skills, and less in privation endurance.

His parents had divorced while he and his sister were in junior high school, and his father had moved to New Jersey. That was five years ago. His mother had not been seen since the power had gone out 15 days ago. He was sure that his mother had not abandoned them, and that she simply had not been able to get back home. On the morning of the bombings, his mother had driven down to see her sister, and had planned to spend the night with her. He had known that this was a lie, and that she was going to visit a man who just happened to live close to her sister, but he and his sister had said nothing about it. His mother had left a microwave-ready supper for them in the fridge, as well as the makings for breakfast for the next morning. Other than that, there had not been a blessed thing to eat in the house.

His name was Colin Richards, and he was 18 years old. His sister, Emily, was 16. They lived together with their mother in a rented cottage that would, under other circumstances, have been a pleasant enough home. Despite the recent and unseasonable cold snap, and lack of heat, the cottage might still have been bearable. But without food…

They had become desperate. It had been 15 days since the electric power went down, and they were quite literally starving. They needed food. Now. Their neighbors were all in the same position. Though he and his sister had been vegetarians since junior high school, mostly thanks to their mother's psychotic and mercurial belief systems, Colin had tried to kill squirrels by throwing rocks at them. He had yet to make his first kill. He had an old double-curved bow that had belonged to his father, and several arrows tipped with points suited for target practice. He didn't want to risk losing an arrow by shooting at a squirrel. Hoping for larger game, he left the bow strung and waiting in the "mud room" entrance of their house.

Emily screamed to Colin that there was a dog in their front yard. He ran to the mudroom, grabbed the bow and several arrows, and slipped quietly out the door. A medium sized dog was examining a particular odor on Colin's front lawn. Though Colin had never shot archery in his life, he notched his arrow the way he had seen it done in the movies, drew back the bow's string—making a mental calculation of distance and direction—and loosed the arrow.

The arrow hit the dog broadside. The shaft pierced its body, glanced off a bone, deflected downward, and pinned the dog to the hard ground. The animal let out a wild and frantic howl, and Colin charged it and began to beat it over the head with his bow.

Colin didn't know that the dog belonged to a woman who lived a couple of blocks away. He also did not know that she and the dog had just begun a 22-mile trek on foot to her sister's house. The woman, a former schoolteacher by the name of Mrs. Davies, heard her dog's cries and ran to her best friend's aid. Colin didn't see her as she approached. He was too focused on the potential meal in front of him. Mrs. Davies withdrew her late husband's .45 caliber Colt 1911 semiautomatic pistol and shot Colin between the shoulder blades as he reared up to hit the dog again. Colin felt no pain as his body collapsed, his face on the cold, hard ground, mere inches from the dog's muzzle. Their eyes met for a moment as the life ebbed from both man and man's best friend.

Mrs. Davies was so horrified by the specter of man and dog bleeding out before her, and by the realization that she had just killed a human being—a starving teenager—for the crime of trying to survive, that she did not hear Emily charge up behind her and plunge a kitchen knife into her back. Emily proceeded to stab Mrs. Davies another 30 times before she realized that she was hacking away at a corpse. Emily dragged the dead dog back to the cottage without a second glance back at the bodies of either her brother or her neighbor.

Chapter 28

CeeCee, or just Cee, which was short for Cecilia, lived in the lap of luxury. CeeCee had entered middle age recently, with most of her good looks still intact. Yes, she had had some "work" done, but not a lot—at least not by Boca Raton standards. Breast implants, some liposuction, facial derma-abrasion, an eyelid tuck and a tasteful nose job. After all, she simply had to be pretty. That was her stock in trade. When CeeCee looked in the mirror, she could quickly look past the permanent expression of surprise that the eyelid-tuck seemed to have given her.

Raised in a Catholic, working-class family, she had worked her way through college. Well, sort of. In truth, she had received a lot of financial aid due to her family's extremely modest circumstances. She had taken on student loans for the balance, and held a couple of odd jobs, mostly to pad her resume. Later, her first husband had paid off these student loans for her. Still, she felt she had earned that money. After all, he had been a working-class-kid-made-good, not a scion of the Kennedys. If he wanted a wife like her, well, he would have to earn it, and she didn't come cheap—or easy. There was nothing easy about CeeCee.

Life with her first husband had been good, and they had produced a daughter and then a son. After deciding that they preferred the weather in South Florida to Chicago, they had moved to that bastion of the nouveau riche, Boca Raton, just south of the famous city of Palm Beach. Unfortunately, the marriage didn't last. Boca Raton was an environment of consumption and material competitiveness—and hubby number one just hadn't been up to the task. She had just turned 30 at the time. Drop dead gorgeous was her claim to fame, and hypergamy was her game. She had decided that the moment had come for her to trade up to a bigger and better deal.

Soon she had a very wealthy man, 15 years her senior, on the line. She then filed for divorce, seeking the house, spousal support, and custody of the kids. Thanks to the vagaries of early 21st-century family law, the Court had awarded her everything she had sought, leaving her free to marry her new man in a private ceremony at The Breakers.

For several years now, everything had been right with CeeCee's world. Her new husband kept her in the style of living that she deserved. They lived in a waterfront mansion, most of which they never used, with a 45-foot Bertram fishing yacht that they also never used moored at their private dock. Her jewelry sparkled. Her cars shined. All *was* right with her world—until now.

Now, the power was off, and for the past 15 days their home's six-figure air conditioning system had not worked. South Florida is a beautiful place to live—but not without air conditioning. It wasn't just hot. It was *fucking* hot. They had a cook and a cleaning lady but had not seen them since the day of the bombing. Water service to the home had ceased when the power went out, a few hours after the first reports of the nuclear bombs in the Middle East. At first, they had used the water in the pool for washing dishes and clothes, but now the pool's water was a bright green color, and as thick and soupy as pond scum. They hadn't even been able to flush the toilets, because they didn't know that they could flush them by taking a bucket or a pot, filling it with water from the pool or intra-coastal waterway, and pouring it into the toilet. They didn't have much practical knowledge about how the physical world worked. What they did know—how to borrow money from a bank to buy real estate, pay the loan back with government inflated dollars, and sell the property for the resulting inflated price—was not particularly useful at the moment. Since they didn't know how to make the toilets flush, they had started to use a section of lawn behind their house, next to a large hedge, as a latrine. For privacy, they had set up a makeshift barrier from a tarp that their landscape contractor had left on the property. Now, when they completed their ablutions, they used the dog's pooper-scooper to throw their own feces into the intra-coastal waterway behind their house.

They found this arrangement somewhat less than acceptable, but they still were better off than most of their neighbors were. After 15 days without power, most of Southeast Florida's seven million people were living in unimaginable deprivation and misery, in the equivalent of a 70-mile-by-10-mile refugee camp. Those seven million people, accustomed to the convenience of grocery stores, refrigeration, municipal water, electricity, and air conditioning, now lived without any of that, in 95-degree heat and 100 percent humidity. It created an environment that had been inconceivable "Before", but which was all too real now.

Today, CeeCee had managed to catch some small fish from the intracoastal waterway that ran behind their home, using her son's fishing rod and tackle box. Her husband had never gutted a fish before, but Cee had seen it done in her childhood, so she set her teeth and did the task. They intended to cook the fish on the patio, which had a massive built-in fieldstone grill on their patio that they never used, and a standard metal grill-on-wheels that they never used, either. They had never bothered to fill the 100-lb. propane tank on the large grill, and even if they had, they would not have known how to fire up the thing. But, a couple of days after the blackout, they had managed to procure a 5-gallon tank of propane for the small grill. "Before", the tank would have been available from any big-box store for $20, but "After", they had had to pay for it with a necklace that had cost them $10,000 retail. Today, that small tank probably was worth more than a human life.

CeeCee turned on the gas to the grill to prepare for cooking, but she forgot to open the grill's cover, so the area under the hood filled with propane. When CeeCee pressed the "start" button, the spark ignited the propane under the hood, which exploded with enough force to send the metal grill hood 120 feet out into the inter-coastal waterway. En route, the hood also removed most of CeeCee's skull above the eyebrows.

The force of the blow knocked her body back onto the dock of her multi-million-dollar waterfront mansion. Her body rolled over and fell into the salt water, face down. CeeCee's five-carat engagement ring, always just a little too big for her perfectly starved finger, slipped off, tumbling into the silt below her husband's fishing yacht.

Her husband ran from the seawall to the dock and looked down at his wife's lifeless body floating in the water. He then walked back into the house and up to their bedroom, where he took a 9mm semiautomatic pistol from his safe and shot himself in the head. Eventually, the tides carried CeeCee's bloated body out through the Boca Raton inlet to the open sea, where it was consumed in the natural order of things.

Chapter 29

Jason awoke at first light and looked over to the LED light on the power strip next to the bed. Nothing there, but a lot had happened since the power went out 15 days ago.

Their homestead had been a whirlwind of activity. Ellen had turned every piece of food in the freezers and refrigerator into canned goods, dug up every stray potato from the garden to use as seed in the spring, and secured the garden seeds, saving them from rodents and insects by packing them in sealed gallon sized food containers. For several evenings, the entire family had helped a neighbor's family to get their pumpkin harvest in.

The kids collected firewood, sawed, cut, and split stove billets and kindling, and stacked it until it covered a wall eight feet high and 36 feet across in their oversized woodshed. The pile of fire logs on the other side of the woodshed could fill half a dozen small dump trucks. In the first few days, Jason, Noah, and Noah's two teenage brothers had worked Jason's hay, stacking it up to the rafters in the hayloft. For the next few days, Jason and his horses had helped Abraham's family get their hay in. Jason and Ellen milked a total of three cows, locking their calves up on the other side of the barn to wean them. They traded the extra milk for some sausage, plus four sides of bacon that they would salt and cure as soon as soon as their neighbor had slaughtered his hogs. The ground meat sausage would be preserved via the pressure canner, since freezing was no longer an option.

The weather had turned unseasonably cold, and it rained for many days without a break, with temperatures never getting above the 30s. Jason could only imagine what was happening on the road to Edinburgh. The bad weather meant that there wasn't much for Jason to do, so to keep his mind occupied, he busied himself organizing his workshop. He was there when he heard Noah's buggy coming up his gravel driveway. Jason stood in the doorway of his workshop and waved to Noah. Noah waved back, and Jason went back to his shop. After a few minutes, Noah appeared in the doorway.

"Good morning, Noah. How about a cup of coffee? We might as well enjoy it while we can."

Noah smiled with his lips and paused just inside the doorway to the workshop. "It's cold in here," he said and nodded to the small wood stove.

"Yeah," replied Jason. "I figure that firewood is going to take a lot more work than it used to. My demands for comfort have been getting a serious adjustment." He held his hands together in front of his mouth and exhaled to warm them.

"Same at our house. And as for coffee, I don't think we will run short anytime soon. Our dry goods store has several hundred pounds of coffee, and there are only 11 families in our community—12 if we include you. My father has put some by for you, enough to keep you in coffee for a long time."

"Well, thank heavens for some good news! And I have some good news, too. I have 200 lbs. of salt in four 50 lb. bags, that I bought for curing hogs. I won't need most of it now, and the same batch can be used over and over for curing if you drain it well and fluff it up. I bet it's worth its weight in gold. Come on, let's go set by the stove and have a cup."

Jason clapped Noah on the shoulder, and Noah followed Jason to the house as the two hunched their shoulders and squinted their eyes for protection from the cold, driving rain. When they came in, Ellen was tending the firebox in the stove.

"Good morning, Noah!" she said.

The men sat down at the table. Ellen set cups before them and poured coffee from a stainless-steel pot that was warming on the stove.

"I wish I could say it was a good morning," Noah began. "I came over to tell you that some of our people said they saw more than a few dead bodies over on 41E heading north outside Edinburgh."

Ellen and Jason turned to each other, and then turned back to Noah.

"How many more than a few?" Jason asked.

"From what I understand, quite a few."

"What the hell?" Ellen demanded flatly.

"The weather," Jason said quietly, as he looked down into his coffee. Noah and Ellen also said nothing and looked away.

"It was in the 30s again last night," Jason said. "And it rained hard all night."

"So?" asked Ellen.

"So, people who are not used to privation die of exposure much more easily than you might imagine. After sitting on a couch and watching TV for their whole lives, they are in no condition for long-term physical challenges. Heck, most Americans are in no condition for a couple of flights of stairs, especially older people."

"Couldn't people sleep in the abandoned cars? From what we hear, there are abandoned cars everywhere."

"Honey..." Jason said in his most gentle voice. "People cannot stay in cars for long. They need food, they need to relieve themselves, and they need to stay warm. Once they get cold, wet, and hungry it doesn't take long—a few days tops—before they succumb."

"I don't think it helped that McCoy O'Neil and his friends broke all the windows in the cars along the highway," said Noah.

"He did what!?" exclaimed Jason.

"People were sleeping in cars over there. The O'Neil farm is close by. I heard some of these people were showing up at his place looking for help. He ran them off and then he and a few others rode horses up and down that stretch of highway

193

and busted the windows of the abandoned cars there and told the people to keep walking."

Ellen looked at Jason with a shocked look of disbelief.

"Let's hope that is all McCoy did," said Jason. "Let's hope that he didn't kill anybody."

"I don't think so," replied Noah. "My father asked our people if they thought those people had been murdered, but all who saw it agreed that there was no blood. They said it looked like they had just laid down on the cold, wet ground and died."

"That makes the most sense," said Jason. "If McCoy were going to shoot people, it would be those who trespassed on his land, or were caught stealing. I wouldn't put that past McCoy for a second."

"What are we going to do when people start knocking on our door and demanding food or shelter?" asked Ellen. "Because you can be sure that is going to happen at some point. What if they come here while you are out in the fields working? What am I going to do if I am here all alone?"

The three fell silent for several minutes. Ellen took a seat next to Jason at the table. Finally, Jason broke the silence.

"It's already been two weeks." He lowered his head toward his coffee, took in a deep breath, and sighed loudly.

"What do you mean?" asked Ellen.

"Well, at first I thought this would be over in a matter of days. But the days kept piling up. Then I thought that people would then be on the move, and that the weather would eventually become an issue, but I wasn't counting on late December weather in mid-November. I guess my crystal ball is broken. I don't think many people will be showing up here on the farm now. People are stranded where they are. But I think that anyone who does find his way here could pose a danger to us. Desperate people do desperate things."

"We have not had any strangers show up in our community," said Noah. "But we have had a steady stream of family and friends coming in from Indiana."

"Why Indiana?" asked Ellen.

"Lots of Amish worked up there at the RV manufacturing plants. They don't work farms. They work at manufacturing jobs. When the plants closed, they got in their buggies and went wherever they have family living in farming communities."

"I don't think strangers walking hundreds of miles are our greatest liability. Former law enforcement officers and military veterans living right here in the county are a risk for their neighbors—though they do not have to be—and they will have all sorts of hardware."

"You mean like McCoy O'Neil?"

"That's exactly what I mean. And the National Guard, the State Police, and Lord knows who else. I am somewhat surprised that the National Guard or the Army has not shown up to confiscate cattle off the farms in the name of national security or national emergency or whatever they come up with. Things must be really bad out there if they have not been able to get that organized. Or they must have a mountain of MRE's. You know, those 'Meals Ready to Eat' packages that the military feeds their people when they are in the field."

"Do you know our neighbor Roy Whitsahl?" asked Noah. "His son, Buddy, is with the National Guard. I saw him carrying firewood into his father's farmhouse on the way over here."

"Hey, I forgot about him," Jason said as he stood up from his chair. "Let's go over there and talk to him."

"You can't leave the kids and me here alone," said Ellen. She was starting to sound as if she were going to be upset. "And we can't go with you. I have bread in the oven."

"I don't think there is any need for us to go over there," Noah said quickly to comfort Ellen. "My father talks to Roy pretty regularly. There is an armory in Edinburgh. Buddy walked there the day after the bombings, and the commander said they had not received their orders yet. Buddy walked all the way back home the next day, and he has not heard from them since."

"Well, that makes absolutely no sense," Ellen said with a sense of relief that she would not be left alone. "What's the point in having a National Guard if two weeks after a catastrophe they are nowhere to be found?"

"Well, that is troubling," said Jason. "Still, there are probably about 5,000 or so National Guard troops in Kentucky, and 4.5 million civilians. If they are operating, I would imagine they are in Louisville and Lexington and perhaps Bowling Green. The *only* reason they would be operating here would be to confiscate livestock to feed themselves. There are just not enough of them to feed 4.5 million people. So perhaps it is a good thing—at least as far as we are concerned—that Buddy has not heard from anybody."

Ellen was about to say something when they heard a voice calling from outside

"Yo!"

Jason knew the voice immediately and came out of his chair like a rocket.

"Yo!" the voice repeated. It was not a happy or enthusiastic voice, but the voice of someone who wanted to expend the minimum effort to make his presence known.

It was Roone! Jason opened the front door and jumped off of the porch. Roone was standing at the end of the walkway, a young woman by his side. Jason's heart jumped for joy.

Roone and his companion stood at the end of the walkway, holding two walking sticks each. They looked a little top heavy, though not from the weight of their backpacks. On closer inspection, Jason saw that they both were wearing makeshift ponchos over several layers of clothing. Jason ran down the walkway to meet Roone. As they approached each other, both men opened their arms and hugged each other tightly. Pilar stood behind Roone and could see the anguished yet relieved look on Jason's face. It brought her parents to mind. They would be worried sick about her, too. But she did not have the luxury of being able to walk home—if one could call her experiences during the past two weeks luxury. When she stepped up beside Jason and Roone, Jason had not yet released Roone from his embrace.

"It's OK, pop. I made it," Roone said in a voice that had no force left in it.

Ellen approached Pilar and said, "Hi, I'm Ellen, Roone's stepmom."

"Hello, how do you do?" Pilar said in a polite and formal tone. "My name is Pilar Martinez. I am Roone's girlfriend."

Even in a state of near exhaustion, Pilar exuded grace and good manners.

Jason was overwhelmed with relief but collected himself and offered to take Roone and Pilar's backpacks, which they shed willingly. Jason, holding the backpacks, and Ellen, holding the baby, led them into the living room, where both Roone and Pilar immediately collapsed on the floor. Ellen went to fill the water pitcher while Jason and Noah sat in wide-eyed wonderment. Ellen returned with two cups and a full pitcher of water, filled the cups, and placed them in front of Roone and Pilar. She then filled plates with bread, butter, cheese, and hard-boiled eggs, and set them on the floor in front of Roone and Pilar. Then she headed back to the kitchen, filled two mugs with broth from the ever-present stockpot that sat on the right side of the wood stove, and brought the mugs to the cold and famished hikers spread-eagled on the living room floor.

Roone opened his eyes and smiled at the food and water. "Thank God. I am sick and tired of caramel peanuts." He tried for an exclamation but just didn't have the strength. He leaned forward, rolled on his side, drained the water, and set the cup back down. Jason refilled it, and Ellen sat next to Pilar, took her hand, and put the cup of water in it. Pilar raised the cup to her lips and drank it all in three gulps. Ellen filled the cup again.

Jason looked his son over carefully. There were no obvious injuries, no bloodstains. Roone looked tired and had lost some weight, but other than that he did not seem much the worse for wear-and-tear. Pilar appeared to be in worse shape. Jason figured there hadn't been much to her when they left on their trek, and that she had been "worked down," as they say about workhorses after the duties of spring. Roone and Pilar were able to eat, and they drank impressive volumes of water, but they did not have the energy for conversation. Both saved the hot broth for last, and it seemed to raise their spirits. Ellen bustled about, putting linens on a bed in the guesthouse, which really was just an apartment that had been framed out into half of the old workshop building. Jason carried their bags and laid them next to the bed, with Roone and Pilar in tow. The two stripped down unceremoniously, fell onto the bed, and crawled under the blankets. In a moment they were gone to the world, and Jason was left standing there with tears in his eyes, relieved beyond words that his son had made it home.

Chapter 30

Roone and Pilar slept through the day and awoke when the kids rang the bell for supper. Roone took a deep breath, and Pilar rolled over and snuggled into him.

"Are you awake?" she asked.

"I'm awake. And I am starved," Roone answered. "And that is the bell for supper."

"Is that what that is? I'd hoped it was."

"There is an outhouse, like a bathroom, right out the back door on your right," said Roone. And then he swung his legs out of bed, stood up, and walked out of the guesthouse backdoor and onto the grass, where he urinated with great satisfaction. He heard the door open and close, and out of the corner of his eye saw Pilar on her way to the outhouse. He waited for her there, looking out over the pasture fields. There must have been 50 head of cattle, and at least as many sheep, scattered there.

Pilar walked up behind him, put her arms around him, poked her head out the side, and took in the view.

"There was toilet paper in there!"

"Really? Well, thank heaven for small favors. I don't think we will have the luxury of toilet paper for very long, no matter how well stocked my father's pantry is. Come on, let's go eat."

Roone and Pilar walked around the workshop/apartment building, passed raised bed garden boxes filled with broccoli and cabbage and garlic, and headed for the commotion on the porch. The kids were outside jumping up and down on a pogo stick, the family's two dogs were tangled together by the thin steel cables used to secure them outside, and Jason was filling up two hurricane lanterns with kerosene. It was all so *normal*. Jason turned around when he felt, rather than heard, Roone's steps on the wooden porch.

"Ah, you're up! How do you feel?" He cast his eyes first to his son and then to Pilar. "Hello, Pilar. We did not have a chance to speak and be introduced when you arrived this morning. I am Jason, Roone's father, as you know."

Pilar's formality kicked in, and she came forward with her hand stretched out in a lady-like fashion, one that signaled Jason to hold her hand for a moment and not shake it as he would a man's. Jason understood the signal perfectly, and liked Pilar immediately.

"Very nice to meet you, Jason. I have heard so much about you from Roone. It is nice to hear a man speak so highly of his father."

This pleased Jason immensely. He and Roone had always been quite close, but just before his 17th birthday, Roone had become impatient, and even prickly with his father. Jason had never understood why, and for the nearly 7 years since, had tried to bridge the gap that had grown between father and son. Until now, Jason had felt that his efforts had come up short. Perhaps he had just been oversensitive. Boys grow into men, and Roone was now a straight-up man, nearly 25 years old. So, to Jason, this report from Pilar was very welcome news.

"Are you feeling better?" Jason directed the question to both of them.

"Another meal, and a good night's sleep, and I think I will be good to go," said Roone.

Jason's eyes went to Pilar.

"I might need a day or two more than Roone. I am very tired, but I will be fine."

"Well, it can wait. Let's feed you and get you back to bed. A day off of your feet and some good eating and you will be as good as new. Come on, I think dinner is ready."

Roone and Pilar took their seats in two chairs, with their backs to the wall, at the long table in the country style kitchen. This left the other side open, with access to the kitchen for serving. The younger children stared at Roone and Pilar as if they were just the most interesting objects that they had encountered during their short lives. Roone said nothing but made funny faces at them. The kids thought Roone was hysterical. He remembered the low threshold children had for humor and enjoyed their response.

Pilar looked around in astonishment. Pots and pans steamed on the wood cook stove in the kitchen, and the heat made the home warm and cozy. A round-wick kerosene lamp on the table gave off a soft and pleasant reddish light. In the living room, a kerosene hurricane lantern hung from a short chain, above a small table that held a checkerboard. Ground beef mixed with ground sausage waited in a large cast-iron pan in front of Jason. Ellen brought another broad cast-iron frying pan to the table with something unrecognizable in it. Jason took that pan, and with a pair of gloves to prevent getting burned, expertly turned it upside down onto a plate. A large round ring of perfectly browned shredded potatoes with onions fell out. Ellen came back with sliced cabbage, fried with a couple of pieces of bacon and a clove of garlic. A fresh baked loaf of bread sat on a wooden board in the middle of the table, along with a pitcher of milk, a small bowl overflowing with soft butter, and a small bowl of canned tomatoes that had been crushed with a potato masher into a puree that looked like ketchup but was lighter in color and not as sweet. Shakers of salt and pepper stood at attention to Roone's left. It looked like a scene from a Norman Rockwell painting.

Roone's stomach growled, and Pilar elbowed him gently. Roone put his arm around her and pulled her close.

"Wow," said Roone, in a humble tone. "This is almost too good to believe."

"Well, there is not much variety in the menu around here at the moment," said Jason, taking a large spoonful of the ground meat and then handing the spoon to Roone, who sat on his right. "But we don't go hungry. Please, dig in."

Roone spooned a large portion of ground meat for himself and Pilar, and then handed the spoon across the table to Ellen, who sat at Jason's left. Jason passed the browned potatoes and then the cabbage to Roone and Pilar. Ellen prepared two small plates for the younger children, Samuel and Sophia, adding a little bit of everything on the table. There was no difficulty in getting the kids to eat. By suppertime they were hungry and ate what they were served without complaint. Ellen cut the loaf of bread into slices and passed the cutting board with the bread around the table. Roone took two pieces, scooped a large dollop of butter onto each, and deposited one onto Pilar's crowded plate. Then he took the ketchup bowl, ladled some of the red sauce onto his hash browns, and offered to do the same for Pilar, but she waved him off.

Ellen poured them large cups of milk in stainless steel mugs. Pilar took a drink. It was cool but not cold, and absolutely delicious.

There was no conversation. Roone and Pilar tucked into their food and hardly looked up. They finished their last bites at the same time, looked at each other, and half laughed, half sighed. Then they looked back to Jason and Ellen who had not taken their eyes off them during the entire meal.

"That was an amazing meal," said Roone. "Thank you."

"Yes, thank you," said Pilar. "And please don't think me rude. I was just so hungry and tired. I am still tired, but now I am full and tired instead of hungry and tired."

They both looked exhausted to Jason. "Well, I think you two should head back to bed."

"No," said Pilar, looking at Ellen. "I will help you with the dishes and cleaning up."

"You can help me tomorrow. Or maybe the next day," Ellen replied. "But right now, you look a little pale. I think a good night's sleep will do you good."

"I am sorry," said Pilar, her voice trailing off. "I am just a little light headed."

Roone put his arm around Pilar's waist. "Can you walk, baby?"

Pilar squinted a little. "Yes," she said. "I am OK. We have not had this much to eat in a while."

"Good," said Jason, not knowing what else to say. "Off to bed with you two. Tomorrow morning you can take a nice hot bath after breakfast."

"A hot bath?" asked Roone, his tone dubious.

"Oh, yeah. First some breakfast and then a hot bath."

"If you say so."

"I say so. Now, off to bed with the two of you."

Chapter 31

12 hours later Roone and Pilar awoke in one of the
bedrooms of his father's guesthouse. The bedroom was still
dark, but outside the first hint of daybreak was gently lifting
the curtain of darkness. The outside temperature had fallen
into the upper 30s overnight, and the guesthouse's small
wood cookstove had not been fired, so it was chilly, except in
the comfortable blanket-covered king-sized bed.

"How are you feeling, baby?" Roone asked Pilar

"Much better." And she looked it. Her eyes were bright,
and her coloring was back. "I am looking forward to that
bath."

"Yeah. I have no idea where my father is getting hot water
from, but I am ready for a bath too."

"I need to use the outhouse."

"Me too. You first. I will wait here."

Pilar climbed over Roone and across the bed. He gave her
a playful squeeze, and she steadied herself after standing by
placing her hand on his chest. Then she was off.

Roone and Pilar had slept for nearly 20 of the last 24
hours. Roone felt that he had gotten over the crushing
exhaustion of the hike, and it looked to him as though Pilar
had, too. She came back from the outhouse, and Roone
departed for it while Pilar got dressed in the clothes she had
worn yesterday. Those clothes needed to be washed—
desperately. Roone came in and grabbed the jeans he had
been wearing, along with a t-shirt that his father had given
him the night before. It was summer wear for nearly winter
weather, but he didn't seem to notice. They left the
guesthouse and headed for the main house.

The main house was a whirl of activity. Samuel was
heading out to split logs from the woodshed into stove billets
and kindling. Sophia was mixing something in a large metal
bowl, and Ellen was stirring something in a cast-iron frying

pan on the wood cook stove, while holding the baby on her belly on a blanket. The house was warm and smoky from whatever Ellen was frying in the pan. Jason was at the table with a pencil and a pad of paper.

When Jason saw that Roone and Pilar were up and about, he stood up, retrieved the coffee pot from the stove, and placed it on a homemade wooden coaster next to the coffee cups that Ellen put out earlier.

"How are you two feeling?" asked Jason as he poured them each a cup of coffee. He wasn't sure that he should trust them to pour their own. They still looked a little shaky. "That's cream there. It might look lumpy, but it will melt in your coffee and taste delicious."

Roone and Pilar helped themselves to the cream.

"I feel great," said Roone. Then he turned to Pilar. "How 'bout you, baby?"

"I am okay. It might take me another day or two before I am all the way back."

"Okay, good," Jason replied. "I didn't want to press you yesterday, but I am dying to know what you saw and heard out there."

"Have you not been off the farm since the power went out?" ask Roone.

"Just in the neighborhood. We have been working from dawn to dusk getting ready for winter."

"So, you don't know?"

"Know what?"

"Dad, it is totally fucked out there. The highways near Atlanta, Chattanooga, and Knoxville are packed with abandoned cars, and there are dead bodies all over the place."

Jason could see that Roone was getting worked up, and that Pilar had gone pale again.

"Hold on, calm down, and start from the beginning."

Roone filled him in on his binge drinking night out with his friends, Pilar waking him up, breaking into the student canteen and Sonny's Sporting Goods, meeting Max

Pennington and his girlfriend Akiko on I-75 in Atlanta, and then hiking to Chattanooga, TN.

"Wait. So, what happened to Max and his girlfriend?"

"We parted company in Chattanooga. They were heading up I-24 towards Nashville, and we were heading up I-75 before heading west."

"What was Chattanooga like?"

"Dad, we didn't see much of Chattanooga. The highway skirts the city. On the fourth day 'After' it got cold—close to freezing—and then it started raining and sleeting. Until then, the people stranded in their cars didn't do much. Some people were hiking on the highway, but I noticed that they were young or very fit. Everybody else seemed to just sit in the cars. The trekkers would walk during the day, and then take shelter in a vehicle along the road at night. We talked with a bunch of them along the way. They were on a day trip, or going to an appointment, or commuting. You know, just going about their lives. As soon as the power went out, it seemed that traffic just locked up around Atlanta. Cars ran out of gas, and then their batteries died—and that was that. None of these people had any food or water with them, and suddenly they were marooned on a highway far from home. I can't even imagine a worse scenario—other than being stuck in an elevator."

Roone told Jason about the workman at the dorm, who had been trying to free students stuck in an elevator car. Jason shuddered at the thought of being trapped in an elevator for two weeks.

"Pilar developed a bad blister on her heel and couldn't walk for a couple of days. We stayed in an abandoned RV on I-40 outside of Knoxville for three days. There was no food or water in the RV, but we had a backpack filled with candied peanut bars, and I had a quart of bleach. On the first day, Pilar locked the door behind me, and I walked down to a river to fill up our water bottles. I filtered it through a sheet I found on the RV. I folded the sheet over several times, ran the water through it, and then added a half-teaspoon of bleach to every 16 ounces of water. I think I used too much bleach, but I didn't have a chart, and I thought 'better-too-much-than-too-little.' We had to air the water out after the bleach sterilized it, but at least we didn't get sick. It seemed that everyone we saw on the road was sick. I guess that was from drinking untreated water.

"Anyway, Pilar's foot healed, and we got back to hiking. There was a first aid kit in the RV, and I taped a gauze pad with some petroleum jelly on to the back of her heel. It worked, and she didn't have any more problems with her feet. We headed west on I-40 from Knoxville, but remember, it wasn't just cold; it was raining, too—a steady, cold, cold rain. We put all our clothes on, layer upon layer, and I took a small tarp that I found and cut a hole for our heads, and we put that over us, poncho style. That kept the rain off us. Then we hiked. Two hours on. Ten minutes of rest. Repeat. We hiked from daybreak to sundown. We saw other people hiking, but by the 10th day, most of the people we saw on the highway were sick, dying, or already dead. It had been cold and wet for five or six days, and between the weather and the lack of food and clean water, well, that took a toll on people.

"Walking 30 miles a day was much more challenging than I thought it would be, and I guess we were weak from having nothing to eat except the peanut caramel bars. I thought we would be able to find food along the way, but there was nothing to find. After the RV, we stopped at a couple of highway rest stops on I-40, but after the second, we didn't bother, especially since there was no water service at either of them. They were filled with people waiting there to be rescued. But there was no rescue. No one came. We saw some emergency service people between Atlanta and Chattanooga, but they were few and far between, and after Chattanooga, by day four, we didn't see any more of them."

Roone paused and looked at Pilar, who was now ashen and perfectly still. "Anything you want to say or add here, baby?"

"It was so dark. We didn't see any violence, other than what Max said he saw, but the nights were terrifying," said Pilar in a small voice. "I can't imagine going through those nights alone."

Pilar was trembling. Roone pulled her close and held her.

"Oh, yeah. Max said that some guy got killed in Atlanta when someone threw a rock or a brick down on the highway from one of the downtown overpasses. Said it knocked the guy's brains out."

Jason winced, and Ellen covered her open mouth with her hand.

"And the nights were freaking scary. It is one thing to be alone in the dark when you know you can flip a switch any time you want to, but it is something else when you are trapped in darkness. We had a flashlight and a headlamp, but the batteries got low, and we saved them for emergencies. Every night, for 12 hours, we couldn't see two feet in front of us. I can't even begin to describe the feeling. We just got in our sleeping bags and waited for daylight. But it wasn't like the TV shows or movies. No one bothered us, and we didn't see any serious violence. Maybe it was like that back in Atlanta. I don't know because we left right away, but it was not like that out on the highway, though we did see several roadblocks on 41E, with armed men just on the south side of Edinburgh. For close to 300 miles there was not a single roadblock. Then we saw three roadblocks within 15 miles. I figured there would be more on the north side, so we doubled back down the parkway and took a two-lane country road north. I just guessed, and it turned out to be the right one. The last night on the road we slept in a barn, got up early and headed north, and we popped out on route 318, 6 miles east of here yesterday morning."

"What about the roads near here? What did they look like?" Jason asked, spellbound. Neither he nor Ellen had moved a muscle. Sophia had lost interest in what the adults were talking about some time ago, and had headed off to supervise her brother, even though she had no interest in swinging an ax. Jason could see through the window that she was now heading back up to the house. Before she got there, Jason asked, "Did you see dead bodies along the roads in the county here?"

"Dad, we saw dead bodies strewn up and down the roads everywhere from just south of Knoxville to here. It was disgusting."

"Is that when the weather turned cold and rainy? Around Knoxville?"

"Yeah, it was the cold and rain that did a number on people, if that's what you are getting at. We didn't see many bodies until after we left the RV, but it had been cold and raining for almost a week by then. We started to see lots of bodies over the next four days; that would be day ten through yesterday. By that time, we were just numb to it and numb to everything else. I kept telling myself, 'one foot in front of the other.' It was survival of the fittest—like something out of a nature documentary. People on the highways were stuck between a rock and a hard place. They had no food or water, so it was either get out of their cars and seek help or stay in their cars and starve. And if they went out, they got cold and wet. Hell, Pilar is young and in excellent shape, and just one bad blister put her out of commission for two days. Imagine the average 40-year-old. These were just average Joes and Janes who happened to be in transit somewhere when WWIII broke out, and the power went down." Roone made a sound that was somewhere between a scoff and a sob. "They just got tired and cold, and then they laid down—and died."

"Oh, my word," said Ellen in a small voice. "What about my parents?"

"Were your parents traveling?" asked Roone.

"Not that I know of, but who knows?!"

"Honey, your parents are probably at home, and your brother has probably gone to their house."

"Oh, great." Ellen's brother was no prize.

"Honey, it's better they are home with family than on the road."

Ellen turned her head away from Jason and stared out into the pasture through the window. Jason turned back to Roone and Pilar.

"The helicopters?" Pilar said to Roone, to jog his memory.

"Oh, right. The next morning after the lights went out, we saw quite a few helicopters going into and out of Atlanta. As we got closer to Chattanooga, the flight pattern changed. But when we got to Knoxville, we only saw a few of them. And by the time we left the RV, I guess that would have been the 10th day 'After,' we didn't see any more."

"What kind of helicopters?"

"I don't know much about helicopters, Dad."

"Well, were they big choppers with big rotors in the front and back? The kind that can carry a lot of people or cargo?"

"Yes," Pilar answered for Roone. "Most of the helicopters I saw were like that. They also flew in groups. Sometimes six at a time, but mostly in groups of three."

"Yeah," said Jason. "Those would be military. I don't know if they were bringing relief supplies or troops to enforce martial law or taking stuff out of Atlanta to supply something else. We have not seen the National Guard or any government relief efforts here. I imagine that they are concentrating their resources in the population centers. I don't know what else to make of that. Is there anything else that struck you or got your attention?"

"Yes," answered Roone. "Regarding the human bodies along the side of the road. With all of the rain, water was draining into ditches and culverts and these drained into the streams and rivers. All of those human bodies are going to wind up in the drinking water."

"Ugh!" Jason responded as if someone had just punched him in the liver. "I hadn't considered that."

"Yeah, well, when we were staying in the RV while Pilar healed up, I walked about a mile to a place where the highway crossed a small river. As I walked down to get water, I could see the water draining from the highway down a culvert and into the river. When I walked back, I saw a body lying on the side of the highway. I threw the water away and was able to fill our bottles when it was raining from runoff from the roof of the RV. But when it stopped raining, I had to get our water from streams and other surface water. That's why I used so much bleach."

"You never told me that," said Pilar, her eyes wild and staring, her color had gone from pale to white.

"You had enough on your plate, baby. You were exhausted, your foot was a mess, and we were hungry. There was no need for me to burden you with anything else. I did my best to find water that was uphill from the highways, and to filter and bleach it. It must have worked because we didn't get sick."

Jason spoke up to change the subject. Pilar had been traumatized enough. He could speak to Roone later in private.

"I'm sorry you went through all of that. But you did the right thing by leaving immediately and coming here. Any hesitation and things might not have turned out so well."

Pilar started to tremble, and then she started to cry.

"She is worried sick about her parents and family, too," said Roone.

"Where are her parents and family?" asked Jason.

"They're all in Argentina."

This snapped Ellen out of her self-pitying trance. Maternal instincts and female solidarity kicked in together, and she left her seat, moved a chair next to Pilar, and put her arms around her. Pilar dissolved into sobs, but was comforted by the satisfied look on the baby's face as she slept in the sling

Ellen held her in. Sophia picked up on this from the living room, came to stand next to her mother, and put her small hand on her mother's back. Jason cocked his head to the side to signal Roone to follow him, and then he stood up and walked out the front door and off the porch without a glance back. Roone met him in the gravel driveway.

"I am sorry about that," said Jason casting his eyes and nodding in the direction of the house.

"That's all right. And it's not your fault. We are all going to have to learn to deal with not knowing about our people until we do. And who knows when that will be."

Jason didn't answer that; he just blinked his eyes, tilted his head, and shrugged his shoulders. Roone had always been a kind child, but as he matured into an adult, a tough, almost nihilistic edge to his personality would sometimes emerge. Jason had the distinct impression that under the right circumstances, Roone could be a ruthless bastard. Well, thought Jason, he came by it naturally. That seemed to be a family trait.

"You know what my father always said?"

"'If you can't talk and work at the same time, don't talk.' That one?"

Jason and Roone shared a smile.

"Yeah, that one. Come on, let's go get some firewood for the kitchen and your bath."

Father and son headed off to a small barn that served as a woodshed and winter chicken coop.

"I could use a good wash. What are you going to do? Fill a bunch of pots with water and warm them on the stove?"

"Ha! Nah, we've gone high tech! You'll see in a minute." They rounded the corner of the shed row, a three-sided barn that functioned as their woodshed.

"Whoa!" exclaimed Roone, confronted by an enormous pile of stacked wood. "You like to put up a little wood for the winter?" he asked sarcastically.

"Yeah," Jason chuckled. "It seems each year we have plenty of firewood left over and then I lay in some more. I always like to have at least two years of supply, in case I get sick or something."

"Yeah, well that looks more like five years' supply, but I expected nothing less. Excess is just how you roll."

Father and son shared a laugh at that, loaded some firewood into a wheelbarrow, and toted it up to the house. They unloaded the wood into the "wood box," a 70-gallon heavy-duty plastic drum that sat in the summer kitchen. Jason grabbed a bucket that was next to the wood box, and motioned Roone to follow him. In a few steps, they arrived at a large plastic tank positioned next to the house and set up on cinder blocks. There were four of these tanks arranged around the house. Jason had rigged them as a rainwater catchment system, with the roof gutters draining into the tanks.

"Believe it or not, if we don't get rain for two weeks these tanks go empty," said Jason.

"That's a lot of water. How much exactly?"

"Each tank holds 330 gallons. It is not as much as you think. So, we drilled a well and installed a hand pump." Jason pointed toward the pasture south of the house. There was an old-fashioned hand pump tapped into a poured concrete base. "It is a lot more convenient to come here and open the tap and fill up a bucket, but we do what we have to. Of course, I wouldn't drink the water coming off the roof unless it was sterilized, but the well water is potable."

Jason filled a bucket from one of the tanks and walked it over to what appeared to Roone to be a large metal barrel. On closer inspection, Roone saw that the bottom half was a firebox with a hinged door, and carbon stains that rose up the side above the door. Roone took the fitted top off and poured the water into a tank that had been fabricated and welded to sit over the firebox.

"It's stainless steel, so it won't rust, and it holds 55 gallons or so if my math is right."

"Wow! How cool is that?"

"Pretty cool, alright. Buying it was Ellen's idea. I think we are all now forever in her debt."

Jason squatted down and opened the firebox door.

"This thing is invaluable to us now. Without it, we would be limited to the saddle tanks and whatever we could fit in pots on the cook stove. But that would be absolutely miserable in the summer heat. With this thing, we can have lots of hot water without baking us out of the house. In the winter we bring it into the laundry room off the guesthouse and hook it up to that metal chimney you see there."

Jason pointed to what looked like a thin and rusted church steeple that rose to eight feet above the roof of the guesthouse. "We will bring it in there soon, now that the cold weather is here. But for now, here's your bucket. Fill up the kettle with water and set a small fire in the firebox. Let me emphasize that. A *small* fire. Time is more important than size with this thing. I would imagine that if we are not careful, we could burn out the firebox, and we wouldn't want that."

"No. We wouldn't," Roone agreed.

"OK, have at it. It will take an hour to warm that much water in this weather. There's the tub we use for outside baths," Jason pointed to the tub he had removed from the original Amish bathroom when he bought the farm a little over three years ago. When Jason bought the place, there had been a single "bathroom" in the house, and the guesthouse—but no toilet in either of them. They were quite literally "bathrooms." The Amish had arranged three outhouses for their comfort. Jason took down the outhouse that sat behind the main house, and installed a single toilet in the farmhouse bathroom, along with a septic drain field. "You can drag that tub back behind the apartment for a little privacy, or you can use the tub in the guest house bathroom. I think a warm soak and some rest will do you and your girlfriend wonders. Come and find me when you are finished. There is work to be done."

Roone set about filling the hot water kettle, setting a fire in the firebox, and dragging the outdoor tub behind the apartment. He thought that perhaps a hot soak under the blue sky and then another nap would help put the experiences of their trek from Atlanta behind them. He walked around the barns and outbuildings and examined his father's equipment. Roone had never taken much interest in his father's farm, but he had a new-found appreciation for the scale of it now. The workshop was stocked with an impressive array of tools, many of them hand-powered, necessary to make repairs to the equipment and buildings. There was a row of horse-drawn implements under the eve of the barn: sickle mowers, hay rakes, plows, discs, harrows, and cultivators. Hay filled the barn's hayloft right to the rafters, and his father's massive workhorses stood tied to the feed boxes in the barn. It was quite an operation.

Roone walked back to the house and collected Pilar from the kitchen, where she appeared to be having a heart-to-heart with Ellen while Sophia braided Pilar's hair. Roone opened the door and leaned his head in, so that he didn't have to take off his dirty boots.

"Come on; I have a treat for us," said Roone, and walked back to the guesthouse. Pilar followed after a few minutes.

"Ellen is worried sick about her parents," said Pilar as soon as she stepped inside. "So am I."

Roone went to her and held her close. "I know you are, baby. But right now, there is nothing we can do about it. Your parents have each other, and we have each other."

Roone could hear Pilar sniffling. In Latin America, "family" is still the cornerstone of society, and a very different construct from what passed for the idea of "family" in the United States. Roone was an only child from a broken family, and he hardly knew his half-siblings. Pilar was the youngest of six children from an intact Latin American family.

"Baby, I know you are hurting. But I have something that I think is going to cheer you up."

Pillar pulled back and looked inquisitively up at Roone. Her eyes were red, and her skin was blotchy. She must have been having a good cry with Ellen in the kitchen.

"There is a hot bath waiting for us out back. Well, not yet. I have to carry the hot water from the kettle to the tub, and then we will have a good long soak and just get the smell of the road off us."

"What are you talking about? What is a 'kettle?'"

"Come on! I will show you. You can help carry the water."

When Pilar saw the hot water kettle, she couldn't believe her eyes. Roone lifted the fitted stainless-steel cover, and Pilar touched the surface of the water. It was hot! She started to cry again.

"What's the matter, baby?" asked Roone.

"When you told me that your father lived on a 'self-sufficient homestead,' all I could see was a crazy person living in a one-room shack with one of those idiotic 'rocket stoves,' guns, and canned beans, waiting for the world to end. You know, like you see on the Internet. But here I see a family with children playing checkers around a kerosene lamp as their mother works in the kitchen, and they have hot water for baths and laundry, and wood stoves to cook and heat their home. There was milk, bread, butter, and a hot meal on the table last night, and again this morning. They have garden boxes outside their kitchen door, filled with cabbage, broccoli, garlic, and lettuce—and we've been eating peanut candy bars and haven't had a bath for two weeks! I don't know what to say. I almost didn't come with you. If you had given me time to think about it, I probably wouldn't have. And then I might have been one of those poor people we saw on the side of the road."

Pilar was working herself up and was almost hysterical. Roone held her and comforted her as best he could.

When the worst of the storm passed, Roone said, "Come on, baby. You had no choice in the matter. You were coming with me one way or another. You think I would have let you stay and starve? I would have carried you if I'd had to."

Roone held her tight and gently nibbled on the side of her neck, and then whispered in her ear, "I love you, baby. You're mine. Now grab a bucket and follow me. This bath is going to be epic."

Pilar had to laugh at his frat boy vocabulary, even as the tears were still on her face, but then she reconsidered. There was no better word to describe the way a hot bath would feel to her right now.

"Epic," indeed.

Roone and Pilar spent the next hour bathing, carrying hot water from the kettle, and refilling it with water from the rainwater tanks. They went through a couple of tubs full, since the cold weather sapped the heat from the water, but the kettle was more than up to the task. Pilar sat in front of Roone in the tub, sitting between his legs and using his chest to rest her head as she watched the steam come off the hot water into the cold air. They were about to remove themselves, reluctantly, from the comfort of the water when they heard a commotion on the other side of the single-story building that contained the guesthouse and workshop.

Ellen was alone in the kitchen when she heard someone pounding on the front door, scaring her half-to-death. She could hear a woman calling her name in between the loud bangs, and as she approached the door, she could see through the glass. It was their neighbor, Belinda Cutliff. Ellen opened the door and signaled Belinda, who seemed to be in distress, to follow her into the kitchen. Ellen pulled out a chair in an unspoken offer to sit, and went back to the stove, rearranging things there before coming back to the kitchen table to find out what the matter with Belinda was.

Roone and Pilar rose from the tub and dashed—naked as the day they were born—into the back door of the guesthouse. When they entered the bedroom, they were pleasantly surprised to see a pile of freshly laundered clothes, stiff from drying on a rack next to a hot stove, waiting for them on the bed. They got dressed and headed for the house. When Roone saw Belinda, he turned around and headed off to find Jason, and Pilar stepped into the kitchen. Roone found Jason in the milking parlor.

"Hey, Dad, some woman just came up your driveway screaming her head off. She's in the kitchen with Ellen and Pilar."

"Well, whatever it is it can wait until I finish milking."

"All right," said Roone. "I am going to go check on Pilar."

By the time Jason finished milking and walked back to the house, Belinda Cutliff had calmed down.

The Cutliff's lived on a small farm on the other side of the street, about a mile east. They were friendly enough, but they were not friends. The Cutliff's eked out a living operating a small dairy with 35 cows. They were not Amish and could not milk their herd without electric power. Their small home had a wood stove, and though it was not designed for cooking, it could be used for frying and boiling a pot or two, and they had plenty of beef and milk to trade, and an Amish community to trade with. They were not starving, but Jason imagined that they were struggling to adjust.

Jason sat down at the table. All three women were in tears. "What's going on?" Jason asked. Ellen answered for Belinda.

"Roscoe got physical with her!"

Jason just looked at Ellen blankly and let a dramatic pause pass, hoping that she would understand that throwing more fuel on this fire was not helpful. Then, looking at Belinda, he asked, "Are you hurt?"

"Roscoe threw me out of the house!" Belinda sobbed.

Jason did not respond immediately but waited to give Belinda time to get hold of herself. He looked her over. There were no signs of injury, no marks on her face, and no scrapes or contusions on her elbows or knees, but she was distraught. That much was plain to see. As Belinda cried and wept anew, Jason signaled for Ellen to follow him. He walked out onto the porch and turned to wait for Ellen.

"What happened?" asked Jason. "And why would she come to us? We have been here for three years, and this is the first time she has been to our home."

"Belinda said Roscoe got physical with her and threw her out of the house!"

"Were those her words? 'Got physical' and 'threw her out'? Because she doesn't look like she got beaten up."

"Does a woman have to look beaten up?" asked Ellen.

"I didn't say that." Jason wanted to change the subject. "What does she want us to do?"

"I don't know. I am going to go back in there and talk to her. Would you go talk to Roscoe?"

"You want me to get in the middle of a domestic dispute?" Jason was incredulous. "The police used to get shot pretty regularly on domestic violence calls."

"Roscoe is not going to shoot you."

"How do you know what is going on with Roscoe right now? All we know about them is that they wave to us and we have had a little small talk. Who knows what went on with these two?"

"Please, go talk to Roscoe, and I will handle Belinda."

"I don't like this at all."

But Ellen wasn't hearing any more and was on her way back into the kitchen. Roone had been listening from the shadows behind the screen door of the apartment.

"Do you want me to come with you?" asked Roone.

"No. No point in both of us getting shot."

"I could bring a rifle and take up a defensive shooting position."

Jason wondered how he had wound up caught between Ellen's concern for Belinda and Roone's willingness to kill to protect his father. No wonder cops got shot in these situations. People should mind their own business.

"No. I don't want you to have blood on your hands, and I don't want anyone to get hurt. I will talk to Roscoe in a little while. No point stirring the pot when the blood is up."

Jason walked to the barn to finish his chores.

*****

As Jason walked down the road, he saw Roscoe walking out of his barn with a milk pail in his hand. That was a good sign. Milking a cow by hand is a calming and meditative activity. Roscoe saw Jason and gave him a friendly wave.

"What the hell?" Jason muttered to himself. Roscoe did not seem to be upset.

"Hey, Roscoe!" Jason called out as he turned off of the road and into the gravel driveway.

"Hey, Jason."

"Hey, I hate to interfere," said Jason, sounding flabbergasted. "But Belinda is up at my house having hysterics in my kitchen."

"Well, I am truly sorry to hear that," said Roscoe. He was as calm as a snake charmer. "She should have gone to her parents' house in Edinburgh."

Jason was having trouble connecting the hysterical woman back at his kitchen to the serene and sensible man standing in front of him with a pail of milk.

"Well, that would be a 20-mile walk," said Jason. He was just trying to keep the conversation going and wasn't sure what to say in this situation.

"Yes, it's a long walk," Roscoe agreed, nodding his head and looking at the ground as he stroked his short beard. After a while, he looked up to Jason and said, "But she can make it before sundown. She will have to make it there eventually."

"Roscoe, I don't know what happened, and it's none of my business."

Roscoe cut Jason off right there.

"You're right about that. It ain't none of your business. But I know you are just trying to do the right thing, especially now that you got caught in the middle. But there's no need for any more drama. Just tell Belinda that I don't want to see her—ever again. Tell her she is not welcome back. There is nothing more to talk about."

"Roscoe, you have children!"

"My daughter's nearly 15 and my son is 13. They ain't kids no more. My daughter's already got herself a man. She's been shacking up with Jacob Yoder. My son doesn't need to be around my wife either. It ain't healthy. She's evil."

"Hold on; your daughter has taken up with one of the Yoder boys? They're Amish."

"Well, you will have to ask them about it. About a week after the power went out, Sally didn't come home. I tracked her down over there, and she says she is staying with Jacob from now on."

"You're kidding me! Is that OK with you?"

"Why? You think the government is going to pull what they pulled down in Waco, Texas? Come up in here and kill a hundred people to protect teenage girls from getting married? I don't think so. They got other things on their minds these days."

"No, I guess I was just surprised is all."

"Well look, Jason, I got no quarrel with you. But I am not spending another second of my life with that woman. Belinda has been a miserable and unhappy person since the day Sally came home from the hospital. And she ain't done a damn thing but smoke cigarettes, drink coffee, spend money, and complain since the kids came along. I won't take her back, and that's that."

"Roscoe, she said that you 'got physical' with her." As soon as Jason said this, he wished he could take it back. What was he trying to do? Redden Roscoe's bottom in front of the class? Use guilt to manipulate Roscoe into taking Belinda back home?

Roscoe just smiled and put the milk pail down.

"She smacked me because I was ignoring her during one of her meltdowns. So, I dragged her out of the house and threw her on the front lawn. I told her if she ever comes near me again, I am going to beat the living shit out of her, or maybe even kill her—that would be the best thing for all concerned—and then I locked the doors.

"But I did her no harm, though I was sorely tempted to beat her within an inch of her life. I can't live with that woman any more, or I will kill her or myself. And you know what? I don't have to. She is a sick, evil, selfish, mean, and nasty bitch—and I am free of her. I can't tell you how relieved I am that I don't have to see her sour face when I walk through that door."

Roscoe nodded at his front door, and it occurred to Jason that the word "relieved" did best describe Roscoe's demeanor.

"Now," Roscoe continued. "If you will excuse me, I gotta cook this milk before it goes sour. I got no more to say about Belinda. She is dead to me. And if you let her into your life, you are going to feel the same way in no time."

Jason didn't know what else to say, so he said "Goodbye," and left for home. When he got back, he knocked on the door to the kitchen. Ellen came out on the porch and closed the door behind her. Jason filled her in on the conversation, including Sally's move to Jacob's house.

Ellen was horrified. "Now what do we do?" she asked.

"She can stay here for a few days or until the weather clears, but then she has to go to her parents. We can't take in every stray that comes in off the road, or we won't have enough food to make it through winter."

Ellen was disgusted, but she understood the situation. "I understand. I will go over and get her clothes."

Jason couldn't believe it. He was expecting a battle from Ellen, but she was perfectly reasonable.

"Well, let's wait until tomorrow, and then I will go over with a team of horses and a hay wagon. I get the feeling Roscoe will be only too happy to give me her things."

"I am going to go talk with Belinda," said Ellen. "She can stay in the other bedroom in the guesthouse."

"No. Roone and Pillar have been through enough hell. Besides, I don't want to make things comfortable for Belinda. She can sleep on the floor in the living room. And I will make sure she knows that we are leaving just as soon as we get a break in the weather."

Chapter 32

The rain pelted Walt, Martin, and company as they tramped westward along I-40 on the outskirts of Greensboro, N.C. Their bodies were dry under their jackets, but their feet were cold and wet. It was the morning of the eighth day since they had left their boat in Washington, N.C., and 15 days since the grid had gone down. They had covered about 180 miles in seven days of walking. It had rained off and on for most of that time. It had been warmer by the coast, or at least everyone agreed that it felt as though the temperature had dropped as they trekked west. Of course, they couldn't be sure, as no one in the group had a thermometer, and the local banks' time and weather reporting signs were dark.

They had decided to go on "half rations" the day they set out on foot, so that they would not run completely out of food. After seven days of strenuous hiking and a constricted diet, all of them felt their clothes getting loser on their bodies. Unfortunately, while they had plenty of water to drink, as many of the service stations they passed had outdoor faucets that still had water service, they had not passed a body of water bigger than a stream. Fish had not been on the menu since the first day of their hike. They were tired, and at this pace and food intake, Walt felt things would soon get rough. They needed to find some food. And of course, some "food" was available—they just weren't hungry enough to go turning over logs for insects or eating dog meat. Not yet, anyway. On the bright side, shelter was everywhere, in the form of abandoned cars on the highway.

They met others on the road and heard compelling stories of misfortune. One young man, Leon Brophy, had worked as a janitor at a hospital in Durham. The hospital had backup generators and packaged food for the cafeteria, and so he had stayed there rather than go home to his "hood". The hospital backup generators had enough fuel for 24 hours, but only powered the surgery rooms and the critical care units of the hospital. Martin thought the backup system had assumed that a power outage wouldn't last more than a day, or that if it did, they would have access to fuel. It had turned out to be a terrible assumption.

When the backup power went down, the patients being kept alive by artificial means had died immediately. Many others had died over the next week. Any patient who could move got up and left, some in frightening conditions or terrible pain, but it was better than living with the smell that permeated the hospital. Leon had helped remove dozens of bodies from the building. He and other hospital staff had wheeled the bodies down the sidewalk to a Little League baseball field and left them lined up on the line between third base and home plate. But the most troubling experience at the hospital had been the people they could not rescue from the elevators. The custodial staff had managed to open the elevator doors and could pull people out of those elevator cars that were near one floor or another. But several elevator cars were stuck right between two floors, and while the custodial staff could get down onto the top of the elevator cars from the floor above, they were not equipped with the harnesses and the other specialized equipment that elevator service companies and firefighters use in elevator rescues, and they feared that they might fall down the shafts. The only way to rescue the people trapped in those elevators was to have them climb out the ceiling hatch and then pull them to safety with knotted bed-sheet ropes or fire hoses. None of the people in those elevator cars had been fit and agile enough to climb out. Leon said he knew several of the trapped people, "But they was big girls. Ain't no way we coulda pulled 'em up and outa there." Leon had become emotional and had to stop talking.

Leon had said that there were over 2,500 elevators in Durham, and only 250 firefighters. There was no way to reach an elevator technician, and even if they could have, the situation was impossible.

Leon's story was making Walt and Martin sick to their stomachs. Martin had taken the elevator—*with his family*—down from his apartment when he began his hike out of New York City immediately after the bombings. What the hell had he been thinking? They could have suffered a terrible death, trapped in the elevator.

New York City had 80,000 elevators. There were 40,000 more in the metropolitan area. Walt was a volunteer fireman; he knew how elevator rescues took place. It takes four or five highly trained rescue workers half a day to execute a safe evacuation rescue from an elevator car trapped between two floors, and that does not include transport time—and now there was no fuel for transport. With the grid down, most people trapped on elevator cars between floors were going to die slow deaths in those elevator cars. Those caught with floor access to the elevator car still needed someone outside to open the elevator shaft's floor door before they could escape; otherwise, they would meet the same awful fate.

As they listened to Leon's story, Walt and Martin looked at each other and shook their heads and rolled their eyes in exasperation. Just thinking about it was painful.

Leon was on his way to family that had rural property "down the hill"—Martin guessed that meant the foothills before the mountains—from Morganton, N.C. He was young and in excellent physical condition, and he left them behind when they stopped to rest.

They saw several people who were in shock from exposure, and lay dying on the grass that bordered the highway's paved shoulder. Walt noticed that Miriam did not stop to render CPR and mouth-to-mouth. It occurred to Walt that Miriam was the very definition of a virtue-signaler. Strident, angry, and overtly hostile to anyone who did not recognize her moral superiority, and conform to her demands for fairness and equality, she contributed nothing but strife to the world she wished so desperately to improve.

Not a word passed between the two.

Still, Walt felt that they could make it to Jason's. They might be in terrible condition when they got there, but they would be alive. He and his brother had been very close. Walt was sure that they would all be brought back to good health if they could make it there before serious illness struck, or the weather turned bitterly cold. He knew that there was skiing in the North Carolina mountains, and that meant snow and freezing temperatures. Walt just hoped that late November was not skiing season down here in the south. The road atlas gave an elevation for the Cumberland Gap of only 1,600 feet, but that was still high enough to get pretty cold at this time of year. They would just have to deal with that when they got there. Walt estimated that it was 200 miles to the Gap, and another 200 from there to Jason's house. He put his head down and walked on, one foot in front of the other.

Chapter 33

Jason was indeed correct that Roscoe was only too happy to remove all evidence of his 16-year marriage to Belinda from the home he shared with his 13-year-old son. After a few days with Belinda as a houseguest, no one in Jason's household wondered why Roscoe had removed Belinda from his life, though they did wonder how he had endured 16 years with a bona fide sociopath. Belinda was a deeply disturbed person. She was in turns manipulative, charming, moody, seductive, impatient, and nasty. Both Jason and Ellen were eager to get her out of the house. Roone and Pilar avoided her as if she were selling cancer. None of them had ever met a person who wore mental illness on her sleeve the way Belinda did.

The weather did not let up for another five days. It took another two days to make the necessary arrangements, but on the 21st day "After", Jason, Roone, and Noah packed Belinda's things in baskets and secured them to the rig on the back of their mule, "Lady." Jason loved Lady, but he was never able to find a match for her, so Lady stayed on and "worked single," an unmatched mule without a regular teammate, for odd jobs. For big jobs, Lady could be teamed up with another horse harnessed together "in the lines," but the horses didn't like her.

"I wish I were going with you guys," said Roone.

"We need you here to keep an eye on things," said Jason.

"I hear you, Dad. I don't think I can leave Pilar alone just yet, anyway."

"That, too," said Jason as he finished tying down the baskets on Lady's back. He had never packed anything by mule before, and he hoped Lady would cooperate. She had pawed the ground, churning the mud around her feet into a liquidly clay goo the consistency of breakfast oatmeal.

The temperature was mild. At daybreak, the thermometer read 40 degrees. That was the warmest dawn temperature in over two weeks. Jason figured it just couldn't rain and sleet forever, so after a full day with no rain, he thought it would be a good bet that they would make the 40-mile round trip on horseback without being soaked through-and-through and catching pneumonia. Of course, they could have taken a buggy or even a spring wagon, but Jason felt that with three horses and a mule, rather than one horse and a buggy, he would stand a better chance of not having to walk back. And since they had no idea what the weather had in store, this was how they had elected to travel. To get Belinda out of his life, Jason would have been willing to walk if necessary. He could not begin to imagine how Roscoe had survived living with this woman for 16 years, and though it was sad, he understood why neither of her children came to visit her or to say good-bye. Belinda was an emotional black hole that sucked in and destroyed the well-being of everyone around her.

Jason was taking no chances. Belinda would ride "Annie," an older warm-blooded, herd-bound Percheron/Standardbred cross mare that would follow the other horses no matter what Belinda did. He wouldn't put it past Belinda to try to steal the horse and take off on her own. Annie made a good broodmare, as well as a good "all around horse," as the Amish called these draft/light horse crosses, but Jason had never been able to break Annie of her separation anxiety. She could work in teams or groups but would not work or ride "single"; this was a severe fault in a horse, but one that Jason thought would come in handy today.

Jason climbed onto his mount, Thunder, a powerful, mixed-breed bay gelding in its prime. Noah was already in the saddle on his mount, Drifter, a chestnut Quarter Horse gelding. Even though there had been no reports of violence on the roads of the county or 41E between the farm and Edinburgh, both men were armed. Noah had a revolver on his hip and a 30-30 rifle in a western style leather holder next to his right leg—he liked to imagine himself as an old west cowboy. Jason was under no such romantic illusions and wore a military-style tactical vest under his wool-lined sheepskin leather coat. The vest held three clips for the 9mm pistol he had strapped under his arm, and another three clips for the CAR-15 rifle he carried in his saddle scabbard. Of course, they were not looking for trouble. They planned to give anything suspicious a wide berth. The hypocrisy of two men of pacifist faiths, riding out armed to the teeth, was not lost on Jason. But it was one thing to mumble platitudes under safe conditions, and another to adhere to their self-destructive mumbo-jumbo when staring into the abyss.

All of their mounts carried saddlebags with a day's food ration for three people, and grain-feed for the horses and mule. Fast food was no longer an option when traveling, and horses need to eat too.

"I think that's it then," said Jason, looking over to Noah.

"I'm ready when you are," said Noah as he nodded once to Jason.

"Good luck. I'll hold down the fort," said Roone.

None of them acknowledged Belinda.

"We should be back no later than 3 pm," said Jason. "If we are not back by sundown, don't freak out, but if noon comes and we are not back, go over to Abraham's and bring the cavalry."

Noah chuckled a little at that.

Jason gave Thunder a light kick in the ribs and made a clicking sound, and the three horses and riders and the pack mule trotted down the long gravel drive to the two-lane highway and headed west for the first leg of their ride to Edinburgh.

Jason and Noah rode west with their charge, Belinda, tasked with depositing her at her parents' house after Roscoe, her husband of 16 years, had evicted her from their home. Jason was not happy about being placed in this situation, but he was not willing to turn Belinda out to the elements, and so she had become his responsibility. After a week in Belinda's company, Jason had developed a profound respect for Roscoe, who had been trapped in a marriage to a sociopath by the vagaries of American family law. Roscoe did what he could to protect his children from Belinda's evil pathology, but in the new disposition of things, Roscoe had seized the opportunity to take his life back, by throwing Belinda out of the house and threatening to kill her if he ever saw her again. Belinda, like any parasite, would have to find a new host. Roscoe had won his freedom without lengthy and draining court proceedings, and without lifetime financial enslavement. He had freed himself, by simply throwing Belinda out. Jason was thrilled for Roscoe but was unwilling to take over Roscoe's former responsibilities to Belinda. Enough was enough.

Marriage and family were taking on a new dimension in the "After" circumstances. Or, perhaps marriage and family were returning to their former dimensions or regaining certain aspects from an earlier time. Most people who had found value in their marriages "Before" still felt that way "After." But suddenly all associations, including marriage, had become utterly voluntary again. In Belinda's case, she had lost more than a husband; she lost her entire life support system. On her own, Belinda could not produce enough firewood to keep warm, or produce enough food to keep from starving, or provide any of the other things necessary to sustain life under the current circumstances. To survive in this new environment, she would need to earn her way, and get along with people, in the ethos of a family and a clan. But she had poisoned her own family environment, and had been shocked to discover that, like any parasite, she needed a new host. So, to survive, she had manipulated her way into dependence on Jason and his resources.

Jason had determined that he would not be placed in this situation again. He had enough responsibility; he didn't want any more. So, for the second time in a week, Belinda was being evicted and rejected. Jason felt that this made Belinda even more dangerous. He wondered if her parents would refuse her, too. Either way, Belinda would not be returning to Jason's farm.

Jason and Noah rode in the lead, with Belinda's mount following behind Jason. Noah "ponied" the mule behind his horse with a lead rope attached to a nose chain on the mule's halter.

"I think we are better off taking Route 1224 south and then crossing over to 41E."

"I wanted to see what happened on 41E for myself," replied Jason, getting right to the point.

"Well, I think you will see enough. We will still have to ride down 41E for the last four or five miles. But weaving through the abandoned cars and the fencing on the side of the road will be hard on the horses and harder on us."

"Is it that bad?" asked Jason.

"Well, I am only going by what I've been told. I think it is harder for a buggy than a horse, but the days are short this time of year. If we want to get down there and back before sundown, this is the way we should ride. We can always take 41E all the way north on the way back if we are making good time."

"That makes sense," replied Jason.

The ride west to Route 1224 was uneventful. The rural county appeared much as it had "Before", with suburban-type houses built along the roadside on small lots carved from the farmland behind them. Dark and empty, with no signs of life, the houses stood in mute witness to a future that was not in the plan, with their warm and dark refrigerators, cold stoves, and silent air conditioning units. On the other hand, these structures would provide an endless supply of materials that the locals who survived could reclaim and repurpose.

The riders trotted on the grass at the edge of the road, sometimes edging onto the pavement to avoid a mailbox or other obstruction, but mindful that road surfaces can be hard on a horse's feet, not to mention on a fallen rider. The party maintained a trot most of the way and arrived at Route 1224 in less than an hour. There was a truck repair business on the southwest corner, and they rested the horses in a patch of grass between the street and the building while Jason relieved himself behind a tree. He then mounted Thunder, and they walked the horses south.

"Well, that was disconcerting," said Jason. "We didn't see a soul."

"I imagine they all left when they ran out of food," said Noah. "Or when they got too cold."

"That makes the most sense."

"We heard that the authorities set up a shelter in the Home Hardware store in Edinburgh for people who needed food and a warm place to sleep, but I don't know what has become of that," said Noah. "I don't think it is operating anymore."

"I guess we will see soon enough," said Jason. He looked back at Belinda, remembered this was not a fact-finding trip, and turned back to Noah and asked, "Ready to ride?"

"Let's go," replied Noah.

Jason's horse set the pace at a lope that was comfortable for both horses and riders. The horses ate up the miles as they bounded across the rural landscape. After another 45 minutes of riding, Jason was just about to pull up and let the horses walk and rest when something caught his eye up ahead in the grass, on the field side of the roadside drainage ditch. He slowed his horse to a walk and approached the objects he saw lying in the grass.

It was two sets of human remains, lying on their backs. The bodies had begun to return to the soil. Their clothes were still in reasonable condition given the circumstances, and the smoked remains of dozens of cigarette butts surrounded their bodies. Several empty cigarette packs littered the ground nearby.

"Brace yourself," said Noah. "You are going to see a lot of this today."

"What the fuck happened here?" Jason asked in a voice that was equal parts frustration and anger. Noah had never heard Jason use profanity. "What did they do? Just sit down and smoke until they died?"

"That looks to be the size of it," said Noah. "I would guess they got tired from walking, and sat down to rest, and never got back up."

"Look at the size of their clothes," Belinda chimed in, her voice critical and unconcerned. "These people were immensely fat. Typical country land whales. I don't think these two walked very far. They must have lived in one of the houses we passed."

Jason ignored Belinda. "What should we do?" he asked Noah.

"Well, there's not much we can do. Some members of the Amish church group that lives on the other side of Edinburgh traveled up to our place, and they said there are more dead bodies than they could count on the road. And that was over a week ago. We need to make tracks if we are going to get home before dark."

Jason responded by asking his horse to walk. Noah rode alongside Jason, and Belinda's horse followed obediently behind.

"Has any member of the Amish community died since the power went down?" Jason asked Noah.

"Not that I am aware of, and no one in our church group has. We are not eating as well as we were, but we are not starving. I imagine it's the same with your family."

"Our pantry is in pretty good shape, especially after we cleared out the freezer and canned everything. There is not much variety, but we won't starve."

"And you won't freeze, either. These people relied on electricity to run their propane furnaces. They were not just hungry. Unless they had a wood stove and lots of firewood, they were cold, too. You know how much firewood it takes to get through a winter. I imagine there is plenty of propane sitting in tanks around the county."

"I can't imagine freezing with a full tank of heating fuel, but there it is. Let's pick up the pace."

Jason brought his horse up to a trot, and the other horses fell in behind. They covered ten miles on Route 1224, and they saw more than a few human remains along the way. At the east-west junction that would take them west to 41E, and then south to Edinburgh, they walked the horses to let them rest. As they approached 41E four miles north of Edinburgh, the enormity of the situation came into view.

Cars and other vehicles clogged 41E on both sides of the highway. Jason had no idea that there had been so many cars in the five-county area, and they were seeing only a fraction of all of the vehicles registered there. Edinburgh was the commercial center of the five counties that surrounded it. Although rural, the five counties were home to nearly 90,000 people.

Human remains dotted the fields along the highway. They could see hundreds of bodies. Jason also was sure that many people had sought more privacy deeper in the fields and woods on either side of the highway for their final moments. Jason hung his head. What morbid curiosity had led him here? Why did he need to see this? Why hadn't he just kicked Belinda off the horse, back on Route 1224, and told her to walk the rest of the way?

Because deep down Jason needed to see it with his own eyes, to understand it, to commit it to memory, and later to paper, so that those who didn't see it, or who came after, would know what had happened in this time.

But what had happened? Mankind had built an industrial society in which almost everyone had become dependent on electrical power to survive. Our dependence had become so complete that we had constructed nuclear reactors, and risked Armageddon in the form of a meltdown, rather than reduce our consumption of electricity. And for what? So that we could watch other people live life on a computer or television screen, while we sat on couches and ate ourselves into limp dicks, and waddled our fat asses into early graves?

How fucking stupid can we be?

Jason answered his own question: *Pretty fucking stupid.*

Jason, Noah, and Belinda arrived at Belinda's childhood home, in a working-class neighborhood two miles east of Edinburgh. 36 years ago, when Belinda's parents had brought her home from the hospital, this community was solidly middle class. Her father worked at the mill and made a decent living, and her mother stayed at home until Belinda and her older brother were in school. Even then, her mother had only worked part-time, and had been home waiting for her children when they walked in the door after school. Since then, things had changed, a lot.

Jason saw a hardscrabble neighborhood of dilapidated houses. Had he arrived here 22 days ago, he would have seen dispirited people, obese, tattooed, and addicted, who had been painted into a smoke-filled corner by life and circumstances. But today, Jason saw no one. Well, he saw no one who was alive. There were bodies on the road to Belinda's house, and Jason was pretty sure there were bodies hidden behind the walls of the houses here.

"How could this happen in just three weeks?" Jason asked out loud, to no one in particular. He dismounted, handed the reins to Noah, and walked into Belinda's old bungalow-style house. There was no one in the home, and there were no bodies. There was no significant damage. Unwashed dishes filled the sink and covered the counter in the modest kitchen. Jason turned the faucet on, but no water emerged. He wondered how long the house had been without water. Jason guessed that the pile of dishes in the sink could be a week's worth for two people. But it had been raining. They would have had access to water.

Maybe they had gone down to the makeshift shelter at the Home Hardware store. It seemed worth a look. Jason stepped outside and reported to Noah and Belinda that no one was home, dead or alive. Belinda got a strange look on her face but said nothing. If anything, she looked relieved. Jason considered this for a moment. Was she relieved that no one was home, or that there were no bodies in the house? He mounted his horse and signaled Noah to join him. They nudged their horses forward a few steps, so that they could talk together without attracting Annie, the horse Belinda was riding. Belinda seemed content to sit in front of her parents' house with that blank-and-satisfied look on her face.

"You feel like taking a ride over to the Home Hardware store to see if there is anybody at that shelter?"

"I think we are running out of daylight. It also occurs to me that if we leave now, we can head up 41E but south of where we got on this morning and pay a visit to the O'Neil farm. I hear they have a foundry and a forge set up, among other things. Maybe she could stay there and work for them, and you can be free of her, and we can get on back home."

"Normally, McCoy O'Neil would be the last person I would want to visit. But under the circumstances, I think that's a good idea."

Jason and Noah, their mounts, and Lady the mule turned back the way they had come. Belinda's horse Annie followed. Belinda seemed to have gone into some form of catatonic state. That was just fine with Jason. They picked up 41E and headed north, toward the O'Neil farm, and home.

Chapter 34

Late on the 21st day "After," Walt, Martin, and company
were getting ready to bed down for the night in the grass off
highway 58. They had passed the sign that said: "Welcome to
Tennessee." With each passing day, the days got shorter and
the nights got longer and colder. They rested or slept from
twilight until dawn, over 12 hours each day. They were still
tired, but not exhausted. Their strategy of stretching their
food supplies had paid off. The fishing had been excellent,
and it seemed that a body of water presented itself at the end
of each day's trek, but Martin wondered if that would come
to an end soon, as the weather got colder, and the days got
shorter. They had perfected an evening program of duties:
Walt turned over logs and rocks for grubs, beetles, and
worms for bait. Martin and Miriam took on fire duties, Jenny
cleaned fish as they were caught, and Manny comforted his
pregnant wife, who was now starting to show just a little.

BLAM!! A gunshot shook their tired bones. Martin set off
toward it, but Miriam called him back, and Manny took off
toward the pond where Walt was fishing. Manny slipped and
slid down the embankment, and towards the stand of scrub
wood that surrounded the pond. Just as he got to the trees,
Walt appeared, about 20 yards to Manny's right, holding a
Canada goose and wearing a big smile.

"You scared the shit out of me!" screamed Manny.

"Here, take this," Walt said, offering the goose to Manny.
"I think I wounded the other one, too. I'm going to see if I
can get it."

"We only heard one shot," said Manny as he took the bird.

"The way they were standing, I am pretty sure the bullet
went through this one and wounded the other. Damn, I'm
good! Go on; I will be right back."

True to his word, Walt was back by the fire in a matter of
minutes with another goose. Then he and Martin stood back

in awe as the women plucked the birds and singed off the pin feathers over the fire. With a little coaching from Manny, they then gutted each bird, retrieved the heart, liver, gizzard, and testicles from the drake, or male, and quartered the birds so that the pieces would roast quickly.

"Now I have seen everything," said Martin. "I just watched my wife help pluck and gut a duck. And my daughters watched with interest rather than being appalled. Let me point out; those are three Jewish girls from Manhattan." He delivered the last line in his best Jackie Mason imitation, where "girls" became "goils."

"It's a goose, but who's counting?" Walt teased. The mood all around seemed to have been lifted by the promise of fresh game to eat. "And I saved the best for last."

"What's that?" Martin asked.

"Salt!"

Chapter 35

On their trip south towards Belinda's parents' home, the sight of so many disabled cars and human remains had overwhelmed Jason's ability for accurate and dispassionate observation. On the return trip north, Jason managed to clear his mind. Reports of broken windows in the cars along the highway had been accurate, but it became clear that McCoy O'Neil and his henchmen were not the culprits.

Jason noticed telltale pockmarks in the vinyl siding on the houses, something he had not noticed on the way into Edinburgh. Each car's roof and hood had dozens of dents, which must have been caused by hailstorms. It's not unusual in the mid-south to have significant hailstorms in spring and fall, and hail big enough to dent a car's hood is big enough to dent a human skull.

"I don't think O'Neil was out here breaking windows, Noah. It looks to me as though the area got smacked with some serious hail."

Noah pursed his lips together and took the scene in for a bit before responding, "Looks that way."

"I have driven past the O'Neil farm many times, but I've never been there."

"Me either," said Noah.

It occurred to Jason that, although Noah was quiet, reserved, and not at all prone to the drama of the TV-raised English people his age, the scene along the highway had disturbed him, as it had disturbed Jason. Noah was just being quieter about it. They rode the next several miles to the O'Neil farm in silence.

The first thing Jason noticed as they walked their horses and mule down the O'Neil farm's gravel drive was the strange, industrial smoke smell. It was a complicated odor that Jason thought he recognized but couldn't place. Jason also found it odd that no one was keeping an eye on the farm entrance, even though it was adjacent to 41E. After dismounting, Jason handed his reins to Noah, and set off toward the door of the sizable outbuilding, from which the industrial smoke was drifting. Belinda remained in her saddle.

Several men were in the shop. Some were wearing welder's glasses around their necks and were working on something on the far side of a massive metal-topped table. The roof had several clear panels that provided a comfortable amount of natural light, but Jason wondered if they wouldn't bake like a solar oven in this building come summer. Jason banged loudly on the door and remained just outside the doorway, in the daylight. McCoy O'Neil appeared from behind a stack of sawn wood that had been set up to dry.

"Well, how 'bout that! What you got to say for yourself, Yankee?" McCoy asked in a friendly and teasing sort of voice.

"Hello, McCoy," said Jason, his voice firm. Jason had resolved to meet O'Neil head-on in their interactions. O'Neil was not the sort to whom you wanted to show any weakness.

As O'Neil got closer, he put up his hands in mock surrender and said, "D'ju come to rob me?"

He had a big smile.

"No. What do you mean?" asked Jason, a confused look on his face.

"Wha'chu got on under that coat?" said O'Neil pointing at the place where Jason's pistol hung under his arm.

"You can tell I'm armed?" Jason was impressed.

O'Neil forced Jason out of the doorway by walking towards him, clapped Jason on the shoulder in a friendly way, and said, "C'mon". They started walking toward the first of several houses built along the driveway. O'Neil stopped when he saw Noah and Belinda.

"You travel in strange company," said O'Neil. He resumed walking toward the house, signaling Jason to follow.

"You know her?"

"Yankee, you are new here. The rest of us have been here for generations. Of course, I know her. I went to high school with her brother." Suddenly, the Kentucky/Appalachian twang was gone. "You just gonna leave your party there?"

"Well, they are not 'mine,'" replied Jason. "Noah can see your hitching post if he wants to use it."

"Suit yourself," said O'Neil, as he opened the front door to the house. "Come on in and have a seat and tell me what's on your mind."

The two men sat down at a small table in a kitchen, or perhaps "lounge" would be a better word to describe it. There was a large room adjacent to it that had a wide entrance way—wide enough so that a person in either room could see most of the other room. It was lined with book-laden shelves. The room had a fireplace, in addition to the cook stove in the kitchen area, and several comfortable chairs. It was as impressive a home library as Jason had ever seen.

"You seem to have lost your 'twang' somewhere between the workshop and here."

"I put the Kentucky 'twang' on extra strength for Yankees. Especially, Yankees who think all people west of the Hudson River are rednecks and morons." Here, O'Neil paused for dramatic effect. "I understand that you and your wife sometimes work as math tutors for kids getting ready for tests."

"Yes, we do. Or we used to."

"Including the higher maths?"

"Well, that would depend. I am proficient in algebra, geometry, calculus, and trigonometry. I have a reasonable understanding of linear algebra, but I would not call myself proficient."

"I have a degree in mechanical engineering from the University of Kentucky. I was 'retired out' of the U.S. Army—as a major—for migraines and vision problems with my left eye, but I spent nearly 11 years in the military, with eight years working for Army Intelligence."

Jason wasn't sure where this conversation was going, but he got the idea that he had misjudged O'Neil and was being dressed down for that.

"I didn't know that. I understood that you were in the military. I assumed you had been an enlisted man, because you ran for sheriff. Officers do not typically go into law enforcement in civilian life."

"A county sheriff is an elected official, not one of these scumbag Nazi police forces the municipalities can't even fire. There is a big difference between the two approaches to 'law enforcement,' but I will forgive and forget your assumptions about me." O'Neil paused again for dramatic effect, this time with an expression that bordered between impassive and seriously pissed off. After a few seconds, all of that melted into a friendly smile. "So, to what do I owe the honor of this visit?"

Jason told O'Neil the story of how he had come into Belinda's company. He then gave O'Neil his assessment of her, in plain language. When Jason finished, O'Neil smiled and shook his head.

"Well, I don't blame you for wanting to be rid of her. She suffers from Borderline Personality Disorder, or BPD for short. So, does her mother, but that was a different time, and her father could handle her mother. Roscoe was playing by a different set of rules. I will make room for her. Maybe she can fool one of the men working here into thinking that she's human."

McCoy chuckled at his own humor.

"How do you know what her mental health status is?"

"Brother, if it takes a medical degree to determine if someone is an evil nut-job, then they ain't. Ain'chu never heard of the 'emperor's new clothes?'"

O'Neil chuckled and was back to his good-old-boy accent. Jason wondered if maybe O'Neil had some sort of personality disorder, too.

"My first wife was a Borderline personality," O'Neil continued. "Half the dictators and bad actors across the world are Borderline personalities, usually associated with homosexual pedophilia and sadism."

Jason winced.

"Oh, you don't like hearing that? Well, the people working in military and civilian intelligence are not in the business of being politically correct. That's for politicians, and for the recently departed cultural Marxists who dominated the now dead-as-fried-frog-legs news media. Didn't you ever wonder why such a high percentage of serial killers murdered and raped men and boys? Never mind. That was rhetorical. That's just the way it is. The evidence supports the idea that BPD is a genetic condition that is passed on from Borderline mother to daughter or gay son. Heterosexual men have other mental pathologies, but BPD is not among them. In my estimation, all exclusively gay men suffer from BPD. The Left managed to suppress lots of research on BPD, by using undergrad students from women's studies programs as 'agenda editors' to control the content of the online encyclopedias. They even managed to edit the diagnosis in the DSM, the codebook for shrinks. Not that the shrinks were worth a shit anyway. You know what the DSM is?"

"Well, I have heard of the 'Diagnostic and Statistical Manual of Mental Disorders,' if that's what you mean," replied Jason. "But that's about it."

"Yeah, that's what I mean. Lovely folks, those cultural Marxists."

The conversation was not going the way Jason had hoped it would. He changed the subject.

"She will be safe here?" Jason's tone was a statement of demand more than a question.

O'Neil looked at Jason as if he'd been blowing bubbles with his spit.

"Will Belinda be safe here? Brother, you are one arrogant jackass, aren't you? You want to be rid of that psychopath, but you don't want to feel guilty about dumping her on me. Well, you are hereby absolved of all responsibility. You know full well, from living with her for only a week, that no one is safe around Belinda. That's why you want her out of your house—and not just you, I reckon. Your wife would prefer to have a cigarette put out in the palm of her hand every day rather than live with Belinda. Am I right? I thought so. You're not worried about Belinda. You're worried about appearances. Well, you shouldn't worry. She has a long career ahead of destroying the wellbeing of everyone around her. She can stay here, but only because the only thing worse than a woman with BPD is no woman at all. I've got a dozen workmen here without a woman. I need to find them some female companionship.

"I always felt bad for Roscoe, and it ain't over for him even if he is rid of Belinda. His daughter is a carbon copy of his wife, and his son ain't never gonna produce any grandbabies for ol' Roscoe, if you know what I mean. But enough of that evil cunt."

It suddenly occurred to Jason that there might be some personal history here.

"Is there more to your relationship with Belinda than going to high school with her brother?"

"Well, alright! Now we're talking! Well done! Shoot, you might have a career in intelligence yet. Yeah, 20 years ago we had a sexual relationship over a summer, and when I went back to college, I broke it off. She stalked me for two years afterward, keyed my car, cut up the leather seats with a knife, threatened to kill my girlfriend, that sort of thing. But she's been civil with me since the day she married Roscoe. Borderlines *hate* the man they are sleeping with, or at least they hate their man during the 'devaluation' stage in their emotional cycle. Of course, they are incredible lovers and charming friends during the 'idealization' phase of the cycle.

But this is all Greek to you, right? Well, that's why their men keep coming back, and it is why BPD exists at all—natural selection. During the idealization phase of their cycle, the sex is so good it would make a porn star blush. Borderlines are just plain more fun in bed than emotionally stable women are, and eventually somebody knocks 'em up. But sooner or later, they destroy the wellbeing of every person in their orbit, and even their own family disassociates from them. If she had been successful in seducing you, you would have been on for the ride of your life."

Something in Jason's expression confirmed McCoy's suspicion. McCoy began to laugh.

"She tried to seduce you, didn't she? Not overtly, but she laid it out there. Good thing you took a pass. She would have destroyed you and your family before moving on to her next victim. Here's another fun fact to know about women with BPD: The majority of police domestic violence calls are to homes with a Borderline, and most female victims of domestic abuse are Borderline personalities. Borderlines instigate conflict, and will always escalate an argument, no matter how trivial; they never back down. Well, not until the 'devaluation' cycle passes, or if they are about to lose their parasitic host."

Jason's head swam. He had nothing more to say to any of this, so he remained silent. McCoy moved on.

"OK. You had enough of talking about Belinda? Good. Me too. C'mon. I want to show you some things. See if I can't make a customer out of you."

And with that, McCoy stood up and motioned for Jason to follow him. As they stepped back outside, McCoy shouted over to Noah, "Hey, tie those horses up over yonder, unpack that mule, and come with us," and he pointed at the hitching post.

"His name is Noah."

"Thank you, Noah!" McCoy called back to Noah. Then to Jason, "I know he's Abraham's boy, I just can't keep track of

all their names. Shoot, he must have 15 kids." Then back to
Noah, "Come on! Meet us in the workshop when you're
done; I got some things I want you to see."

Chapter 36

If spring in the country is the celebration of life and rebirth, then the character, look, and feel of the rural American landscape in late autumn is the melancholy of mourning. The cycle of birth, life, death, and then rebirth is writ large. Roone and Pilar looked at the gun-steel grey sky, bare trees, brown-green grass, and wood-smoke mists in the still morning air and saw a blatant reminder of their mortality. The young lovers sensed the foreboding shadow of winter closing in and felt a primal fear of cold winds to come. In this new "After" world, winter was the dying time. They could feel, if not hear, the trials and struggles of their ancestors echoed across the eons.

Roone and Pilar took the morning off to explore the farm. Roone had been away at college when his father had bought this property. He had only visited here three times before. He used the tour to rediscover the farm himself, and to tell Pilar about his childhood farm experiences. During his childhood, Roone had spent most of his summers and school vacations at his father's first farm and had been as much a country boy as any kid from metropolitan New York or South Florida could be. For his 11th birthday, his father had bought him a .22 rifle, and had insisted that Roone take over the milking duties for the summer. For his 13th birthday, Roone's father had bought him a well-bred quarter horse, a roping saddle, and a lariat, and assigned Roone the task of putting up enough firewood for the winter. For his 16th birthday, Jason had given him a 12-gauge pump shotgun and had spent many hours teaching him to shoot it well. He also had made Roone responsible for all the repair work around the farm—fences, roofs, barns, wagons, and every other piece of equipment or building, all of which mother nature seemed to wear down and break constantly. The repair work had compelled Roone to learn carpentry, welding, masonry, plumbing, and even some electrical skills, though Jason called in a professional electrician to do the high-voltage electrical work. Father and son had a healthy respect for the dangers of electric power.

Pilar was amazed by these new insights into Roone's personal history. Suddenly, Roone was no longer a puzzle to her. She had known that Roone was no snowflake. He was willing to tackle anything, manifestly confident that he would succeed. But here, the life experiences that had created the man she loved came into view. He had always been so different from the other boys at school. Her Latin culture had an expression for young men like Roone: "Eres un hombre hecho y derecho, un verdadero macho"—"You are a man made and straight, a real man." The phrase seemed to have been fashioned with Roone in mind.

Roone and Pilar strolled along the border of the woods and hayfields. A small tornado had toppled several trees by the roots and knocked the tops off several more.
Roone pointed to them.

"My father does not cut down trees for firewood. He says he only takes what nature has already harvested."

"It seems he will have plenty of firewood."

"You mean 'we' will have plenty of firewood," Roone said, laughing. "I will be the one getting this wood in, though Samuel is old enough to help now."

"How old is Samuel?" Pilar asked.

"He's 10. But my father has always insisted that his sons are able to handle every job on the farm by the time we are 14. He got that brilliant idea from the Old Order Mennonites who lived near his first farm."

"Your father demands that you accept the responsibility of your manhood."

"Something like that."

Roone loved the amusing formality of Pilar's English. He reached for her hand, and she turned her face up and smiled at him. They climbed a short hill and came to level ground. There was a barbed wire fence about 100 yards ahead. On the other side was the "back 80"—80 acres of fenced pasture where they ran their cow herd, along with fifty or so sheep.

"It's beautiful," said Pilar.

"It took a lot of work to get that ground producing. The previous owner rented it out to grain farmers. They killed everything and planted corn for three years in a row. It is unusual to plant corn more than two years in a row because it depletes the soil, and usually farmers alternate corn one year and beans the next. For some reason that did not happen here. My father bought it in late spring three years back. It took him two seasons and a lot of seed to get it producing grass and clover again."

"Is that all the cows eat? Grass and clover?"

"City girl," Roone teased as he squeezed her hand. "It is all they are really supposed to eat. We feed them grain, like corn, oats, and wheat, also legumes like soybeans, but that is not their natural diet. Man feeds them that to fatten them up before the slaughter."

"Oh," said Pilar with a frown.

"My father says that cattle farming is really grass farming, and that if you take care of the grass the cattle will take care of themselves. For the most part, I think that's true."

"Does your father milk all those cows?" Pilar asked, looking out at the herd.

"No. Most of those are beef cows. Dad keeps a half dozen Jersey milk cows. He is milking three now, but he typically milks one at a time. But he likes to have several around to feed the calves that lost their mamas, and he likes to dry up his family milk cow every six to eight months so that the cow can fatten up before calving. So, he needs to rotate a few cows through that process."

"There's a lot to running a farm."

"More than I could ever explain. You have to see it to get the idea, and you have to do it to understand it. Come on, I want to show you something."

They walked across the hayfield, back to the houses and barns, down the fence line on the other side, and into the "horse barn". Four massive workhorses, a draft mule, and two light horses were standing in tie-stalls; the feed boxes in front of them were empty.

"These horses are fed twice a day, every day, and three times a day if they are being worked. My father grows, harvests, and stores all of their hay on the farm, and in return these horses do all of the heavy work. Here, help me untie them."

Roone showed Pilar how to release the first horse's halter from the clip on the end of a chain that was secured to the stall. Then he stood back and directed her to the next horse. After she unclipped the horse, the beast backed up and walked down the alleyway to the door and out to the barnyard. Pilar unclipped the other horses and watched each leave the barn on its own.

"If you feed and handle a horse every day," said Roone. "It gets into a routine, and it becomes your horse. All of these horses will be waiting outside the door to be let in for their afternoon meal."

"What work do these horses do?" asked Pilar.

"They pull. That's all they do. They pull stuff, and then they stop or turn when they are told. The equipment does the rest. Come on, I'll show you."

Pilar followed Roone down the feed aisle that separated the horses from the people feeding them and crossed to the barn on the opposite side from the barnyard. They walked around to the front, where an awning had been constructed to shelter the equipment and implements necessary to work the land. Roone began at the east side of the barn and worked his way west.

"This is a sickle mower. It cuts the grass to be cured for hay. This is a hay rake, and it rakes the hay into windrows. This is a hay loader. It picks up the hay and throws it on a wagon. This is a moldboard plow. It turns the earth over and breaks up sod. This is a disc plow. It cuts the soil and loosens it for planting. This is…" Pilar couldn't keep up with it all. There were twenty pieces of equipment, all pulled and powered by horses.

"It all looks so old. Where did your father get all of this stuff?"

"At auctions mostly. He's been at it for almost 15 years. Most of this stuff is 85 to 100 years old. But it was designed to last, and to be repaired by the farmer. There is no reason that most of this stuff won't be working in another 100 years."

"Is all of this equipment necessary?"

"Well, you can't run a real farm—feed a family and have a surplus to sell—with just a garden fork, a spade, and a hoe. Mankind bred workhorses and oxen, over thousands of years, because he needed them. If those survivalists and preppers in our class back at school don't have all this stuff, plus seed to sow, livestock to work and produce meat and dairy, a barn full of hay to feed the livestock through the winter, wood stoves, and lots of seasoned wood for cooking and keeping warm, they are going to freeze and starve to death, crowded around one of those silly rocket stoves they bought online."

"But your father was a banker! What made him do this?"

"Well, he's been a banker, a broker, a salesman, a construction worker, a ditch digger, and a lot of other things. But he's been a farmer for almost as long as I can remember."

"It seems so strange. What drove him to this life?"

"I don't know. When I was a kid, my Dad and I did some adventure travel. One day, when I was 10 years old, he came to me and said, 'these one-week adventures are fun, but let's do a real adventure, one that we can live in and not just visit for a week. Let's buy a farm and some horses and live off the land.' And then *he did*. I was only 10, so I didn't know how crazy that sounded. Last year he was talking about buying a sailboat and sailing around the world, but then Ellen got pregnant. I've learned you have to take what my father talks about seriously, because he is probably going to do it. Whatever it is."

Pilar and Roone shared a good laugh.

"Well," said Pilar. "I hope he can still have his sailing adventure."

"It doesn't look good, does it?"

Chapter 37

A tremendous racket came from a machine under a lean-to type structure outside the workshop on the O'Neil farm. O'Neil led Jason and Noah around the building to the machine and stood out of the way so that his guests might inspect it. It was an old but powerful diesel tractor, powering a generator via its PTO, or "power take off," which connected the engine to other implements or equipment via a splined drive shaft at the back of the tractor. PTO generators were great for localized electric power—if you had a tractor and fuel. Cables ran from the generator into the building.

It was too loud for McCoy to talk, so he signaled for Jason and Noah to follow him. They stepped inside the building, where it was quiet enough to be able to carry on a shouted conversation. McCoy led them to a large propane tank—it must have been 12 feet in length—that had been arranged to sit vertically in a metal bracket. Two welders were working on the bracket. McCoy led Jason and Noah across the workshop and out a wide door on the other side. Once outside, he pointed out into a cattle pasture to a small "nodding donkey" well pump.

"We got two oil wells on the property. See that collection tank up yonder?" He pointed to a pair of rusty 5,000-gallon vertical collection tanks. "They are half full of crude oil. And that well produces between 50 and 100 gallons of crude per day. It ain't running now. We need a generator or a windmill, or even a horse-powered treadmill, but it ain't nothing. We got plenty of juice to get started."

Jason put it all together in an instant. He was stunned.

"Holy smokes," said Jason. "That's smart."

"It won't be very efficient," said McCoy. "But it don't gotta be. This is only one design. We have been able to refine some serviceable product with a simpler set up using non-pressurized tanks and 55-gallon drums."

Noah had no idea what McCoy and Jason were talking about. He just shot Jason a bewildered glance and shrugged his shoulders a little.

"They are going to take the crude oil from these wells and refine it in that old propane tank, into useful products like gasoline, diesel, and kerosene," Jason said to Noah.

"Well, it will be a little more complicated than that. But all we need is enough to run a few tractors and light a few lamps," McCoy said. "I hope to trade the rest. I expect y'all will need kerosene and lubricating oil for your equipment. We are going to set up to do metal fabrication for hardware and parts."

Jason was speechless. He had misjudged McCoy O'Neil in just about every respect. Jason still had some reservations about him on a personal level, but O'Neil clearly was an educated and experienced man with important skills.

"Well, McCoy, I have to say that this has been a pleasant surprise. I am impressed."

"Come on with me," said McCoy, bouncing along like a proud and happy schoolboy who had just taken first place in the school science fair. He walked around his workshop and headed back to the house that served as his office and library, with Noah and Jason following close behind.

McCoy sat down in the same chair he had used before and said, "Have a seat, gents."

Noah and Jason sat on either side of McCoy around the small table in the kitchen area.

"You fellas saw what went on over at 41E," said McCoy.

"Yes," Jason and Noah replied in unison.

"If you look on either side of the highway, you see corn and bean fields for almost as far as the eye can see. And them dumb motherfuckers in those cars starved and froze themselves to death. That make any sense to you?"

"I hadn't thought about that," said Jason.

The three men looked down at their hands on the table.

"I don't think dried corn kernels as hard as rocks were going to do much for them," said Noah.

"Well, not now." McCoy always seemed to enjoy a mordant sense of humor. "But it's worth everything to us. Y'all got endless labor in your community, right? Hell, the average family has 12 kids. I know y'all been busy since this all happened, but if your community organizes harvest teams, we will all be glad of it come winter, not to mention next year."

"You can't get enough fuel for your equipment?" asked Jason.

"Well, it ain't that. I got a time problem just like y'all do. We can use up the fuel we got in the farm tanks, but I would rather save that to run the generators until we get the refining process up and running, because you can be sure that there will have to be lots of trial and error. But that corn and bean crop is going to go bad if we leave it in the field. I been up to y'all's place a couple of times, and ain't nobody took me up on my offer. But I think y'all are going to want to trade with me, and one of the things we all need, and that y'all can trade, is corn and beans. Y'all fill up my bins, and I'll give y'all enough kerosene to keep your lamps lit so y'all won't have to sit around in the dark, and enough lubrication oil to keep your equipment running."

"I will talk to Abraham as soon as I get back," said Jason. "We will get a harvest party organized. And not to change the subject, but I guess you don't think the power is coming back on anytime soon."

"No, you're right. I don't. Not the way it was. Nothing will be the way it was. Maybe in a year or two we will get local power plants generating again. It all depends on what infrastructure damage was sustained. If they did extensive damage to the step up/step down transformers across the system, it could be quite a while."

"Who is 'they'?"

"The 'enemy.' When nuclear bombs get tossed around you tend to make 'enemies,' and all bets and all restraints are off. We don't know who fired first, and we don't know if there wasn't some sort of coup, but it doesn't matter. Once nuclear weapons are engaged, there is no incentive to maintain the status quo of international trade and finance, because neither of those things can survive even a limited nuclear war. But to answer your question, I suspect Iran."

"How could it be Iran? You think that they would be capable of that after a nuclear attack?"

"Well, Iran is a big country, and they have been hardening against a nuclear attack by the U.S. or Israel for many years, so yes, I think Iran is the likely culprit. After getting nuked, they had absolutely nothing left to lose. But it could have been Russia, or Iran and Russia working together. And China has the capability, but they would be cutting their own throats, as they rely on grain shipments from the U.S. to feed their people—but maybe their elite wants to thin the population some. Who knows? China and Russia don't want to provoke a full-scale exchange with the U.S., but they have every reason to feel threatened, and might have felt the need to respond, and put the U.S. back on its heels. The best way to do that is to cripple the economy and create a domestic national emergency. There will be no half measures. This is not Ukraine, where Russia fooled around and shut off power to a couple of cities for a few hours. This is all out. I bet the 'enemy' did a lot of damage. The SCADA systems that control most of the gird, including the nuclear generating plants, were developed years before cyber security was an issue. Perhaps they damaged the big transformers throughout the grid by shutting down their cooling systems with malware. Transformers always generate heat. Turn off the cooling system, and you get insulation failure pretty quick, and if you don't do something about it fast, the transformers will experience catastrophic damage that would take years to fix. I'm a mechanical engineer, not an electrical or software engineer. So, I am just speculating on how they did it, but the fact is that the grid is down for three weeks now, so something big happened. If the grid stays down, 80% to 90% of the population will die over the winter of exposure, starvation, suicide, or disease from dirty water and unsanitary conditions."

"I thought that many local water systems were gravity fed and that many of those have several months of supply in elevated storage," Jason said.

"Well, under normal operating conditions, that is probably so. But the first good freeze is going to empty out those water towers 1, 2, 3."

"How's that?"

"Without domestic space heating, water pipes in the houses will freeze and bust open and leak. The water will drain out of those towers in a day or two."

Jason rolled his eyes and slumped in his chair.

"You okay?" asked McCoy. "You're sweating like a dyke holding a baby."

"What the hell is that supposed to mean?"

"You ever seen a lesbian holding a baby?"

"No."

"Well, I'm not surprised. One doesn't follow the other, does it? I imagine it wouldn't be comfortable for them. Anyway, I bet 10% to 20% of the population died in the last 21 days. Hell, we probably lost close to 1% of the American population just in elevators."

"Wait a minute... wait a minute... Dykes, babies, elevators. You've lost me."

McCoy smiled and said, "That's 'cause you got no sense of humor. But let's get back on track. The U.S. has nearly a million elevators. Let's say more than half were empty. If the 500,000 occupied elevators held an average of six people, that's three million people. Can you imagine being stuck in a crowded elevator when the grid went down? No light, no food, and human excrement piling up around you before dying from dehydration?"

"Holy shit!" exclaimed Jason.

"No pun intended, right?" McCoy asked with a chuckle. Neither Jason nor Noah laughed. McCoy looked back and forth between his two guests. "You know, elevators don't have bathrooms..." McCoy paused to see if anything registered. "Some people got *no* sense of humor. Anyway, I expect half the people who were traveling when the grid went down are dead, all but the young and extremely fit—those capable of walking long distances. People who were at home will stay there until they run out of food. When something like this happens, it is best to be at home. But you gotta ask yourself: what happened to the hordes of roving gangs, killing and raging across the country like in all those Hollywood movies and TV shows? How many of them did you see on the way down here?"

"None at all," Jason looked at Noah for confirmation. "We didn't see anyone on the roads."

"Some of the other big farming families set up roadblocks with armed men to protect against that sort of thing. My family helped. After a week they were bored to death. It's been a week since they abandoned that idea, and no one has come here looking for trouble. We've had a dozen kin show up. They walked from Nashville and Louisville. And a dozen local young men came here looking for work and food. Not one was interested in fighting. They were too damn hungry to fight. We post a guard at night, but that's only because we are right on 41E, and that is the extent of our security. Hollywood would be very disappointed."

"My son and his girlfriend walked here from Atlanta," said Jason.

"How old is your boy?"

"He's 24."

"From Atlanta to here is a hell of a walk. At least he had the good sense to bring his woman with him. I don't know where the local girls went off to, 'cause we got too many men and not enough women. And my kin brought their women but left the old folks in the city and walked here by themselves. I hear the same thing from the other farming families. They all got young kin straggling in from all over the place. It's a terrible thing, but I guess it's just as well. I ain't got the resources to be runnin' no nursing home."

Jason let that last comment go. Noah's eyes widened perceptibly, but McCoy didn't notice.

"What about the National Guard and the military?" asked Jason. "What about FEMA and the rest of those agencies?"

"Well, the military has its hands full with logistical problems right now. They have people scattered across the planet that needs to be provisioned while maintaining battle readiness in case of a million different contingencies. They will be lucky to keep everybody fed and supplied. Oil shipments are going to grind to a halt, and all of those ships, planes, tanks, and other vehicles burn a lot of oil. And as for the National Guard, I would bet the farm that they are busy keeping the nation's 100+ nuclear plants from melting down and cooking off."

An alarm went off in Jason's head, and he filled O'Neil in on Roone's reports about the large transport helicopters flying into and out of Atlanta.

"Yeah. I bet they were flying back and forth between Atlanta and the nuclear power plants over in South Carolina. That's a whole other can of worms. But let me bring y'all back to the here and now. That's their problem, not ours. Ain't nothing we can do about any of that, so let's focus on us and our situation for a moment. Look out at the corn and bean crop right here in the county. Most of it is going to rot in the fields. If that is happening here, it is happening everywhere in the U.S. But there is enough out there to keep us, our families, and our livestock fed, IF we can harvest it, and figure a way to store it so that rats and mice don't eat it all, because it will be impossible to load it into the metal grain bins without power for grain elevators. Next year, there won't be any fertilizer, even if there is fuel. This is a worldwide disaster, but in percentage terms, the U.S. and Canada will suffer the most significant losses."

"You know, on the day after the power went down, Abraham said he feared 'Seven Years of Famine,'" said Jason.

"Abraham got the famine right and the time frame wrong. I don't think this famine will last seven months, let alone seven years. I don't expect more than 10% to 20% of the American population to survive through to spring. The survivors will be the lucky people who just happened to be in the right place at the right time, the young and fit, the highly motivated and skilled, and people living in cooperative and interdependent communities, like the Amish and Mennonite communities here. Also, the Mormons, as they have a year's food supply on hand as a general practice. Everybody else, especially the people living in the big urban centers, will die. There won't be a soul left in Chicago, New York City, Philadelphia or Boston.

"But we will have another problem next year. Without natural gas distribution and grid power to make ammonia fertilizers, each acre we plant next year will yield 20% to 25% of what these industrial farms yield now. Even if we could plant all of the acres that got planted in the past, and we can't, the food supply would drop by 80%. It is just math, Yankee. The faster the population declines, the sooner the famine will end."

Chapter 38

Walt, Martin, and their families were three days behind
schedule when they arrived at the Cumberland Gap, but Walt
figured that that was a small price to pay for taking the time
to take good care of their feet. Walt had made sure that they
took regular rest breaks, and that they all took off their shoes
and socks when they did so. His Boy Scout training had
come in handy again and again on the trek.

Winter was closing in fast. The nights were long and the
days short, and they had to push themselves harder each day
to cover the same distance. They needed to get through the
Cumberland Pass, and out of the mountains, before the
weather became an issue. All the adults had lost significant
body weight. The twins looked much as they had 20 days
earlier, when they had left the sailboat, but the adults were
swimming in their clothes. The ropes that Walt had taken
from the sail-lines had become useful in a very unexpected
way—as belts to hold up the adults' pants. They were always
hungry, but they were not yet starving. They had stretched
the candy, beef jerky, and peanut butter from Walt's
convenience store, and had supplemented that supply with
fish, fowl, insects, and other catches, including one very
large rattlesnake that they had found hibernating under a log.
The snake must have weighed 10 pounds, and it had fed them
for two days. Walt mused that, while the adults in the party
were all fitness conscious professional types, they all had
carried a few extra pounds at first. Their fitness and those
extra pounds had come in handy in their new circumstances,
and while he felt that they couldn't survive like this
indefinitely, he also hoped that they wouldn't need to. They
just needed to keep going for another seven to ten days to get
to his brother's farm.

They found themselves confronted by a highway sign
saying that that the Cumberland Gap Tunnel was up ahead.

After consulting the road atlas, they estimated that the tunnel was about a mile long. They sat on the ground in silence, and contemplated walking that far underground while relying only on their flashlights. Manny spoke first.

"Who knows what we might find in the tunnel. It could be blocked. We don't need to get hurt climbing over a wreck in the dark."

The unanimous decision was to double back and take the path to the scenic route and the "Wilderness Road", which the pioneers had taken across the Appalachian Mountains in the 18th and early 19th centuries.

"Ah, what the hell," said Walt. He would have taken the tunnel, but he kept his opinion to himself. "Daniel Boone's got nothing on us. Let's just get this done. I am tired of walking uphill."

Chapter 39

Jason drove a team of horses, pulling a wagonload of just picked corn, up the drive to the new corncrib that they had built into the unused end of their woodshed. After what had seemed like endless rain and cold, the weather had turned clear and even colder. The corn was as dry as a bone. The kids and Ellen, who held the baby nursing and napping in her sling, lay on top of the corn, tired but happy. Roone and Pilar drove the other team, pulling another wagonload, and Pilar sat in Roone's lap on the forecart as he drove the horses. Ellen watched as Roone held the reins in his right hand and held Pilar around her waist with his left hand. When he needed to use both hands to guide the horses, he squeezed his knees together to keep Pilar secure in his lap. Jason and Ellen just loved watching the two young lovers revel in each other's company, and Jason was often reminded of the biblical exhortation, "O, young man, rejoice in thy youth!"

Roone needed no encouragement in this matter. Nor did Pilar. They spent their days working side by side in the fields, barns, and workshops of the farm, and their nights making love by the soft light of a kerosene lamp, and the warmth of the wood stove, in the guesthouse. Their youthful vitality and joy in life, so evident in everything they did, was infectious. In the midst of crisis, life went cheerfully on.

This load finished their grain harvesting project. It was early December, and the chill in the air chapped the skin on their hands and sapped the strength from their bodies. They had been working the corn harvest for the past twelve days. Huge tractors and planters had set the seed in the ground in May. Today, nearly six months later, 80 pairs of hands picked the ears, shocked the stalks, and saved the husks for use as "toilet paper." Over 90% of the corn and 98% of the bean crop was left in the field unharvested, but even that wouldn't all go to waste. Cattle owners had taken to branding their cattle and turning them and their hogs out of the fenced pastures, so that they could graze on the corn and beans in the fields. Hay had become a precious commodity, and there just wasn't enough of it in their barns to get their cattle through winter if they were confined. Only the dairy cows remained confined and were fed in the barnyard and milked in the parlors. The dry cattle and hogs were turned out to fend for themselves. In the greatest famine America had ever known, a head of beef was worth a fortune in a major city, but here in farm country, it wasn't worth much. Without transportation to a market, the farm-country people had far more cattle than they needed, while the people in Atlanta, Nashville, Louisville, and other cities starved.

Thousands of years ago, Mankind had domesticated the familiar American and European farm ungulates—cattle, sheep, and goats—to turn the grass, vetches, and clover that humans couldn't eat, into nutritious meat and milk. The ungulates' unique digestive tracts and four-part stomachs are much more efficient at turning forage into meat than the systems of horses or bears or even pigs are. So, while people throughout the ages would eat their horses at the end of their useful lives, they never raised horses for the sole purpose of providing meat.

Grains such as corn, wheat, and oats provide supplemental calories to give working horses extra energy, and to fatten slaughter animals, but those grains are not part of their natural diet. Over the millennia, Mankind had developed "grains" from selective breeding of local grasses, and that had enabled Mankind to discard its original nomadic hunter-gatherer lifestyle in favor of agriculture, in which people coaxed food from the soil, and from their domesticated livestock. The livestock benefited from feeding on grain, but if they had to, they could live without it.

The day after Jason and Noah visited the O'Neil farm, Jason and his Amish neighbors set about building corn cribs, scavenging materials from decrepit barns and woven wire fencing. As agreed, the community delivered a dozen wagonloads of corn to the O'Neil farm, and in return, O'Neil sent them north with several reclaimed industrial vegetable oil tanks, holding several hundred gallons of a serviceable distillate from his refining operation for their kerosene lamps. O'Neil also gave Jason 25 gallons of gasoline, which is an unavoidable byproduct of refining crude oil into diesel and kerosene, to run Jason's workshop generators and chainsaws. O'Neil promised them more fuel to run the diesel engine at their sawmill, so that they could mill enough lumber for the community's—and O'Neil's—needs.

Jason's gravel driveway ran straight away from the road at a 90-degree angle, wound through 100 yards of woods, and then went up a hill to the farmhouse, barns, and outbuildings. As Jason's team pulled its load out of the woods and started up the hill, he saw a rag-tag group of people sprawled on the ground under the maple tree in front of the house. He stopped his team and waited for Roone to drive his team up next to Jason's. Jason and Roone took in the strangers lounging on their front lawn, and were making mental calculations of fight or flight, when Jason heard a familiar voice.

"Yo!" called Walt, squinting his eyes. He was mildly nearsighted, which meant, at his age, that he didn't need reading glasses, but things were a little fuzzy at a distance.

"Yo!" Jason responded, more on reflex than anything else. He didn't recognize the skinny and bearded men walking toward him. When they got to within 20 yards, Jason had a vision of his late father, but with a beard. It was his brother Walt! Walt and Martin approached slowly, with quizzical looks on their faces. Since their physiques and clothes had degraded just a little each day, Walt and Martin had no idea how different they looked today, compared with the way they had looked a month ago. Jason, however, wash shocked by the transformation. He stared at his brother, and at the specter he now realized was his old friend Martin, while he tried to cope with his astonishment.

"Wally? Marty?" His mouth hung open. "What the hell? How did you get here?"

"We walked," said Walt. "And what kind of welcome is that?"

Chapter 40

Walt, Martin, and their families made it to Jason's farm just in the nick of time. Murphy's law states that "Anything that can go wrong, will go wrong. And Murphy was an optimist." Walt, Martin, and their families had managed to avoid Murphy, but most of the American people who lived above 30 degrees north latitude had not. For them, Murphy was spot on. Winter set in hard within days of Walt and Martin's arrival, with unusually low nighttime temperatures in the low teens. And this was only early December.

Jason and Walt planned on building another house on the farm come spring, but for now, Manny and Danielle were assigned to the other bedroom of the guesthouse, and Martin and Miriam and their girls set up in one of the upstairs bedrooms of the main farmhouse. The old farmhouse had steep pine steps coated in polyurethane, and Miriam worried that somebody would break his neck walking down those stairs in the middle of the night when nature called. After a couple of nights of this, the family asked Roone and Pilar and Manny and Danielle if they could sleep in the living area of the guesthouse, near the wood stove. Everyone did their best to cooperate, given the tight quarters and lack of privacy, and Martin's family decamped to the guesthouse. That left only Walt and Jenny with Jason's family in the main house, and that was okay with Jason and Ellen.

With eight new mouths to feed at the farm, the first order of business was to slaughter a steer. Jason had a small diesel tractor with a front-end loader that could lift the steer for butchering, but they could not get it started in the cold weather. The tractor did have a block warmer, but that required electricity. Jason also had a small hoist, but it was built for a 200-pound deer, not a 1200-pound steer. So, they would have to butcher the steer on the ground, right where it fell after the slaughter, and they would have to carry the carcass, piece by piece, to the house for processing.

The steer was lured out of the pasture by the promise of some corn in a feed bucket, and the pasture gate was closed behind it to keep the rest of the herd safely out of the way. The steer dutifully followed Jason, and the corn in the bucket, up to the fence closest to the house. The entire clan was in attendance, so that they could learn about home butchering. Martin had been trained in kosher ritual slaughter during his rabbinical studies, but those procedures were impossible under the current circumstances. They would have to use old-fashioned methods. Jason poured the corn on the ground, and when the steer lowered its head to eat, Jason shot it once in the center of the imaginary "X" between its eyes and its ears. The steer dropped immediately to its belly, and then rolled onto its right side. Jason put his left knee on the steer's left shoulder and used a sharp knife to cut the steer's throat, all the way to the spinal column. The still-beating heart pumped the steer's blood out onto the ground.

Roone, Walt, and Martin rolled the steer on its back, and held the steer's legs straight up to hold it in that position. Jason began by using a skinning knife to open the carcass along its belly, from its severed throat all the way to its tail, taking care not to puncture the digestive tract. Then Jason skinned the carcass, laying the hide on the grass, but leaving it attached to the steer's back. He pulled the guts out to one side and cut the liver away. Ellen came forward with a pot and collected the liver, while Jason removed the heart and kidneys and put them in the pot too. Ellen took the pot up to the house. Lunch would be liver and kidneys, with onions and sliced and fried heart.

Next, Jason severed the head with a hatchet, used a knife to cut the last strip of hide that connected the head to the body, and removed the tongue. Ellen returned from the kitchen, picked up the tongue, and took it up to the house to add to her pot. Sliced tongue and cornbread made a fine sandwich.

Jason then sliced the flesh of the flank and laid the meat on the hide next to the ribs. Miriam, Danielle, and Pilar picked up these cuts at Ellen's instruction, and headed off to the kitchen to put the meat through the hand-cranked meat grinder. Jason then removed both hocks—the rear legs and hips all the way up to the spine. Roone and Martin hefted these—they must have weighed well over 100 pounds each—over their shoulders and headed off to hang them on the hoist support that Jason had built for deer processing. Jason went back into the cavity to slice out as much fat as possible, setting it aside so that they could render it into tallow for Martin's Shabbos and Chanukah candles. Next, Jason removed the steer's forelegs, and with them, the chuck and the brisket. Roone and Martin hung these with the hocks. Then all four men worked together to strip the meat from the ribs, back strap, and tenderloin. Roone went to work on the stripped skeleton with a hatchet, and then sawed the bones into short sections, so that they would fit in Ellen's large stockpots, to be cooked down to a concentrated beef broth.

With the benefit of Jason's experience, the butchering process took the four men a little over four hours. The grinding process took the women an entire day, and the canning operation—browning all of the ground beef and preserving it in quart jars in the pressure canner—would take two and a half days and would require about 300-quart jars and lids. Labor-intensive as it was, the grinding and canning process still gave safer and more certain results than either dehydration into jerky or salting and curing, which were the only other options they had for preserving meat without refrigeration. Fortunately, Ellen had over 500 canning jars and over 900 sealing lids in inventory. The jars could be used over and over again, but the lids could only be re-used if they were opened very gently to prevent bending.

The newly enlarged clan would consume all the cold weather vegetables in the raised bed garden and the root cellar within a week or two, and they wouldn't have a spring harvest of these crops again until March or early April. These vegetables—cabbage, broccoli, brussels sprouts, and lettuce—had two growing seasons and were planted in late winter and again in late summer. Onions and garlic also were cold weather veggies, but onions only grew into bulbs in spring, and garlic was planted in the fall and harvested in spring.

So, their winter diet would consist of meat, dairy, and corn—and then still more meat, dairy, and corn. They would make corn cakes, corn bread, mashed corn, and succotash—but with soybeans instead of lima beans—creamed corn, and corn fritters. Jason had some "feed wheat" that he had bought as livestock feed, but now it was too valuable to use for livestock feed, or even for bread. They needed to use it as seed for next year's wheat crop. For variety, Ellen had planted lettuce seeds indoors, and hoped it would grow in the cold frames, but even that harvest was at least six weeks away. Jason and Ellen figured that they had enough tomato sauce in jars from last year's garden to make pasta and marinara sauce at least once per week, and they had enough canned potatoes so that they could serve them several nights per week.

"How long will this meat last us?" Miriam asked Ellen, as they cut the meat into cubes for Pilar to crank through the grinder.

"Well, let's see. I expect we will harvest about 600 pounds of meat from a 1,200-pound steer; that's what Jason guessed the steer weighed. We figured that, given our limited diet, all of us together would consume about 15 pounds of meat per day, so the meat from this steer will last us 40 days or so."

"I had no idea that 12 adults and three children would eat a massive animal like that every 40 days."

"Keep in mind that I'm just estimating," said Ellen.

"Yes," said Miriam, as she continued cutting meat into chunks for the meat grinder. "But it's close enough. What the hell are my people in New York City going to do? They don't have 50 cows in their backyards! They don't have pressure canners and 500 quart sized jars waiting in the pantry!"

"Oh, I can't even imagine it!" cried Danielle, as she dropped bones into the stock pots. She was tearing up. "I'm sorry. Since I've been pregnant, I get so emotional."

Ellen, who was closest to Danielle, came and put her right hand around Danielle's shoulders, holding a bloody handful of meat in her left. "It's okay, honey. I don't even want to think about you sailing in a boat for a week, especially in the dark, and then walking for a month when you're three months pregnant!"

"Don't remind me. And I think I am 18 or 19 weeks now! I was sick every morning on that damned boat and scared to death every night."

"I can only imagine," replied Ellen. "But thank God you did it. The future depends on you and your babies."

"And who is going to deliver this baby?" asked Danielle, in tears again.

Pilar wanted to say something, but the timing didn't seem right.

"Miriam, you're a doctor, right?" asked Ellen, hopefully. "You can deliver this baby, right?"

"I'm not that kind of 'doctor,'" said Miriam. "I have a Ph.D. in sociology. I teach women's studies."

"But you study about women, right? You must have studied something about childbirth."

"I'm afraid not," said Miriam.

"Well," said Ellen, turning back to Danielle. "Jason has delivered lots of babies—foals, calves, kids, and lambs—and he was there in the delivery room for all of our babies. If anyone can do it, he can."

With that, Miriam stood up, tossed the meat she had just cubed into the large mixing bowl in front of Pilar, and walked out the front door, headed for the guesthouse.

Ellen watched Miriam leave, a confused look on her face. She looked at Jenny, Pilar, and then Danielle. Jenny and Pilar said nothing, but Danielle, tilting her head to the side and shrugging her shoulders a little, said "It's okay. You didn't say anything wrong. She's some kind of super-feminist. I think she is having a hard time."

"Well," Jenny piped in. "She's not special. We're all having a hard time. We all are worried sick about our families, especially now that we see just how much food it takes to keep a family from starving." Jenny stopped what she was doing, put down the knife she was using, and started to cry. "Can you imagine what is happening back in New York right now? There are tens of millions of people there, and they are hundreds if not thousands of miles away from any source of food!"

"And it was 12 degrees here last night!" Danielle said. "And we are several hundred miles south of New York. My mother and father live in Vermont. They have a wood stove, but I don't know how much food or firewood they have."

Pilar could barely contain herself but managed to remain silent and let the older women talk. Even Danielle was ten years older than she was. Pilar, nauseous and trembling, kept cranking the grinder, taking cubed meat out of one mixing bowl, grinding it, and then catching the ground beef in another mixing bowl. Ellen continued to brown the ground meat in a cast-iron pan on the wood stove, and then pack it into quart-sized canning jars, for processing in the pressure canner.

"She should appreciate her husband," said Pilar, more to take the social pressure off than anything else. "I have never seen a more patient and hardworking man."

As if on cue, Martin stepped into the kitchen with an armful of firewood, placed it in the wood stove's firebox, and headed back outside like a man on a mission. He WAS on a mission—all of the men were. They hauled over 100 gallons of water by hand each day for the kitchen and kettle, fed the livestock first thing every morning and last thing every evening, and shoveled manure in between. They also were busy putting up next year's firewood, harvesting fallen trees in the woodlot, sawing limbs where they had fallen, splitting them by hand with a maul, stacking the pieces on a wagon, driving the horses to pull the loads to the woodshed, and then unloading and stacking the split firewood so that it could dry. While the women worked in the warm kitchen all day, the men were outside doing heavy work in the cold.

"Well, he is a Rabbi," said Jenny, as if that explained Martin's patience and good nature. She had regained her composure. "But I think all of us are being forced to recognize just how precarious our lives have become. Perhaps we even feel a little guilty that we are here, safe, well fed, and warm. Miriam is handling that in her own way. She'll come around. She doesn't have a choice. We are all she's got."

Ellen sat at the table with Jenny and Pilar, in the seat that Miriam had left empty, holding her baby girl in her sling. Pilar took one look at the contented face of Ellen's daughter nursing at her breast and couldn't hold it in any longer.

"I think I am pregnant."

All motion stopped in the kitchen. All eyes fixed on Pilar. Danielle came and joined the others at the table. Pilar surprised even herself with that admission. When she looked up, the three women looked at her with the expressions of wonder and astonishment that the mere mention of a new life seems to bring in these situations.

"You haven't told Roone yet, have you?" asked Jenny.

"No, I haven't."

Ellen leaned forward, carefully selecting her words and softening her countenance, remembering the fear she had felt with her first pregnancy. "Well, a woman knows when she is pregnant. How amazing this is! I am so happy for you."

"I'm scared to death," cried Pilar. "I don't know how this happened."

Jenny and Ellen laughed. Danielle was crying.

"I'm sorry," Danielle sniffled.

"Oh, my," said Ellen as she clapped her hands in celebration. "Two pregnant ladies in the house!"

"Hold on," said Jenny. "How sure are you?"

"I am at least three weeks late, and I have been sick for the last several mornings."

Now it was Jenny's turn to clap her hands and laugh in celebration. "Well, that's that!"

Pilar and Danielle seemed unable to join in Ellen and Jenny's festivities. They looked back and forth at the older women, unable to feel whatever it was that they were feeling at the moment. Jenny sensed the disconnect and said, "We know you are scared. Both of us have been there. And I know that the circumstances between 'then' and 'now' are very different. But we will get you through this." Jenny made sure to make eye contact and to smile confidently at both expectant mothers.

"When are you going to tell Roone?" asked Ellen.

"Tonight."

Ellen reached across the table and held Pilar's hand. "Don't worry. None of us will say a word to the men until you make your announcement." Ellen smiled and nodded her head to affirm her connection to Pilar. "A grandchild! Welcome to the family, Pilar."

Chapter 41

That evening, Pilar and Roone retreated to the bathroom
of the guesthouse, carrying two 5-gallon buckets that they
had filled with warm water from the wood-fired kettle, to use
for their evening "shower." The young lovers had developed
a system in which Roone would strip first and stand in the
tub, and then Pilar would pour water over Roone's body,
using an old bleach bottle that had been cut in half to form a
scoop. Roone then would lather himself with soap that they
had made from lard, lye, and sheep's milk. When Pilar's turn
came, Roone would pour the water over her, and then would
help with the lathering as well. Of course, Pilar didn't need
any help, but she enjoyed the intimacy of Roone's hands, as
he explored her body from head to toe. On this night, Roone
started at Pilar's neck and shoulders, and then went down to
her breasts, kissing her as he went. As he slid one hand down
to her stomach, with the other hand at the top of her buttocks,
she held his hand over her belly and said, "Be gentle here,"
as she looked into his eyes and gave him a coy smile.

He smiled back, at first unable to decipher the expression
on Pilar's face, but when her countenance did not change,
and she did not look away, but held his hand still over her
lower belly, it hit him. His head cocked up and to the side,
and his eyes widened, and he opened his mouth. Pilar nodded
to him and smiled with her lips and her eyes, without
showing her teeth.

"Oh, my God! You're kidding me! How did that happen?"
Pilar hit him in his belly with the back of her hand. His smile
stretched across his face. "Come here, baby." Roone kissed
her as his hands ran over her body and back to her belly over
and over again. "I told you, you're mine."

The following day, after the morning chores, the clan gathered around the table for their breakfast of cornbread and butter, ground meat, farmer's cheese, corn grits, and milk. Lunch and dinner would be more of the same, although potatoes and onions were served at supper on Tuesday, Thursday, and Saturday evenings. Burdock leaves were still available, but soon wouldn't be, and though they were bitter, they were edible, and the clan welcomed a little change in flavor.

Roone waited for the lull that came after everyone had finished eating, and before the women began to clear the table. The signal came when the kids headed outside to play. He reached for Pilar's hand and stood up.

"Pilar and I are expecting our first child."

First child?! The words stunned Pilar. She was still grasping at the idea of being pregnant, and Roone was already looking past this baby to a larger family. Pilar got over it quickly and loved her man all the more for his vision.

Jason looked over at Ellen. She was nodding her head in short quick bursts with a silly smile on her face. Jason realized then that he was the last to know. Roone looked at his father, seated to his immediate left at the head of the giant table. Jason stood up, and the two men embraced.

"Well done, big daddy!" Jason said into his son's ear.

When their embrace broke, they held each other's shoulders with their hands, and Roone said, "Ya happy there, grampa?"

"You fucking bet I am."

The women crowded around Pilar in a display of the maternal camaraderie and solidarity that women have known since the beginning of time—and of which men have remained clueless.

Martin rose and embraced his old friend and said, "Generations and generations to you, my brother. To life!"

"Thank you, Martin," said Jason.

Walt came to Jason, hugged his younger brother, and said, "In the midst of catastrophe, life goes on."

They paused and remembered that they had family out there enduring the famine. Jason hesitated, and then said, "I thought I was entering the age of irrelevance—and then Sarah was born. And now a grandchild is coming my way. I guess our job here is not done."

"I guess not," said Walt.

Manny came to Jason and hugged him and said, "Thank you. For everything."

"Manny," replied Jason, loud enough for all to hear. "There is an old saying, 'God has no grandchildren.' Our lives are only a single leg in a long, long relay race that has been going on for thousands of generations, and each generation must hand off the baton of *life* to the next. I wish for you and Danielle, and Roone and Pilar, a house full of children, and a long life to see those children through. And your father and I will do what we can to help provide a path to the future for your children."

Then Jason sat back down and took a deep breath, as did the other men. The women gathered around Pilar and Danielle. Miriam's lack of enthusiasm was not lost on any of them.

Chapter 42

The daylight hours were nearing their shortest of the year, and the men hustled about the farm to complete their chores after the happy news over breakfast that Roone and Pilar were expecting a child. Roone and Martin went to work firewood in the woodlot, Manny went to feed livestock, and Walt and Jason went to milk the cows. The sun would set a little before 4:30 pm. Ellen kept "clock time" for the household, using a wind-up watch that she had received as a gift before she met Jason. Everyone else knew only mealtimes, sunup, noon, and sundown as the measure of the time of day.

At twilight, just after sundown, some riders appeared out of the woodlot on their driveway. They were walking their mounts; the horses' heads hung low in fatigue. The children, the twins Aviva and Hanna, and Samuel and Sophia saw them first, and ran to the house to tell their parents. The adults all spilled out of the house and onto the front porch except Roone, who crossed over to the guesthouse, retrieved a .270 short-mag bolt-action rifle, and stood in the shadows. But there was no need for his precautions. It was McCoy O'Neil and his son, Trevor, trailed by four horses that appeared to be carrying two people each.

McCoy did not call out or hurry his horse up the drive. His travel companions trailed about 50 yards behind him. When he got to end of the walkway, McCoy dismounted and walked stiffly up to the porch.

"Howdy. I am applying to you good people for food and shelter for the night."

"Well, of course," said Jason, concealing his bewilderment at the sight of 8 very young women, sitting astride four exhausted horses, in the company of McCoy and Trevor O'Neil.

Roone came out of the guesthouse and walked towards McCoy and his party, to gather the horses and take them to the barnyard to be fed and watered. In spite of his exhaustion, McCoy smiled at Roone, winked at him, and said, "You're a careful bastard, ain't ya?" McCoy had seen him separate from the others and go to the guesthouse and had understood Roone's tactic immediately. Roone only nodded and went to help the women down from their horses. When one of the women leaned on him, Roone was surprised by how little she weighed. Roone, Manny, and Walt led the horses to the barn.

"Please come in," said Jason.

"Hello, sir," said Trevor.

"Hello, Trevor," Jason responded.

McCoy and Trevor stood next to the dining table that sat just to the right of the front door, while Ellen and Jenny led the eight women into the living area. The women sprawled on the floor without a word. Ellen left them there and walked to McCoy and Trevor for an explanation. Before she could say anything, McCoy said, nodding to the women on their living room floor, "Ma'am, those girls are hungry. Damn near starved."

Ellen shook her head in exasperation and looked at Jason.

"Who are they?" Jason asked.

"I don't know much about them. I guess we will have to wait for them to tell us their story."

"How'd they come to be in your company?" asked Jason.

"We ponied four horses up to E'town to see if we could find supplies, and maybe see if we could find some womenfolk who might be interested in meeting some of our menfolk."

"You mean you were out to kidnap women for your harem!" Miriam shrieked at them.

"Miriam! Stay out of this!" Martin roared at his wife.

McCoy looked at Martin and Miriam calmly, observing Martin's tzitzit hanging at his waist, and his kippah, the skullcap worn by orthodox Jews, and Miriam's ferocious expression.

"Who the hell are they?" McCoy asked Jason.

"Friends of mine. They live here with us."

McCoy just shrugged, ignored Miriam, turned to Ellen, and said, "They need whatever food you can spare 'em, Ma'am."

"Yes, of course!"

"I'll help," said Jenny, following Ellen to the summer kitchen. They poured two gallons of milk into a large pot and set it on the stove to warm. Then they filled 10 bowls with broth from the stockpot, opened several jars of the ground beef they just recently canned, scooped the meat out, and deposited it into the hot broth. Each of the women, including Miriam, grabbed two of the bowls. Ellen set hers down on the table for McCoy and Trevor and told the others to try to feed the girls where they were, lying on the living room floor. Ellen headed back to the kitchen, retrieved some stale cornbread that she had been saving to use in a pudding, brought it to the living room, instructed the women to dip it in the soup and feed it to the famished arrivals. Though weak, the girls were ravenous, and consumed the soup, meat, and bread without saying a word. Jenny retrieved the milk from the stove, and Ellen brought cups. The women drank the milk greedily, and then fell back to the floor, breathing heavily. Jenny, Danielle, and Pilar stood silent, mortified by the scene. Martin used this moment to whisper to his wife,

"Have you lost your mind? This is not the women's studies department at school! Keep your mouth shut."

Miriam responded by glaring at her husband, shooing the twins out the door, and leading them over to the guesthouse.

Walt watched the drama and felt terrible for his friend and erstwhile traveling companion, but now everyone was gathering around the table to hear McCoy describe his adventure to E'town, or Elizabethtown, a small city south of

Louisville, Kentucky. Miriam reappeared in the doorway of the summer kitchen, without the twins.

McCoy took no notice of the people sitting around him at the table until he had finished his soup and bread. He looked around, grabbed the cup of milk in front of him, slugged it down, wiped the milk off his mustache, looked at Ellen, and said, "Much obliged, Ma'am." Then he fell silent and slouched in his chair. Trevor finished up his soup and bread and did the same.

"Okay… so what happened?" asked Jason.

"This was our first trip out of the county. As you know, we've got a bunch of people living with us just like y'all got here. Only all y'all got mates. I got over a dozen young men without a woman. So, we figured we'd take a ride up to E'town and see what was going on in the world and see if we could meet anyone. We were not prepared for what we saw."

McCoy looked over at his son, who met his eyes for a moment, and then looked down at his empty soup bowl.

"Are any of you familiar with the Ukrainian Holodomor?"

"I am," Martin said.

McCoy looked at him and nodded. "Well, that's what we saw. It's the American Holodomor. That's what it is."

McCoy fell silent. Jason looked up at Martin and signaled with his hands, "What?"

"In the Soviet Union in the early 1930's, Josef Stalin engineered the greatest manmade famine in history. Millions died from starvation. He…"

"Not no more," McCoy interrupted. They waited for him to complete his thought, but it appeared McCoy was finished.

"'Not no more' what?" Jason asked McCoy.

"Ukraine's Holodomor ain't the world's greatest manmade famine no more. This one is. Go look at those girls in there. There ain't nothing to 'em, and they was better off than the others. From what I gather, after their families died, they took up residence at the high school. I ain't never seen nothin' so pathetic in my life. There's a bunch more kids there, but lots of 'em couldn't even get up. At first, I was afraid someone might shoot my horses, they was so hungry lookin'. But they was so weak, ain't no chance they could've held up a rifle, let alone butcher a horse. We took the ones we thought most likely to live."

"I notice you didn't 'save' any young men." Miriam just couldn't help herself.

McCoy made a sound between a scoff and a chuckle, nodded his head a few times, and said, "I guess that's so. We got enough mouths to feed. We don't need any more men. And we don't need no old ladies, neither." Here McCoy paused and regarded Miriam, who met his eyes without flinching, using all the contempt she could muster. Martin rolled his eyes in exasperation. McCoy addressed Miriam.

"I don't know who you are or what's goin' on with you. But what we saw out there was a human die-off. The next generation, if there is one, won't be coming from women your age, lady. My people need women who can make babies, not old ladies who ain't nothin' but trouble."

Then McCoy turned to Jason and said, "Yankee, I am sorry to have troubled you. But I ain't getting any younger either, and I gotta get some sleep."

"Yes, of course." Then he turned to Ellen and Jenny and said, "I guess we will stoke up the big stove to keep everybody warm and they can all sleep on the living room rug."

"That'd be fine with us," said McCoy. He and Trevor stood up, walked over to the living room, slid onto the rug, and then rolled over on their backs. They were asleep almost immediately.

Jason's clan stood there and looked on in stunned silence at the refugees sleeping on their living room floor.

Chapter 43

Ellen and Jason got up before first light, to stoke the fire in the kitchen cook stove, and then the fire in the big stove in the living room. McCoy and Trevor were still asleep, but some of the girls were awake. Ellen had a terrible thought that maybe they had died with their eyes open, but then she saw their eyes blink, which told her that they were alive.

Jason went to the workshop to retrieve a salted and cured side of bacon. There were four sides of bacon hanging out there. They were saving them for special occasions or emergencies. Jason felt that eight starving teenagers qualified as an emergency. When he came back to the house with the bacon, Walt was sitting at the table, and Jenny and Ellen were holding milk for the girls on the floor to drink. Ellen left Jenny with the girls, went to Jason, and said, "I think we can afford to grind some wheat for them, too."

Jason shook his head. "They won't know the difference between cornbread and wheat bread. We need to keep the wheat for crop seed. I will take a jar of tomato sauce over to the Millers' house and see if I can't trade it for eggs."

The Millers, an elderly Amish couple who had never had any children, lived halfway to Roscoe Cutliff's dairy farm.

Ellen said, "Take a jar of ground sausage and a jar of tomato sauce and ask for two dozen eggs. Tell them what's going on here."

"Alright, I'll ask. If it was summer and the chickens were laying heavy, I am sure that wouldn't be a problem. But chickens don't lay well in winter. I doubt they will have that many eggs."

"It can't hurt to ask."

"Okay. I'll be back in 20 minutes."

Ellen sliced the bacon from the hide as Jenny mixed corn flour and milk in a stainless-steel mixing bowl. The cook stove was up to temperature, so Ellen retrieved the big cast-iron pans from the rack in the summer kitchen, placed them on the stove, and dropped a dollop of butter in one. In the other, she placed a handful of fatty bacon slices. Jenny stood next to her and poured the corn paste into the pan with the butter. By the time the bacon was cooked, Jason was back from the Millers' house with two dozen fresh eggs.

"They were pretty excited about the tomato sauce," said Jason as he handed the eggs to Ellen.

Ellen went back to the stove and flipped the cornbread from its pan into the pan that held the bacon fat. The pan smoked as the bread soaked up the bacon fat. Ellen then loaded some butter into the other pan and used it to scramble a dozen eggs. In a few more minutes, Ellen, Jason, Walt, and Jenny were sitting on the floor of the living room, helping the young women from E'town eat a breakfast of scrambled eggs, bacon, and fatty cornbread, all washed down by vast quantities of milk. It was the most food the girls had eaten in 40 days, and the response was immediate. They sat up on their own, and then got up and went outside to relieve themselves. They were a mess. Their clothes were soiled, and the wool hats that they wore made them look more like homeless drug addicts than high school cheerleaders and athletes.

McCoy and Trevor didn't stir until one of the girls slammed the door when coming back into the house. When they finally got up, Ellen pointed them to the table, and fed them the same fare that she had given the girls.

Ellen pulled Jason to the summer kitchen and said, "I don't think these girls are in any condition to travel."

"Well, they don't have far to go, maybe a two-hour ride. We can't afford to feed them. They have to go."

"We can afford to feed them one more meal and wash their clothes for them. They need a bath."

"Well, that's fine, but then they gotta go. We have our own problems."

Ellen frowned. "I don't know how I feel about this."

"Oh, yeah?" Jason was losing his patience. "How would you feel about your own children looking like those girls? Enough! Feed them, wash them, but they are out of here after lunch." Jason walked out of the summer kitchen and over to the table where McCoy and Trevor were eating their breakfast. Jason was hungry himself, and the smell of the food, and the sight of McCoy and Trevor chowing down, was getting to him. When he sat down, McCoy looked up at him.

"Much obliged here, Jason." McCoy didn't call him "Yankee." "I know I brung a burden down on you here. Just let me say that I 'preciate it and that I will return the favor."

McCoy looked as sincere as an Eagle Scout, and Jason believed him. Jason also felt bad that he had continued to misjudge this man. You might not like what came out of McCoy's mouth, but no one could accuse him of trying to deceive.

"I hope it all works out for you, and for them," said Jason as he cocked his head towards the girls still sitting in his living room.

"Well, they look a whole lot better than they looked yesterday," said McCoy.

"That's for sure," said Trevor.

Ellen came to the table and said to Jason, "I only have enough hot water on the stove to wash the dishes. I need a kettle full of water and a fire. We can give them all a bucket of hot water and a few minutes in the tub. There's not enough time to wash their clothes and get them dry, and it's too cold to ride in wet clothing."

Roone heard this and said to his father, "I'm on it."

"Hey, Jason," said McCoy. "Ask your son here if he will lend his hunting rifle to Trevor." And then to Trevor, "Hey, sit yourself up on the hill behind the farmhouse in among those hay rolls. You'll have a clear shot of the tree line for 300 yards east and west."

Jason just nodded to Roone, and Trevor said, "That ain't a bad idea."

"Yeah, I bet our new friends and our hosts wouldn't mind greasin' their chins with some venison ribs for lunch."

"Honey," Jason called to Ellen. "See if you can figure out who among those ladies would best be willing to talk and tell us what happened to them."

Then Jason stood up and said to no one in particular, "I got chores to do."

McCoy and Jason were on their way to the barn when they heard the report of the rifle. The men looked at each other, wide-eyed and all smiles.

"Trevor never misses," said McCoy; his demeanor had gone from tired to energetic in the split second of the rifle shot. "Let's go see what he got."

The two men turned back towards the house and walked to the hayfields behind it, climbing the hill to the place where Trevor had hidden among the large round hay bales. Trevor was at least 200 yards up the pasture from where they walked; a deer carcass lay on the ground 50 yards farther up.

"I told you. That boy's been hunting since he was ten years old. His nickname should be 'one shot.'"

After Roone filled the kettle with water and set a proper fire in the firebox, Ellen had him start a fire in the wood stove in the guesthouse. She also asked Roone and Manny to get whatever they needed from their bedrooms, as the women would be commandeering the use of the guesthouse for their female guests.

They let the water in the kettle get almost hot enough to boil, and then mixed cold water from the rainwater tanks with hot water from the kettle until the temperature of the bathing water was comfortable. This would give them about 100 gallons of warm water, enough for each of the visitors to enjoy a luxurious pour over shower. Ellen, Jenny, and Pilar hauled water into the guesthouse in 5-gallon buckets, and Ellen retrieved the first of their guests for her shower. They were not prepared for what they saw.

All of the women wore wool hats and had not taken them off since they had arrived. When the girl removed her hat, they saw that she had only stubble for hair. When she undressed, they saw that her pubic hair had also been shaved, and her undergarments were soiled. The smell of body order, feces, and urine permeated the air.

"Who did this to you?" Miriam asked, a little too sternly for Ellen's taste.

"I did," the girl answered in a monotone voice.

"Why would you do this to yourself?" Miriam asked in disbelief.

The girl stood naked and perfectly still before them, like a sick animal at a livestock auction. She gave a one-word answer to the question,

"Lice."

"Oh, you poor thing!" cried Jenny. Ellen and Pilar were also in tears.

"Let's get you cleaned up," said Ellen.

Ellen turned to Pilar and said, "Please go find Jason, have him wait outside the door, and then come and get me."

Pilar, relieved to be sent on an errand away from what she saw here, took off. She returned quickly and signaled to Ellen that Jason was waiting at the door.

Ellen left their charge to Jenny and Pilar and went to Jason.

"Please," she said, her eyes filled with tears. "I need you to go over to Abraham's and ask him to collect eight dresses from the women in their community. We will bring them back in a few days."

Jason began to object, but Ellen put her hand to his mouth and said, "They've got lice and have soiled their clothes with diarrhea. And they are emaciated. They won't live…" Ellen was shaking as she said this, unable to finish her thought.

Jason made no more objections. He nodded his head and walked off to the barn, where he saddled his horse Thunder, harnessed his mule Lady with pack baskets, and set off for Abraham's farm.

Jason returned with full-length Amish style dresses for eight women. The women were welcome to keep the clothes if they wished, but if they chose not to wear them again, the Amish wanted them returned. They also gave Jason a 5-pound bag of rice and a 2-pound bag of dried black beans. As always, Jason could only marvel at their kindness and generosity.

By the time Jason arrived back at the farm, the last of their visitors was in the tub, scrubbing with strong homemade lye soap as Jenny poured water over her head. Trevor was in the grass next to the raised bed garden, roasting venison joints on a metal grill over an open fire. Walt had finished milking the three cows alone. Roone and Martin were driving a team of horses up the hayfield from the woodlot, hauling a load of firewood. Jason knocked on the door of the guesthouse, and Pilar appeared. Jason handed her the bundle of clothes and left for the kitchen, where he deposited the rice and beans on the counter. When Jason looked out the kitchen window, he could see Trevor slicing meat from the joints on the grill. Pilar collected the meat on a plate, and when she turned, Trevor's eyes followed her as she walked back to the guesthouse with the meat for their guests.

It occurred to Jason that young men without female companionship, left to their own devices, were a disaster waiting to happen. He now accepted McCoy's reasoning on the subject as sound.

Ellen walked into the kitchen. Jason turned to her, held up the rice and beans, and said, "Courtesy of Abraham."

"Oh! Wasn't that nice of them," answered Ellen. "We boiled their underwear and hung them on a drying rack by the stove in the guest house, and we've got their clothes out in a burn pile in the pasture, if one of the men could set fire to it."

"How are they doin'?"

"Well, they're young and strong. But they are ravenous, gorging on deer meat and sitting around the stove in their new Amish dresses. It's quite a sight."

"I'd like to talk to them."

"Two of them seem positively chatty. The others are pretty far down. They are going to need some time."

"Well, let's bring those two in here, the other six can settle in the living room and join in if they feel like it. And let's keep feeding them as you cook up the rice and beans. Make it feel like we are just visiting over lunch. I am not trying to traumatize them any more than they are already. I'll meet you back here in a bit. I'm going to round up McCoy, Martin, and Walt."

Chapter 44

Martin found his way to the house without Jason and sat next to Miriam at the table with Tara and Suellen, the two young women who Ellen felt were most willing to talk. Jason and McCoy opened the front door, but Ellen stopped them there and told them to take their boots off before coming in. The other girls were sitting on the floor in the living room. Martin was cranking the grinder, making corn flour from corn. Everyone took turns running the grinder, as it took a couple of hours each day to grind a day's worth of meal for the clan. Martin was fascinated by the mill, and while grinding was impressively laborious, he wondered what they would do if they didn't have the thing. He figured they would think of something.

Jason smiled and said, "Hello," to the two young women seated at his table with their crew-cut hair and Amish dresses.

They responded, "Hello," in unison.

"This is my husband, Jason," Ellen said to the young women from across the kitchen.

"Yes, Ma'am," said Tara. The two women looked at Jason, and said his name, "Jason," together, and nodded to him.

"Well, I see you are feeling better today," Jason said hopefully. "Would you like some more milk?"

"Thank you, no," said Tara. "I've been eating all morning, and for the first time in over a month I feel like I've had enough to eat."

Jason smiled, more to acknowledge Ellen's assessment of "chatty" than in response.

"I am glad to hear that. You frightened us last night."

"I hardly remember anything from yesterday," said the other woman, Suellen. "I remember getting on a horse with Tara and holding on. I remember getting off and being fed on the floor and then waking up this morning and being fed again. But it was like a dream. I feel like I am just waking up."

"I think you will be okay now. Do you remember what happened?"

"You mean after the lights went out?"

"Yes."

"I remember everything," said Suellen. "It's just that in the last, I don't know how many exactly, maybe ten days or so, we got so weak that it was hard to tell when we were sleeping and when we were awake."

Tara kept her eyes down on the table and nodded as her friend spoke.

"We had basketball practice. But then somebody came into the gym and said WWIII just started, or something like that. The coach called practice, and I drove Tara home. We waited there for her mother to come home, but after a while, we decided to go over to my house. Just as we pulled into the driveway, the electricity went out. And it never came back on."

"And my mother never came back home," Tara added in a low tone.

"Was your mother at work?" Miriam asked Tara. "What about your father?"

"Yes," said Tara. "She is a Registered Nurse at General Hospital in Louisville. My parents are divorced. My father drives a truck cross-country. He never came home, either."

Martin and Miriam looked at each other but remained silent. Walt stepped into the house from the summer kitchen entrance but did not take a seat. He leaned on the counter and listened in on the conversation at the table.

"So, you stayed at Suellen's house?" asked Miriam.

"Yes."

"And your parents were home, Suellen?" Jason asked.

"My mom and my step-dad. My father lives in Indianapolis."

"Okay," Jason continued. "But you had people, your family, around you."

"For a while."

"What happened then? What did you do?"

Suellen shrugged and said, "We did the same thing that everybody else did."

Tara and Suellen's eyes were glued to the table. Jason looked around, finally making eye contact with Ellen by the stove. She nodded for him to go on.

"What was that? What did everybody do?"

"We sat around and waited for the lights to come back on," said Suellen.

"I walked home to my house every day looking for my mother," said Tara. "But she never came home."

"In less than a week, there wasn't even a cracker left to eat in the house," said Suellen. "Then the water to the house stopped running. We went out looking for food, but there was nothing to find. Then the weather turned cold and rainy. We ran out of gasoline in the car after about a week, too. We would sit in there to get warm and charge our cell phones, hoping to get a signal. The house was freezing."

"What did your parents do?"

"What could they do? My mom and step-dad were not healthy people. My step-dad was obese, and my mom was morbidly obese. On the 21st day 'After,' my step-dad died. We found him in his recliner in the morning. We couldn't even budge him, he was so big. So, Tara and I went out to look for help. We found some classmates, boys, but when we got back home, we found my mother dead in the garage. She put some twine around her neck, hung it from a coat hook, and sat down and strangled herself."

Miriam gasped. Ellen and Jenny were already in tears. Tara and Suellen did not cry. They never lifted their eyes from the table.

"How did you come to be at the high school?" asked McCoy.

"After Suellen's parents died, we went with our classmates," said Tara. "They had a thing they called a 'rocket stove' for cooking in an emergency. They managed to kill a few cats and a dog with guns, but they never got a deer or anything. By the 30th day of the blackout, there wasn't a pet left in E'town. The boys tried to keep warm by setting up the rocket stove in one of the locker rooms and venting it outside, but it didn't work. The locker room was warmer than our house because it was half below ground, but it was still freezing. We went out dumpster diving and trash can picking but we were starving. We were sleeping most of the day, just waiting to die, when someone in the locker room said there were men with horses outside. Most of the kids were too weak to stand up and walk, but the rest of us wandered outside. We had been in a trance for days by then, and we didn't wake up from that until this morning."

Jason was sure there was much more to their story, but he didn't want to press them. It would all be known in due time. Jason looked around and noticed that Roone and Pilar were not there. He guessed they had seen enough out on the road and didn't need to hear any more.

Miriam was less thoughtful than Jason.

"So, what are your plans now?"

"Miriam…" Martin said softly, but he was interrupted before he could finish.

"Plans?" asked Tara. "We don't have any plans, Ma'am. Right now, I am thankful to be alive. This gentleman here," she gestured towards McCoy, "has offered us food and fellowship with his family at his farm. I don't think we would have survived if he hadn't found us."

"Have you given this any thought?" Miriam was becoming agitated. "Eight young girls living with strange men?"

Suellen and Tara looked around at the other people gathered in the kitchen, and then back at Miriam.

"You're not from here, are you?" said Suellen.

"What does that have to do with anything?"

"Miriam..." said Martin, losing his patience.

"And you haven't listened to a word I said. We've been living in a freezing high school locker room with our starving classmates. Our parents, and most of the people their age in E'Town are dead. We need food and a place to sleep. We need fellowship, family, and men to protect us. What would you have us do? Build a log cabin in the wilderness with our bare hands and hunt for rabbits? Rub two sticks together to make a fire? These men came to rescue us, and their neighbors took them in without question and fed and washed us. Obviously, y'all think very highly of these men, or you wouldn't have taken them, and us, into your home."

"I think you are naïve. What do you think they want from you? Their men are going to want to have sex with you," Miriam hissed.

Suellen regarded Miriam with an expression of bewilderment.

"I hope the good Lord sends me a man who wants me, and who will protect me, and take care of me. And I will take care of him. My stepfather was a helpless wimp who couldn't protect and care for my mother. That's why she killed herself, isn't it? She had a real man, but she got herself involved with women who sound an awful lot like you, and she lost him. If she still had a real man who could take care of her, would she have killed herself? And you're worried that these men came looking for me because they need women in their lives? That they have resources and are willing to work hard to provide for me in exchange for the pleasure of my company? Thank the Lord for such men. I grew up in the country. My grandfather was a farmer. I know a real man when I see one. And look at you! You got yourself a real man to take care of you, to put food on the table, and to keep you safe and warm. I haven't once seen you put wood in that stove, but I watched your husband do it. I see a real man out there in the cold squatting over a fire cooking deer meat for us girls to eat as we sat around a warm stove. That's the kind man I want. You didn't come looking for us, and I'm damn sure you didn't shoot that deer, gut it, and drag it back here to feed us. What do you do for anyone besides you? You can't even respect your husband by keeping quiet when he was trying to keep you from embarrassing yourself."

Miriam fumed and glared at Suellen, but Suellen wasn't having any of it, and glared right back. Everyone else traded embarrassed glances, except for McCoy, who kept his head down and his eyes on the table, and tried hard not to smile, but just couldn't help himself.

"A country girl will speak her mind," McCoy said with a chuckle. "And you're worried about her?" He directed his question to Miriam.

"I can't speak for anyone else," Suellen said to McCoy. "But I am grateful to you and would be honored to go with you and see if I can fit in with y'all. I need help, and I will be helpful, too."

"Me, too," said Tara.

Miriam stood up from the table and stormed out of the farmhouse, with Martin in pursuit. He caught up with her in the guesthouse. He shooed the twins outside and closed the door behind him.

"Have you lost your mind?!" Martin shouted at Miriam. "These people have been living here for 200 years. They walked here—fucking barefoot!—after they took a rickety boat across the ocean. And when they got here, they didn't have a fully stocked farm and a warm stove waiting for them; they had to carve a life out of the wilderness. Lots of them perished. These people are the descendants of the survivors. And you are going to come out here and tell the women they don't need their men?"

"Martin, we can't stay here with these people! They're sick! They are treating those girls like heifers in a herd, ready for breeding! Our daughters are not safe here!"

"Not safe here? Are you kidding? This is the only place they *are* safe! Do you understand what is going on out there? It is *winter*! There's no food! No fuel! No electricity! People are freezing and starving to death, and our daughters are enjoying pony rides and playing in the hayloft!"

"Oh, yeah?" Miriam was hysterical now. "How long before they are going for a roll in the hay with one of the local rednecks?!"

Martin became stark raving calm again. This was only the second time he had ever raised his voice back at Miriam, and he was disappointed in himself for sinking to her emotional level. He waited for her to recognize the change in his demeanor.

"Well, I am deeply disappointed to hear you disparage these good people in that way. These 'rednecks,' to use your words, broke their bread with us, protected us, watched over our children, and took us into their home."

"Martin, they're not Jewish! We can't stay here! We are a people apart! We are God's chosen people! These people, your friend and his family, they might be good people, *but they are not our people!*"

Just then, Roone opened the door to the bedroom he shared with Pilar. Martin and Miriam forgot that Roone and Pilar had not been in the kitchen as they listened to Suellen and Tara. Miriam was horrified. Martin could only blink at Roone a few times, like a moose in the headlights. Martin was too big to be a deer.

"Miriam," Roone began. "Perhaps a thousand years from now, *our people*, yours and mine, will tell the story of your Exodus before the storm. How our Creator led you out of the darkness, to a family who became your family. How you survived a perilous journey by sail and by foot, to find a new promised land. And how our children, yours and mine, became a great people who resettled a continent after the Creator wiped the land clean."

Pilar came and stood by her man and took his hand in hers. Roone continued.

"It appears to me that *we* are the chosen people—chosen to survive. Or perhaps it is the end of the line for your family. 10,000 generations before you, who passed you the beauty of life, could very well end with your children. I don't know what you've done exactly, but I can guess. You have to find a way to forgive yourself. What's done is done. You have other children. Encourage them to love their men. When their time comes, let them enjoy the buoyant surge of new life that only a *man* can fill them with. Give them generations and generations to come. Your daughters don't need to know what you have done, but you must stop filling them with your anger and hatred, or all is lost for them, and for you. You will need your children and grandchildren to care for you in your old age, and your daughters will need their children and grandchildren. As my father said, 'God has no grandchildren.'"

Miriam turned on Martin, and half hissed, half pleaded, "What did you tell them?"

Martin's mind reeled with Roone's penetrating analysis. If a 24-year-old kid could see it all so clearly, there must have been many others along the way who had seen it too. All of the anger and rage in Miriam's life was little more than a thinly veiled coping mechanism for the guilt and the feelings of inadequacy she carried. If you surrounded yourself entirely with women who also had aborted a child, well, it was possible to think that killing an unborn child must be right and just. But here they were confronted by people who didn't think it was right and just, and who couldn't be intimidated into silence. In the aftermath of the greatest man-made cataclysmic event in human history, human life suddenly had become manifestly more precious.

Ever since Miriam had left her Manhattan apartment, the raw difficulties of survival had exposed the philosophical contradictions, logical fallacies, and intellectual failures of her brand of bloodthirsty man-hating Feminism. Now she was choking on the enormity of her failures. Miriam had no idea how to fry an egg, to say nothing of how to care for a chicken. She didn't know how to fish, and cutting bait was beneath her. Miriam was helpless. Worse, without the inherent violence of a government that was willing to use force in exchange for votes, she was *powerless*.

"I never betrayed your confidence," Martin said, his voice soft and sad.

"I hope you will reconsider," said Roone. "You are a good man, Martin. My father always valued your friendship. He will be very sad if you leave us. And so, will I. But right now, there is work to be done, and we are losing daylight."

Tara and Suellen followed Ellen and Jenny out of the farmhouse and back to the guesthouse, passing Martin and Roone on the way. Martin headed for the house, but Roone peeled off for the barn, where the horses were tied, still hitched to the wagonload of firewood. When Martin stepped into the kitchen, he saw McCoy, Walt, and Jason still seated at the table.

"Come on and have a seat, Martin," said Jason. "You look like you could use a cup of coffee."

"Yes, I think I will. I hate to leave all the firewood to Roone."

"He'll live without you," said Jason.

Martin collapsed into one of the chairs and Walt poured him a cup of coffee.

"It's smokin' hot, brother," said Walt.

Martin leaned his huge frame over his elbows on the table, the muscles on the top of his shoulders bulging up to his ears. With his short grey beard, skull-cap, frayed and greying white shirt, and coffee cup held in his thick hands, he looked like a Viking who had gotten lost in the wrong costume shop.

"I want to go to Louisville," said Martin.

"For what?" asked Walt. "We just got here."

"Martin," said Jason. "It's almost 100 miles to Louisville, and it's winter."

"That's why I have to go immediately. I am not asking you to go with me. I am asking you for a horse."

"You don't even know how to fuckin' ride a horse," said Walt. "Are you back on that 'my people' stuff? Is that why you wanna go to Louisville?"

McCoy looked back and forth at the three of them. He seemed thoroughly amused, but he kept quiet.

"If people are starving… maybe I could help."

"Oh, yeah?" asked Walt. "How? Are you going to call in the U.N. with a relief effort for 'Martin's people' of Louisville? We don't have enough to feed the mouths we've got. There are plenty of people right here you can help. Your *new* people."

"Walt, I appreciate everything you've done for me. But I need to know what is going on out there."

"Bullshit. You're back to worrying about a bunch of strangers and not giving a fuck about us, the people who saved your ass."

There was silence around the table as Walt fumed and Martin refused to address Walt. It was McCoy who broke the silence.

"Whoa. You two fellas oughta get married."

Jason shot McCoy a look. McCoy put his hands up in mock surrender and averted his eyes to the table as he pretended to try to not to smile.

"I'm just teasing 'em. You Yankees argue like married couples, is all. Why can't you two just get to the dang point?"

"The point here is that Martin wants to go riding off to look for trouble because he feels guilty that he ain't starving to death," said Walt.

"Martin, what about your wife and daughters?" asked Jason. "They need you. We need you. We've got enough responsibility around here. What if something happens to you? Do you want your daughters to be raised in a fatherless home in a Gentile community?"

The question caught Martin up short. Jason pressed on.

"I guess this is as good a time as any to talk about it. We are okay for this winter, but that was because we were surrounded by a sea of corn and soybeans that got planted before the grid went down. That fortunate circumstance no longer exists. We will need to plant, cultivate, and harvest a year's worth of food in the upcoming 12-week growing season. If anything goes wrong, we will suffer in ways I don't even want to think about. Some of it is beyond our control. A drought could kill us all. We need to make a plan for the growing season, and then execute the plan perfectly."

"Jason," said Martin. "At some point, the grid will come back up. McCoy is already refining crude oil and fabricating metal parts. Thousands of other people are reestablishing production. Industrialization is not dead. The world is not coming to an end. Markets will reestablish themselves."

"No, industrialization not dead. But you forgot something."

"What's that?"

"Economics. By all reports, we've lost a significant percentage of the population. By the end of winter, I think you can essentially count on the loss of all human life in places like New York City, Chicago, Philadelphia, and Boston, in fact, in all of the big northern states. Famine in Southeast Asia or sub-Saharan Africa takes time to kill. But famine and winter is a deadly combination. It won't take any time at all."

"What the hell does that have to do with economics?" asked Martin with some impatience.

"First, this is the ultimate deflationary event. The value of almost everything, except food, oil, and perhaps coal, has already dropped to zero. The money supply dropped to zero, credit creation dropped to zero, and the velocity of money dropped to zero. Second, the system is going to rapidly corrode in place because the maintenance workers who kept it up are all dead."

Jason and Martin's eyes met, and Jason just nodded his head over and over.

"I can tell you my gold and silver coins ain't worth nothing," said McCoy.

"English, please," said Walt.

"If you want a car," Jason answered Walt. "You can have your pick out on 41E for free. Want a house? Most of the houses in the county are vacant. Just move in, and it's yours. Need a set of steak knives? Or a pair of shoes? By the end of winter, 90% of the people will be gone, but all their stuff will still be here."

Then Jason addressed McCoy. "Yes, indeed. Precious metals might be precious again in a decade or two, or maybe not. Right now, horse-drawn turning plows and hay mowers and such are the only metal worth anything. Those lunatic survivalists or preppers or whatever they call themselves now, with their guns and silver, will not survive the winter."

Then Jason turned back to Martin. "I am not telling you your business, my old friend, but it is just supply and demand. We've got an infinite 'supply' of everything but food and subsequently people, at least in the short term. And 'demand' is starving to death—or is already dead."

"So?" asked Walt. "More for us, right?" He looked back and forth between Jason and Martin. McCoy sat perfectly still, but he was listening intently and taking it all in.

"More of the stuff we don't need," said Jason. "And disaster for us if anything goes wrong with our food supply. There is only one growing season per year."

"Yes," said Martin. "I see what you are getting at."

"Great," said Walt. "Now will someone please tell me what the hell you're getting at?"

"My assertion that power will be reestablished soon from the three major grids, the east coast, west coast, and Texas electrical grids, is probably wrong," said Martin. "Local grids will reestablish themselves at some point over the next couple of years, as will local markets for everything from apples to zinc, but long supply lines are years away."

"Years away?" asked Jason. "Would you trust a bridge in five years? All the infrastructure, the bridges, tunnels, ports, railroads, and sewers and drainage systems, are going to fall apart without maintenance, and there is no shot that the surviving population can maintain an infrastructure system of this size. But let's get back to the 800-pound gorilla in the room. We—and our livestock—can only eat what we produce during the growing season, at least until we can establish a surplus. So, if anything goes wrong during the growing season here, we will have to live with what we've got for a year, until the next growing season. And even if by some miracle a large portion of the American population survived the winter, without nitrogen-based fertilizer the grain and bean crop will shrink 80%, even if we planted the same number of acres, and that's not going to happen. In all the history of civilization, it was grain production that determined population levels. We are not hunter-gatherers."

"All the more reason for me to try to see if any of my people are alive in Louisville," said Martin.

"Martin…" Jason was speaking gently to his old friend. "We have a much bigger demographic problem than 'your people' to contend with. Except for the Amish community, I see almost no children between the ages of one and ten in the county, few between 11 and 20, and too many of us are in our 40's and 50's. If we don't do something about it, this place is going to look like an old-age-home wrapped around an elementary school in just a few years. We are missing an entire generation of people. I think McCoy understands that. His solution is over in the guesthouse."

"Miriam seems to think you are treating those girls like breeding heifers," Martin said to McCoy.

"I haven't treated 'em like anything. All I did—with y'all's help—was save their lives. I left the men to die. I reckon these girls got a bargain. But I tell you what, there Martin. Y'all better get your heads out of your asses. Wait 'till you see what's goin' on out there before you pass any judgments. Jason understands me, and he understands the situation. He's still just too damn much of a politically correct Yankee to say so."

"So, what is the situation?" asked Martin.

"Your wife's right about one thing. Every good rancher understands herd management. This ain't no different than that. We need young'uns, and we need women for that. We need men to work, and there's a lot of work to be done. You can have women without a man, but you cannot have men without a woman, or they will set to killing each other to get the ratios back in order. I don't want to lose my son any more than you wanna lose your'n. You know why warfare came into existence? To kill off enough men to even out the deaths of women in childbirth, so keep that in mind when you start looking down your nose at me."

"I am sorry if it appeared that way," said Martin. "I assure you, I meant no disrespect."

McCoy looked at Martin for a few moments before answering. Then he said, "No, I guess you didn't. I can't be blaming you for your wife. I can see that you're an earnest son-of-a-bitch. It's hard to get a fix on you."

"Martin is a Rabbi and a very learned man," Jason said to McCoy.

"Oh, yeah?" said McCoy, visibly irritated. "Well, I'm pretty smart myself. Both y'all are mathematicians, right? Well, us engineers got a lot of math under our belts, too. And the mathematics of demographics just ain't that complicated. I can run one bull with 25 cows and build an empire, but if I run 25 bulls with one cow, within a year, I'll have a dead cow and 24 dead bulls. We all know the rules if we want our families to survive into the future. Men are expendable. Women are invaluable—if they make babies—but their politics became an unmitigated disaster for our culture."

"Some people might be offended by that," said Martin. "They might even think you're a sexist asshole."

"Well, who would 'they' be? It seems to me that the people given to such notions are all dead. So, I expect it's a moot point. Maybe it's supposed to be this way. Maybe the Creator used a flood last time, and famine this time, if you believe such things. But it seems to me, given the political environment of the past century, that women are incompatible with liberty. They will happily vote away all of our God-given rights, to an Authoritarian State, in exchange for a sense of security—and for control over men. Maybe we won't let that happen again."

"What the hell are you talking about, McCoy?" asked Martin.

"Civilization has been around for what? 12,000 years? How long have men had the right to vote?"

"Don't change the subject!" said Martin.

"I'm not! Answer the fucking question!" McCoy responded. "Never mind. Men have had the right to vote for only a little over 200 years in the 12,000 years of civilization. Men handed the right to vote over to women without a shot fired almost 100 years ago. It's just math, fellas. Men did not have the right to vote for over 98% of the timeline for civilization—and we bled the ground red to get it—and women did not have right to vote for 99%. Where is the oppression in that? It's a 1% difference. That's a rounding error."

"Huh," said Walt. "Is that true?"

"Please," Martin said to Walt. "Don't encourage him."

"Encourage me to do what?" asked McCoy. "We're just talking. All the PC police are dead! From my perspective, since the day women began voting they have voted to injure liberty at every turn. Prohibition, the War on Drugs, gun control, the onerous family law that destroyed the fabric of society, and endless wars that murdered millions of men. Who voted for all that? When the war in Afghanistan started to lose public support, a photo of an Afghan woman who had her nose cut off by her husband suddenly appeared everywhere in the news. American women responded by sending another couple thousand of their sons off to die. Not their daughters—their sons. American women seem perfectly willing to send their sons off to kill and die to make the world fair for women they never met. Think about that one for a moment. Like I said, women's politics seems utterly incompatible with male liberty."

"I am not going dignify that with an answer," said Martin.

"Of course not. I haven't said anything that you can refute. What did I say that offended you? That men had no right to vote for 98% of civilization? And women were the driving force behind the prohibition of alcohol and drugs that created black markets and filled our prisons and killed hundreds of thousands of men? That millions of men died in wars that women voted for? You should be offended. But not at me. Shit, I ain't even got to religion yet.

"But hold on a second. Thanks to y'all I got a better handle on the demographic big picture. I want to ride north to E'town on another rescue, but I don't need to risk my son's life. If Martin wants to see what's going on out there, he can ride with me. If what he sees in E'town doesn't satisfy him, he can ride on up to Louisville by hisself and look for 'his people.'

Then McCoy turned his attention to Jason.

"You are dead right—pun absolutely intended. Winter is going to kill the hungry and kill them fast. If you can feed these girls for another two days, I will reimburse you for everything they eat, and then some. Martin doesn't need to borrow one of your horses. He can ride Trevor's."

Chapter 45

The rough wind that had blown the night before was gone as they rode in the calm air of dawn. Jason's farm was now six miles behind them, and Martin and McCoy turned north on the two-lane country road that would take them to E'town. McCoy hadn't been trying to be generous when he had lent Martin his son's horse. The O'Neils used their horses every day on their ranch, and all of their horses were fit for a day's work. Most of Jason's horses were working stock, with heavy bones and big feet, and his light horses were not in condition for several days of hard riding. Martin outweighed Trevor by 50 pounds, and McCoy feared this might be a problem. He would have to keep a close eye on the horse, and if the need arose, move Martin onto one of the horses they were ponying.

The morning ride was uneventful. It was cold; Martin guessed that it was just above freezing, but at least it was not raining. McCoy planned to make it to Hodgenville, not far from the birthplace of Abraham Lincoln. He reckoned that would be a good place to spend the night, and maybe give Martin a good look at the situation, if the bodies they passed on the road were not enough to curb his enthusiasm for trying to rescue a city of more than a million residents, using only his good intentions. McCoy could only roll his eyes at such Yankee do-gooder nonsense. Didn't they know that there was no one left to virtue signal to?

"Notice anything?" asked McCoy.

"What's that?" asked Martin.

"No animal road-kill. Just people."

"Well, no. I didn't notice the absence of road kill. But now that you mention it…"

McCoy sniffed loudly and exhaled.

"Smell that?"

Martin sniffed. "I don't smell anything."

"Exactly, nothing but fresh air. No car or truck exhaust. No coal emissions. Too bad all your Yankee friends couldn't be here to see what wonderful thing zero carbon emissions is for the environment."

"There is no need to mock me," said Martin.

"Sure, there is," McCoy winked at Martin. "I got no one else. It ain't nothin' personal."

"Are you sure about that?"

"I ain't sure of anything. Well, except you virtue signaling do-gooders out on the coasts done fucked everything up in rural America."

"Is that a fact?" Martin asked, more to keep McCoy amused then to express real interest. "It seems to me that you are much better off than New York City at the moment."

"Yeah, but the term that comes to mind is 'in spite of, not because of.' Besides, that's only 'cause you ain't never been here before, and you ain't been off Jason's farm since you got here. My bet is Kentucky and Tennessee were not vacation destinations for y'all."

"No. You're right about that."

"And the only time you seen the middle of the country was from an airplane."

"What's your point, McCoy?"

"Your sort don't have any idea about life out here in 'fly-over-land,' but you sure as hell got opinions 'bout what we need and how we should live."

"I was wondering where this was going. By 'your sort,' do mean the Jews?"

McCoy pulled his horse to a stop. Martin stopped his mount and turned to McCoy who was red-faced with anger.

"What the fuck does religion got to do with this?"

"I was wondering that myself. What did you mean by 'your sort?'"

"Bullshit. You was trying to play that victim card again. If you could, you'd cue up some sad music and black and white photos of the Holocaust and stamp 'redneck' on my forehead.

You got to get over yourself, brother. I ain't no redneck. And you ain't no victim. All of the victims are dead. You're a survivor and a damn lucky one at that. You got friends that care about you. So, I figure you must be a good egg. But please, don't be playin' any of that shit with me. Because I know the truth of it."

Martin had no idea what to make of this man. He had never met someone so mercurial in his life. McCoy asked his horse to walk again, and Martin fell in next to him.

Oh, yeah?" Martin chuckled. "What truth would that be?"

"The truth is, you don't believe your shit any more than I believe mine. I been a Southern Baptist all my life. Went to church every Sunday. You think any of my fellow church members believed any of that? Ain't none of them could pass a polygraph. And neither could you."

McCoy was smirking at Martin.

"Everyone questions his faith at some point."

"Bullshit. There's a reason they say, 'everyone wants to go to heaven, and ain't no one willing to die to get there.' And here we are, in the aftermath of a nuclear World War Three, set off by a couple of countries fightin' over who owned the 'Word of God'. Ain't that an ironic sumbitch? And I get it. People need faith. They need something to believe in, and to feel they belong to, a family, a community, a church, and a country. They need ideals, and a moral and ethical framework to help them steer their lives. And they need common expectations of behavior and conduct, to help them fit in and belong. Your multiculturalism was an unmitigated disaster."

"What? So now I have to abandon my culture and my identity and take up yours?"

"Man, sometimes I think I'm the only normal person left. You got some chip on your shoulder, ya know that? What is it about nuclear war in the Middle East that you don't understand? And what the hell are you talking about? We, you and me, my friend, *are* the same culture. Or at least, that's where it was going until the multiculturalists got up a head of steam. But they're gone now. This is a new day."

Martin paused for a minute. He wanted to wind the conversation back a bit.

"Okay, so if it isn't the Jews' fault, whose fault is it?

"I meant the coastal elites. And what'd I say? Don't give me that victim-class bullshit anymore. There ain't no anti-Semitism here; there never was, and you ain't no victim. And tell me this; how is it that all you folks came to the conclusion that the people here in fly-over-land are all racist anti-Semites? When the closest you came to the people here was an airline seat at 30,000 feet? You drank the Kool-Aid, that's how. This is rural Kentucky. None of the people here have ever even met a real live Jew. And if they did, y'all would be an honored guest in their homes." McCoy was exasperated. "Shit, more than half the churches in the county here fly an Israeli flag under their American flag; they send lots of money Israel's way, and their favorite political pundit is an orthodox Jew who went to Harvard Law School. I am talking about the liberal elite. They controlled the media, the message, and the policy. And it was a gotdamn disaster for the people out here."

"In what way?"

"You sure you wanna have this conversation?"

"What? You think you've got something to say I haven't heard before? I'm a New Yorker. We've heard everything."

"Haha! You ain't heard shit. But since you asked, they destroyed our people, our families, and our economy."

"Oh, yeah?" Martin looked at McCoy as if he had two heads. "How's that?"

"I'll start with abortion. Do you have any idea what abortion is really all about? Not the bullshit and fabrications comin' out of the radical Feminists. Lord knows they ain't at any risk of unwanted pregnancy. A woman can't get pregnant without a man if you follow me. And don't be givin' me that homophobic bullshit. Feminists *hate* men, and they *hate* the product of men—children—even more. Their maternal instinct wiring got shorted out with the other wiring."

"What the hell does abortion have to do with what is happening in rural America?"

"Well, I'm glad you asked that, brother. Abortion is about one thing, and one thing only: The woman's estimation of the social and economic status of the father. If his status is high enough, the woman will keep the baby. If his status is too low, the woman will kill the baby."

Martin felt as if a heavyweight fighter just punched him in the chest.

"Women *do not* abort the children of dot-com billionaires, NFL quarterbacks or NBA superstars, hedge fund fat cats, or of one of the Kennedy men. The children of these men are celebrated, and the women are congratulated on the fine match. Women only abort the children of low-status men. These unborn children are murdered, unmourned, then unceremoniously thrown away in a medical waste 'red bag,' and incinerated. Well, out here in rural America, the men just don't have the social and economic status of you Ivy Leaguers. Our women are killing our babies, and abortion is killing rural America. And it's the same story in Black America. Now what were you saying yesterday about the ethical nature of women's politics?"

Martin went pale and had no response.

"Wassa matter there, Martin? Cat gotcha tongue? Well, take a few deep breaths, 'cause I ain't done. Let's do this logically. Two things. Feminism is an Engels/Marxist philosophy. And Feminism cannot exist without abortion."

Martin looked like he was going to be sick.

"Ah, you see where this is going, dontcha?" McCoy seemed to be enjoying Martin's discomfort. "Dang! It sure is nice to have a learned man around to talk to. I figured an economist would be familiar with Engels's work. Well, Feminism is a collectivist belief system, right? Feminism rejects private property rights, marriage, family, and inheritance as the underpinnings of the patriarchy, right? And Feminism utterly depends on abortion as its raison d'être. But the thing is, the women who are aborting their children are making that life or death decision based on the socio-economic status of the father, and that status is measured by the *private property rights* of the father and the father's *family*! Is that not the most delicious irony and hypocrisy ever, or what? You just can't get more full of shit than that! Haha!!"

McCoy had a good laugh. He waited a moment to see if Martin had anything to say. He didn't.

"Well, at least you are smart enough not to try to defend the indefensible. But hold on. Abortion is one side of the family and fertility coin, Martin. Divorce is on the other side."

"I've been through a divorce," said Martin.

"What you are trying to say is that you have been through a marriage that was infected by Feminism. Feminism insists that women have no responsibilities in a marriage. None. Women can work or stay home, have sex or refuse sex, have babies or refuse to produce babies, and abort their husband's child for any reason or no reason, with no input from him. So, what's the point of marriage? The removal of all responsibility gave women tremendous incentive to trade interdependence with their husbands for dependence on the government. If a husband is successful, his wife can skin him alive in divorce court, using government violence to seize his private property—in spite of Feminism's rejection of the legitimacy of private property rights! If her husband isn't successful, she can throw him out—and get what she can from him—and the government will subsidize her decision, no questions asked. Feminists are pretty flexible on the subject of private property versus socialism when it suits them, wouldn't you say? But women are not any more independent than they were—they just got more violent. They moved their dependence from their husbands and family to the government and used the government's thugs and guns against their men. Violence by proxy is still violence. And the government was thrilled—the government loves violence. Why would any man in his right mind sign up for that?

"Feminism needs women to be angry and unhappy, and they did a hell of a job, because one in three American women over the age of 35 is, or was, on anti-depressants or anti-psychotics. The Feminists also insisted that women don't need men—as if society can survive without children—and that most men are unworthy of being husbands and fathers. Feminism is the most anti-social belief system in history, and because of it, our fertility is inadequate, the idea of family has been destroyed, and the few children we manage to produce grow up in broken homes without the influence of a father. Instead of a father's influence, our kids are subjected to endless propaganda in the public-school system— organized and staffed by Feminists!

"Along with destroying our families with divorce and our future generations with abortion, y'all destroyed the economy in rural America by obliterating small businesses, rolling them up into these huge publicly traded corporations where all the profits get shipped off from the people here to the coastal elites. The local hardware store got put out of business by the big box corporations; the local diner got put out of business by these fast food restaurants you see on every corner and all like that. Y'all needed taxes to fund your do-gooder social programs, and the big public corporations are the perfect tax collection vehicle for funding those grand social programs—and small businesses ain't. So y'all destroyed them with occupational licensing and bureaucracy and forced their profits into entities that collected and paid taxes better than the little guys. Now the only worthwhile employment out here is working for one government agency or another. We got no choice. We're a bunch of chicken-fried socialists. Y'all made socialism as country as cornbread.

"Then y'all made it so that young people ain't 'qualified' to work for these corporations unless they graduate from 'elite' colleges with important degrees—ya know, like 'women's studies.' So, our best and brightest young people don't stay. They go off to college, get deep in debt to y'all, and get their heads filled with socialistic nonsense, and afterward, they move to the cities to work for corporations or government bureaucracies to pay off the debt. But they don't really get ahead. And then they don't have any children! Feminists have convinced our young people that they shouldn't have children until they are too old to have children, and they have convinced women they shouldn't have babies until they need fertility drugs, Petri dishes, and 'in vitro' fertilization! Half those women are so old when they finally become mothers that they are going to die before their children are raised. The other half will remain childless. The brutal fact is that most of our young people who moved to the city got mixed up in the politics of tryin' to make the world fair, and this gender war nonsense y'all got started, because of the indoctrination they suffered in school and college.

"Our young men, and now women, who do not go to college have no other option but to join the military. That's the only jobs program we got. And y'all ain't doin' that for us out of the goodness of your hearts. None of your kids get killed or get their limbs blown off in these wars. Y'all talk a lot of shit about peace, but without our massive military empire, the U.S. dollar will not enjoy worldwide hegemony, and without U.S. dollar hegemony, you can't fund the deficits that pay for your gotdamn, do-gooder social programs. Ain't that right, mister Ivy League economist?

"Then came the United States Department of Agriculture, and all their asinine regulations that the big corporations wrote for their own benefit. There are very few farmers left in rural America because y'all put the little guy out of business with paperwork, regulations, insurance, and licenses. The only farms left are industrial. And most of the food is processed. It is a federal crime for me to sell a gallon of fresh milk at my farm stand. Hell, it is illegal for me to butcher a steer and sell the meat to my neighbors! Did you know that? I gotta go through a USDA approved packing plant. Regulations forced farmers to specialize and sell their products into the commodity market, where they can't make a living, and that reduced the offerings of local food products. And if anything goes wrong with that system, everybody starves to death. Well, things sure went wrong. You still with me?"

Martin met McCoy's eyes but said nothing.

"Of course," McCoy continued. "TV didn't help. Not everyone can live in a mansion in California or New York and come home from their job as a movie star or a hedge fund manager and jump into a hot tub filled with champagne. The nice folks in Hollywood created an image of an ideal life and beamed it into every American living room. When their own lives didn't measure up to what they saw on the TV, people got depressed, and the obesity and addiction epidemic followed. And here we are!

"The greatest irony of rural America is that most of the people here are on food stamps. They call it 'S.N.A.P.' now. Catchy, ain't it? Can you believe that? Great climate, fertile soil, and open land as far as the eye can see. But now that the government feeds them, the people don't know how to do anything for themselves. They can't garden, slaughter a hog, milk a cow, or put up food for the winter. All they know how to do is watch TV—and now they are going to starve. You coastal elites should be ashamed of what you did to the people of rural America. All the dead bodies you see along the road ain't nothin' compared to what's in these houses."

McCoy gestured with his hand to the side of the road. Smoke curled out of the chimney of a farmhouse set back off the road in the middle of a pasture in a cluster of barns and other outbuildings. Human activity was evident at some of the farms Martin and McCoy passed, but the houses built on the small lots along the highway were dark and empty.

"You got any other questions there, Mr. 'I'm a New Yorker?' 'Cause I can talk about this stuff all day long."

When Martin didn't answer, McCoy seemed to lose interest in speaking, and they rode on in silence.

The riders stopped at mid-day in the hamlet of Magnolia, Kentucky. McCoy hobbled the horses so that they could not run, took the bits out of their mouths, retrieved the grain he had packed in feed bags on each horse, and laid it on the winterkill grass in six piles spaced about 20 feet apart. Then he set the horses loose in a field next to the Magnolia Fire Department.

"We'll let the horses graze for an hour or two, and then we'll get on up to Hodgenville," McCoy said.

"For an hour or two? It's getting late already."

"You ain't watchin' no John Wayne western! In real life, horses have to stop and eat. Go on and have a look around if you want to. See the bank sign there?" McCoy pointed to the local bank on the street on the other side of the field. "There are some houses along that street; I saw them back when the road forked. Go knock on a few doors."

"Won't that be dangerous?"

"You want to go to Louisville to look for your starving people, but you're afraid of the good people of Magnolia, Kentucky? You best go have a look around before you do anything foolish. I'm gonna collect some kindling and make a fire. You might want to watch me and learn how to make fire without matches or a lighter. Never mind that. Next time. Go on. When you get back, we can eat."

The fire was more for entertainment than anything, though they might warm their hands by it. The rations they packed did not require cooking.

"Okay. I'll go have a look around."

McCoy didn't respond.

Martin headed off in the direction of the bank. When he got there, he saw a dozen houses on the street to his right. He walked south on the east side of the street past the six houses on that side, crossed the road and walked north on the west side past the other six houses. There was no sign of life. Martin walked around behind the houses on the west side heading south. No people, no dogs, no sounds. Nothing. But there were a few burn patches from fires. On closer inspection, there were charred bones in and around the remains of the fires. He walked back to the road and headed north, screwing up his courage he walked up to one of the houses.

"Hello!" he called out. "Hello! Is anybody home?"

Martin could hear the blood surging in his neck. His heart was pounding. He knocked on the door several times. Then he banged on the door. Soon he was beating on the frame. Still nothing. He looked back at the empty street.

"Is anybody here?!" Martin shouted. The silence was overwhelming.

Martin turned back to the house and opened the screen door. It occurred to him that the residents hadn't taken down the screens and put in storm glass for the winter. The heavy wooden door had a handle and a thumb lock. Martin grabbed the handle and depressed the latch, and the door opened. The smell of decay struck him like a slap in the face, forcing him to hold his breath. But panic overcame that reflex, and Martin pulled the door shut and began to heave the air in and out of his lungs, nearly to the point of hyperventilating. He calmed himself and held his breath for a moment, but then he pulled his shirt and undershirt out of his pants, rolled them up to breathe through, opened the door, and stepped into the small house. To his right were the decayed remains of a grey-haired woman in a yellow housedress, slumped in an upholstered chair, with a knitted wool blanket over her legs. A dull brown bloodstain covered her entire torso. A walker was next to the chair, standing sentry just in case the woman needed it. But she wouldn't need it. Her walking days were behind her.

Martin could see a pair of legs protruding from a doorway on his right. On this side of the door, the floor was carpeted. On the other side, he could see the bright yellow linoleum floor of the kitchen. As he stepped farther into the room, Martin saw the remains of an elderly, grey-haired man. He was dressed in comfortable shoes, blue slacks that reminded Martin of a work uniform, a buttoned shirt, and an unbuttoned sweater and jacket. The man had been shot in the chest too. But there was no gun near either body, so Martin continued into the house, still holding the rolled bottom of his two shirts over his mouth and nose. There was a door half ajar, opposite the kitchen entry where the old man's body lay, and when Martin pushed it open, the mystery was solved. It was a bedroom, and on the bed were the bodies of a man and a woman. They were facing each other in an embrace, she on her right side and he on his left. The heads of both bodies were lopsided and misshaped, and lay in a dull brown dried bloodstain. A large handgun was on the floor where it had landed after it bounced off the bed. There was no note on either nightstand. Martin picked up the gun and walked out of the house.

Martin breathed the fresh air in and out several times, put the gun on the ground between his feet, and shook and billowed his jacket and shirts to get the stink of decay out of them. When he finished airing himself out, he looked down at the gun, thought about leaving it there, but picked it up and walked north. For some reason he could not explain to himself later, he stepped up to the last house on the left and opened the door. The stench of decay slapped him again. He did not enter the house.

Walking north and then turning west into the field where their horses grazed, Martin saw McCoy seated on something that kept his butt off the ground, next to a small fire. Martin walked up to McCoy, handed him the gun, and told McCoy everything he had seen and done since he had departed. McCoy listened, but made no expression, or any effort to make eye contact. When Martin finished, McCoy held the handgun up and said, "Ruger .357 Magnum. Stainless steel. Hell of a gun. Look familiar?" McCoy stood and pulled his jacket up over his belt, and held up the gun that Martin had found, next to the weapon on his belt. They were the same in every respect.

"Did you know what I would find when you sent me off to 'have a look?'" asked Martin.

"If you're askin' me if I been in these houses here, no I ain't been in these houses. But I been in more than a few houses between my spread and E'town, and I've seen a bunch of suicides. It makes sense if you think about it."

"Nothing makes sense," said Martin in a far-off voice. "Nothing adds up."

"Sure, it does," replied McCoy. "You just don't like what it adds up to. In the year 1800, the world population stood at 1 billion people. By 1900, there were 1.6 billion—a gain of 60%. By 2000 there were 6 Billion of us. Last year we were closing in on 8 billion—a 400% increase in 120 years. I believe you mathematician types call what we see here a 'reversion to the mean,' right? Well, a bullet beats starving, every day all day."

"But they lived out in the country!"

"What do you expect them to eat? Some of us kept the old equipment around just for fun, and of course, the Amish and Old Order Mennonites do everything the hard way, but the rest of the people here sit on the couch and watch TV, courtesy of your do-gooder social programs. Every year they gain a few more pounds, and every year they get a few more tattoos. They mar their bodies with this piercing bullshit, and some of them look like they got a bone in their nose. By the time they're 40, they don't even look human. Imagine, if your whole life—everything you ever experienced—came out of a TV or a computer screen, and then one day… ain't nothing coming out no more. What then? Imagine the farthest you walked in years was to the car in the driveway, and then you took a motorized scooter around the big box store 'cause you was so big you can't even push a grocery cart. Now imagine there ain't no gas for the car, no food at the grocery store, and no life coming out of the TV. Is there any wonder why they's killing themselves? Shit, if I was them, I'd a shot myself years ago. Living out in the country only helps if you've been providing for yourself and are fit and used to this way of life. But rural America is filled, bursting at the seams, with obese depressives pullin' a check."

"'Pulling a check?'"

McCoy felt he was being put on, but the sincere expression on Martin's face said otherwise. He checked the urge for sarcasm.

"Most of the people in rural America are on disability or welfare, or they are old and on social security. 'Pulling a check' from the government. Like I said before, you virtue signaling do-gooders really fucked these people up. It ain't just food stamps."

"I don't know what you're talking about." Martin's breath was coming in big gulps like he was trying hard not to cry.

"Well, you got that right. You don't know what the fuck you're talking about when it comes to all of the things you people did to Americans living in 'fly-over land.' After y'all destroyed them by getting them on public assistance, you put them in prison for using drugs, and when they got out you sold them opioids, but first, you dismissed them with that phrase—'fly-over land.' Nice touch. And you ain't seen nothin' yet. Wait 'till we get up to E'town and you see kids that ain't had nothin' to eat for a month and a half. In this cold, I don't know if any will still be alive."

Martin began to weep. Then he began to wail and flail his arms about as he paced back and forth. McCoy, fearing

Martin's mental state, stood up and walked 20 yards away. Martin was a large and powerful man, and McCoy didn't know if he was entirely safe to be around. Martin continued to storm about, but after a few minutes he sat back down, still quietly weeping and rocking back and forth. McCoy used this time to check on the horses. When the storm raging within Martin seemed to pass, McCoy walked back to where he was sitting, and asked Martin if he was all right.

"I don't need to go to Louisville," said Martin in a small voice. "Anyway, I don't want to go to Louisville. I want to go home to my family, back to Jason's farm."

"I think that's a good idea," said McCoy.

It was almost sundown when McCoy and Martin appeared back at Jason's farm empty-handed. Martin lurched as he got down, and Trevor took possession of his horse. Roone led the horses in the pony line, Walt took McCoy's horse, and men and horses headed back to the barn. Miriam came to meet Martin as he stumbled towards her and the twins. They accompanied him into the guesthouse. The women McCoy had brought to Jason's from E'town stood on the front porch of the farmhouse in their Amish dresses, and upon seeing the four riderless horses, several of them started to cry. Jason stepped off the porch and moved to McCoy's side.

"What the hell happened?" Jason asked McCoy.

"Nothing happened. But I don't think your friend has any interest in visiting Louisville anymore."

Epilogue

Winter had come on early, and it was a particularly bitter season indeed, but it lightened up in the second week of February. One hundred days had passed since the electric grid ceased to function. People no longer spoke of "the bombings." If it had happened, it had happened in another world, long ago. The community of survivors where Jason, Abraham, and McCoy lived had more important things to consider.

The calendar said that spring was still over a month away, but already the clan was busy planning and preparing. Jason and Ellen still had family out there. Refugees from the urban centers still straggled into the community occasionally, often in horrific condition. Jason hoped to see his other brothers, or his sister walk up the gravel drive to the house someday, but he realized that the odds dropped with each passing day.

Jason, Abraham, and McCoy organized a committee of local farmers and experienced workers to plan the planting, cultivation, and harvest seasons. They impressed upon the people the brutal truth of local agriculture: without long supply lines of food from other regions, and proper management of local resources, one hail storm, tornado, late frost, or drought could spell disaster. They had to produce, in this growing season. If they blew it or missed it, there would be no "do-overs." If they failed, they would have to try to their existing food supplies through the coming winter and into the following year. Last year's corn and bean crop— there was no local wheat crop—had been seeded before the grid went down, with tractors, fuel, fertilizers, and herbicides. This year's crop was going to require a great deal more effort.

The "Big Four," in order of harvest size and importance, were corn, hay, soybeans, and wheat. The corn and hay crops were absolute "must haves." They could not survive without them. Soybeans and wheat, while not luxuries, were not a matter of life and death. The men from Jason's clan, Abraham's Amish church group, and a dozen other farming families within riding distance, all agreed to work together on shares in some fields, and then exclusively on their own land. The women would see to the family gardens of potatoes, legumes, fruits, and vegetables, along with dairying and cheese making. Abraham's wife Ruth invited all the women in the community to meet in her husband's workshop twice each week, so that they could cooperate to make sure that no family's "kitchen garden," as the Amish called these sizable operations, failed. Healthy kitchen gardens also would provide some redundancy for both production and seed collection.

All foodstuffs in the county, except meat, corn, and dairy, were in critically short supply before the spring growing season, but materials and tools were not. More than nine out of ten homes and at least half the farms in the five-county region were vacant, and these properties contained all manner of useful items, which soon found their way to productive uses.

McCoy and his brother made several successful rescue efforts, so his growing clan spent the winter deconstructing abandoned houses and barns and using the materials to build smart little cottages along the entrance to their farm. Suellen, one of the young women McCoy had rescued from Elizabethtown, married McCoy's son, Trevor. Her friend Tara married Trevor's cousin Bark, short for Barclay. Suellen was 16, and Tara 17 years old. Trevor and Bark were both 20. Both women thought they were "with child" already.

Not everyone who came to the McCoy farm was a perfect fit. Georgia Fox, one of the young women rescued along with Suellen and Tara, refused to have anything to do with the men, and left the O'Neil farm with Belinda Cutliff, on a stolen horse, three weeks after her rescue. The following morning the horse returned to the O'Neil spread, wearing its saddle and bridle. McCoy had almost immediately regretted taking Belinda into his clan. He hoped she was now gone for good; he would gladly have given up an old horse to be free of her. When the horse came back, McCoy was quietly disappointed; it meant that Belinda might have decided to lurk somewhere near.

Martin and Miriam and their daughters took up residence in a small, abandoned house on the main highway, about a quarter mile walk from Jason's farmhouse. A wood cook stove, which McCoy's people fabricated in their shop, had made the move possible, since the house would have been un-livable without the stove's heat and cooking energy. It had taken six men to move the stove into the house. In exchange for the stove, Jason had given McCoy two heavy-bred heifers, and also had agreed to part with another heavy bred heifer, in exchange for a 55-gallon hot water kettle for Martin and Miriam's house. McCoy's crew was fabricating the kettle from several scrounged 8-foot by 4-foot sheets of 18-gauge stainless steel, using Jason and Ellen's kettle as the model. Until the new kettle was ready, Martin's family were producing hot water by putting two five-gallon stock pots and a ten-gallon saddle tank set atop their cook stove, where the saddle tank's top also serving as a warming tray. This worked, but in the summer, it would make the house unbearably hot.

Barter transactions like this were less efficient than cash and credit cards had been "Before", but "After", without electronic currency, barter was the only trading currency they had. For the most part, the people cooperated by bartering their labor.

Miriam and her daughters, Aviva and Hanna, developed a close relationship with the expectant mothers, Danielle and Pilar. Miriam had assisted the Amish community's midwife in all of the Amish births—six so far, with five more expected before Danielle was due. Two of the births had occurred on the same day, when an Amish woman delivered her 12th child, and then helped the midwife and Miriam deliver her teenaged daughter's twin girls. Miriam spent much of her time studying medical textbooks that McCoy's brother Liam had turned up in his travels. Danielle and Pilar found Miriam's efforts very comforting, especially since Danielle's due date was coming up fast.

Roone was becoming a first-rate horseman. He gelded their stallion, Duke, and then broke Duke to work and ride. He also broke Lady the draft mule and the other draft horses so that they would work together. With Lady and Duke in the lines, they now had three well-broken teams to use around the farm. Roone made sure that the four mares got to visit with a neighbor's big grey Percheron stallion when they came into season, so that the clan could expect a good foal crop next year. Pilar loved to sit on top of the panels of the round pen and watch her man work the horses, and Roone loved to come to Pilar and rub her growing belly as she sat there. She was just starting "to show." Soon she would have to watch Roone work his horses while standing on the ground outside the pen.

Ellen, inspired by the women she had met when visiting with Abraham's wife Ruth, had another little surprise for Jason. Sarah would be almost 19 months when this baby was born, and Ellen was waiting for the right moment to tell Jason.

Since the grid failure, the Amish community had opened up a great deal to the other farm families and clans, and now worked closely with many of them. Jason noticed that the "English" women living on the nearby farms often wore ankle length Amish dresses. He wondered how that came to be, and if they would still dress like that in the heat of summer. Jason also wondered how long the Amish could control the marriage decisions of their young people. With everyone working in such proximity, Jason felt the answer was "not very long."

McCoy and his son Trevor came into view on the two-lane highway that ran through Jason's farm. McCoy was riding his horse, and Trevor was driving a team of massive Belgian draft horses, which were hitched to a forecart and pulling a small harvest wagon, which was loaded with Martin and Miriam's new stainless-steel wood-fired hot water kettle. Walt and Martin were on the south side of the highway, in the bottomland of Jason's farm, removing boards from the wall of an old tobacco barn. The men intended to refit the barn into an equipment shed and were removing the paneling of the south wall so that they could back their horse-drawn equipment in and out without having to move other implements around. Martin and Miriam's house was directly across the highway from the barn, so it would be easy for them to keep an eye on the equipment.

Trevor pulled his team into the front yard of the home and parked his rig under the bare maple tree that stood in front of the cement front porch. McCoy rode his horse right up to the porch but did not dismount. The men waited there patiently as Martin crossed the street to greet them. Miriam stepped out the front door onto the porch, with her daughters right behind her, their faces beaming with delight as they looked at the kettle and thought about how dramatically it would improve their hot water supply.

"Good afternoon, Ma'am," Trevor and McCoy said in unison. Then McCoy said, "Is your husband about, Mrs. Weiss? We could use his help. This here kettle weighs a ton."

Miriam had been unpleasant towards McCoy when they first met, but McCoy had held no grudge, and now treated Miriam with respectful deference.

"I'm here!" said Martin as he stepped onto his front lawn behind them.

"Hello, Rabbi Martin," said Trevor.

"Hello, Trevor," Martin responded.

McCoy dismounted from the "off-side" of his horse, and when he came around, he saw Martin approaching.

The two men shook hands and McCoy said, "I'm glad to see you feelin' better."

"Well, I don't know how I feel," said Martin. "I never thanked you for making sure I got home okay. Thank you."

"Well, you was my responsibility. I brung ya. I damn sure had to bring ya back home. It's a helluva thing, to see something like that."

"I hear you have been busy," said Martin, changing the subject.

"Yessir, busier than a one-legged man in an ass kickin' contest."

Martin had to laugh. "That's a heck of an image. I understand you and Jason are heading down to Shady Grove to see the Old Order Mennonites."

"Yeah, that's what I understand too. Jason seems to think that the corn seed we got is all 'hybrid' seed and might not produce next year. That would be a disaster. I think he's right to be worried. We're going to pony a couple of horses down there and see if we can't come up with a couple hundred pounds of heirloom field-corn seed. That should seed 10 or 12 acres. It won't be enough to feed livestock, but it would get us through the winter if the other seed don't grow. And we can save seeds from the best ears and get our own strain goin'. Anyway, I see Jason and Ellen comin' this here way."

Jason stepped into the front yard and up to the harvest wagon with Ellen, Jenny, and the kids right behind him. Walt had finished stacking the boards he and Martin removed from the barn wall and was on his way over too.

"Wow!" said Jason looking at the kettle. "It looks exactly like ours!"

"It better," said McCoy. "That was the whole idea."

Roone joined Martin and Trevor, and with the two young men on one side and the hulking middle-aged man on the other, they lifted and carried the kettle from the wagon.

Miriam was leading them to the back yard and directed the men to put the kettle down in the grass about 20 feet from the back door. Roone departed to get his father's horses.

Jason asked McCoy if he wanted them to hitch the heifer, which they had agreed to exchange for the kettle, to the back of Trevor's wagon.

"Well," said McCoy. "I was hopin' to trade something else with Mrs. Weiss here in exchange for the kettle."

"Oh, yes? What's that then?" asked Miriam.

"Well, Ma'am," said McCoy. "I expect we are going to need your services. I expect to be a grandfather this year. And a great-uncle, too."

A "whoop!" went up from the clan as they crowded around to offer their congratulations. When the celebration quieted down, Ellen looked quizzically at Jason. He gave her a nod and a blink in the affirmative.

"Well," Ellen said with a big smile. "I guess this is as good a time as any. Jason and I also are going to have another baby."

Another "whoop!" erupted from the clan assembled there on Martin's front lawn, with happy faces all around.

When the crowd quieted down, Martin said to Miriam, "It looks like a busy year for you."

Miriam looked at McCoy and asked, "Is it the two girls that I met here who are pregnant?"

Suddenly the festive atmosphere evaporated.

"Uh, yes Ma'am. That would be Suellen, my son's wife, and Tara, my nephew's wife."

All eyes turned to Miriam. The silence was painful.

"Well," said Miriam. "I would be honored to help bring their children into the world."

"Mazel Tov, McCoy!" said Martin. "Generations and generations to you!"

The festive mood and celebration returned. Roone had just arrived from the horse barn, riding his father's horse and ponying the two young riding mares. After a minute, Jason spoke over the noise from the throng.

"Well, I am glad everyone is happy and enthusiastic about our future. But McCoy and I have a long ride ahead of us. We made it through this winter, and though this winter isn't even over yet, it's time to prepare for next winter."

McCoy was on his horse and ready to go by the time Jason finished speaking.

"Thank you again for the kettle," Miriam said to McCoy. "Just let me know when you need me."

McCoy tipped his hat to Miriam, pointed to Martin, and smiled. Then he turned to Jason and said, "Well, Yankee. I got a notion to git in motion. Let's go see your Mennonite friends and the good people of Shady Grove."

"I hope to be back by noon tomorrow," Jason said to Roone. "With any luck, I will have four feed bags of seed corn with me."

And with that McCoy gave his horse a little kick, and he and Jason and the two pack horses were off. The clan was quiet as they watched the men and horses head east and then south.

Martin spoke first, quoting Ecclesiastes 3:

"To every thing, there is a season and a time to every purpose under the heaven. A time to be born, and a time to die; a time to plant, and a time to pluck up that which is planted; A time to kill, and a time to heal; a time to break down, and a time to build up;" Here Martin paused and looked at Walt. Walt shrugged a little and winked at Martin. Martin gave him the hairy eyeball and continued. "A time to weep, and a time to laugh; a time to mourn, and a time to dance; A time to cast away stones, and a time to gather stones together; a time to embrace, and a time to refrain from embracing; A time to get, and a time to lose; a time to keep, and a time to cast away; A time to rend, and a time to sew; a time to keep silence, and a time to speak; A time to love, and a time to hate; a time of war, and a time of peace."

About a quarter mile down the road, Jason turned back and looked at his family and friends, still gathered on Martin's front lawn. McCoy looked at him closely but came to the same conclusion he had come to regarding Martin. It was impossible to get a fix on this man.

"Congratulations there, big daddy," said McCoy when Jason turned forward. "Not many men get a grandchild and father a child in the same year."

"Congratulations yourself. The child will be your first grandchild, right?"

"Yes, indeed."

"I was just thinking, as I looked back at everyone, that in 100 years none of the people alive then will have any personal memory of the catastrophe that has befallen us. This will all just be a part of their history. Ancient history, if you think about it. Like the American Civil War is for us."

"From your lips to God's ears."

"What do you mean?"

"We ain't survived it yet. This ain't over. Not by a long shot."

"Maybe not. But I'm hopeful."

"Shoot, I'm hopeful too. The act of putting seeds in the ground, or a baby in a woman's belly, is the ultimate expression of hope. And faith. It means you plan to be around to harvest the fruit of those seeds, and to care and provide for that baby and woman until they can take care of themselves. In times like these, that takes a lot of hope and faith."

Jason didn't answer McCoy. There was no need to belabor the truth. Every survivor grappled with despair in his or her most private moments. All had lost family and friends. All recognized that there was little more than luck standing between them and the abyss. But here they held, bringing new life into the world by the passions of the flesh, and from the soil by the sweat of their brows, and by bending the toiling beasts of Creation to their will. They knew what it was to feel hunger, to shiver in the cold, and to fall asleep before they could lay their heads down. They looked to the future, to the growing season and the harvest, and to the birth of their children. The crisis would pass. They would endure. Life, precious life, would go on.

To the Reader:

"Seven Years of Famine" is the first of what I hope will be four books in this series. The second book, "Stones in the Garden," is available now at Amazon, and "Born of the Flesh" is scheduled for publication in the spring of 2020. I have much more to say about the sovereignty of the individual, the natural rights of man, our moral imperative to reject the use of violence and coercion for personal, moral, or political agendas (especially violence by proxy, i.e., "The War on Drugs," the endless Wars for Oil, and the regulatory-judicial complex that has criminalized essentially all forms of economic freedom and in the process has enslaved us), and the ideals of Simplicity, Integrity, Community, Equality, and Peace that are at the foundation of my personal philosophy.

Individual Liberty and Freedom has become sacrilege, Free Speech has become a nuisance and a provocation, and the Free Thinkers of Western Culture and Civilization have become the adversary—but only if good people do nothing.

"The best revenge is not to be like your enemy." – Marcus Aurelius

Gregory Thomas Jeffers

www.Gregorytjeffers.com

Made in the USA
Monee, IL
08 February 2021